WHERE LOVE HAS GONE

HAROLD ROBBINS

The scorching bestseller of an amoral tempt-
ress who believed her only responsibility was
to her own insatiable appetites . . . a rich and
beautiful San Francisco artist who would
sacrifice anyone—her daughter, her lovers,
her ex-husband—to get and keep what she
wanted!

HAROLD ROBBINS

WHERE LOVE HAS GONE

PUBLISHED BY POCKET BOOKS NEW YORK

POCKET BOOKS, a Simon & Schuster division of
GULF & WESTERN CORPORATION
1230 Avenue of the Americas, New York, N.Y. 10020

ISBN: 0-671-44595-2

First Pocket Books printing July, 1963

55   54   53   52   51   50   49   48   47

POCKET and colophon are trademarks of Simon & Schuster.

Printed in the U.S.A.

CONTENTS

THE PURPOSE
OF
JUVENILE COURT LAW.

"To secure for each minor under the jurisdiction of the juvenile court such care and guidance, preferably in his own home, as will serve the spiritual, emotional, mental and physical welfare of the minor and the best interests of the State; to preserve and strengthen the minor's family ties whenever possible, removing him from the custody of his parents only when his welfare or safety and protection of the public cannot be adequately safeguarded without removal; and when the minor is removed from his own family, to secure for him custody, care, and discipline as nearly as possible equivalent to that which should have been given by his parents."

Section 502, Chapter 2 of the Welfare and Institute Code of the State of California.

PART ONE

LUKE'S STORY
Friday Night

1

It was a day for losers.

In the morning I blew my job. In the afternoon Maris hit the long ball, and as the television cameras followed him around the bases you caught glimpses of the expressions on the faces of the Cincinnati Reds and somehow you felt the Series was over even if there were four more games to play. And that night the telephone rang, getting me out of the sleepless bed where I'd been lying staring at the gray-black ceiling, trying to be very quiet as I listened to Elizabeth pretending sleep in the next bed.

The impersonal voice of the long-distance operator sang hollowly, "Mister Luke Carey, plee-uhz. Long distance calling."

"Speaking," I said.

By now Elizabeth had her light on. She was sitting up in bed, her long blond hair tumbling down over her bare shoulders. "Who is it?" she mouthed silently.

I covered the mouthpiece with my hand. "Don't know," I said quickly. "Long distance."

"Maybe it's that job in Daytona," she said hopefully. "The one you wrote about."

A man's voice came on the phone. It had a faint Western twang. "Mr. Carey?"

"Yes."

"Mr. Luke Carey?"

"That's right," I said. I was beginning to get a little annoyed. If this was someone's idea of a joke, I wasn't having any of it.

3

"This is Sergeant Joe Flynn of the San Francisco Police." The twang was more noticeable now. "You have a daughter named Danielle?"

A sudden fear clutched at my insides. "Yes, I have," I said quickly. "Is anything the matter?"

"I reckon there is," he said slowly. "She just committed murder!"

Reactions are funny things. For a moment I almost laughed aloud. I'd had visions of her broken bleeding body lying torn up on some lonely road. I bit my tongue to suppress the words, "Is that all?" Instead, aloud I asked, "Is she all right?"

"She's okay," the sergeant's voice came back.

"May I talk to her?"

"Not until morning," he replied. "She's on her way to Juvenile Hall."

"Is her mother around?" I asked. "Can I talk to her?"

"Nope," he said. "She's upstairs in her room, having hysterics. Reckon the doctor's about giving her a shot now."

"Is there anyone there I can talk to?"

"Mr. Gordon's on his way to Juvenile Hall with your daughter."

"Is that Harris Gordon?" I asked.

"Yep," he replied. "The lawyer man himself. He was the one asked me to call you."

Harris Gordon. The lawyer man. That was what they called him out there. The best there was. And the most expensive. I ought to know. He had represented Nora in our divorce and had made a monkey out of my lawyer. I began to feel a little better. At least Nora wasn't so hysterical if she had called him.

A curious note came into the policeman's voice. "Don't you want to know who your daughter killed?" The way he said it, it sounded like "kilt."

"I don't believe it yet," I said. "Danielle couldn't hurt anyone. She's not even fifteen."

"She killed him all right," he said flatly.

"Who?" I asked.

"Tony Riccio," he said. Something nasty came into his voice. "Your wife's boy friend."

"She's not my wife," I said. "We've been divorced eleven years."

"She hit him in the stomach with one of them sculptor's chisels your wife has in her studio. Sharp as a razor it was. Ripped him apart like a bayonet. There was blood all over the place." I don't think he'd even heard what I'd said. "Looks like one a them cases where the man's been making out with both of them and the kid got jealous."

I could feel the nausea coming up in my throat. I swallowed hard and pushed it back down. "I know my daughter, Sergeant," I said. "I don't know why she killed him or even that she did, but if she did, I'd stake my life on it that that wasn't the reason."

"It's been more'n six years since you seen her," he persisted. "Kids have a way of changing in six years. Growing up."

"Not to murder," I said. "Not Danielle." I hung up before he could say another word and turned to the bed.

Elizabeth was staring up at me, her blue eyes wide.

"You heard?"

She nodded. She got out of bed swiftly and slipped into her robe. "But I can't believe it."

"I can't either," I said dully. "She's still a kid. She's only fourteen and a half."

Elizabeth took my hand. "Come on out to the kitchen. I'll make some coffee."

I sat there in some kind of a fog until she placed the

cup of hot coffee in my hand. It was one of those times
when a person thinks about everything and yet really
thinks of nothing. Nothing that is remembered anyway.
Maybe little things. Like a little girl's first time at the
zoo. Or laughing at the spray coming up from the sea at
La Jolla. And the small voice of a child.

"It's so much fun to live on a boat, Daddy! Why can't
Mommy come down here and live in a boat with you instead of the big old house on top of the hill in San Fwancisco?"

There was a kind of smile inside me as I remembered
the way Danielle had of saying San Francisco—San
Fwancisco. It used to annoy Nora. Nora always spoke
so properly. Nora was always proper in everything.
Everything that people could see. She was a lady on the
outside.

Nora Marguerite Cecelia Hayden. In her flowed the
proud blood of the Spanish dons of old California, the
hot Irish blood that laid track on the Western Railroads,
and the ice-water that circulated through the veins of the
New England bankers. Stir them all together and they
made a lady. With wealth and power and land. And a
strange wild kind of talent that lifted her high above
everyone else.

For whatever Nora touched, stone or metal or wood,
it took on a shape, a life, of its own. And whatever she
touched that had a shape, a life, of its own, she de-
stroyed. I knew. Because I knew what she had done to
me.

"Drink your coffee while it's hot."

I looked up. Elizabeth's eyes looked at me steadily. I
sipped at the coffee. I could feel its warmth creeping into
the cold that had been my belly. "Thanks."

She sat down opposite me. "You were far away."

I forced my mind back to her. "I was thinking."

"Of Danielle?"

I nodded silently, feeling a guilt creeping up inside me. That was another thing that Nora had. A way of creeping into your mind and pre-empting thoughts that should be of someone else.

"What are you going to do?" Elizabeth asked.

"I don't know. I don't know what to do."

Her voice was warm and gentle. "The poor kid."

I didn't speak.

"At least her mother is with her."

I laughed bitterly. Nora was never with anybody. Only herself. "Nora was having hysterics. The doctor was knocking her out for the night."

Elizabeth stared at me. "You mean Danielle is alone?"

"Their lawyer went down to Juvenile Hall with her," I said.

Elizabeth looked at me a moment longer, then got to her feet and walked over to the cabinet. She took down another cup and picked up a spoon from the drainboard next to the sink. Her hand was shaking. The spoon clattered to the linoleum floor. She started to pick it up and then she stopped. "Damn!" she swore. "I feel so clumsy."

I picked it up as she took another spoon from the rack. She filled her cup with coffee and sat down again. "What a hell of a time to be pregnant."

I smiled at her. "You're not the only one to blame. I had something to do with it."

Her eyes didn't waver from mine. "I feel so stupid and useless. Like a clod. Especially now."

"Don't be silly."

"I'm not being silly," she said. "You didn't want this baby. I wanted it."

"Now you *are* being silly."

"You had a daughter," she said. "That was enough for you. I wanted to give you a child, too. I was jealous of her, I guess. I had to prove that at least in one way I was just as good as Nora."

I walked around the table and sat down beside her. She was still looking at me. I took her face in my hands. "You don't have to prove anything. I love you."

Her eyes still didn't leave mine. "I saw the expression on your face when you talked about Danielle. You missed her. I thought if we had a baby you wouldn't miss her so much."

Suddenly her eyes filled with tears. She caught at my hand and moved it down to her full, hard belly. "You'll love our baby, won't you, Luke? Just as much as you love Danielle?"

I bent and pressed my face against the life within her. "You know I will," I said. "I love her now."

"She may be a boy."

"It doesn't matter," I whispered. "I love you both."

Her hands raised my head to her breasts. She held me tight against her. "You've got to go out there."

I twisted out of her arms. "Are you nuts? With you two weeks from the hospital?"

"I can manage," she said quietly.

"And what'll we use for money? I lost my job this morning, remember?"

"We've got almost four hundred in the bank," she said. "And you still have your last week's paycheck in your pocket."

"A hundred and sixty bucks! We'll need that to live on. It may be weeks before I can get another job."

"It's only three and a half hours by jet from Chicago to San Francisco," she said. "And round trip tourist is less than a hundred and fifty dollars."

"I won't do it. I can't. We need that money for the hospital."

"I've made up my mind," she said. "You're going. I know that's the way I'd want it if Danielle were our baby."

She reached up for the wall telephone. "You go upstairs and pack while I call the airport. And wear your charcoal-gray flannel. It's the only decent suit you've got."

2

I was staring down at the open suitcase spread on the bed when Elizabeth came into the bedroom. "There's a plane out of O'Hare at two-thirty," she said. "It makes one stop and gets you into San Francisco at four in the morning, Coast Time."

I just stood there looking down at the small canvas bag. I felt kind of numb. The news was still sinking in.

"Grab a quick shower," she said. "I'll pack."

I looked at her gratefully. Elizabeth never had to be told. Somehow she always knew. I went into the bathroom.

I looked at my face in the mirror. My eyes had deep hollows under them and seemed sunken far into their sockets. I reached for my razor. My hand was still shaking.

"There was blood all over the place." The sergeant's words leaped into my mind. The hell with the shave. I could do that in the morning. I went into the shower and turned on the water full force.

When I came out the bag was already packed and closed. I went to the closet.

"I packed your suit," Elizabeth said. "Wear your slacks and sport jacket on the plane. There's no sense wrinkling your suit."

"Okay," I said.

I had just finished knotting my tie when the telephone rang. Elizabeth picked it up. "It's for you," she said, holding the receiver out to me.

10

"Hello."

I didn't have to be told who was on the other end of the line. I'd recognize that quiet voice anywhere. My former mother-in-law. As usual she wasted no time on preliminaries. "Mr. Gordon, our attorney, thinks it would be a good idea if you came out here."

"How is Danielle?"

"She's all right," the old lady said. "I've taken the liberty of reserving a suite for you and your wife at the Mark Hopkins. When you pick up your tickets at the airport, wire your flight number and I'll have a limousine at the airport."

"No, thanks."

"This is no time to be proud," she said testily. "I know your financial position, but it seems to me your daughter's welfare is more important."

"Dani's welfare has always been more important."

"Then why aren't you coming?"

"I didn't say I wasn't coming. I merely said no to your offer. I can pay my own way."

"Still the same, aren't you?" she asked. "Will you ever change?"

"Will you?" I retorted.

There was a moment's silence, then her voice came back—a little colder, a little clearer. "Mr. Gordon wants to speak with you."

His voice was rich and warm. It would fool you if you didn't know him. There was a mind like a steel trap working behind that friendly sound. "How are you, Colonel Carey? It's been a long time."

"Yes," I said. Like eleven years in divorce court. But I didn't have to remind him of that. He probably knew the time down to the minute. "How's Dani?"

"She's fine, Colonel Carey," he said reassuringly. "When the judge saw the state of shock the poor child was in, he remanded her into my custody. She's upstairs, here at her grandmother's, asleep. The doctor gave her a sedative."

Like him or not, I was glad he was on our side.

"She has to be returned to Juvenile Hall tomorrow morning at ten," he said. "I think it would be a good idea if you were here to accompany her."

"I'll be there."

"Fine. Would it be possible for you to join us here for breakfast at seven o'clock? There are a number of things we ought to discuss that I'd rather not mention on the phone."

"Okay," I said. "At seven for breakfast."

There was a pause, then Mrs. Hayden came back on. It seemed to me the old lady was making an effort to be friendly. "I do so look forward to meeting your wife, Luke."

"She's not coming."

I could hear the surprise in her voice. "Why not?"

"Because she's having a baby," I said. "Like any day now."

After that we had nothing more to say, so we said goodbye. But no sooner had I put down the phone than it rang. It was Harris Gordon again.

"Just one thing more, Mr. Carey. Please don't talk to any reporters. It's important that you make no statement until after we've talked."

"I understand, Mr. Gordon," I said, and hung up.

Elizabeth started toward the bathroom. "I'll get dressed and we'll drive out to O'Hare."

I looked at her questioningly. "Do you think you should? I can call a cab."

"Don't be silly." She laughed. "No matter what you told the old lady, it's still a good two weeks."

I like driving at night. The world comes to a stop at

the end of the beam of your headlights. You can't see where you're going, so you're safe, at least as far as you can see, which is better than average for anything in life. I watched the speedometer hit fifty, then slow down to forty. There wasn't any rush. It wasn't even midnight yet.

But we didn't feel like sitting around the house waiting. Out at the airport there would be movement, people. We would feel that we were doing something, even if there was nothing to do.

Out of the corner of my eye I saw the match flicker and cast a brief glow across Elizabeth's face. Then she reached out and put a cigarette between my lips. I dragged deep.

"How're you feeling?"

"Okay," I said.

"Want to talk about it?"

"What's there to talk about? Dani's in trouble and I'm going out there."

"You say that as if you had expected it," she said.

I glanced at her with a kind of surprise. Sometimes she was too good. She dug right inside me and came up with thoughts I wouldn't even admit to myself.

"I didn't expect this," I said flatly.

Her own cigarette glowed. "What did you expect?"

"I don't know."

But that wasn't quite the truth either. I knew what I'd expected. That one day Danielle would call me on the phone and tell me she wanted to be with me. Not with her mother. But eleven years had worn that dream kind of thin.

"Do you think there was anything in what that policeman intimated?"

"I don't think so," I said. I thought for a moment. "In fact I'm pretty sure there wasn't. If that had been the case, Nora would have killed him. Nora wouldn't share anything she figured was hers."

Elizabeth was silent and I went on with my thoughts. That was the way Nora was. The only thing important to her was keeping what she wanted. I remembered that last day in court.

Everything had been settled by then. She had the divorce. I was broke and beat and could hardly support myself, while she had everything in the world that she wanted. The only question left was Danielle's custody.

We went into the judge's chambers for that. It was supposed to be only a formality. We had already agreed that Dani would spend twelve weekends a year and half the summer with me on the boat at La Jolla.

I sat in the chair opposite the judge while my lawyer explained the agreement. The judge nodded and turned to Harris Gordon. "It seems an equitable arrangement to me, Mr. Gordon."

I remembered that just then Danielle, who had been playing with a ball at the far end of the office, suddenly turned and yelled, "Catch, Daddy!"

The ball rolled across the floor and, as I knelt to pick it up, I heard Harris Gordon's reply: "It definitely is not, Your Honor."

I stared at him in disbelief, still holding the ball in my hand. This was something we had agreed on just yesterday. I looked at Nora. Her violet-blue eyes seemed to look right through me.

I rolled the ball back to Dani.

Harris Gordon went on, "It is the contention of my client that Colonel Carey has no parental rights."

"What do you mean?" I yelled, straightening up. "I'm her father!"

Gordon's dark eyes were inscrutable. "Didn't you ever

think it strange that the child was born only seven months after your return from Japan?"

I fought to keep my temper. "Mrs. Carey and her doctor both assured me that Dani was premature."

"For a grown man you were rather naïve, Colonel Carey."

Gordon turned back to the judge. "Mrs. Carey wishes to inform the court that the child Danielle was conceived some six to seven weeks prior to Colonel Carey's return from service. In view of this, which she is sure that Colonel Carey has long admitted to himself, she asks for sole custody of her daughter."

I spun toward my attorney. "Are you going to let them get away with this?"

My attorney leaned toward the judge. "I am terribly shocked by this action on the part of Mr. Gordon," he said. "Your Honor must be aware that this is contrary to the agreement I reached with him yesterday."

I could tell from the way the judge spoke that he too was shocked, though his language was studiedly impartial. "I am sorry, Counselor, but you must realize that the court cannot enforce any agreement that is not reached in the presence of this court."

My temper finally blew. "The hell with the agreement then," I shouted. "We'll go back and fight the whole thing out again!"

My lawyer caught at my arm and looked at the judge. "May I have a moment to talk with my client, Your Honor?"

The judge nodded and we went over to the window. We stood there, our backs to the room, looking out.

"You know what that would mean?" he whispered. "You'll be admitting publicly that your wife cuckolded you while you were still overseas!"

"So what? The whole town knows she's screwed her

way through San Francisco from Chinatown to the Presidio!"

"Stop thinking about yourself, Luke. Think about your daughter. What will this mean to her if it gets out? Her own mother labeling her a bastard?"

I stared at him. "She wouldn't dare."

"She already has."

His reply was irrefutable. I didn't speak. Then a small voice came from across the room: "Catch, Daddy!"

Almost automatically, I bent again to pick up the ball. Danielle came hurtling across the room and flung herself into my arms. I lifted her up. She was laughing, her dark eyes sparkling.

Suddenly I wanted to squeeze her tight against my chest. Nora was lying. She had to be. Somehow I knew inside me that Dani was my daughter.

I looked across the room. At the judge, his secretary, at Harris Gordon, at Nora. They were all watching us. All except Nora. She was staring at some point over my head.

I studied the tiny smiling face opposite mine. I felt a sick, beaten feeling rise up inside me. My attorney was right. I couldn't do it. I wouldn't take the chance of hurting my own child.

"What can we do?" I whispered.

I could read the sympathy in my attorney's eyes. "Let me talk to the judge."

I stood there with Danielle in my arms while he went over to the desk. After a few minutes he came back.

"You can have four weekends a year. And two hours every Sunday afternoon if you come up to San Francisco. Is that agreeable to you?"

"Do I have any choice?" I asked bitterly.

He shook his head almost imperceptibly.

"Okay," I said. "God, how she must hate me."

With the unerring instinct of children, Danielle knew what I was talking about. "Oh no, she doesn't, Daddy," she said quickly. "Mommy loves you. She loves both of us. She told me."

I looked down into her little face, so earnest, so wanting to be sure. I blinked my eyes to keep back the quick, salty tears. "Of course, darling," I said reassuringly

Nora came toward us. "Come with Mommy, darling," she called. "It's time to go home."

Danielle glanced at her, then at me. I nodded as Nora held out her arms. For the first time Nora looked at me over Danielle's head. There was a curious kind of triumph in her eyes.

The same kind of triumph I'd seen when she had completed a piece of sculpture that she'd been laboring over. Something she had struggled to give shape to. Suddenly I realized what Danielle meant to her. She wasn't a child, she was just something Nora had made.

She put Danielle down, and hand in hand they started toward the door. As Nora opened it, Danielle looked back at me.

"You coming home too, Daddy?" she asked.

I shook my head. Tears had come into my eyes, partly blinding me, but I managed to say, "No, darling. Daddy has to stay here and talk to the nice men. I'll see you later."

"Okay. 'Bye, Daddy."

The door closed behind them. I stayed only long enough to sign the necessary papers, then took the train down to La Jolla and boarded the boat and got drunk.

It was a week before I was sober enough to accept a charter.

I paid for my ticket and checked my bag through, then we went to the cocktail lounge. Despite the hour, the place was busy. We got a small table and I ordered two Manhattans.

I sipped at my drink. It was a good one. Cold and not too sweet. I looked over at Elizabeth. She was beginning to look tired.

"Are you all right?" I asked. "I shouldn't have let you come all the way out here."

She lifted her glass and swallowed some of the cocktail. "I'm okay," she said, a little color coming back into her face. "Maybe a little nervous, but that's all."

"There's nothing to be nervous about."

"I'm not nervous about the plane," she said. "Just about you."

I laughed. "I'll be all right."

She didn't smile. "You'll have to see her again."

Then I knew what she meant. Nora had a way of cutting me up, and it always took a while to get the pieces back together again. I'd been in that kind of state when Elizabeth and I first met six years ago. And that was five years after I had been divorced.

It was at the tail end of the summer. Danielle was eight and I was just back from San Francisco after delivering her to her mother after one of our infrequent weekends.

Dani had run into the house while I waited outside

18

for the butler to come and get her bag. I never went into the house after the divorce.

The door opened but it wasn't the butler. It was Nora. We looked at each other for a moment. There was no expression in her cool eyes. "I want to talk to you."

"About what?" I asked.

Nora was never one to waste time. "I've decided that Dani's not going down to visit you any more."

I could feel the hackles rise. "Why?"

"She's not a child any more," Nora said. "She sees things."

"Like what?"

"Like the way you live on that filthy boat. The Mex women who come around, the drunken brawls. I don't care to have her exposed to that side of life."

"You're a great one to talk. I suppose it's better the way you do it? With clean sheets and martinis?"

"You ought to know. You seemed to like it pretty well."

The crazy thoughts that jump into your mind. The fascination of what you know to be evil. She knew me all right. She knew what she was talking about. I fought the memory down.

"I'll talk to my lawyer about that," I said.

"Go ahead—if you can find a lawyer who will talk to you. You're broke and dirty, and if you go into court, I've got a private detective's statement about the way you live. You won't get anywhere."

She turned and closed the door in my face. I stared at it a moment, then walked down the patio steps to my beat-up old jalopy. I didn't get home until late the next day and I got on the boat with half a case of whiskey.

Two days later I heard a knock on the cabin door. I pushed myself up from my bunk and staggered over

to it. I threw open the door and for a moment I could
feel the shock of pain travel from my eyeballs along
the optic nerves to my brain. The harsh blue sky, the hot
sun, the white dress and sun-blond hair of the girl who
stood there. I blinked my eyes for a moment to cut out
the light.

The girl spoke, her voice big and warm. "They told
me at the bait store that you charter."

I kept on blinking. The light was too much for the
whiskey.

"Are you the captain?" she asked.

The pain was easing off now. I squinted at her. She
was as good to look at as she sounded. Blue-eyed and
tan, generous wide mouth, and a clean jaw.

"I'm the whole crew. Come on in and have a drink."

The hand that gripped mine as she came down the
narrow steps was strong and firm. She looked around
the cabin curiously. It wasn't much to look at. Empty
whiskey bottles and disheveled bunks. She didn't say
anything.

"Excuse the mess," I said. "But I drink between
charters."

A faint smile wrinkled her eyes. "So did my father."

I looked at her. "Was he a charter man?"

She shook her head. "He was captain of a tug on the
East River in New York. He hit the bottle hard between
jobs."

"I don't drink when I'm working," I said.

"Neither did he. He was the best tugboat captain in
New York."

I pushed some of the clutter off the table and took
down a couple of clean glasses. I picked up the bottle of
bourbon. "I got water. No ice."

"That's good whiskey," she said. "Don't weaken it."

I hit the tumblers to the halfway mark. She drank the

whiskey like it was water. A girl after my own heart.

"Now to business," she said, putting down her glass.

"Fifty dollars a day. Out at five in the morning, back at four in the afternoon. No more than four passengers."

"How much for a week? We want to go up to L.A., lay over for the weekend and come back."

"We?" I asked. "How many?"

"Just two. My boss and myself."

I looked at her. "This is the only cabin on the boat. Of course I can bunk down on the deck if I have to."

She laughed. "You won't have to."

"I don't get it," I said. "Is there something wrong with the guy?"

She laughed again. "There's nothing wrong with him. He's seventy-one years old and treats me like his daughter."

"Then why the charter?"

"He's a builder from Phoenix. He had some business out here and up around L.A. Since he's seen nothing but sand for a long time he thought it might be a good idea to get a little salt air, maybe do some fishing."

"He won't get much fishing done. It's the wrong time of the year. The fish have all gone down Mexico way."

"He won't mind."

"All meals on?" I asked.

"Except the weekend."

"Would five hundred be too much?"

"Four hundred would be more like it."

"You're on," I said. I got to my feet. "When do you want to leave?"

"Tomorrow morning. Eight o'clock all right? Do you want a deposit?"

I grinned at her. "You got an honest face, Miss . . ."

"Andersen," she said. "Elizabeth Andersen."

She got to her feet. The swell from a passing boat

rocked the deck beneath us. She put out a hand to steady herself and started up the cabin steps.

I called after her. "By the way, Miss Andersen, what day is this?"

She laughed. A warm friendly kind of laugh. "Just like my father. That was always the first thing he asked after tying one on. It's Wednesday."

"Of course," I said.

I watched her walk down the dock to where her car was parked. She turned and waved to me, then got in and drove off. I went back into the cabin and began to clean up.

That was the way I met her. We weren't married until almost a year later.

"What are you smiling at?" Elizabeth asked.

I came back to the present with a start and reached across the table and put my hand over hers. "I was thinking about how you looked when we met," I said. "A blond goddess cast in gold and ivory."

She laughed and sipped at her Manhattan again. "I don't look much like a blond goddess now."

I signaled the waiter for two more drinks. "I'm still ahead."

Her face was suddenly serious. "You're not sorry you married me, are you?"

I shook my head. "Don't be silly. Why should I be?"

"You're not blaming me for what happened? To Dani, I mean."

"I'm not blaming you," I said. "There's nothing I could have done to stop it. I know that now."

"You used to think differently."

"I was a fool," I said. "I was using Dani as a crutch."

The waiter came and put the drinks down. Time has a way of dragging when you're waiting for a plane.

Maybe it's because you have a feeling that everything should move fast, like the six-hundred-mile-per-hour planes. But your feet are on the ground and nothing seems to move except the desire inside you to be off, to be somewhere else.

I hadn't felt like that this morning—rather, yesterday morning. The wind was warm off the lake as I got out of my car at the construction site. The last house in this unit would be framed today and I was certain that we'd get the okay to start on the next group. With the kind of weather we'd be having, I was sure we could get the new bunch framed up before the bad weather set in. That way all the inside work could be completed during the winter.

I went into the trailer that served as our construction office and checked the gang sheets. Everything was right on schedule. This job would take me into December. By that time the baby would be old enough to move down south. Davis was starting a new project just outside Daytona, and the chances were pretty good that I could pick up the construction supervisor's job down there.

So I wasn't an architect like Nora had always thought I should be. With an office and secretaries and clients who came in to bother me about whether they should put gold hardware on their kitchen sinks and pink telephones in their johns.

Instead I wore work shirts and Levis and walked in mud all day and built houses for ten, twelve, fifteen grand. Not fancy, but good for the money. And houses for people to live in. People who needed them. Not neurotics whose only reason to build a home was to show off to their friends.

I felt pretty good. Useful, too. I was doing something. Something I wanted to do. The something I went to college for, to architect's school. The something I planned for before I went off to war.

I was just about to start my first inspection tour of the morning when Sam Brady came into the trailer. Sam was the builder, the boss.

I smiled at him. "Just in time to watch them frame up the last house in this unit."

He didn't smile back. I began to get the feeling that something was wrong. "Hey, what gives? Didn't you get the money for the next unit?"

"I got the money."

"Then cheer up. We'll get them up before the first snowfall. Next spring you'll be walking around with thousand-dollar bills sticking out of your pocket."

"It's not that, Luke," he said. "I'm sorry but I gotta put you down."

"You're crazy," I said, not believing him. "Who's gonna put the houses up for you?"

"The mortgage company's got a man." He looked over at me. "They made it part of the deal, Luke. No man, no dough." He fished a cigarette out of his pocket and lit it awkwardly. "I'm sorry, Luke."

"Sorry?" I said, lighting up my own cigarette. "That's a real gas. How do you think I feel?"

"Yuh hear anything on that Davis job yet?"

I shook my head. "Not a word."

"It'll come through."

I dragged on the cigarette silently.

"Look, if it's just a question of time, I can put you on one of the gangs."

"No, thanks," I said. "You know better than that, Sam."

He nodded. He knew. If I went back on the gangs there wasn't a builder in the country would put me back up. The word got around real fast.

I let out a gust of smoke and pressed the butt out in a tray. "I'll finish off the day and pick up my time."

"The new man will be coming on this afternoon."

I got the message. "I'll clear out by lunch then."

He nodded, then he gave me my pay envelope and went out. I stared after him for a moment, then set about getting my things out of the beat-up old desk.

I didn't go right home. Instead I went into a bar and watched the Reds blow the Series. I stayed away from the whiskey and stuck with the fifteen-cent beer. Maris hit the long one just as I came back from my fifth trip to the john. There was a shot of the Cincinnati manager staring glumly down the line after Maris had come home.

The bartender wiped down the bar in front of me. "Losers," he said, staring up over his shoulder at the set. "That's what they are. Born losers. They might as well quit now."

I threw some change down on the bar and walked out. There was no sense in putting it off any longer. I had to tell Elizabeth sometime.

Actually it was easier than I thought. I guess she kind of knew it the minute I walked into the house early. She didn't say anything when I told her, just turned and put the roast she had been preparing into the oven.

I stood there waiting for her to say something. I don't know what. Anything. Be angry maybe. Instead she acted just like a woman.

"You better go inside and wash up," she said.

4

I was just about to order another round of
drinks when I caught Elizabeth looking at me. I switched
to coffee. She smiled.

"That's another thing for you not to be nervous
about," I said.

"This is no time for you to get back on the sauce.
You'll need all your wits if you're going to help Dani."

"I don't know what I can do."

"There must be something," she said, "or Gordon
wouldn't want you out there."

"I guess so," I said.

The place of fathers in our society. The old man had
to be good for something. Even if it was to play straight
man on television.

I was restless. The hands on the big clock on the wall
pointed to a quarter to two. I wanted to be moving.
"How about coming out for some air?"

Elizabeth nodded and I picked up the check and paid
it on the way out. We came out on the observation deck
just as a big jet came roaring in for a landing. I could
see the big double-A on its side as it taxied over to its
station.

The loudspeaker over our heads blared, "American
Airlines, Flight 42, arriving from New York at Gate 4."

"That must be my plane," I said.

All sleek and shining and big. Four huge engines
balanced precariously on delicately swept-back wings.

While we watched, the doors opened and passengers began to disembark.

"For the first time I'm beginning to feel alone," Elizabeth said suddenly.

I looked at her and her face seemed pale in the blue-white fluorescent lighting from the field. I reached for her hand. It was cold. "I don't have to go."

"You have to go and you know it." Her eyes were somber.

"Not according to Nora," I said. "Eleven years ago she said that I haven't any right there."

"Is that what you believe?"

I didn't answer. Instead I took out a cigarette and lit it. But she wouldn't let me off the hook that easily.

"Is it?" she demanded, a curious harshness in her voice.

"No," I said, looking down onto the field. They were unloading the baggage from the plane. "I don't know what to believe. Inside I feel like she's my daughter all right. But sometimes I wish I could believe it was the way Nora says. Everything would be so much easier then."

"Would it, Luke?" she asked softly. "Would it wash away the years you had with Dani, the years she belonged to you more than to anyone else, even her mother?"

Again I could feel the choking come up inside me. "Lay off!" I said hoarsely. "Even if I am her father, what good was I to her? I couldn't take care of her. I couldn't support her. I couldn't even protect her from her mother!"

"You could love her. And you did."

"Yeah, I loved her," I said bitterly. "That was a big help. A fat lot of good I am to her even now. Still broke, still scratching " I could taste the bile rising in my throat.

"I should never have let Nora have her!"

"What could you have done?"

"Taken her and run," I said. "I don't know. Anything."

"You tried that once."

"I know," I said. "I was broke and I was a coward. I thought it took money when all that Dani really needed was love."

I turned to look at her. "Nora never loved her. Really, I mean. Nora had her work and Dani was just something to have around when she wasn't in the way. But if there was any inconvenience, off she went to her grandmother's or I'd take her down on the boat. And you know the topper to the whole story?"

She shook her head.

"Dani was always so glad to see her mother," I said. "She was always trying to make up to her. And Nora would just give her an absent-minded pat on the head and go on with whatever she was doing. I would watch the child coming back to me with a kind of sad expression on her face underneath the baby laughter and it was all I could do to keep from crying."

Tears were welling up in Elizabeth's eyes. I felt her move closer to me. "You were her father," she whispered gently. "You couldn't be her mother too. No matter how hard you tried."

The loudspeaker over our heads blared again. "American Airlines, Astrojet Flight 42 to Denver and San Francisco now loading at Gate 4."

I rubbed my neck. Suddenly I was tired. "That's us," I said.

"I guess it is, Daddy."

I looked at her in surprise. It was the first time she had ever called me that. She smiled. "You'll have to get used to it again."

"That won't be hard."

We started to go back inside. "You'll let me know when you arrive?"

"I'll phone myself person-to-person from San Francisco. If you don't have anything to tell me, say I'm not there. That way we'll save the cost of a call."

"What could I possibly have to tell you?"

I put my hand on her stomach.

She laughed. "Don't worry, I won't have the baby until you come back."

"That's a promise?"

"That's a promise."

There weren't many people around Gate 4 by the time we got there. Most of the other passengers had already gone aboard. I kissed Elizabeth goodbye and gave the passenger agent my ticket.

He looked at it, stamped it, tore the top section off and gave it back. "Go right on through, Mr. Carey."

I didn't get off the plane at Denver to stretch my legs as the stewardess suggested. Instead I sat in the lounge and had a cup of coffee aboard. It was hot and black and I could feel its steaming warmth creep down inside me and loosen up the muscles in my gut.

Six years. A long time. Many things could happen in six years. A child could grow up. She could be a young lady now. High heels and bouffant skirts. Pale, almost colorless, lipstick, and green or blue eye shadow, and that funny pile-up of twisted hair on top of her head, like an artichoke, that would make her look taller. She would appear very mature until you saw her face, and only then would you realize how young she really was.

Six years is a long time to be away from home. The child you left behind could grow and be many things that you never wanted for her. Like her mother. Six years and your child could grow up to—murder?

I heard the cabin door lock and the lights flashed on. I ground out my cigarette in the tray and fastened my seat belt. The stewardess came back and gave me an approving nod, then went about her task of checking the rest of the passengers.

I looked at my watch. It was four-thirty Chicago Time. I set it back two hours. Now it was two-thirty Pacific Coast Time.

I smiled to myself. It was so easy. Just turn back the clock and you've got the two hours to live all over again. I wondered why, if it was so easy, no one had invented a machine that would do it for the years.

I could turn the clock back six years and Danielle would not be where she was tonight. No, I'd turn it back almost fifteen years, back to the night she was born. I remembered those hours in the hospital. It was just about this time of the night and Nora had just come down from the delivery room.

"Don't stay too long," the doctor said as I started into her room. "She's very tired."

"When can I see the baby?"

"In ten minutes. Just tap on the nursery window. The nurse will show you your baby."

I stepped back into the corridor and closed the door behind me. "I'll see the baby first. Nora will want to know what she looks like. She'll be angry if I can't tell her."

The doctor looked at me quizzically, then shrugged. It wasn't until a long time later that I learned that Nora wouldn't even look at the baby up in the delivery room.

When the nurse rolled up the shade and held up my daughter, I flipped. With her tiny red screwed-up face and glistening black hair and little fingers tightened into angry little fists . . . I flipped.

Something inside me began to ache and I could feel all the pain of being born, all the shock that that tiny body had known in the last few hours. I looked down at her, and I knew even before she opened her eyes and then her mouth what she was going to do. We were in tune, we were on the same wave length, we were like locked-in to each other, and she was mine and I was hers. We went together and belonged together. And the tears came to my eyes for the tears she could not shed.

Then the nurse rolled down the shade and suddenly I was alone. Alone as if I were standing at the edge of the sea and a wave of dark night flooded over me. I blinked my eyes for a moment and I was back in the corridor of the hospital.

I knocked at Nora's door softly. A nurse opened it. "May I see her now?" I whispered. "I'm her husband."

With that peculiar look of tolerance that nurses seem to reserve for fathers, she nodded and stepped aside. "Don't be too long."

I walked over to the bed. Nora seemed to be sleeping, her black hair spread across the white pillow. She seemed pale and tired and somehow more frail and helpless than I had ever imagined she could be. I leaned over and kissed her gently on the forehead.

She didn't open her eyes but her lips moved. "Up the oars. The Free French Navy will never say die."

I looked at the nurse across the bed and smiled. I put my hand on Nora's lying on the sheet, and pressed it lightly.

"The Free French Navy will never say die."

The nurse was smiling now. "The pentothal, Mr. Carey," she said. "Sometimes it makes them say funny things."

I nodded and pressed Nora's hand again.

A strange look of fear crossed Nora's face. "Don't

hurt me, John!" she whispered hoarsely. "I'll do anything you want! I promise. Only don't hurt me!"

"Nora!" I said quickly. "Nora! It's me. Luke."

Suddenly her eyes opened. "Luke!" The faint shadow
of the fear disappeared. "I was having a terrible dream."

I put my arm around her. Nora was always having
terrible dreams. "It's all right, Nora," I whispered.
"Everything's all right now."

"I dreamed someone was breaking my hands! I
couldn't stand that. You know I couldn't! Not my hands.
Without them I would be nothing!"

"It was just a dream," I said. "Just a dream."

She raised her hands and looked at them. Long and
slim and graceful. She looked up at me and smiled.
"Aren't I silly? Of course they're all right." She closed
her eyes and went back to sleep.

"Nora," I whispered. "Don't you want to hear about
the baby? She's a little girl, a wonderful, beautiful little
girl. She looks like you."

But Nora didn't move. She was asleep.

I looked at the nurse. This wasn't the way it should
have been. It was never like this in books.

I guess the nurse noticed the puzzled look on my face,
because she smiled sympathetically. "It's the drug."

"Sure," I said. And I walked out into the corridor.

I glanced out the plane window. I thought I could see
the haze of light from the city far into the front of the
plane. San Francisco.

It would not be enough to turn the clock back fifteen
years. That wouldn't have stopped anything. Twenty
years would be more like it.

1942. Summer. And the battered P-38 that I was
flying screaming down into the wind as I dived at the
funnels of the gray-black Jap battleship. I had a sudden

and strange urge. Like dropping the bombs but not pulling back on the stick afterward, following them into the funnels of the warship and dying in the cool sea with it.

Then there would be no Air Medal, no Silver Star, no Purple Heart. Maybe there would be a C.M.H. like they gave Colin Kelly, who had done the same thing a short while before. There would be no hospitals afterward, no hero's tour, no bond drives, no publicity.

Because then there would be no me and I wouldn't be coming to San Francisco now as I came to San Francisco then. For I would be dead and I never would have met Nora and Danielle would never have been born.

Almost twenty years. And maybe even that would not have been enough. I was so young then. I was tired. I closed my eyes for a moment.

Please, God, give me back the time.

PART TWO

The Part of the Book
About NORA

1

It is trite, but it is true. Time lends perspective. When you are trapped in the emotions of the present, you cannot really see because you are like a leaf driven before the autumn winds by the demons that possess you. Time dulls and sometimes kills the demons of love and hatred leaving only the tiniest thread of its memory so that you can peek through the keyhole to the past and see much that you could not see before. I looked down from the window as the plane swung wide across the city to enter its landing pattern. I saw the lights of the city and the string of pearls that was its bridges and suddenly I realized that the pain and fear that had been mine at the thought of returning no longer existed. They lay dead in the past with the other demons that had possessed me.

At that moment I knew why Elizabeth had insisted that I come and I was grateful to her. She had chosen this way to exorcise my devils, so that I could once again be my own man, free of my guilts and tortures.

The reporters were there with their cameras but they were as tired as I at that early hour of the morning. After a few minutes they let me go. I promised them a full statement later in the day.

I went over to Hertz and rented the cheapest car they had, then drove into the city to a new motel they'd built on Van Ness, just across the street from *Tommy's Joynt*. The room was small but comfortable in that antiseptic style that motels go in for.

I picked up the telephone and called Elizabeth. When I heard her voice, warm from our bed, as she told the operator I was not at home, I wanted to thank her. But the connection was broken before I could utter a word.

The morning was at the windows and I went over and looked out. North toward the hills in the gray mists I could see the tower of the Mark Hopkins rising to the sky. I tried to see beyond, a few blocks to the west, to a familiar white façade and an Italian blue stone roof. The house where I used to live. The house where, even now, Nora was probably sleeping. Sleeping in that strange dream-filled peculiar world all her own.

From somewhere far off in the fog of dulled sleep, the telephone was ringing. Nora heard it and didn't hear it. She didn't want to. She pushed her face deeper into the pillow and her hands pressed it tighter against her ears. But the telephone still kept ringing.

"Rick! Answer it!" And the thought woke her. Because Rick was dead.

She rolled over and stared balefully at the instrument. Now its ringing came from far away and all she heard was the soft peal of the chimes that had been installed on her bedroom extension. Still she made no move to answer it.

After a moment the chimes stopped and again the house was quiet. She sat up and reached out for a cigarette. The sedative the doctor had given her the night before still pounded dully in her head. She lit the cigarette and drew in deeply.

There was a click as the house interphone came on, bringing the voice of her butler. "Are you awake, Miss Hayden?"

"Yes," she answered, without moving from the bed.

"Your mother is on the phone."

"Tell her I'll call her back in a few minutes, Charles. And bring me some aspirin and coffee."

"Yes, mum." The interphone clicked off, then a moment later clicked on again. "Miss Hayden?"

"Yes?"

"Your mother says it's very important that she speak with you immediately."

"Oh, all right," she said truculently. She reached for the telephone. "And, Charles, hurry with the aspirin and coffee. I have the most frightful headache." Then, into the telephone: "Yes, Mother."

"Nora, are you awake?" Her mother's voice was bright and penetrating.

"I am now," she answered resentfully. She didn't know how her mother did it. She was well over seventy and her voice sounded as if she'd been awake for hours.

"It's half-past six, Nora. And we expect you at seven. Mr. Gordon is already here."

"Is Luke there yet?"

"No. But he'll be here."

"You're so sure," Nora said. "How do you know? Have you heard from him?"

"No."

"Maybe he didn't come."

"He'll be here," her mother said definitely. "He said he would."

"You always believed him rather than me, didn't you?" Her voice filled with resentment.

"That doesn't matter. You're my daughter."

"And that's all that matters," Nora added bitterly.

"That's right," her mother said with crisp finality. "And if you haven't learned that by now, you'll never learn."

There was a subdued knock, then the door opened and Charles came in. He was carrying a small silver service tray.

"Mr. Gordon wants you to wear a simple suit and a cloth coat, Nora. And no makeup, only pale lipstick."

"Mr. Gordon thinks of everything."

Charles put the tray down on a small table next to the bed. He filled a cup with coffee and handed it to her, along with three aspirins on a small plate.

"You can thank God we've got him," her mother said.

"Do I have to come? I feel terrible this morning. I've got a frightful headache . . ."

"Nora!" Her mother's voice was shocked.

"What good can I do? I couldn't stand those questions again this morning. And the reporters will be there—"

Her mother's voice went cold and hard. "You'll go to Juvenile Hall with your daughter this morning. This is one thing I can't do for you. Her father will be there and you'll be there, like it or not."

She felt the vise of the headache tighten on her temples. "All right, I'll be there."

She put down the telephone and picked up the aspirin. She placed all three on her tongue and washed them down with a swallow of coffee.

"And how is Miss Danielle?" Charles asked softly, an inquiring look on his shining round face.

She looked up at the butler with a kind of surprise. She hadn't asked. But then there'd been no real reason to. If anything had been wrong with Danielle her mother would have told her. "Fine," she answered automatically.

Charles waited for her to go on.

"My mother said she was still asleep," she added, lying. Then she was angry with herself. She owed no explanations. Charles was nothing but a servant. No matter how long he had been with her.

"Tell Violet to draw my bath," she said sharply.

"I'll send her right up, mum."

The door closed behind him and she finished her cup of coffee. She got out of bed and poured herself another. As she turned, she caught her reflection in the large mirror over the dresser. Still holding the cup in her hand, she walked toward it.

She studied herself carefully. She didn't look her thirty-eight years. She was still slim, still straight. There was no fat on her hips, and her breasts, though never large, were still round and firm.

She sipped at the coffee, still looking at herself. She liked the way her flesh shone through the sheer white silk and lace of her gown. She leaned closer to the mirror, peering at her face. There were faint blue hollows under her eyes but other than that there were no signs of what she had been through. Her eyes were clear, not bloodshot, and the flesh across her cheekbones was taut and held no trace of puffiness.

She began to feel better. There would be no one who would see her today who would not find it difficult to believe that Danielle was really her daughter.

The sound of water running into the tub began in the bathroom next door. Quickly she finished her coffee and, leaving the cup on the dresser, went into the bathroom.

The colored maid looked up from the large sunken marble tub. "Good mornin', Miss Hayden."

Nora smiled. "Good morning, Violet."

"Y'all rest well, Miss Hayden?"

"I don't remember a thing after Dr. Bonner gave me the sedative."

"I didn' sleep too good myself. Them policemen kep' me up half the night with their questions."

Nora looked at her curiously. "What did you tell them?"

"What could I tell them?" Violet answered, getting

to her feet. "The same whut I seen when I came into the studio." She reached for a bottle of bath salts on the shelf over the tub and began to sprinkle the scent into the water. "When I come into the room there you was on the flo', bendin' over Mr. Riccio. An' Miss Dani, she was huddlin' against the wall."

"I don't want to talk about it!" Nora said coldly.

"Yes'm. Neither does I. I don' ever want to think about it no more." She capped the bottle and placed it back on the shelf. The fragrant musky odor of the perfume began to rise with the steam from the tub. "Be a few minutes befo' the tub is full. Would yuh like me to give you a rub? It'll relax you."

Nora nodded silently and removed her nightgown over her head. Violet moved quickly, taking the gown and folding it neatly across a chair as Nora stretched out on the narrow massage table.

She rested her chin on her crossed arms. It was so good to stretch. Really stretch out until you felt every muscle in your body pulling. She breathed deeply and closed her eyes.

After her bath she pressed down the button on the interphone. "Charles?"

"Yes, mum."

"Would you please get the car from the garage? And would you mind driving for me today? I don't feel quite up to it."

"Of course, mum."

She released the button and got to her feet. She studied herself in the long mirror before she left the room. Harris Gordon knew what he was doing. The right impression was so important in situations like this.

The black suit she was wearing was perfect. It made her look slim and young. And the simple cloth coat she carried over her arm added the final touch, what her

going along with it. She was having fun being a little girl
again for a few moments, when some instinct turned
our eyes toward the doorway.

Dani was out of her chair before any of us could
move, and by the time she reached Nora she was no
longer a little girl. The transition was swift and shock-
ingly complete. She was a young woman.

I looked around the table to see if the others had
noticed. I couldn't tell. Harris Gordon had a faint smile
on his face as if he were thinking how good this would
have looked in court. My former mother-in-law was
looking at me, a thoughtful expression in her bright blue
eyes. Then she too turned toward the doorway.

Nora had her arms around Dani. "Baby," she was
saying softly, turning her cheek so that Dani could kiss
her. "My poor baby!"

"Are you all right, Mother?" Dani asked anxiously.

"I'm fine, darling. And you—?"

"I'm okay, Mother. I'm just—just frightened, I guess.
I had such nightmares last night."

Nora stroked her hair. "There, there, don't be
frightened. Mother wouldn't let anything happen to you.
It'll all be over in a few days. You'll be home again as
if nothing had ever happened."

"I know, Mother. Do you know why?"

Nora shook her head.

Dani came over and took my hand. "Because Daddy's
come to help me," she said with a proud smile. "He
came all the way from Chicago!"

Nora stared at us. I could tell from the expression in
her eyes that it was as if the six years Dani and I had
been apart had never happened. I could tell from the
trusting warmth of my daughter's hand that it was as it
had always been between us. We were so much alike

that Nora always felt somehow on the outside when we were together.

"You've grown thin, Luke." She came toward me, holding out her hand, and I sensed her resentment. "Thank you for coming."

"Chains couldn't have kept me away," I said quietly. I took her hand, making it brief and impersonal. Not at all as it used to be.

She withdrew her hand quickly and touched her forehead in that gesture I remembered so well. The headache warning, I used to call it. And the peculiar shadow that came into her eyes confirmed it. "Suddenly I feel old," she said. "You look so young standing there next to Dani."

"You'll never be old," I said politely.

But she looked at me and knew better. And knew that I knew better too. The shadow deepened and furrowed her brow. Abruptly she turned to her mother. "Do you have any aspirin, Mother? I think I have what they refer to as a sedative hangover."

Her mother gestured. "On the sideboard, Nora."

I watched her cross to the sideboard and shake three tablets out of the small bottle. Then she put one back and I knew that she'd already taken three before she arrived. She glanced at me just before she swallowed the aspirin, and again there was that peculiar flash of recognition between us.

Suddenly I felt sorry for her. Don't ask me why; it was just there. Sometimes it is terrible to know so much about another human being. I knew that she was filled with a new and inexplicable fear and that she felt very much alone. For this was tomorrow. The empty tomorrow of her secret nightmares. This was the tomorrow she had told herself would never come.

And I was the same in that tomorrow as I had always been. Before she ate out my eyes.

2

In September 1943 the war in Italy was almost over. MacArthur had begun his long march back to the Philippines and I was in San Francisco winding up a tour of defense plants and factories. The wheels had decided that would be an ideal way for me to recover my strength before going back to duty.

Nora was giving her first showing of the work she had done in the twenty-one months since we had been at war. The little studio that had formerly been the greenhouse in back of her mother's house was crowded with people. She looked around appraisingly. She was pleased with the turnout.

Even the newspapers had sent out their art critics and they seemed impressed. She couldn't help feeling an inner glow of pride. It helped make up for all the long wearying nights she had spent in the studio after working at the aircraft factory all day.

The war. It was a fool thing she had done. But she had been trapped like everyone else. Caught up in the hysteria of patriotism. The newspapers made a big thing of it—Nora Hayden, prominent debutante, daughter of one of San Francisco's leading families, and one of America's most promising young artists, sets aside her career for the duration.

She had felt like a silly fool when she'd read that. But early in 1942 she had never thought the war would drag on so long. By now she had had it. She was bored with getting up at six-thirty and driving fifteen miles to

47

work six days a week, with doing the same stupid thing day after day.

Stop the conveyer belt. Solder wire number one to wire number two. Start the belt so that the girl at the next bench can solder number two to number three. Stop the belt so that she can start over again. Nora was tired of playing Rosie the Riveter.

The whole thing was entirely too mechanized, too planned, for her. Even lunch hours were organized. It wasn't bad enough that she had to eat a lousy sandwich, but every noon hour, along with her sandwich and the sugarless muddy coffee, she had to swallow exhortations to increase her production.

That noon there had been a rally complete with war hero. She hadn't even gone outside. Instead she had gone upstairs to the lounge and perched on a bench near the window. She lit a cigarette and stretched out. She closed her eyes. The temporary quiet of the factory was a blessed relief. She could use the rest. She hadn't gone to bed until four that morning, making sure that every-thing would be ready for the show that afternoon.

A roar came from the crowd outside the window. She sat up and looked out. An olive-and-tan Army Chevrolet had pulled up next to the stage just beneath the big blue and white factory *E* flag.

The crowd roared again as a man got out of the back seat and clambered up onto the platform. The man, of course, was me.

I did nothing but the applause stretched out into embarrassment. Helplessly I looked away. I was still new enough at it to feel like an idiot. I turned and looked up.

A girl was standing in the window just above the building entrance. At first my gaze swept on past her, then by reflex, or precognition, or kismet, or what have you, my eyes came back to her. In that fractional moment our eyes met.

Nora turned angrily from the window. It was too much. She didn't belong here, she should never have come to work here in the first place. She hesitated a moment, then went downstairs to the personnel office. She was bound to quit some day, why not today, the day of her first show?

So now it was all different. She was alive once more and the world was happening all around her. She picked up the thread of a conversation. Sam Corwin, the art critic of the *Examiner,* was talking to a man she didn't know.

"Assemblage is the art of the future," he was saying. "We're finding out every day that this war goes on that the only true art is the result of accident. War is destroying man's avowed purpose and the only thing that will be left when all this is over will be the result of accident. So assemblage will be the only art form that reflects the attempt of Nature to arrange itself into something of meaning."

She plunged headlong into the conversation. Any time she could find herself on the opposite side of an argument with Sam, she was ready for it. She remembered when she too had been impressed with his erudition. She had been not quite seventeen and an enthusiastic art major the night she had gone to his apartment for a few words of wisdom.

They had ended up taking their differences of opinion to bed in order to resolve them. She still remembered the frightened expression on his face when she'd told him afterward that she was below the legal age of consent.

Now she turned and looked into Sam's face. "I disagree, Sam. Art without purpose is nothing. It merely ex-

presses the emptiness of the artist. Especially in sculpture. A finished work must have something to say, even
if its creator is the only one who can hear it."

She smiled at the man she didn't know and apologized,
holding out her hand. "I'm Nora Hayden and sometimes
Sam gets me going."

The small middle-aged man with the pleasant smile
took her hand. "I suspect Sam does that sometimes to
get a rise out of people. I'm delighted to meet you, Miss
Hayden. I'm Warren Bell."

She raised her eyes in surprise. Warren Bell was one
of the leading art teachers in the country. "Professor
Bell, this is an honor." She turned to Sam accusingly.
"You should have let us know that Dr. Bell was coming,
Sam."

"Don't scold him, Miss Hayden. I hadn't expected to
be here, actually. I had a luncheon date with Sam and
he suggested I tag along. Since I'd heard so much about
your work, I couldn't resist."

"Professor Bell is planning a contemporary American
sculpture show down at U.S.C.," Sam said. "I told him
that no show would be complete without something of
yours in it. So you see I'm not as much against you as
you think."

She held up her hand in mock surrender. "Sam, you're
absolutely right. Assemblage is the art of the future!"

They all laughed.

"I'll get Arlene Gately to show you around," she said
to Dr. Bell. Arlene Gately, who ran a small gallery
downtown, was acting as her sponsor and agent.

"That won't be necessary. I'd really much prefer to
poke around on my own."

"Please do." She smiled. "If there's anything you
want to know, please ask me."

The professor bowed slightly and wandered off. Nora

turned back to Sam. "You stinker!" she whispered. "You might have tipped me off."

"I wanted to. But every time I looked for you, you were surrounded." He fished a pipe out of his jacket and stuck it in his mouth. "By the way, is it true that you may have a show at the Clay Club in New York next month?"

She looked at him curiously. "How did you know that?"

"Arlene. Where else?"

"Sometimes Arlene talks too much," she said. "It's not definite yet." She looked after Professor Bell. "Do you really think he'll take something?"

"Who knows? We'll keep our fingers crossed. It's time San Francisco came up with another real sculptor besides Bufano."

"Do you think I'm real, Sam?" she said, a sudden seriousness in her eyes.

"You're the realest there is," he said, equally serious. "And I have a hunch Bell will agree with me."

She took a deep breath. "Then I'll keep both my fingers and toes crossed."

He turned back to her and smiled. "If it works, maybe for a change I won't have to listen to an artist who claims that the only true inspiration is to be found in Marxism."

She laughed. "Poor Sam, you do have your troubles, don't you?"

"How would you know?" he asked wryly. "I haven't seen much of you lately."

She put her hand on his arm. "It isn't that I love you any the less, Sam. It's just that I've been doing my bit. Between the aircraft factory and the studio I haven't been able to get around very much."

"You seem sort of tense. What you need is one of my famous relaxing treatments."

She looked at him thoughtfully. Neither of them was a fool. And favors were favors. It meant nothing and it meant everything. That was the kind of world they lived in. "It has been a long time, Sam, hasn't it?"

"Too long," he replied.

"Do you think the doctor could find time for me tonight?"

"I think he might manage. About eight, at my place?"

"I'll be there."

She watched him as he walked up to Professor Bell. She tried to hear what they were saying but a hand on her arm turned her away.

"How is it going, my dear?"

"Fine, Mother."

"I'm glad." Cecelia Hayden smiled. She didn't smile very often, and it lit up the bright blue eyes under her carefully combed white hair. "I was wondering if you had time to do me a little favor."

"What is it, Mother?"

"There's a young man, the son of a friend of your father's. I had forgotten about your show when I invited him for cocktails this afternoon. He'll probably stay for dinner."

"Oh, Mother!" Nora said in an exasperated voice. "This just isn't the time. I've got too many things on my mind."

"Please, dear."

Nora looked at her mother. Those two words left no room for argument. Despite her frail appearance, Cecelia Hayden was hard as a rock.

"He seems such a nice young man," she continued. "A war hero. And he has just three days before he returns to duty. I'm sure you'll like him. I told Charles to bring him over when he arrived."

Nora nodded and turned just as Sam came over to her, an excited expression on his face. "He wants *The Dying Man.*"

"Not that one!" Her voice filled with dismay.

"He likes it."

"Talk him out of it," she begged. "I didn't even want to have it on display. I wouldn't have if I hadn't needed a big piece to fill up that corner. I don't even work that way any more."

"It doesn't matter. That's the one he wants."

She turned and looked through the crowd at the large iron figure. It was a man half sunk to the ground, leaning on his elbow with one hand across his heart, an expression of agony contorting his features. She remembered the excitement of working on it, but it somehow seemed ugly to her now.

"Please, Sam, talk him into something else!"

"Not me, not after he told me that this was the first time he'd ever seen an artist capture the exact moment of death in sculpture."

She stared at him. "He really said that?"

Sam nodded.

She looked toward the statue again, trying to see in it what the teacher had. "All right," she said finally.

"Good. I'll tell him he can have it."

At least it was a big piece, she thought consolingly. And that was better to have in a mixed show than a small one. People couldn't miss seeing it.

She was standing like that with a thoughtful expression on her face when her mother brought me over. Mrs. Hayden touched her arm and Nora turned toward us. She raised her face and I saw that she was the girl I'd seen that noon in the factory window.

I saw her eyes grow large in a curious kind of surprise and I knew that she had recognized me too.

"Nora. This is Major Luke Carey. Major Carey, my daughter Nora."

3

Wars are the whetstones that man uses to sharpen his appetites.

I looked at her and I knew I was gone.

Some girls are bitches, some are ladies, and once to every man there is one who is both. I knew that as soon as I touched her hand.

The dark-blue eyes were almost violet, hidden by long heavy lashes, and the thick black hair was pulled up and away from her forehead. Her creamy translucent skin, taut across the high cheekbones, and the slim, small-breasted, almost boyish, figure added up to all the wrong kinds of arithmetic. But it was just right for me.

This was the deep end. Life and death. Over and out.

Her mother wandered off somewhere and I was still holding her hand. Her voice was low and had that carefully cultivated affectation that is common to girls who go to the good Eastern schools. "What are you looking at, Major Carey?"

I let go of her hand quickly. It was like losing touch with a peculiar kind of reality, like beating your head against a wall because it feels so good when you stop. "I'm sorry," I said. "I didn't mean to stare."

"How did you know where to find me?"

"I didn't. It was just a lucky accident."

"Are you always this lucky?"

I shook my head. "Not always."

I saw her eyes move across the ribbons on my blouse. I knew what she saw. Besides the Purple Heart and

Cluster, there was enough color there to brighten up a small Christmas tree.

"At least you're alive."

I nodded. "I guess I have no complaints. I've made it this far."

"You don't believe you'll make it all the way?"

It was more a statement than a question. I laughed. This girl wasn't one to waste time, she zeroed right in.

"I've been lucky twice," I said. "There's no three times lucky."

"Are you afraid of dying?"

"All the time."

She glanced at the ribbons again. "I'm sure they wouldn't send you back if you told them."

"I guess not," I said. "But I wouldn't."

"Why not?"

"I guess I'm more afraid of chickening out than I am of dying."

"That can't be the only reason."

I was beginning to feel uncomfortable. She never stopped pressing. "Maybe it isn't," I admitted. "Maybe it's because death is like a woman you've been chasing for a long time. You want to find out if it's as bad or as good as you thought it would be."

"Is that all you think about?" she asked. "Death?"

"For almost two years now I haven't had much time to think about anything else." I glanced toward the statue I had noticed as I came in, *The Dying Man*. I felt her eyes follow mine. "I'm like the man in that statue over there. For every moment that I live."

I saw her study the statue for a moment, then she took my hand again. I felt her shiver.

"I didn't mean it to sound so bloody awful."

"Don't apologize," she said quickly. Her eyes were dark now, almost purple-black, like the heavy wine grapes in the vineyards near Sacramento. "I know exactly what you mean."

"I believe you do." I smiled and then looked away. I had to.

"You know," I said, "when I first heard about this shindig, I thought it was going to be pretty dull. Another society girl playing at the arts." I felt it was safe to turn back to her now. "But I've got a hunch you're pretty good."

"She's better than that, Luke." The familiar voice came from behind me. "She's very good."

I spun around. It had been more than three years since I'd heard that voice. "Professor Bell!"

He sounded excited and pleased as he shook my hand. "Luke was one of my boys just a few years back," he said to Nora. "He majored in architecture."

"Building." I grinned, reviving the old argument between us. "Architecture is something for pigeons to sit on, building is for people."

"The same old Luke." He looked into my face and I saw the shock in his eyes. I had seen that look before in the eyes of old friends. The tiny crisscrossed shrapnel scars in my coppery leathered skin somehow didn't belong on the pink-cheeked boy who had gone away to war.

"Not quite the same, Professor," I said, trying to make it easier for him. "It's been a long war."

And all the while we stood there talking I felt her hand growing warmer and warmer in mine.

Dinner was served in the big dining room looking out over the hill toward the bay. Everyone else had gone. There were just the three of us—Nora, her mother and I. I looked towards the head of the table where the old lady sat.

She seemed so right sitting there. Everything belonged. The rich oak paneling, the large round table, the candles glowing in the gleaming silver candelabra. She sat straight and tall, and there was something about her that reminded me of a shining blade of steel.

She was strong and sure of her strength in her calm, quiet way. You were aware of the wisdom that was in her, though there was never any need for her to assert it. From what my father had told me, a lot of people had been surprised when they'd had to deal with this quiet young widow who had inherited two large fortunes.

"My late husband often spoke of your father." She smiled across the table at me. "They were such good friends. It seems strange that we should never have met."

I nodded silently. It wasn't so strange to me. Until Dad retired last year, he had been the postmaster in the small Southern California town where I was born. He no more belonged in Gerald Hayden's world than Hayden belonged in his. All they shared was the memory of having been in the same platoon in the First World War.

"Your father saved my husband's life during the first war, you know."

"I heard the same story. But it was the other way around when my father told it."

She picked up a small silver bell from the table in front of her. It tinkled gently. "Shall we have coffee in the solarium?"

I looked over at Nora. She glanced down at her wrist watch. "You and Major Carey go ahead, Mother," she said. "I have an eight o'clock appointment downtown."

A hint of a frown crossed Mrs. Hayden's face and disappeared. "Do you have to, dear?"

Nora didn't look at her mother. "I promised Sam Corwin I would go over his plans for a show on modern sculpture."

Mrs. Hayden glanced at me, then at Nora. Her tone implied only the mildest protest but I had the feeling that she was choosing her words carefully. Whether it was because I was there or not I didn't know. "I thought you were beyond that sort of thing," she said. "It's been such a long time since you've seen Mr. Corwin."

"I have to, Mother. After all, it was Sam who was responsible for bringing Professor Bell to my show."

I turned to the old lady. "Please don't be upset on my account, Mrs. Hayden," I said quickly. "I'm due back at the Presidio at eight-thirty myself. I can drop your daughter off, if you'd like."

"I don't want to be any trouble," Nora said.

"It won't be. I'm using an Army car, so I don't have to worry about gas rations."

"All right," she said. "Just give me a few minutes to change."

We watched her leave, and when she was gone I turned to her mother. "You have a very talented daughter, Mrs. Hayden. You should be very proud."

"I am," she answered. Then a curious expression came into her bright blue eyes. "But I must confess, I don't always quite understand her. At times, I feel completely bewildered. She's so different from the young girls of my time. But then Nora is an only child and I had her late in life."

"It's the war. We're all very different."

"Nonsense. I hear that all the time," she said sharply. "It's poppycock. Your generation isn't the only one that fought a war. Mine did. And so did the young people of my parents' generation."

I could have argued about that but I didn't. "Your daughter is very talented," I said again. "Professor Bell often told me that talent isn't always the easiest thing in the world to understand, or to live with."

Her eyes brightened in amusement. "You're a nice young man. I hope you'll come to see us again. I have a feeling that you'll be very good for us."

"I hope to. But I'm going back overseas. Perhaps we'll make it when the war is over."

She looked directly into my eyes. "It may be too late then."

I guess the astonishment showed in my face, because she grew even more amused. I reached for a cigarette.

"I've heard you were a very promising young architect before you went into the service, Major Carey."

"Apparently you don't miss very much, Mrs. Hayden."

"I try not to, Major Carey. It's very important for a helpless widow to keep her eyes open."

I started to protest. Helpless widow indeed! Then I saw her smile again and I knew she was having me on. "What else did you find out about me, Mrs. Hayden?"

"Before the war you applied for a position with Hayden and Carruthers. They were quite impressed with you."

"The Army was more impressed."

"I know that, Major Carey," she said. "I also know your war record—"

I held up my hand. "Spare me that, Mrs. Hayden. What are you getting at?"

She looked directly at me. "I like you, Major Carey," she said. "Under the right circumstances there could be a vice-presidency for you at Hayden and Carruthers."

I stared at her. That *would* be starting at the top. Pretty good for a guy who never held a job after graduation. Hayden and Carruthers was one of the leading architectural concerns on the West Coast.

"How do you know that, Mrs. Hayden?"

"I know," she said quietly. "I own the controlling interest in the firm."

"And what would you consider 'the right circumstances'?"

She glanced at the doorway and then back at me. Her eyes were bright and steady. "I think you already know the answer."

Just then Nora came back into the room. "I hope I didn't keep you waiting too long."

"Not at all," I said.

"The Major and I were having a most interesting little chat, Nora."

I caught the quickly curious glance Nora threw at her mother. I looked down at the old lady. "Many thanks for the dinner, Mrs. Hayden," I said formally.

"You're quite welcome, Major. You just think about what I said."

"I will, ma'am. And thank you again."

"Goodbye, Major."

"Night, Mother," Nora said.

Her mother's voice caught us at the door. "Don't stay out too late, dear."

I caught the fragrance of Nora's perfume as she settled back in the seat. It bugged me. It wasn't the kind of perfume one wore to a business meeting.

"Where to ?" I asked.

"Lower Lombard Street. I'm not taking you out of your way, am I?"

"Not at all."

She moved closer and I felt her hand on my arm. "Did Mother talk about me?"

"No." I wasn't exactly lying. Or for that matter, telling the truth. "Why?"

"No reason," she said casually.

We drove silently for a few blocks.

"You're not really due back at the Presidio by eight-thirty, are you?"

"No," I said. "What about you? Can you get out of your date?"

She shook her head. "Not now. It's too late." She hesitated. "It wouldn't be fair. You understand, don't you?"

"I read you loud and clear."

She looked at me. "It's nothing like that," she said quickly.

"I didn't say anything."

I stopped the car for a traffic light. Its red glow turned her skin to flame. "What are you going to do now?" she asked.

"I don't know. Go down to Chinatown . . . tie one on maybe."

"That's pure escape."

The light changed and I started the car again. "The purest," I agreed. "But it's still the best way I know to turn things off."

I felt her hand tighten on my arm. "Is it that terrible?"

"Sometimes."

I could feel her fingernails through my jacket. "I wish I were a man!"

"I'm glad you're not."

She turned toward me. "Will you meet me later?"

I felt the hardness of her small breasts against my sleeve. I knew then that I had been right. She was everything I'd thought and it was there for the taking, but something held me back.

"I don't think so," I said.

"Why?"

"No reason." I was annoyed with myself. "It doesn't matter."

"It does to me. Tell me."

I sensed the angry harshness creeping into my voice. "I know at least a dozen places in this town where I could get seconds if that was all I was looking for."

She let go of my arm and moved away. I saw sudden tears forming in her eyes.

"I'm sorry," I said. "I've been away so long, I'm afraid I've forgotten how to act."

"You don't have to apologize. I deserved it." She looked out the window. "Turn here. It's in the middle of the next block."

I pulled the car to the curb.

"You have three more days of leave?"

"That's right," I said.

"Will you call me?"

"I don't think so. I'm going down to La Jolla to get in some fishing."

"I could come down there."

"I don't think that would be wise."

"Oh! You've got a girl there?"

I laughed. "No girl."

"Then why—"

"Because I'm going back to war," I said harshly. "Because I don't want any ties. I don't want to have anything to think about but making the next day. I know too many guys who lost all their tomorrows looking behind them."

"You're afraid."

"You're damn right I am. I told you that before."

Her tears were for real now. They rolled slowly down her cheeks. I put my hand on her shoulder. "Look, this is silly," I said gently. "Everything is screwed up right now. Maybe, some day, when the war is over. If I make it—"

She interrupted me. "But you told me yourself that no one is three times lucky."

"That's about the way it figures," I admitted.

"Then you really don't believe you'll call me. Ever." There was a strange sadness in her voice.

"I always seem to be apologizing to you. I'm sorry."

She stared at me for a moment, then got out of the car. "I don't like goodbyes."

I didn't have a chance to answer as she ran up the steps without looking back. I lit a cigarette and sat there watching as she rang the doorbell. After a moment a man came and let her in.

When I got back to my hotel, around three in the morning, there was a message under my door.

Please call me in the morning so that we may continue our discussion.

It was signed Cecelia Hayden.

I crumpled the note angrily and threw it into the wastebasket. I went down to La Jolla in the morning without bothering to call her.

Within the week I was on my way back to Australia and the war. If I ever thought that the old lady was hung up waiting for me to call I would have only been kidding myself.

There were some things she couldn't wait for. The next day she called Sam Corwin.

4

"Mrs. Hayden," Sam Corwin said, coming into the room where the old lady waited for him. "I hope I haven't kept you waiting."

"Not at all, Mr. Corwin," she replied crisply. "Please sit down."

He sank into the chair and looked at her with curiosity. Ever since she had called that morning, he had been wondering what it was she wanted to see him about.

She came right to the point. "Nora's been nominated for the Eliofheim Foundation Award for Sculpture."

Sam looked at her with a new and sudden respect. There had been rumors to that effect. But the names of the nominees were very closely guarded. Especially since this was the first award to be given since the war.

"How do you know?" he asked grudgingly. Even he hadn't been able to get any confirmation.

"It doesn't matter," she said briskly. "What is important is that I do know."

"Good. I'm very happy for Nora. I hope she gets it. She deserves it."

"That's what I wanted to see you about. I want to be sure that she does get it."

Sam stared at her. He didn't speak.

"Money can be a terrible handicap sometimes," Mrs. Hayden continued. "Especially in the arts. I would like to make certain that my daughter's wealth doesn't adversely affect her chances."

"I'm sure it wouldn't, Mrs. Hayden. The judges are above that sort of thing."

"No one is above prejudice of one sort or another," she said definitely. "And at the moment it seems to me that the whole liberal arts world is oriented to the Communistic ideology. Almost everything accomplished by anyone outside that group is automatically rejected as bourgeois and unimportant."

"Aren't you rather oversimplifying it?"

"Am I?" she countered, looking directly at him. "You tell me. Almost every major art award during the past few years has been won by an artist who if not actually Communistic was at least closely aligned with them."

Sam had no reply. She was very nearly correct. "Supposing I did agree with you. I still don't see what can be done about it. The Eliofheim can't be bought."

"I know that. But we both know that no one is beyond influencing, beyond the power of suggestion. The judges are only human."

"Where would I start? It would take some very important people to make them listen."

"I was talking to Bill Hearst at San Simeon the other day," she said. "He felt very strongly that Nora deserved the award. He felt it would be a triumph for Americanism."

Now it was beginning to make sense. He should have known right away where her information had come from. "Hearst could be helpful. Who else?"

"Your friend Professor Bell, for one," she said. "And Hearst has already talked to Bertie McCormick in Chicago. He's very much interested too. There must be many others, I'm sure, if you'd put your mind to it."

"It would take a lot of doing. This is February, so we have less than three months before the awards are announced in May. Even then we couldn't be sure."

She picked up a sheet of paper from her desk. "Your salary at the newspaper is about forty-five hundred. In addition to that you average approximately two thousand dollars for magazine articles and miscellaneous pieces." She looked over at him. "That's not really very much money, is it, Mr. Corwin?"

Sam shook his head. "Not very much, Mrs. Hayden."

"You have expensive tastes, Mr. Corwin," she continued. "You have a nice apartment. You live well, even if not entirely within your means. For the past few years you've been running into debt at an average of a little more than three thousand dollars a year."

He smiled. "I don't worry too much about my debts."

"I realize that, Mr. Corwin. I understand that a good deal of that money is never repaid in cash, but in favors. Would I be too far off if I assumed that your overall income is in the neighborhood of ten thousand a year?"

He nodded. "You wouldn't be far off."

She put the sheet of paper back on the desk. "I'm prepared to pay you ten thousand dollars for your assistance in securing the Eliofheim Award for my daughter. If she gets it, we will enter into a ten-year contract guaranteeing you twenty thousand a year, plus ten per cent of her gross earnings."

Sam calculated swiftly. At Nora's present rate of output she should be able to gross between fifty and a hundred thousand a year if she won the award. "Make it fifty per cent."

"Twenty-five per cent," she said quickly. "After all, my daughter still has to pay her gallery fees."

"Just a moment, Mrs. Hayden. This is going a little too fast for me. Let's see if I understand what you're saying. You're hiring me as a press agent to help Nora get the Eliofheim Award?"

"That's right, Mr. Corwin."

"And if she gets the award, we then enter into an agreement whereby I become her personal representative, agent, manager or whatever for a period of ten years? For this I will be paid twenty thousand a year plus twenty-five per cent of her gross earnings from her work?"

Mrs. Hayden nodded again.

"What if she doesn't get the award?"

"Then there wouldn't be much point in any agreement, would there, Mr. Corwin?"

"No, of course not," he said. He looked at her shrewdly. "If we made the agreement, who would pay the guarantee?"

"My daughter, of course."

"It might happen that she wouldn't gross enough to make it worth her while."

"I doubt that would worry her." The old lady smiled. "Nora is a wealthy woman in her own right. She has an income of more than a hundred thousand a year from a family trust."

Sam stared at her. He had known that Nora had money but he'd never realized it was anywhere near that much. "I'm curious about one thing, Mrs. Hayden. Have you talked to Nora about this?"

She nodded. "Of course, Mr. Corwin. I wouldn't have discussed it with you unless I had Nora's full consent."

Sam took a deep breath. He should have known that. But he couldn't keep himself from asking another question. "Then why didn't she speak to me herself?"

"Nora felt it would be better if you and I discussed it first," the old lady replied. "Then, had you not agreed, her relationship with you would not have been disturbed."

Sam nodded. "I see." He fumbled in his pocket for

his pipe and put it in his mouth thoughtfully. "Of course, you both realize that if I undertake this job, my decision on all business matters would be final?"

"Nora has the greatest regard for both your integrity and acumen, Mr. Corwin."

"You've just made a deal, Mrs. Hayden."

"Nora will be very pleased."

"Where is she? There are a number of things we'll have to discuss."

"I'll have Charles call her," Mrs. Hayden said. "I believe she's in the studio."

She pressed a button and the butler appeared in the doorway. She asked him to call Nora and turned back to Sam. Her voice was deceptively gentle. "I too am very pleased, Mr. Corwin. It will be a great comfort to me to know that someone besides myself is concerned with Nora's welfare."

"You can be sure that I'll do my best, Mrs. Hayden."

"I'm sure that you will," she said. "I won't pretend that I always understand my daughter. She's a very strong-willed person. I don't always approve of her behavior."

Sam didn't answer, just sat there sucking at his pipe and looking at her. He wondered just how much she really knew about Nora. Her next statement made it clear that there was very little that she didn't know.

"I imagine I might be considered old-fashioned in many ways," she said, half apologetically. "But at times my daughter seems—shall I say—quite promiscuous?"

Sam studied her cautiously for a moment. "May I speak frankly, Mrs. Hayden?"

She nodded.

"Please understand, I'm neither defending Nora nor condemning her. But I think it's most important that you and I understand what we're talking about."

She was watching him as carefully as he had watched her. "Please go on, Mr. Corwin."

"Nora is no ordinary person," he said. "She's highly talented, perhaps a genius. I don't know. She's finely strung, acutely sensitive and highly emotional. She needs sex the way some people need liquor."

"Are you trying to tell me politely that my daughter is a nymphomaniac, Mr. Corwin?"

"That's not what I'm trying to say, Mrs. Hayden," he said, choosing his words carefully. "Nora is an artist. She finds both a certain stimulus and an escape in sex. She told me once that it helped bring her closer to people, to know more about them, to understand them better."

The old lady was still watching him. "Have you and Nora—?" She left the question hanging in the air.

He met her eyes squarely. He nodded without speaking.

She sighed softly and looked down at her desk. "Thank you for your honesty, Mr. Corwin. I didn't mean to pry into your personal relationships."

"It's been over for a long time," he said. "I found that out the last time she came to my place."

"That was about six months ago? Just about the time of her show?"

He nodded. "She seemed very upset. She'd been crying. It seems that young major who drove her over had been pretty rough on her."

"Major Carey," she said. "He seemed such a nice young man."

"He said something that upset her. Anyway, I sent her home in a cab a half hour after she arrived."

"I wondered why she got home so early that night. I'd like to ask one favor of you, Mr. Corwin."

"Anything I can do, ma'am."

"Nora has a high regard for your opinion. Help me —help her keep out of trouble."

"I'll try, Mrs. Hayden. For all our sakes."

"Thank you," she said. Suddenly she seemed very tired. She leaned back in her chair and closed her eyes. "Sometimes I think the best thing for her would be to get married. Perhaps then she would feel different."

"It might be." But inside, Sam knew better. Girls like Nora never changed, married or not.

They sat silently until Nora came into the room. "Mr. Corwin has agreed to our proposition," her mother said.

Nora smiled. She held out her hand. "Thanks, Sam."

"Don't thank me," he said. "You may be sorry before all this is over."

"I'll take my chances."

"Okay," he said, his voice brisk and businesslike. "Now—what are you working on?"

"I'm getting ready for a show that Arlene Gately is giving in April."

"Cancel it."

"What on earth for?"

"We can't afford it."

"But I promised—"

"Then you'll have to break your promise," Sam said gruffly. He turned to her mother. "Make out a check for ten thousand dollars. Nora and I are going to New York."

"New York?" Nora asked. "Why?"

Her mother was looking questioningly at Sam. "New York," he repeated. "I want Aaron Scaasi to give her a show in April."

"I—I couldn't do that."

"Why not?" he asked harshly.

"Because Arlene has always been my agent. She's put

on every show I've ever had. I can't just walk out on her after all this time."

"You can and you will. Arlene Gately may be very nice but she's nothing but a small-time, small-town dealer and you've outgrown her. Aaron Scaasi is recognized as one of the leading dealers in the world. A show at his gallery will do more toward getting you that award than anything else right now."

"But how do you know he'll do it?"

"He'll do it." Sam smiled. "Your check for ten thousand dollars says that he will."

All this, of course, took place while I was still in the Pacific.

I was a big man for the Somerset Maugham kind of story. The sweating, steaming jungle lulling the white man into a torpor, then seducing him with the aid of a lovely brown-skinned maiden to a happy way of life never dreamed of in dear old Blighty. It never was like that for me. I guess I was in the wrong jungle.

It was always cold and dank at the airstrip north of Port Moresby, and no matter how many layers of clothing you wore, the chill ate its way into your bones. Your teeth always chattered, and your nose always ran, and it was easier to catch the flu than malaria. We spent most of our spare time huddling around the pot-bellied stove in the pilots' ready room, debating the serious tactical aspects of the war—like would Pat make the Dragon Lady before she copped Terry's cherry, or would Daisy Mae ever succeed in freeing Li'l Abner of Momism.

In between these high-level discussions, we ran out to our planes when the siren shrieked and went up and came down again, then sent our drawers to the little black Fuzzies who did our laundry so that we would be ready for the next flight. There is something very unesthetic about dying in stained underwear. Almost un-American you might say.

I made it to Lieutenant Colonel the hard way. My flight commander was shot out of the sky in front of me and I was moved up into his place. I remember what I thought when they swapped my gold oak leaves for silver. Like everybody dies, now it's my turn.

But I'd been lucky. I still remember the surprise I'd felt at the sudden needle-like pain lacing up my back. The instrument panel disintegrated before my eyes as the Jap Zero spun out over my head and into the water, while I tried to get away from the one beneath me. I don't know how I made it back to the airstrip. I seemed to be floating in a sea of jelly, and then the plane hit the ground and rolled over. Somewhere in the distance I heard someone yelling and felt hands pulling at me. They were warm hands, comforting hands, even though they were trying to take me away from the beautiful heat that surrounded me.

I closed my eyes and gave myself up to them. It was about time I got to that jungle I'd read so much about. I smiled to myself.

This was more like it. I was lying on the beach at Bali Bali and a thousand bare-breasted beauties all looking like Dorothy Lamour were parading up and down and the only problem I had was to decide which one of them I would choose for that evening.

This was one dream I would never give up. MacArthur would just have to learn to get along without me.

I was shipped back stateside as soon as I was well enough to travel.

5

I didn't learn that Nora had won the Eliofheim Award until the second week in July, and then only when I happened to see her picture on the cover of *Life*.

Since February, when I'd been hit, I'd put in five weeks in a hospital in New Guinea, then seven more in the Veterans' at San Diego, after which I'd been discharged as good as new. I had a thirty-day leave coming before returning for reassignment, so I went back to La Jolla, renting a small boat on which I could eat and sleep and begin to soak up a little sun.

I'd been dozing on a deck chair when the thud of a bundle hitting the deck woke me. I opened my eyes to see a boy standing at the edge of the dock grinning at me. I made it a point not to read the daily papers I'd had enough of the war. But I had asked the newsstand to drop off a few magazines every week.

I stuck my hand in my pocket and spun a half-dollar in the air. He caught it with all the grace of Joe Di-Maggio pulling down a high fly ball.

I leaned over and picked up the bundle and pulled the string that held it together. The magazines slid to the floor and I picked up the first one that my hands touched.

I stared at the picture of the oddly familiar-looking dark-haired girl on the cover, and I remember thinking how nice it was that they'd finally gotten off the war kick. Then I realized why the girl seemed so familiar.

It was there in small white block letters: Nora

HAYDEN—WINNER OF THE ELIOFHEIM FOUNDATION AWARD FOR SCULPTURE.

I looked at the picture again and the old itch came back. The luminous dark eyes, the oddly sensual mouth over the proud, almost haughty, chin. It was like yesterday, though it had been almost a year since I'd seen her.

I opened the magazine. There were more pictures inside. Nora working in the small studio out in back of her mother's house. Nora smoking, while sketching out an idea. Nora sitting at a window, her face silhouetted by the light behind her. Or stretched out on the floor, listening to a record player. I began to read.

The slim Miss Hayden, who looks more like a model than an artist, leaves no doubt in your mind where she stands in regard to her work.

"Sculpture is the one true life form in art," she maintains. "It is three-dimensional. You can walk around it, see it from any angle, touch it, feel it as you would any living thing. It has shape, form and reality and it exists in life all around you. You can see it in any stone, in the flowing grain of every piece of wood, in the tensile, yielding strength of every strip of metal.

"It remains only for the artist to bring forth this buried vision from the raw material, to fuse it into shape, to breathe it into life . . ."

I could hear her voice echoing in my ear.

I turned back to the cover of the magazine and studied her picture. That did it. I dropped the magazine to the deck and got to my feet. So I changed my mind. What difference did it make if it was a year later?

I stood in the cramped, narrow telephone booth at the foot of the dock, hearing the phone ring at the other end of the line in San Francisco. Her mother answered.

"This is Luke Carey," I said. "Remember me?"

The old lady's voice was clear and firm. "Of course I do, Colonel. How are you?"

"I'm fine, Mrs. Hayden. And you?"

"I have never been ill a day in my life," she answered. "I read about you in the papers. That was a very brave thing you did."

"The newspapers made too much of it. I really had no choice. There was nothing else I could do."

"I'm sure there was more to it than that. But we can discuss that at another time." I could hear her voice soften. "I'm sorry that Nora isn't here. I know that she will be disappointed."

"Oh," I said. "And I did so want to congratulate her on winning the Eliofheim Award."

"That's why she went away. The poor child hasn't had a moment's rest since the announcement was made. I insisted that she go down to La Jolla to get away from it."

"Did you say La Jolla?"

"Yes." A sudden awareness came into her voice. "Where are you calling from?"

"La Jolla. I'm spending my leave down here."

"Isn't that a fortunate coincidence, Colonel? Of course, now I do remember seeing something in the papers about your being there. Nora's at the Sand and Surf Club."

"I'll call her," I said.

"If you can't reach her, Colonel, get in touch with Sam Corwin. He'll know where to find her."

"Sam Corwin?"

"Yes," she said. "You remember him. The newspaperman friend of Professor Bell's. He's taken over the management of my daughter's affairs. The poor child has no head for business."

The old lady's voice changed again. "I do hope we won't have to wait another year to see you, Colonel. I still feel we have something to discuss. It seems to me that Hayden and Carruthers would be an excellent place for you to resume your career."

"Thank you for thinking of me, Mrs. Hayden. We'll talk about it real soon."

"You're welcome, young man. Goodbye."

The phone clicked and I hesitated a moment before putting in another nickel. This time Corwin answered.

"Is Miss Hayden there?" I asked.

"Who's calling?"

"Luke Carey."

It seemed to me that his voice grew friendlier. "Colonel Carey?"

"Yes."

"Just a moment, please. I'll see if I can find her."

I held onto the telephone a moment, then I heard her voice.

"Colonel Carey. This is a surprise. How did you know where to reach me?"

I laughed. "Your mother told me. I thought we might meet for a drink."

"Are you in La Jolla?"

"About three miles from where you are," I said. "How about it?"

"I'd love to. But Aaron Scaasi, my agent, is due in from New York any minute now. We have a cocktail thing set up for the press at five o'clock."

I waited for her to suggest another time but she didn't. Fair enough, I thought, she had no reason to. I hadn't exactly been the politest the last time we'd seen each other.

"I'll try again," I said.

"Please do," she said politely and hung up.

I squinted up at the sky as I moved off down the dock. It was a good sky. Blue, like in the postcards, with a few high-running clouds. The sun was nice and warm; later it would get hot and heavy, but by then I wouldn't care—I'd be out on the water.

That was the end of it, I thought. But, then, I didn't know what Sam told her after I hung up the phone.

"You weren't very cordial," Sam said as she put down the telephone.

"Damn. A whole year. Who does he think he is?"

Sam walked back to her sketch pad and looked down at it. The sketch was of a young man about to dive. He was nude. Sam knew the face. It was the high school boy who worked as a lifeguard at the club.

"He's not one of these kids," he said drily.

"That has all the earmarks of a crack. Do you have any objections?"

"Not personally," he answered. "I don't give a damn whom you go to bed with. But when it becomes public knowledge it affects our business."

Her voice grew cold. "Where did you hear about it?"

"It's the big noise down on Muscle Beach. You're too much for the kid to keep to himself. He's been filling in his buddies, blow by blow. The kid left nothing out."

Angrily she tore the sketch from the pad and crumpled it. "The little bastard!"

"I told you to be discreet," he said patiently.

"What am I supposed to do?" she demanded, throwing the crumpled paper on the floor. "Become a nun?"

Automatically he picked the wad of paper off the floor and threw it into the wastebasket. He dug his pipe out of his pocket.

"I wish you'd get rid of that damned pipe! I can't stand its stink."

Silently he put it back in his pocket and started for the door. She stopped him. "Sam." Her anger had left her and suddenly she seemed young and helpless. "Sam, what do you think I ought to do?"

"I don't know," he said thoughtfully. "But I'd start by leaving these kids alone."

"I will, Sam," she said quickly.

"And another thing," he added. "It wouldn't hurt if you were seen with someone like your soldier boy who just called. It might help drown out the gossip."

When I got back, the ancient watchman seated on the bench in front of the dock office waved a tired hand at me. "Hi, kunnel."

"Hi."

"Hear tell they seen some marlin off'n Coronado. Might pay yuh to give it a look-see."

"Might do that," I said, giving him his daily bread.

He slipped the half-dollar into his pocket. "Thanks, kunnel." He squinted up at me with his watery eyes. "By the way, they's some gal out to your boat. I told her you was about due back from lunch."

I went down towards my boat. Nora must have heard my footsteps because she was standing on the deck when I came up. She was wearing a pair of blue polka-dot shorts and a halter, and she looked like a kid with her black hair tied behind in a pony tail.

"Hello," she said.

"Hello."

Her eyes crinkled against the sun. "It's my turn to apologize, Colonel."

I studied her for a moment, then I jumped down to

the deck beside her. "You didn't have to come all the way down here for that, Nora."

She put her hand on my arm. It was warm on my flesh. "But I wanted to, Colonel. I wanted you to know I was sorry."

She was so close I could smell the fragrance in her hair. It was good and clean and fresh—like the pines up in the hills, and all the makeup she wore was a faint shade of lipstick. I looked down into her eyes. It seemed like forever. Then I kissed her.

Her mouth was warm and sweet and her teeth were hard and sharp behind her soft lips. I felt her arm around my neck and the press of her body against mine. I dropped my hand to her waist and I could almost count every rib on the way down. It was the way I knew it would be between us.

I let her go as suddenly after I'd kissed her again, and reached for a cigarette. I spun the wheel of my Zippo but I couldn't get the damn thing to work. "Look, I'm shaking."

"I'm shaking, too," she said softly.

I took a drag on the cigarette I'd finally managed to get lit and then gave it to her.

She took one puff from it, then turned. "I wanted you to kiss me that very first time."

"I wanted to," I said.

"Then why didn't you?" Her eyes were like the shadows in the water between the boat and the dock. "You knew I was ready."

I turned away. "I thought you were—for somebody else."

"Did it matter that much even then?"

"It did to me," I said. "You took a long time making the scene. I wanted everything to be right between us."

"You weren't exactly the early bird yourself."

"No."

"Does it matter now?"

I took her into my arms again. "Nothing matters now."

Then the tears were in her eyes and wet against my cheeks. "Oh, Luke, Luke!"

I know what has been said about a woman's tears but I don't buy any of it. It's the greatest sop to a man's ego ever invented. I felt ten feet tall as I kissed her tears away. I never did get out to see if the marlin were really off Coronado that afternoon. Instead I climbed into my uniform for the first time since I'd come down here and trotted along after her to her press conference.

I was glad when it was almost over. It was deadly. The reporters were all over us the minute they saw us together.

They made us pose for pictures. They asked questions. Were we engaged? When were we getting married? How had we met? Was she going to Washington with me for the citation? Did I come down here to be near her or was it the other way around?

After a while they got tired of asking questions for which we had no answers, and the party got down to the business for which it had been organized. That was to listen to Aaron Scaasi expound on why he thought Nora was the greatest thing to happen to American sculpture since the totem pole.

I must say he was convincing. He even sold me. He was a bald, thickset man who looked more like an ex-pug than one of the most prominent art dealers in the country. He kept mopping at his head with a baby-blue handkerchief. Nora looked like a little child sitting there on the couch beside him.

Sam Corwin wandered over and sat down. "He

knows what he's talking about," he said, nodding toward Scaasi. "She's really very good."

I looked at Sam. He was a thin, almost delicate-looking man, whose appearance might fool you if you didn't notice the firm mouth and decisive chin. Inside, this lad was as hard as nails. "I believe him," I said, wondering just how deep Corwin's interest in Nora went.

It was as if he knew what I was thinking. "I've known Nora ever since she was in school. I always had faith in her, and I was very happy when she and her mother suggested I take charge of her affairs."

He studied me with his dark eyes. "I owe you a vote of thanks."

"Oh?" I said.

He nodded. "For coming to the party. Nora was very upset after she spoke to you and was all set to call it off if she couldn't find you to apologize. She's very emotional, almost like a child about things like that."

The party was beginning to break up and Corwin went off to exchange some final words with the newspapermen. Maybe the bourbon was dulling my senses, but I had the feeling that there had been more that he wanted to tell me.

Scaasi and Nora came over then and I found myself resenting the way he let his hand rest familiarly on her shoulder. "Perhaps you'd join us for dinner?"

I hesitated a moment, looking at Nora, then made up my mind. "No, thanks. You people have business to talk over and I don't want to intrude."

"You wouldn't be intruding," Nora said quickly. I saw the disappointment in her eyes.

For a moment I almost changed my mind. Then I thought better of it. I smiled, making my excuse. "I promised myself a crack at some marlin. I think I'll take the boat out tonight and lay up off Coronado. That way I'll be ready for them when the sun comes up."

"What time will you be back tomorrow?" she asked.

"Late."

"Then I won't see you. I'm due back in San Francisco the next morning."

"I'm sorry," I said.

Sam called to Scaasi and they left us alone. "Are you going to call me?" she asked.

"Of course."

"No, you're not," she said after a moment. "I know you won't. It will be just like the last time. You'll go back and I won't ever hear from you. I'll know nothing about you except what I read in the newspapers."

"Don't be silly. I said I'd call you."

"When?"

"First time I'm in San Francisco."

"That might be never," she said gloomily.

I took her hand. It seemed warm, soft and helpless. "I'll call you. I promise."

She looked at me strangely. "What if something happens to you? How will I know?"

"Nothing will happen to me. I'm convinced now. You know the old saying about being born to be hanged?"

The last of the reporters filed out. It was time to go. I shook hands all around.

"I'll walk to the door with you," Nora said.

We walked out into the patio. It was already dark and a thousand tiny stars were lighting up the night. I closed the door behind us. "I thought you didn't like goodbyes," I said. I knew I could have kissed her but I chose not to. If I had I never would have gone.

I think she knew it too. "This isn't goodbye," she whispered, her hand touching mine briefly. The door closed behind her and I went down to the cab.

Scaasi had gone to his room to wash up so Sam was alone when Nora came back in. He looked at her questioningly.

"Fix me a drink," she said.

Silently he got out of his chair and got her a Scotch and soda. She put it down. "I'm going to marry him," she said, almost defiantly.

Corwin still didn't say anything.

"Well, haven't you anything to say? It's what you and Mother want, isn't it?"

He was surprised. "How do you know?"

"I'm not that much of a fool," she said, picking up her drink again. "I knew it the minute you told me to call him back. Then when he said that Mother had given him my number, I was sure."

Now that she had said it, he was not too sure that he was happy about it. "Marriage is a serious business."

She finished her drink and put it down. "I know," she said.

"He seems like a nice guy."

"What you really mean is that I'm not!"

"I didn't say that."

"I know you didn't. But that's what you're thinking, isn't it? Because I am the way I am, I won't be a good wife to him?"

He was silent.

"Why can't I be?" she demanded. "I'm the right age. I'm not hard to take. I've got all the money we'll ever need, and after the war I can arrange it so he can do whatever he wants. Is that so bad?"

"Are you asking me or telling me?"

"I'm telling you!" she said angrily.

He pulled out his ever-present pipe. "In that case, I have just one question. Do you love him?"

She stared at him. That was the last thing she'd expected him to say. "Of course."

"All right, then." He smiled. "When is the wedding going to be?"

She saw his smile, and the anger and defiance slipped away from her. She smiled back. "Just as soon as I can get him to ask me," she answered.

6

I got out of my uniform and back into a pair of Levis when I got back to the boat. The gas tanks were full—I'd seen to that earlier in the day when I planned to go out after marlin—but I didn't like the way some of the plugs were firing, so I set about cleaning them. In turn that led to cleaning the rings, then the valves, and before I knew it, it was almost ten o'clock. Suddenly I realized that I was hungry.

I checked my stores but there was nothing I really felt like eating. Besides, I would have to lay in some supplies if I wanted to stay out all the next day. I found a little grocery store that was still open, picked up what I needed, and went to the Greasy Spoon for a very bad steak and the inevitable bottle of chili. There was no other way to make it go down.

Suddenly even the chili couldn't kill the lousy taste of the food. I looked down at my plate, disgruntled. If I hadn't been such a fool I might have enjoyed a decent dinner.

But not me. I had to be independent. No ties for little old Luke. He walked alone. I took another bite of the steak and chewed it reflectively. What was the matter with me anyhow?

The trouble was that I always tried to make more out of anything than it really was. I didn't know enough to take things as they were. I had to make it deep and take it big. What was it? Her money? The fact that the old lady had practically spelled it out for me? It couldn't be that. I remembered back in school they used to have a saying: It's just as easy to fall in love with a rich girl as it is with a poor one. And much better.

Then I knew what it was. I wasn't eager to get involved because I was afraid. Afraid that if I let myself fall for her, I'd really be gone. She was everything I'd ever wanted. Class and style and charm, all bright and shining with a veneer that only the years could achieve. All this plus an artistic talent and the wild fierce bitchiness that I sensed running deep within her. Life with a girl like that wouldn't be easy. Besides, how did I know she felt the same way? What did I have to offer?

I took another bite of the steak, but it was cold now and I pushed the plate away. I went back to the counter and picked up my two bags of groceries.

I had no ice locker so I put the groceries down on the floor of the cockpit and looked up at the sky. It was clear and the moon was so bright it seemed almost like daylight. I looked out at the sea. It was as smooth as the proverbial millpond. I checked my watch. It was half-past eleven. I could drop anchor off Coronado by a few minutes after one. I reached over and hit the starter button and went out on deck to cast off.

The trip took no longer than I thought. As I cut the engine and tossed out the anchor the spray came up to hit my face. It felt good. So I dropped my clothes on the deck and followed the anchor overboard.

There's something about swimming in deep water that's like being rocked in a cradle. The ocean has a swell to it, a body that you can feel. You rise with it and fall with it as you do with a woman; the motion soothes you and rests you and untangles all the knots.

Later I climbed back aboard and padded down the deck in my bare feet to the cabin. I pushed open the door and went in. I reached for a towel but my hand hit the empty rack. I'd just turned to tap the light switch when a voice came out of the darkness.

"Looking for a towel, Luke?"

One came hurtling out of the darkness, hit me and fell to the floor. I bent to pick it up.

I couldn't see her. She was in the shadows of the bunk but I heard her laugh. "My God, you're skinny. I watched through the porthole. I could count every bone."

Quickly I wrapped the towel around me. I heard her move, then her head blocked out the moonlight coming through the porthole. I felt the touch of her hands on my shoulder, and as she turned the moonlight caught her face. I reached out for her and I knew even before my fingers touched her that she was as naked as I.

I don't know how long we stood there in the tiny cabin, our lips touching, our bodies molded so that I could not tell where I left off and she began.

"I love you, Nora," I said.

I felt her stir slightly in my arms. "I love you, Luke." She laid her cheek against my chest. "I told you it wasn't goodbye."

I picked her up and carried her back to the bunk. "We'll never have to say goodbye again, you and I," I whispered. Her arms reached up and led me down into a wonderland I never had known before.

How sweet the flesh of love.

She was sleeping on her side when I awoke in the night, her back against the wall, her knees drawn up as much as space allowed. Her eyes were closed and even in the moonlight I noticed how long and dark her lashes were, and how like a little girl she looked when asleep. Slowly her eyes opened.

She closed them again for a moment, then opened them slowly. A mischievous smile came over her face.

She drew my head down to her breast. "Come here, baby."

Her breasts were like small ripe fruit, sweet and firm and warm, like the yellow clings on the trees in July. I kissed them and I heard her soft sensual cry of delight.

Later, much later, she lay with her face buried in my shoulder. "Luke," she whispered. "It was never like this for me before. Never."

I stroked her head gently. I didn't answer.

She raised her head to look into my eyes. "You do believe me, don't you?"

I nodded without speaking.

"You must believe me. You must!" she said fiercely. "No matter what people may say."

"I do believe you."

To my surprise she began to tremble and was suddenly very close to tears. "There are people who hate me! Who envy everything I have and everything I do. They're always making up stories about me. Telling lies."

I remember how very, very wise, how much older than she, I felt at that moment. "Forget about them. There are always people like that. But I know you. And anyone who knows you knows better than to listen to them."

I pressed her head down to my shoulder again, and after a while her trembling stopped. "Luke, what are you thinking?" She looked up into my face. "Luke, I have one terrible confession to make."

A sudden fear came up inside me. If she had been lying about anything, I didn't want to know. I didn't want anything to change between us. I didn't speak.

I think she knew what was going through my mind because she began to smile teasingly. "I can't cook."

The relief that went racing through me was almost

comic. I began to laugh. Then I crawled out of the bunk
to go and make coffee.

When I came back I saw that she had found an odd
length of wire. She sat quietly toying with it while I
drank the strong black coffee. I sat there fascinated as it
came to life and took on the outline of a man about to
dive into water. She noticed and put the wire down.

"Don't stop," I said. "I wish I could do things like
that."

She smiled. "Sometimes I wish I couldn't. I'd like to
stop but I can't. I keep seeing things in things and it's as
if they had to come out. Do you know what I mean?"

"I think so. You're one of the fortunate ones. Many
people see things but they can't make them come out."

She looked at the wire figure for a moment, then flung
it casually aside. "Yes, I'm one of the fortunate ones,"
she said, almost bitterly. "And you? What are you?"

I shrugged my shoulders. "I don't know. I never
thought about it. I'm just a guy, I guess, waiting for the
war to end."

"And what will you do then?"

"Find a job. Maybe if I'm lucky I can get to build a
few houses before I'm too old to get a kick out of it. I
don't know whether I'm really any good at it. I never
had a chance to prove myself. I went right out of college
into the Air Force."

"Professor Bell says you're very good."

"He's prejudiced," I said. "I was his favorite."

"Maybe I can help. I have a cousin who is a fairly
well-known architect."

"I know," I said. "George Hayden. Hayden and
Carruthers. . . ."

"How did you know?"

"Your mother told me."

She looked at me thoughtfully, then held out her hand

for a cigarette. I held the light for her. She took a deep drag. "Mother doesn't waste any time."

I didn't answer.

She leaned back. "It's so quiet out here. So big and empty and so far away from things. No noise to tear at your ears, no people to bug you. Just a tremendous deep calm. As if you're alone in another world."

I didn't speak.

"Luke." She didn't look at me. "Do you want to marry me?"

"Yes."

Now she did, her eyes light and dark all at once. "Then why don't you ask me?"

"What could I offer a girl like you?" I asked. "I've got nothing. No money, no job, no future. I don't even know if I'll be able to support a wife."

"Is that so important? I have enough—"

"It is to me," I said, interrupting her. "I'm old-fash-ioned like that."

She knelt down beside me and took my hands. "That doesn't matter, Luke. Believe me, it doesn't. Ask me to marry you."

I studied her silently.

Her eyes fell away from mine. "That is—if you really want to. But you don't have to just because of what hap-pened between us. I want you to know that."

I reached out and turned her face up to mine. "I love you," I said. "Will you marry me?"

She didn't answer, just looked at me and nodded, the tears bright in her eyes. I leaned over and kissed her gently on the lips.

"I'll have to let Sam know."

"Sam?" I asked.

"I have to. It's part of his job. He'll have to issue a press release. It's better than having some gossip columnist getting it first and making something dirty out of it."

I didn't answer.

She put a hand on my arm. "Sam's a good friend."

"Sam was your date the night I met you," I said.

"Oh, so that's it. You're jealous of him."

I didn't answer.

"You don't have to be. Sam's been a good friend to me for many years. Since I was in school."

"I know. He went to great lengths to tell me."

She stared at me for a moment. "And that's all he's been. A good friend. There was never anything between us, no matter what people say."

"Is that one of the things you were trying to warn me about?" I asked.

"Yes. But it's just another of their dirty lies!"

Right there I made the first mistake of our marriage. It was a lie all right, but the lie was her own. I don't know how I knew it but I did. Maybe it was the honest, candid look in her eyes or the straightforward tone of voice. Something about them didn't belong. This kind of thing I never felt in her; it didn't fit.

But the mistake was my own and there's no going back and doing it over. One lie leads to another, not only for the liar but for the pretending believer, until the truth becomes too terrible a thing for either to face. But I didn't know that then.

Instead, I thought that whatever it was that she didn't want me to believe had been over for a long time. It had happened before I knew her and it didn't matter now. I loved her and she loved me and everything else was yesterday. I leaned over and kissed her cheek lightly.

"I believe you," I said.

7

I glanced at Dani, sitting next to me, then across the table at Nora seated between Harris Gordon and her mother. Without making a point of it she managed studiously to avoid my gaze after our polite words of greeting. I wondered if the demons of memory ever returned to plague her as they had me.

Harris Gordon glanced at his watch. "I think we'd better get ready," he said. He looked down the table at Dani and smiled. "Run upstairs and get your coat, child."

Dani looked at him for a moment, then silently left the room. An awkward kind of silence fell upon us as if she had taken with her the invisible means that made communication amongst us possible.

Gordon cleared his throat. "Dani can ride with her mother and grandmother." He turned to me. "I'd appreciate it if you'd come with me, Colonel. It will give us a chance to talk."

I nodded. That was what I wanted. I still knew no more than I had last night after his telephone call. All through breakfast we had carefully avoided talking about the one thing that had brought us together.

"We can go in my car, Mother," Nora said. "Charles will drive us."

A soft sigh escaped Mrs. Hayden as she got to her feet. She looked at me with a faint grim smile. "Growing old is a painful process. It's never quite as graceful as we'd like it to be."

I returned her smile, nodding. I knew just what she meant.

When Gordon followed the old lady out, Nora and I were left alone. She picked up the coffeepot. "More coffee?"

I nodded.

"Cream and sugar?"

I looked at her.

She flushed. "How silly of me! I forgot. Black. No cream. One sugar."

We were silent a moment. "Dani's very pretty, don't you think?"

"Yes, she's very pretty," I said, sipping my coffee.

"What do you think of her?"

"I don't know what to think. It's been so long and I've only seen her for a few minutes."

A trace of sarcasm came into her voice. "I didn't think you'd need time to make up your mind. You used to say that you were both tuned in."

"We used to be," I said. "But that was a long time ago. She's grown up now and so much has happened to us both. I don't know, maybe it will come back in time."

"You used to be more sure of your daughter."

I glanced at her. "There were many things I used to be more sure about. Like right now, I'm sure you're deliberately making a big thing out of the word *daughter*. If you're trying to tell me something, this is as good a time as any."

A veil fell across her eyes. "You're exactly the way you were when we first met. Painfully blunt."

"It's too late for polite lies, Nora. We took that trip a long time ago and it didn't work. The truth is simpler. Nobody stumbles over things that way."

She looked down at the tablecloth. "Why did you

come?" she asked bitterly. "I told Gordon we didn't need you. We were getting along all right."

I got to my feet. "I didn't want to. But I'm sure if you had geen getting along so well, there wouldn't have been any need."

I turned and went out into the foyer. There was a peculiar knot in my gut. Nora hadn't changed a bit.

Dani was just coming down the stairs. I looked up at her and everything inside me stood still. It wasn't a little girl coming down the steps now. It was a young woman. Someone I had known very well. Her mother.

She was wearing a suit, her coat flung casually across her shoulders. Her hair was fluffed up, bouffant I think they call it, the lipstick fresh on her young mouth. The child that had sat next to me at the breakfast table disappeared again.

"Daddy!"

The ice inside me vanished. The voice was still a child's voice. "Yes?"

She came down and spun around in front of me. "How do I look?"

"Like a living doll." I smiled, reaching for her.

"Don't, Daddy," she said quickly. "You'll muss my hair."

The smile left my face. She was still a child if that was all that worried her. But maybe it wasn't that at all. Nora acted like that when she wanted to preserve what she called her *image*. I wondered if my daughter had grown to think like her too.

Dani seemed to sense my uneasiness. "Don't worry, Daddy," she said, in the same oddly reassuring voice she had used when Nora had come into the room. "Everything will be all right."

I looked down at her. "I'm sure it will."

"I know it will, Daddy," she said with a curious emphasis. "Some things just have to happen before people can grow up."

I stared at her.

The old lady came into the foyer then, followed by Gordon and Nora.

"Tell Charles to follow my car," Gordon said, as he opened the front door for them.

"What time are we due in court?" Nora asked as they walked past.

He looked at her quizzically. "We don't go to court today. We're merely returning the child to the custody of the juvenile authorities."

"I'm glad. I don't think I'm up to appearing in court."

Gordon didn't answer, just nodded as she walked on down toward the cars. "After you, Colonel," he said politely.

Charles was holding the door of Nora's Jaguar as I came up. A wrinkled smile came to his face. "Colonel Carey."

"Charles." I smiled and held out my hand. "How have you been?"

"Fine, Colonel." His voice took on a warmth. "Despite the circumstances, it's good to see you again, sir."

"Close the door, Charles," Nora said from inside the car.

Charles nodded and shut the door. He shot me a look as he hurried around and got in behind the wheel.

"Did you drive, Colonel?" Gordon asked.

I pointed to the little rented Corvair, a pygmy between two giants, his black Cadillac and Nora's gray Jag.

"Then I'll have my chauffeur follow us," he said. "You may want it when we're finished."

He signaled with his hand and we began to move down the long driveway, the other cars filing along behind us. The gardener opened the gates and we passed through. There was a group of reporters standing outside, but they scattered to their cars when they saw we weren't going to stop. Gordon signaled again and we turned west along California Street past the Grace Cathdral.

We both reached for the dashboard lighter at the same time. He laughed and gestured. I lit my cigarette, then held it for him.

"Thanks." He didn't look at me. "I hope you carry no grievance against me because of our previous encounter?"

I glanced at him. I remembered a picture I had once seen of Gene Tunney and Jack Dempsey at some sports dinner—Tunney was smiling but Dempsey's face wore a black scowl. I knew now how he had felt.

No matter how long ago it may have happened, nobody likes to remember a beating. I was no exception. I didn't like it, but like everyone else I had to learn to live with it.

"Just see that you do as good a job for my daughter. I'll have no complaints."

He didn't miss my evasion but he chose to disregard it. "Good. You can be sure that I will."

I waited until we swung into Gough Street, then said, "All I know is what you told me over the telephone or what I've read in the papers. Perhaps you can fill me in."

"Of course." He glanced at me curiously. "I trust I don't have to elaborate on Nora's relationship with Riccio?"

I shook my head. I knew Nora.

"They'd been quarreling all day," he said. "From what I gather, Nora wanted to end their relationship, both business and personal. She asked him to leave the house immediately. He had a good thing going for him and wasn't about to give it up."

"Nora find another boy?" I asked.

Again the side glance. He shrugged his shoulders. "I don't know and I didn't ask. The police were already on the scene when I arrived. I didn't think it prudent to inquire."

"I see," I said.

We turned west again on Market Street. "Apparently Riccio had followed Nora down to the studio from her room, still arguing. Dani was in her room trying to study when she heard her mother scream. She ran downstairs and saw Riccio advancing threateningly on her mother. Picking up the sculptor's chisel from the table, she ran between them and stabbed Riccio in the stomach. When Riccio fell to the floor bleeding, the child got hysterical and started to scream. Charles came running into the room, followed by Nora's maid. Nora told Charles to call the doctor on the house phone, then called me on the studio phone. I asked her to notify the police and to cooperate with them, but to make no statement until I arrived. I got there in about twenty minutes. The police arrived at least ten minutes before I did."

I ground out my cigarette in the ashtray. "Now for the big one."

"Did Nora kill him? Is that what was on your mind?"

I nodded.

He answered very slowly. "I don't think so. I spoke to both of them before any statements were made. Their separate stories were too mutually corroborative to be disputed."

"They had time to agree on their stories."

He shook his head again. "I've had too much experience with this sort of thing to be taken in. Besides, neither of them was in any condition to cook up a phony.

They were both close to hysterics. It would have been impossible for them to be coherent enough to fabricate a story."

"There were no other witnesses?"

"None."

"What happened then?"

"Dr. Bonner, who arrived before I did, took Nora upstairs and gave her a shot. Then I had Sergeant Flynn call you while I went down to Police Headquarters with Dani where she gave a statement. I read it to her and despite my advice she insisted on signing it. From Police Headquarters I went to the juvenile detention home, where Dani was given into custody of the juvenile authorities. Fortunately, I was able to persuade the probation officer to call the Juvenile Court judge who, upon hearing Dr. Bonner's recommendation, sent Dani home for the night. I took her to her grandmother's and it was from there that I called you."

We were on Portola Drive now, climbing up into the hills. I looked back. Nora's Jag was right behind us, and off to the left I could see almost the whole city sprawled out. On the right I noticed the familiar sights of construction. We were coming to a big billboard.

THIS IS DIAMOND HEIGHTS

This was where I had come to buy our Christmas trees when Nora and I were first married. I remembered I had once considered it as a building site for my first project, but there had been a shoring problem because of the hills, and the city would not cooperate. But land was less plentiful now and more valuable. Apparently the authorities had seen the light.

I looked at the houses with a critical eye. They were doing a good job.

I turned back to Gordon. "Exactly what made you decide to call me?"

He shrugged his shoulders. "I don't really know. I had a hunch, I guess. I had the feeling that you'd be a good man to have around in a spot like this."

"You thought that even after what Nora said the last time we were in court?"

He didn't answer right away. When we reached the top of the hill we made a sharp right turn onto Woodside Avenue. A series of dull-green buildings loomed up on our right. We turned into a driveway and up and around behind the buildings. I noticed a small sign, CHILD IN-TAKE DIVISION.

Gordon stopped the car and shut off the motor, then turned to look at me. His voice was level and his eyes met mine squarely. "What I think doesn't matter. It's what you think that counts. The responsibility is yours. Either you're her father or you're not."

He opened the door and got out. I heard an automobile come up behind us. I looked in the rear-view mirror and saw Nora's Jaguar. Slowly I reached for the door handle.

The reporters and photographers were all around us before Nora's car came to a stop. Gordon gestured toward a door behind him. "Get her in there as quickly as you can."

I nodded and pushed my way through to the door of the car. Nora got out first. I took her hand to steady her. The flashbulbs went off. She turned and both of us helped Dani out. Her hands were cold as ice; I could feel them trembling in mine.

"Don't look at them, sweetie. Just come with me."

Dani nodded silently and we started for the door. The reporters pressed against us, forcing us to stop.

"Hold it for a picture, please!" one of them called.

I sensed Dani's almost instinctive obedience to the voice of authority. I kept nudging her. "Keep moving, honey."

Gordon managed to join us and we made a tight knot around Dani as we pushed our way to the door.

"Lay off, fellows," Gordon pleaded. "Give the kid a break!"

"That's what we want to do, lawyer man!" a voice from the back of the crowd shouted raucously. "A front-page picture of the youngest murder defendant you ever had!"

Dani's face went white and her knees sagged. I locked one arm around her waist and flailed out angrily with the other. "Leave her alone or I'll break your cruddy necks!" I shouted.

Suddenly they were quiet. I don't know whether it was

my anger or their own embarrassment over that stupid remark, but those closest to us fell back. I half dragged Dani through the doorway and Nora and Gordon followed. Gordon turned and closed the door.

Dani was sagging against me, her eyes half closed. She was so pale that the small amount of makeup on her face stood out sharply. I pressed her head against my chest and held her tight. "Take it easy, baby."

I could feel her trembling. She tried to speak but no words came out. She shivered violently.

"There's a bench over there, Mr. Carey," a white-uniformed nurse said. I hadn't seen her come up.

I led Dani to the bench and we sat down, her face still against my chest. The nurse bent over, a bottle of smelling salts in her hand. "Give her a whiff of this, Mr. Carey," she said sympathetically.

I took the bottle and passed it under Dani's nostrils. The faintly pungent odor came up to me. Dani sniffed, then coughed.

The nurse took the bottle and gave me a glass of water. I held it to Dani's lips. She sipped, then sipped again slowly.

She looked up at me. Some of the color had come back into her face. "I'll—I'll be okay, Daddy," she whispered huskily.

"Sure?"

She nodded. Her eyes were a deep violet like her mother's, though softer and somehow gentler. But now they were suddenly old and tired and hurt. "I'll get used to it, Daddy. It will just take a little time."

"You don't have to get used to anything!" I said angrily.

She smiled. "Don't worry, Daddy. I'll be okay."

I caught Nora's eye. I knew that look. I'd seen it many times before when she looked at Dani and me. As if we were two people from another planet. A flash of the old bitterness crossed her face.

"Do you feel well enough to come to the desk, child?" the nurse asked.

Dani nodded. As she got to her feet I took her arm. She pushed my hand away and I knew she had seen the look on her mother's face. "I can manage, Daddy."

I followed her to the small registration desk. There was a sign on the painted bare wall—GIRL INTAKE. It looked a little like a cheap hotel.

Under that sign was another, smaller.

Girls will be allowed no makeup except one pale lipstick. Everything else must be checked at this desk before proceeding to the cottages.

A quiet-looking gray-haired woman sat behind the desk.

"Your daughter doesn't have to sign in again, Mr. Carey. She was already signed in last night. All she has to do now is check her valuables."

Dani placed her small purse on the desk. "I can keep a lipstick and a comb?"

The woman nodded.

Dani opened the bag and took out a lipstick and comb. Then she took off her wrist watch and put it in the purse. She reached up and unclasped a single strand of pearls and put that in too. She started to take the ring from her finger, but it wouldn't come off. She looked at the woman questioningly.

"I'm sorry, Dani," the woman said gently.

Dani sucked her finger for a moment. Finally the ring came off, leaving a white band. She held it hesitatingly over the open purse for a moment, then turned and gave it to me. "Will you keep it for me, Daddy?"

There was something in her voice that made me look at the ring. I could feel the knots around my heart. Like it was a hot afternoon in La Jolla and she was six years old and I blew my last fifteen bucks on a fourteen-carat gold ring for her birthday. I'd had her initials engraved on it—D. N. C. Danielle Nora Carey. I noticed where it had been expanded to make it larger as the years went by. For a moment I couldn't speak. I just nodded and put the ring carefully into my pocket.

Just then the door opened again and old Mrs. Hayden came in. "Those wretched reporters! I gave them a piece of my mind!"

As she came toward us she looked at Dani. "Are you all right, child?"

"I'm all right, Grandmother."

"Time to go, Dani," the gray-haired woman said quietly. "Miss Geraghty will take you to the cottages."

Suddenly Dani seemed very much alone. A look of apprehension came into her face. Her eyes shadowed and darkened with fear.

Miss Geraghty spoke reassuringly. "Don't be afraid, child. We'll take good care of you."

Dani took a deep breath. She walked toward her mother and raised her lips to kiss Nora's cheek.

That was the moment when Nora chose to go dramatic. "My baby!" she cried. "I won't let them take you away from me!"

That was all the child needed. In a fraction of a second, she was weeping hysterically in her mother's arms. In a moment everyone was around them, clucking sympathetically. That was another talent Nora had. Even the nurse, who must have been used to scenes like this, had tears in her eyes.

Quickly and professionally the nurse disengaged them

and led Dani, still weeping, through another door. Over it was another sign—TO THE GIRLS' COTTAGES.

Nora turned to Gordon, still weeping. He gave her his handkerchief and she covered her eyes quickly. But I got a glimpse of the triumph in them. I watched them go out the door, then turned to old Mrs. Hayden.

Her face was grim and sad. "Would you like to come back to the house for lunch, Luke? We have so much to talk about."

"No, thanks," I said. "I think I'll go back to the motel and get some rest. I didn't get any sleep at all last night."

"Then tomorrow for Sunday dinner? No one else will be there. Just the two of us."

I wondered what she had on her mind. The old lady never did anything without a reason. "I'll see," I said. "I'll call you."

She stared at me silently for a moment, then drew a deep breath. "You don't have to be afraid of me, Luke. I love the child. I really do."

There was a kind of pleading in her eyes that made me sure that she was telling the truth. It was the first time I'd ever seen her asking to be believed. "I know you do, Mother Hayden," I said gently.

She looked at me gratefully. "Please call me either way."

"I will."

She turned and I watched her go out the door. It closed and I turned to the gray-haired attendant who had gone back to her typewriter. "When can I visit my daughter?" I asked.

"The usual visiting hours are from two-thirty to three on Sundays. But exceptions are sometimes made for new arrivals."

"I can make it at that time."

"Stop by the desk when you come, Mr. Carey. I'll have a pass waiting for you."

"Thank you."

I went out into the driveway. Nora's car was gone and most of the reporters had left, but Gordon was standing near his black Cadillac talking to the two who remained. He gestured and I walked over.

"John Morgan of the *Chronicle*," Gordon said, indicating the taller of the two, "and Dan Prentiss, AP."

"I'd like to apologize for that stupid remark, Mr. Carey," Morgan said. "I wouldn't want you to think that all of us were like that."

"That goes for me, too, Colonel," the AP man said quickly. "You have my sympathy, sir, and if there's anything I can do to help, don't hesitate to call me."

"Thank you, gentlemen."

We shook hands and they walked away. I turned to Gordon. "Now, what?"

He looked down at his watch, then back at me. "I have to get back to my office. I'll be jammed up all afternoon. Where can I reach you about six?"

"I'll be at the motel."

"Good. I'll call you there and we'll set a time to finish our talk." He smiled suddenly. "I was right, you know. You are a good man to have around in a squeeze. You did very well back there."

"I didn't do anything."

"Yes, you did. You reacted just right. You've gotten every legitimate reporter on our side."

The way he said it got me. "Legitimate? What kind of a reporter made that stupid crack?"

He grinned. "That wasn't a reporter, that was my chauffeur. For a moment I was worried that he wouldn't get here in time."

I stared at him, my mouth hanging open. I should

have known. They didn't call him lawyer man for nothing.

He opened the door of his car. "That reminds me. Here are your keys. Your car is parked down the street. I'll pick my man up a few blocks from here. I didn't want to take a chance on anyone recognizing him."

I took the keys from his outstretched hand and watched as he got into his car. I stood there for a moment until his car disappeared around the side of the building, then slowly began to walk towards my car.

I passed by a wire fence behind which were a series of long green quonset-type huts. I reached out and touched the wire and stood there for a while. Somewhere inside that fence was my daughter. I began to feel emptier and emptier. She must be so alone.

I wondered if Nora felt all the same things about Dani that I did. Then, in the insidious way she had of stealing my thoughts, Nora took over and it was the past I was thinking of.

9

The three weeks left of my leave was our honeymoon. And in a way, I guess, they were our marriage too. For it was almost two years before I got back. The war had been over a year by then, and we were never able to pick up where we'd left off.

Nora hadn't come down to the airport to see me off because she didn't like goodbyes. Nor was she at the airport when I returned. But her mother was.

The old lady was standing on the field when I came down the ramp. No waiting in the terminal for her. She held out her hand. "Luke, welcome home. It's good to have you back."

I kissed her cheek. "It's good to be back," I said. "Where's Nora?"

"I'm sorry, Luke. Your cable didn't arrive until yesterday. She's in New York."

"New York?"

"Tonight is the opening of her first postwar show. We didn't have any idea that you were returning." She read the disappointment in my face. "Nora was very upset when I told her about your wire on the phone. She wants you to call her as soon as we get to the house."

I grinned wryly. It figured. Just like everything else the last year. Each time I thought I was getting out something came up and I had to stay on. I'd have been better off if they'd never made me a chicken colonel and transferred me to general staff. All the other men that I'd flown with had been out for six months.

"Is she all right?" I asked. Nora hadn't been exactly the most faithful correspondent in the world. I was lucky if I averaged one letter a month from her. If it hadn't been for her mother I'd have been completely out of touch. The old lady wrote me regularly, at least once a week.

"She's fine. She's been working very hard to get ready for this show. But you know Nora." She looked at me quizzically. "She wouldn't have it any other way. She always has to keep busy."

"Yeah."

She took my arm. "Let's go to the car. Charles will fetch your luggage."

We made a lot of small talk on the way home. I had the impression that the old lady was more nervous than she showed on the surface. In a way that was normal. This was really the first chance we'd had to test our new relationship. I felt kind of strained myself.

"Scaasi's number is on the desk in the library, next to the telephone," she said as we came into the house.

She followed the butler up the stairs with my bags and I went into the library. The slip of paper was exactly where she'd said it would be. I picked up the telephone and gave the number to the operator. The call didn't take long to get through.

"Scaasi's Gallery," a voice said. In the background I could hear a great deal of noise, people talking.

"Miss Hayden, please."

"Who's calling, please?"

"This is her husband calling from San Francisco," I said.

"Just a moment, please, I'll try to locate her."

I waited for what seemed an interminable time. After a while the voice came back on the line. "I'm sorry, Mr. Hayden. I can't seem to find her."

Mr. Hayden. That was the first time I'd heard that. It wouldn't be the last though. After a while I would get sick of it, but at the moment it was amusing.

"Carey's the name," I said. "Is Sam Corwin around?"

"I'll see. Just a moment."

A moment later Sam was on the phone. "Luke, old boy. Welcome home."

"Thank you, Sam. Where's Nora?"

"I don't know," he said. "She was around here a minute ago. She was waiting for your call. You know how an opening is. Maybe she went out to eat. She hasn't all day. Things have been really hectic here."

"I can imagine. How's it going?"

"Great. Scaasi had already sold most of the important pieces before the show opened. He's working on some very important commissions for Nora."

There wasn't much else to say. "Have her call me as soon as she can." I looked at my watch. It was six o'clock here, which would make it nine in New York. "I'll be here all evening."

"Sure thing, Luke. You're at Nora's mother's house?"

"That's right."

"I'll have her call as soon as I locate her."

"Thanks, Sam," I said. "Goodbye."

I put down the telephone and walked out of the library. Mrs. Hayden was waiting in the foyer. "Did you talk to Nora?"

"No. She'd gone out to dinner."

My mother-in-law didn't seem surprised. "I told her you'd call about six."

I found myself defending Nora. "She's had a rough day, Sam says. You know how those New York openings are."

She looked as if she were about to say something, then seemed to change her mind. "You must be exhausted after your flight. Why don't you go upstairs and freshen up? Dinner will be served shortly."

I went up to my room while she went into the library and closed the door behind her. What I didn't know then was that she called Sam right back.

He picked up the telephone wearily, knowing who it would be. "Yes, Mrs. Hayden."

The old lady's voice was sharp and angry. "Where's my daughter?"

"I don't know, Mrs. Hayden."

"I thought I told you to make sure she'd be there to take his call."

"I gave Nora your message, Mrs. Hayden. She said she would. Then I looked for her and she was gone."

"Where is she?" the old lady repeated.

"I told you. I don't know."

"Then find her. Right away. And tell her that I want her to call home immediately!"

"Yes, Mrs. Hayden."

"And I want her on the next plane out here! You make sure she's on it. Do you understand that, Mr. Corwin?" Her voice had a cold, steely quality.

"Yes, Mrs. Hayden." The phone clicked off in his hand. Slowly he put it down. He massaged his temples wearily. He had all the makings of a good headache. Nora could be at any one of a hundred different places.

He pushed through the crowd into the night. Fifty-seventh Street was almost empty. He looked up and down the street, mentally tossing a coin. After a moment he made up his mind. He crossed the street and began to walk downtown on Park Avenue. If he had to start someplace he might as well begin at the top and work his way down. El Morocco was as good a place as any.

Then the bright lights of a drugstore beckoned him as he crossed Lexington on Fifty-fourth Street. Acting on impulse he went in and called a private detective he knew.

It was after two in the morning when they finally caught up with her. In a third-floor walkup down on Eighth Street in the Village.

"This must be it," the detective said. He sniffed the air. "You can get high just standing out here!"

Sam knocked at the door. She had to be here. She'd met the boy at a bar on Eighth Avenue where unemployed actors hung out. Sam was surprised to learn that she'd been seeing him almost constantly since they'd arrived in New York. And he'd thought he had every moment of her time accounted for.

After a moment, there was a voice on the other side of the door. "Go away. I'm busy."

Sam knocked again.

This time the voice was angry. "I said beat it! I'm busy."

The detective measured the door with his eye, then placed his foot squarely against the lock. He didn't seem to push very hard, but the door flew open with a vicious splintering crash.

A young man came charging at them from out of the darkness. Again the detective didn't seem to move very quickly, but suddenly he was between Sam and the young man and the young man was on the floor. He glared up at them, his hand nursing his chin.

"Is Nora Hayden here?" Sam asked.

"There's nobody here by that name," the young man said quickly.

Sam looked at him for a moment without speaking, then stepped over him and started for the other door. Before he reached it it opened.

Nora stood in the doorway, completely nude, a cigarette between her lips. "Sam, baby." She laughed. "Come

down to join the party? Things must be getting a little
dull uptown along about now." She turned her back and
started back into the room. "Come on in," she called
over her shoulder. "There's enough tea in here for the
whole Mexican Army."

Sam moved after her quickly and spun her around.
He pulled the cigarette from her mouth and threw it on
the floor. The acrid smell of the marijuana was strong
in his nostrils. "Get your clothes on."

"What for?" she asked truculently.

"You're going home."

She began to laugh. "Home, sweet home. Be it ever so
humble, there's no place like home."

Sam's hand flashed against her face. The resounding
slap sent her reeling back. "Get dressed, I said!"

"Wait a minute!" The young man was on his feet now.
He hitched at his tight black trousers as he walked toward Sam. "You can't do that! You her husband or
something?"

Nora began to laugh again. "That's a good one. My
husband? He's just a watchdog my mother hired. My
husband's five thousand miles away!"

"Your husband is home. He just got in tonight. He's
been trying to reach you."

"He's been away two years. A few days more or less
shouldn't make any difference."

"Maybe you didn't hear what I said," Sam said quietly. "Luke is home."

Nora stared at him. "Great. When do we hold the pa-
rade?"

Suddenly her face began to turn white and she rushed
to the bathroom. Sam could hear her heaving and retch-
ing, then the toilet flushed and the water began to run in
the basin.

After a few minutes she came out, still holding a wet towel to her face. "I'm sick, Sam, I'm sick."

"I know."

"No, you don't," she said. "Nobody does. Do you know what it's like to go to bed alone night after night, wanting it and not being able to have it?"

"It's not that important."

"Maybe not to you!" she said angrily. "But after I'm through working I'm all keyed up. I can't sleep. I have to do something to unwind!"

"Did you ever try a cold shower?"

"Very funny!" she said. "Do you think all those things I do come out of here?" She touched her forehead. "Well, they don't! They come out of here!" She touched her naked body. "That's where they come from, and every time I feel a little bit emptier. And I have to get something back to fill me up again! Do you understand that, Mr. Art Critic?"

Sam gestured to her clothing lying on the rumpled bed. "Get dressed. Your mother wants you to call Luke right away."

She looked at him strangely. "Does Mother know?"

He looked at her steadily. "Your mother's always known. She told me the day I agreed to take you on."

She sank to the bed. "She never said anything to me."

"Would it have done any good if she had?"

The tears began to well up in Nora's eyes. "I can't do it," she said. "I can't go back!"

"Yes, you can. Your mother told me to put you on a plane after you called Luke."

She looked up at him. "She said that?"

"Yes."

"What about Luke? Does he know too?"

"As far as I know, he doesn't. I gather your mother wants to keep it that way."

Nora sat silently for a moment, then took a deep breath. "Do you think I can make it? Now that Luke's home I won't be alone nights any more."

She reached for her clothing and began to dress. "Do you think you can get me on a plane tonight?" She sounded like a breathless, excited child.

"I'll get you on the first plane out."

She was happy now, smiling. "I'll be a good wife to him, you'll see!" She shrugged into her brassiere and turned her back to him. "Hook me up, Sam."

He went over and fastened her brassiere. She slipped into her dress and went back into the bathroom. When she came out a few minutes later, she looked as fresh and clean as if she had just stepped from her morning shower.

She came over to him and suddenly reached up and kissed his cheek. "Thanks, Sam, for finding me. I was afraid to go back. Afraid to face him. But I know it will be all right now. I wanted you to find me and you did."

He looked down at her face for a moment, then shrugged.

"If you wanted me to find you, why didn't you leave a message?"

"It had to be like this," she said. "Or it wouldn't have mattered. Somebody besides myself had to know."

He opened the door. "Let's go."

She went into the other room and through the outer door without a look at the young man who sat in the chair.

10

Charles put the orange juice on the table in front of me. It was a couple of months later. I picked the glass up and began to drink as my mother-in-law came into the room.

She smiled at me. "Good morning, Luke." She sat down and unfolded her napkin. "How is she this morning?"

"She seemed all right," I said. "She had a good night. I guess the morning sickness is about over."

She nodded. "Nora is a strong, healthy girl. She shouldn't have any trouble."

I nodded in agreement. I hadn't been home more than six weeks when Nora discovered that she was pregnant. I'd come home from the office one evening and found her in raging hysterics. She was sprawled across the bed in our room, sobbing angrily.

"What's wrong?" I was already used to some of her temperamental outbursts, like when the forms she thought should come alive so easily refused to take shape.

"I won't have it! I don't believe it!" She sat up and screamed.

I stared at her. "Take it easy. Won't have what?"

"That damn doctor! He says I'm pregnant!"

I began to grin in spite of myself. "Such things have been known to happen."

"What's so funny? You men are all alike. It makes you feel big and proud and virile, doesn't it?"

"It doesn't exactly make me feel bad," I admitted.

The tears were gone now and all her anger was directed at me. "Having a baby won't interfere with *your* work. Having a baby won't twist *you* all out of shape, make *you* big and fat and ugly so that nobody will look at you any more."

She glared at me. "I won't have it!" She screamed again. "I'll get rid of it! I know a doctor—"

I went over to her. "You won't do any such thing."

"You can't stop me!" she shouted, getting off the bed and starting for the door.

I caught her shoulders and turned her toward me. "I can and I will," I said quietly.

Her eyes clouded with anger. "You don't care anything about me! You don't care if I die having it. All you care about is the baby!"

"That's not true. I do care about you. That's why I want you to have the baby. Abortions are dangerous."

Slowly the anger in her eyes faded. "You do care about me, don't you?"

"You know I do."

"And when the baby comes, you'll still care more about me than—than it?"

"You're the only thing I've got, Nora. The baby is something else completely."

She was silent for a moment. "We'll have a son."

"How do you know?" I asked. "Babies aren't made in a studio like statues."

She looked up into my face. "I know. Every man wants a son and you're going to have one. I'll make sure of that."

"Don't worry about it. A little girl would be okay with me."

She slipped out of my arms and walked over to the mirror. She dropped her negligee on the floor and, turn-

ing sideways, looked at her naked reflection in the glass.
"I think I'm getting a little tummy."

I grinned. She was as flat as a washboard. "It's a little
early for that."

"Oh, no, it's not! The doctor says it shows earlier on
some women. Besides I feel heavier."

"You don't look it."

"I don't?" she asked. Then she turned and saw my
grin. "I'll show you!"

She laughed and threw herself across the bed at me.
We tumbled together, she on top of me. She kissed me,
letting all her weight rest on me. "There. How does that
feel?"

"It feels fine."

"It does, does it?" I knew that suddenly hungry un-
dertone in her voice. She kissed me again, her body beginning to move.

"Wait a minute," I said cautiously. "Are you sure it's
okay?"

"Don't be silly! The doctor told me everything should
go on as usual. Just not to place too much weight on
me. He recommended the position of female superior."

"Female superior?" I questioned, feigning ignorance.
"I thought males were superior."

"You know. It means the woman on top."

I acted as if I were learning something new. Then I
couldn't help myself. I threw my arms and legs ecstati-
cally into the air. "Take me, I'm yours!"

We collapsed in a gale of laughter.

But the next few mornings had been rough. She had
been sick almost every day since.

"How's the work in the office going?" my mother-in-
law asked.

"Okay, I guess. They're still getting used to me and

I'm trying to find out what's going on. Actually, I have very little to do as yet."

"These things take time."

"I know." I looked at her. "I've been thinking maybe I ought to go back to school and brush up. So many new concepts have developed while I was away. There's a whole new field in the use of aluminum as a structural component. I don't know anything about it."

"There's no point in rushing."

I knew what it meant when she spoke like that. It meant that she knew something that I didn't. But there was no use asking her. She would tell me when she was ready. Or she wouldn't tell me at all. I'd have to learn it for myself.

She was quite a woman, this mother-in-law of mine. She had her own way of doing things. Like that first morning I had gone to the office.

She'd called me into the library and taken an envelope out of the desk and given it to me silently.

I'd opened it curiously. Several eleborately printed stock certificates fell out. I picked them up from the floor and looked at them. They represented twenty per cent of the stock of Hayden and Carruthers. On the back of each she had endorsed the shares over to me.

I put them back on the desk. "I didn't earn them."

She smiled. "You will."

"Maybe I will," I said. "But right now, I couldn't take them. I'd feel like a damn fool. There are people in that office who have worked there for years. They'd resent it."

"You haven't seen the morning paper?"

"No."

"Then maybe you'd better look at it," she said, handing me the *Chronicle*.

It was already folded to the financial page. I read the

small headline: HAYDEN AND CARRUTHERS APPOINT NEW VICE-PRESIDENT. Alongside the story was my picture. I read the item quickly.

"That's really starting at the top," I said, giving the paper back to her.

"There's nowhere else a Hayden can start."

There was no point in telling her that I wasn't a Hayden. She was quite clear in her thinking. She hadn't lost a daughter, she'd gained a son.

"I hope my demotion isn't as rapid."

"You've a strange sense of humor, Luke."

"Easy come, easy go," I said.

"Don't talk like that!" Then she smiled. "You'll do all right. I know you will."

"I hope so." I turned and started for the door.

Her voice stopped me. "Wait," she said. "You forgot the stock."

"You keep it. When I think I've earned them I might ask for it back."

A kind of hurt crept into her eyes. That wasn't what I'd intended at all. I came back to the desk. "Please understand," I said. "It isn't that I don't appreciate what you're trying to do. It's just that I'd feel a lot better if I could make it on my own."

She stared at me a moment, then slipped the certificates back into the desk. "I understand. And I approve heartily. It's the way I'd expect a Hayden to act."

I had no reply to that one.

"Good luck."

I returned her smile. "Thank you."

I'd been uneasy about it ever since.

When Nora came down we were just finishing our coffee. She was already dressed to go out. I raised an eyebrow. Any time Nora got down before noon it was a miracle.

Her face was excited. "Do you have to be at the office early?"

"I guess not," I said. If I didn't show up for a year I doubt that anyone would have missed me.

"Good! I have something to show you."

"What is it?"

"It's a surprise."

"Tell me," I said. "I've had enough surprises in the short time I've been home. I'm not sure that I can take another."

She laughed. "You'll like this one." She looked at her mother and they both smiled. "A friend of mine wants you to do her house over."

"Well, now," I said. That was more like it. Something to do at last. "Where is it?"

"Not far from here. We'll go over and look at it and I'll tell you what she's got in mind."

"Great. I'm ready to go whenever you are."

"I'm ready right now. I had my breakfast upstairs."

It was a dream house. Three wings and seventeen rooms, at the top of Nob Hill looking out over the bay. There was a wonderful old marble staircase curving up off the large entrance foyer. The rooms were tremendous, like nothing they ever built today. Out in back there was a three-car garage, with servants' quarters above. The house itself was greystone, beautifully patinaed with age, and there was a blue tile roof that seemed to soak up its color from the sky.

"It's beautiful. I hope they don't want to do much to it. They'd only spoil it."

"I think it's mostly modernizing the bathrooms and the heating plant, perhaps doing a few rooms over."

"That makes sense," I said, still studying the house.

"They'll need a nursery. And a large studio for the wife in the north wing, to catch the light. Maybe a combination den and office for the husband, when he wants to work at home."

I wasn't altogether dumb. "Exactly who is this house for?"

"Haven't you guessed?"

"I'm afraid to."

"Mother bought it for us," Nora said.

"That's great!" I exploded. "Do you know what it would cost to run a house like this? More in a month than I make in a year!"

"What difference does that make? We don't have to worry about money. The income from my trust fund alone is more than enough to take care of us."

"You think I don't know that?" I said. "But didn't you ever once stop to think that I might like to support my own family? All you and your mother ever think of is money. I'm beginning to feel like a gigolo."

"You're acting like a damn fool! All I'm interested in is having a decent place to live, a proper home to bring up a baby."

"A baby doesn't need a seventeen-room house on Nob Hill to be brought up properly. If you want a place of your own, there are lots of houses we could buy. Houses that I can afford."

"Sure," she said sarcastically. "But I couldn't afford to be found dead in any of them. I have my position to consider."

"Your position? What about my position?"

"You made your position clear when you married me," she said coldly. "And when you went to work for Hayden and Carruthers. As far as San Francisco is concerned, you belong to the Haydens. Whether you like it or not, you're one of us."

I stared at her. The realization spilled over me like the shock of ice-cold water. What she said was true. The war was over, and as far as anyone else was concerned, Colonel Luke Carey might as well be dead. The only identity I had left was associated with them.

"I want this house," Nora said quietly. "And if you don't want to remodel it, I'll find an architect who will."

I didn't have to look at her to know that she meant what she said. I also realized what it would mean to me. I might as well look for a job as a truck driver if I let it happen. "All right,' I said reluctantly. "I'll do it."

"You won't be sorry, darling." She threw her arms around me. "You'll be the biggest architect in San Francisco when everyone sees the wonderful things you'll do with this house!"

But she wasn't quick enough to hide the glimmer of triumph in her eyes. And that night, for the first time since I'd come home, she did not seek my embrace.

11

In the end it wasn't I who did the house. I got all the credit, but it was was only a technicality. Actually, it was all Nora. All I did was translate her ideas into their proper architectural concepts.

But she was right about one thing. It was a showplace. We'd scarcely moved in before *House Beautiful* did a spread on it, and the month after the magazine came out I was the hottest architect in town.

Everyone who was anyone on the Coast wanted me to do their houses. I could have had more commissions than a five-percenter on a field day in Washington.

Instant success. I suppose I should have been content with it, but it bugged me. I guess that it showed, because the first time I turned down a client, George Hayden came into my office.

I looked up in surprise. George was a big man. Heavyset, florid-faced, very solid and dependable. It was the first time he'd come down to see me instead of calling for me.

"How's it going, Luke?"

"Okay, George," I said. I turned off the light over my drafting board. "What can I do for you?"

"I thought we might have a little talk."

"Fine." I waved to a chair.

He sat down. "I've just been looking over the monthly report. I get the feeling that you're being overloaded."

"I don't mind," I said easily. "It's a pleasant change from having nothing to do."

He nodded. "I've been thinking it's about time we

gave you a department. You know, a few boys to do all the preliminary work so you can have a chance to keep an eye on the big ones."

This language I understood. The Army spoke like that. I played it ignorant. "What big ones, George? All I'm doing is small stuff."

"There's a good margin in your field," he said. "Much better than in the big stuff. That's why I hate to miss out on anything just because you're too busy. If somebody has his mind made up to build and one architect can't do it, he'll find one who can."

"You mean like Mrs. Robinson who just left?"

"I don't mean only Mrs. Robinson. There will be others. They are coming to you for your ideas. They won't care who does the actual drawing."

"Let's stop kidding ourselves, George. They're not coming to me because of my ideas. Most of those idiots wouldn't know an architectural idea if it hit them in the face. They're coming to be because all of a sudden I'm the fashion."

"So what, Luke?" he said, looking at me shrewdly. "The main thing is to keep them coming."

"And how long do you think that will last? Only until they find out that their houses won't make the magazine like mine did. Then they'll be after someone else."

"It doesn't have to be like that. We can keep things alive. That's why we have a P.R. man."

"Oh, cut it, George," I said disgustedly. "We both know it's Nora's house."

He looked down at his hands for a moment without speaking. They were soft and white and well manicured. Then he looked up at me, his eyes unblinking. "You and I both know that I'm not half the architect Frank Carruthers was. But I've managed to keep this a going business and maintain our reputation."

"But the Robinson house isn't my kind of thing. I've been over the whole layout. The land. Everything. It's nothing special. No matter what you do it's just another house."

"It's not just another house. They're willing to spend a couple of hundred thousand on it. That means at least ten thousand in fees and commissions for what amounts to a few weeks' work."

"It's not the kind of house I want to build," I said stubbornly.

"That's why I want you to have a department. You'll be able to concentrate on what you do want to do. But the client will be happy, too, just knowing that you're around."

I reached for a cigarette. His idea had merit. Maybe it would work. There was something I wanted to try. More in my line. "What do you want me to do?"

"First, call Mrs. R. and let her know that you've found time in your busy schedule to work on her house." He got to his feet, he had what he had come after. "Then check with my secretary and we'll set a date for lunch to talk over your plans."

I watched the door close behind him. I knew that if I waited to eat lunch with him I'd be lucky if I didn't starve to death.

I walked over to my drawing board. I'd been working on a sketch for a giant-sized bathroom and dressing room, off the master bedroom. The house was for the president of a local bank. I'd sketched out a Finnish style bath with a sunken tub six feet wide and eight feet long.

It was big enough for the whole family at one sitting and I wondered if that was what the lady of the house had in mind. There were two of everything—his and her shower stalls, washbasins and toilets, all complete with gold hardware. All that was missing was a sterling silver bidet and the only reason for that was that no one had thought of it. Yet.

Yet. That was the key word. Suddenly my whole life rolled out in front of me. Years and years of bathrooms like this. My claim to fame. Carey builds the greatest bathrooms.

It was too much. I pulled the sheet from the drawing board and crumpled it up and went down the hall to George's office. There was no point in waiting for a lunch that would never take place to find out what would never happen.

His secretary held up a warning hand as I came into the outer office. "Mr. Hayden's on the telephone."

"I don't mind," I said, walking past her into his inner office.

George was just putting down the phone. He looked up in surprise. "What is it, Luke?" he asked testily. He didn't like anyone walking in unannounced.

"Did you mean what you said?"

"Of course, Luke."

"Then why can't we talk about it now?"

He smiled at me. "This isn't the time."

"How do you know?" I asked. "You don't even know what I have in mind."

He looked at me steadily. He had no answer for that. After a moment he waved me to a chair. "Exactly what do you have on your mind?"

I dropped into the chair opposite him and fished out a cigarette. "Low-cost homes. Mass production on a basic design that could be used three ways to vary the monotony of a large-scale development. The houses would sell in the ten-, eleven-thousand-dollar range."

He nodded slowly. "You'd need a lot of acreage to make a thing like that pay off."

I had thought of that. "There's eighty acres off 101 near Daly City. It would be just right for it."

"Sounds like a good idea," he said. "Have you got a builder for it?"

I looked at him. "I thought it might be something we could do."

He was silent for a moment, his fingers playing with a pencil on the desk in front of him. "You're forgetting one thing, aren't you?"

"What's that?"

"We're architects, not builders."

"Maybe it's time we branched out. Others are doing it."

"I don't care what the others do," George said. "I don't think we should. As architects we're reasonably free of financial risk. We collect our fees and we're out. The builder has all the other headaches."

"The builder also makes the big money."

"Let him," George said. "I'm not greedy."

"Then I take it you're not interested?"

"I didn't say that. I just said that under the present circumstances we shouldn't do it. Of course, if you should come up with a builder who was willing to underwrite a project like that, we'd be more than happy to accommodate him."

I got to my feet. I knew the score. He did too. There wasn't an architect in the country who would turn down a job like that. It would be worth a hundred and fifty thousand in fees alone. "Thanks," I said. "I kind of thought that would be your answer."

He stared up at me. His voice was deceptively soft. "I just had a thought, Luke. I think you should make up your own mind exactly what you'd like to be—an architect or a builder."

It was as if the lights suddenly came on in a dark

room. George was absolutely right. I remembered the reason I had studied architecture in the first place. Because I wanted to build things. Then I became so involved with the practice that I forgot the purpose. To build. That was it. To build homes that people could afford to live in.

George didn't understand my sudden happy smile. Maybe he even thought I was being sarcastic, but if he did he was completely wrong. I had never been more sincere in my life. "Thank you, George," I said warmly. "Thank you for making everything so simple."

The news made it home before I did. My mother-in-law and Nora were waiting for me. "I see George didn't waste any time," I said.

Nora's face was frosty. "You might at least have discussed it with us before you quit."

I walked over to the sideboard and poured myself a bourbon. "What was there to talk about? I'd had it. Up to here."

"How do you think it will look?" Nora asked.

"I don't know." I shrugged, taking a sip from my drink. "How do *you* think it will look?"

"They'll think it's an outright insult to Mother and me," Nora said angrily. "Everyone knows what we've tried to do for you."

"Maybe that's why it didn't work." I looked at Nora's mother. "I didn't intend it as an insult. It was my fault. I let myself be rushed right into it when I got out of the Army. I should have taken a little time, looked around, decided what I really wanted to do."

She looked at me calmly. "Was that why you refused the stock?"

"Perhaps. Though I didn't know it then."

"What are you going to do now?" Nora asked.

"Look around. Get a job with a builder and learn something."

"What kind of a job do you expect to get?" she asked sarcastically. "Seventy dollars a week driving a bull-dozer?"

"I have to start someplace." I smiled at her. "Besides, what different does it make? We don't need the money."

"So all you want to be is a common laborer? After all the trouble I went to to get this house just right, so you could make a reputation."

"Let's stop kidding ourselves, Nora. It wasn't my reputation that you were considering. It was your own."

She stared at me for a moment, then raised her hands in a helpless gesture. "I give up." She turned awkwardly and stalked out of the room.

I watched her leave. Despite her pregnancy she hadn't gotten very big. She had watched her diet carefully; she wasn't going to allow pregnancy to ruin her figure. I turned back to the sideboard and freshened my drink. When I turned around, my mother-in-law was still standing there.

"You mustn't pay too much attention to Nora. Pregnant women are apt to be more emotional than logical."

I nodded. That was as good an excuse as any. But I knew my wife well enough by now. Pregnant or not, she wanted her own way.

"George mentioned that you had some idea about a building development," she said. "Tell me about it."

I dropped into a chair. "What difference does it make? He won't do it. It's against policy."

She sat down opposite me. "That doesn't mean you won't do it."

I stared at her. "I'm not kidding myself. I don't have that kind of money."

"How much do you have?"

That was easy enough to answer. After I paid out the seven thousand for the boat I'd bought in La Jolla, I had exactly nineteen thousand left. Fifteen thousand was from the insurance on my father, the rest I had saved from my Army pay.

"Would you put all your money into a project like that?"

"Sure. But it would be only a drop in the bucket. The land alone would cost two thousand an acre. That's a hundred and sixty thousand dollars right there."

"The money is unimportant," she said quietly. "I could arrange for the money."

"Uh-uh." I held up my hand. "I don't want your money. I'd only wind up in the same boat."

"Now it's you who are being foolish, Luke. You'd take the money if it were a total stranger's, wouldn't you?"

"That's different. That would be pure business. Personal relationships would never enter into it."

"Our relationship has nothing to do with it," she said quickly. "You believe in what you want to do, don't you? You'd expect to make a considerable profit."

I nodded. "If it works out the way I think, there could be as much as half a million profit."

"I don't object to making money." She smiled. "Why should you?"

Her logic was faultless. Besides how could I argue against my own desires? I bought the land the next day. Two days later Danielle was born.

I had a few bad moments because she arrived almost two months ahead of schedule. But the doctor told me there was nothing to worry about, the baby was absolutely perfect.

I hadn't seen many babies before but I had to agree with him. Dani was the most beautiful baby in the world.

12

The sounds of night were different now. There was always the soft whisper that seemed to come from the baby's room next to our own. Occasionally she would cry in the small hours of the morning and we could hear the shuffle of the nurse as she gave her a bottle and then the soft crooning of her voice as she held Dani while the baby drank herself back to sleep.

Unconsciously I fell into the routine and began to listen for the sounds in my sleep, finding reassurance in their regularity, knowing that everything was normal. It was different for Nora.

Nora came home from the hospital tense, highstrung and nervous. The slightest sound in the night would wake her. I knew something was going to happen but I didn't know what. I could sense it in her mood. Something in her was lying just below the surface, waiting for the final provocation, and I was wary, determined not to give it to her.

I moved through the days carefully, hoping that in time the mood would pass. But I was only kidding myself and I realized it the moment the lamp on the night table flashed on one morning at two o'clock.

I had been out in the field all day with surveyors. The air and the excitement had slugged me to sleep but suddenly I was wide awake behind my closed eyelids. I came up, still pretending sleep. "What's the matter?"

Nora was sitting up in bed, her back propped against the pillows, staring at me. "The baby's crying."

I looked at her for a moment, then, still not letting her see I was fully awake, swung my feet off the bed. "I'll go see if everything's all right."

I got my feet into my slippers, pulled on my robe and went through the door into Dani's room. The nurse was already there, holding Dani in her arms, giving her a bottle. She looked at me, her eyes startled in the soft night light of the nursery.

"Mr. Carey."

"Is everything all right, Mrs. Holman?"

"Of course. The poor little thing was just hungry."

I walked over and looked down at Dani. Her eyes were already closed and she was sucking on the bottle contentedly. "Mrs. Carey heard her cry," I said.

"Tell Mrs. Carey not to worry. Dani's just fine."

I smiled at her and nodded.

"Dani was just hungry," I said as I climbed back into bed and turned off the light. I turned on my side and lay there for a few minutes, waiting for her to speak. But she was silent and sleep was heavy on my eyes.

Then the light came on again. I climbed up the tricky ladder of wakefulness again. "Now what's the matter?"

Nora was standing at the far side of her bed, a pillow and blanket clutched in her arms. "You're snoring."

I stared at her without answering. I felt like a punchy fighter who has been congratulating himself on avoiding his opponent and suddenly finds himself on the wrong end of an uppercut. There was no way of avoiding the fight now. Suddenly I was angry. "Okay, Nora," I said. "I'll give up sleeping. What else do you want?"

"You don't have to get nasty."

"I'm not being nasty. You've been looking for an argument for a long time. Now, what do you want to hang it on?"

Her voice rose. "I was not looking for an argument!"

I glanced toward Dani's room. "You'll wake the baby."

"That's just what I thought!" she exclaimed triumphantly. "You always think about the baby before you do me. Every time the baby cries, you're in there worrying about her. You never worry about me! I don't count, I'm only her mother. I've served my purpose!"

There was no arguing with that kind of stupidity and I made the mistake of telling her so. "Don't be stupid! Turn off the light and go to sleep."

"You're not talking to a child!"

I raised myself on one elbow. "If I'm not," I said, "then stop acting like one!"

"That's what you'd like, wouldn't you? You'd like nothing better than having me here all day to wait on you both hand and foot whenever you chose!"

I laughed. The whole idea was so completely ridiculous. "I know you can't cook," I said. "So how would you wait on us? I've never seen you do so much as warm the baby's bottle, much less feed her."

"You're jealous!"

"Jealous of what?"

"You're jealous because I'm an artist and an individual. All you want to do is subjugate me, have me play second fiddle to you like an ordinary housewife."

I lay back wearily. "There are times, I must admit, when I find the idea appealing."

"See?" she crowed triumphantly. "I was right!"

I was exhausted. "Cut it out and come to bed, Nora. I've got to get up early and go out to the project."

"I'm going to bed all right," she said. "But not in here! I've had all I can stand of your snoring and the baby crying."

Still clutching the pillow and blanket, she went into the bathroom. Before I could move from my bed, I heard the door to the guest room slam shut. By the time I got there, she had already turned the key in the lock.

Slowly I went back to my own bed. Maybe it was all for the best. Let her get whatever was bugging her out of her system. Maybe by tomorrow night everything would be normal again.

But I was wrong. When I got home the next evening the workmen had already started redecorating the other bedroom and Nora had moved her clothing out of our closets.

I went downstairs and Charles gave me a message that Nora had gone downtown to have dinner with Mr. Corwin and several visiting Eastern art critics. I had dinner alone and worked in the den until eleven-thirty, going over the access road plan for the project. Then I went upstairs and looked in on the baby, as I usually did before I went to sleep.

Dani was sleeping on her side, her tiny eyes screwed tight, her little thumb worrying the corner of her mouth. There was a noise behind me. I turned around. It was the nurse with the bottle.

I moved back and let the nurse pick her up. Dani found the nipple on the bottle without even opening her eyes.

"Let me give it to her," I said suddenly.

Mrs. Holman smiled. She showed me how to hold the baby and I took Dani into my arms. She opened her eyes for a moment and looked at me. Then, evidently deciding I was trustworthy, she closed her eyes again and went back to work on the bottle.

I got into bed a little after twelve and Nora hadn't yet come home. I fell into a restless sleep. I never did know what time she came home that night. I didn't see her until I came home from work the next day. By then Nora's mood had completely changed. She greeted me at the door, smiling. "I've got cocktails ready in the library."

I kissed her cheek. She was wearing elaborate black hostess pajamas. "You look different," I said, following her into the library. "Somebody coming for dinner?"

"No, silly. I just had my hair done."

It looked the same to me. I took the drink from her hand. "You have a good day?"

She sipped at her drink, her eyes sparkling. "Wonderful! It was just what I needed. To get out and begin to be active again."

I nodded, smiling. At least the storm had passed.

"I had dinner with Corwin and Chadwinkes Hunt, the critic, last night. They feel that the sooner I get back to work, the better. Scaasi told Sam he'd like me to have another show, no later than this fall."

"Do you think you'll have enough time to get ready?"

"More than enough. I've been sketching all day. I have a thousand ideas."

I held up my glass. "Here's to your ideas."

"Thank you." She smiled and kissed my cheek. "You're not angry about last night?"

"No," I said easily. "We were both a little wound up."

She kissed me again. "I'm glad. I thought you might not like my moving into the other room. I don't why I didn't think of it sooner. Mother and Dad always had separate rooms. It's much more civilized."

"It is?"

"Of course. Even though people are married they're still entitled to a certain amount of privacy." She looked at me earnestly. "Besides I think it preserves that little bit of mystery that is so important in any marriage."

That was news to me. I'd never heard my parents

complain about any lack of privacy. "What do I do when I want to get laid?"

"Now you're being vulgar." Then she smiled mischievously. "All you have to do is whistle."

"Like this?" I asked, raising my fingers to my lips.

"Stop. Charles will think you've gone mad!"

I finished my drink. "I'll run up and wash my hands and look in on Dani."

"You can wash down here. Mrs. Holman has already put Dani down."

I looked at her. "How was she today?"

"Mrs. Holman said she was an angel. Now, hurry and wash up. I had Cookie make a roulade of beef, just the way you like it, and I won't have it spoiled. After dinner I thought you might come up and see how you liked my room. I had Charles leave an iced bottle of champagne up there."

I began to laugh. So that was how it was done. Maybe she wasn't as far out as I'd thought. I had to admit that it did add a pleasant little touch of the illicit to the whole affair.

Sometime in the middle of the night I said, "Won't the servants think it kind of queer that with two bedrooms we wind up using only one?"

"You're silly. Who cares what the servants think?"

"I really don't," I said, pulling her close to me again. "But I insist that tomorrow night you be my guest!"

But it was always in her room that we made love, never in mine. I always wound up having to cross the cold bathroom floor that lay between our rooms. I learned to turn the knob of her door slowly so that she would not hear me, for there were times when I found her door locked. There were times, too, when I fell across my own bed in exhaustion from my work and didn't know whether her door was unlocked or not.

I began to feel like a man forced to turn into a one-way street that he knows can lead only to a dead end. I began to dread the rejection of that locked door. A few good jolts of bourbon before I undressed always seemed to ease the tensions so that I had no desire even to try the door.

I began the habit of giving Dani her midnight bottle and that seemed to help too. Somehow the softness of her filled a void inside me of which I had never really been aware. I would kiss her and put her back in her crib, then go to my room and find sleep.

On the surface everything was normal. Nora and I acted like any other married couple. We went out several times a week, were asked to parties, had our friends come to our house. She seemed everything a young bride should be. Loving and attentive.

But when it was time for bed, I'd make an excuse that I had some last-minute work to catch up on. I'd go into the den and have a few quick ones to give her time to go upstairs and fall asleep so that she wouldn't know whether I tried her door or not.

If anything about this seemed strange to Nora, she never said a word about it. Time drifted by and she seemed content with the way things were. She was engrossed in her work, and several nights a week she went to art meetings or dinners. On other nights she would work in her studio, so that I never knew whether she came up to her room or slept in the small bedroom that she had fixed up down there.

Routine is a deadly thing. After a while it seemed to me that this was the way it had always been and always would be. Like nothing.

What I didn't know was that in her own peculiar dream-filled world Nora was almost as much afraid of me as I was of her.

She remembered the pain. The terrible tearing pain that seemed to move down from her stomach as the baby tore its way out of her. The pain and the bright white lights staring down at her from the soft green ceiling of the delivery room. Every color was clear and distinct. The blood on the white rubber gloves of the doctor. The black knob on the grey metal tank beside the anesthetist. It was always like that in her dreams. Even in that she wasn't like other people. She dreamed in technicolor.

The doctor's voice whispered reassuringly in her ear. "Bear down, Mrs. Carey. Bear down and it will all be over in a few minutes."

"I can't!" she tried to scream up at him but no sound escaped her lips. "I can't, it hurts too much." She felt the tears dribbling down from the corners of her eyes. She knew how they must look rolling down her cheeks. Like tiny sparkling diamonds.

"You must, Mrs. Carey," the doctor whispered again. She could see the purple-red veins on the side of his nose as he leaned over her.

"I can't!" she screamed again. "I can't stand the pain. For God's sake, do something or I'll go out of my mind! Cut it up and take it out in tiny pieces! Make it stop hurting me!"

She felt the prick of a needle in her arm. She looked up at the doctor in sudden fear. She'd just remembered that he was a Catholic and Catholics believed in letting the mother die and saving the child. "What are you doing?" she screamed at him. "Don't kill me, kill the baby. Please, I don't want to die."

"Don't worry," the doctor said quietly. "Nobody's going to die."

"I don't believe you!" She struggled trying to get up but there were hands pressed against her shoulders holding her down. "I'm going to die. I know it. I'm going to die!"

"Count down from ten, Mrs. Carey," the doctor said calmly. "Ten, nine—"

"Eight, seven, six." She looked up into his face. He was getting all fuzzy around the edges. Like in the movies when the picture was out of focus. "Eight, seven, six, five, four, seven, five, three."

The dark came up. The soft rolling dark.

13

A sound coming from the studio next to the small bedroom in which she slept woke Nora. She sat up suddenly. "Is that you, Charles?"

Footsteps came to the door. It opened to admit Sam Corwin. "What are you doing in here?" he asked.

"I worked late last night." She looked at her wrist watch. It was almost ten o'clock. It had been only five when she'd sprawled across the bed too tired even to take off her coveralls. "What are you doing up so early?"

Sam lit a cigarette. "I've got big news for you."

She got to her feet wearily. She ran her fingers through her hair. It felt gritty and dirty. "What news?"

"Your United Nations sketch has been approved. Yours will be the only statue by a woman in the United Nations Plaza in New York!"

The weariness disappeared, displaced by a sudden elation. "When did you find out?"

"An hour ago. Scaasi called me from New York. I came right over."

She felt a surge of triumph. She had been right. Even Luke would have to admit that now. She looked at Sam. "Have you told anyone yet?"

He shook his head. "No. But we'll have to get a release out this morning."

She walked into the studio. "I want to tell Luke about it before he hears it anywhere else."

"Well," he said, "it will be on the wires from New York by afternoon."

"Then let's tell him now."

Sam followed her down the corridor to the foyer. Charles was just coming down the steps.

"Has Mr. Carey left yet, Charles?"

"Yes, mum. He left shortly after eight o'clock, with the baby and Mrs. Holman."

"They went with him?" Nora exclaimed in surprise. "What on earth for?"

"He said something about it being his big day, mum. This is the day the first group of houses will be completed and there's to be a ceremony. He left a message suggesting that you come out if you had the time."

"Thank you, Charles. He did mention something about it. I had forgotten."

The butler nodded and stood aside to let them pass. Sam followed her up to her room. He closed the door behind them. "You didn't know about it, did you?"

She didn't answer.

He looked around the room. For the first time he was aware that this wasn't the room she shared with Luke. "What's the idea of separate rooms all of a sudden? Is there anything wrong between you and Luke?"

"There's nothing wrong."

"Wait a minute," he said softly. "This is your old friend Sam, remember? You can talk to me."

Suddenly she was weeping against his chest. "Oh, Sam, Sam," she cried. "You don't know how horrible it all is. He's sick. The war's done something to him. He's not normal."

"I don't understand."

The words came tumbling from her lips as if she could no longer keep them to herself. "You knew about his wound, of course? Well, it makes him want to do all kinds of crazy things."

"Like what?"

"You know. Perverted things. He makes me do them. It's the only way he can get stimulation. Without that he's almost impotent! I don't know what I'm going to do. Sometimes I think I'll lose my mind."

"I didn't know he was wounded there. Did you suggest he see a doctor?"

"I begged him. But he just won't listen. He tells me to mind my own business. All he wants is for me to have babies so that he can prove he's a man!"

Nora pulled herself away and took a cigarette from a box on the table. Sam held a match for her. "He's always doing things to annoy me," she said. "He knows that the pediatrician told us not to take Dani out of the house. She has a cold. So he took her out there in all that muck and dirt and cold just to annoy me."

"What are you going to do about it?"

She stared at him. "I'm going out there and bring her back. She's my baby and I won't let anybody, even him, harm her." She somehow sensed Sam's vague disbelief. "You don't believe me, do you?"

"I believe you."

"Maybe you'll believe me after I show you something."

She turned and led him through the bathroom into Luke's room. Dramatically she opened the small door of the night table beside his bed. "Look!"

His eyes followed her pointing finger. There were two full bottles of bourbon and one half-empty standing on the shelf. He looked at her in surprise.

"It goes on every night. He drinks, then he comes after me. Then he drinks again until he falls asleep in a stupor!"

She kicked the door shut and Sam followed her back into her room. He studied her silently for a moment. "You can't go on like this."

"What else can I do?"

"You can divorce him."

"No."

The vague skepticism rose in him again. Suddenly everything seemed too pat, too well fitted together. "Why not?"

"You know as well as I. Mother doesn't believe in divorce and would be terribly upset to have the family name dragged through the law courts."

"And?"

She met his gaze steadily. "My baby. I've seen too many children maimed by a broken home. I don't want anything like that to happen to Dani."

He didn't know whether to believe her or not. "I'll go out to the project with you," he said suddenly.

Nora looked at him in surprise. She had become so engrossed in the drama that she was creating that she had completely forgotten about going after Dani.

"To bring you and the baby back," he said.

She smiled at him suddenly. He believed her. She knew that he believed her. And why shouldn't he? The truth was obvious enough. She placed her hand on his arm. "Thank you, Sam. Go downstairs and have a cup of coffee while I dress. I'll be down in a few minutes."

14

Dani was having a ball. Her dark eyes sparkled and she screamed with delight as I let her go and she slid down the slide into Mrs. Holman's waiting arms. When I took her, she squirmed around in my arms, reaching back to the slide. I laughed and put her up on it again.

"Hold her there a moment, Colonel!" one of the photographers called, raising his camera. "That will make a wonderful shot."

Dani froze, posing for the picture as if she'd been doing nothing else for all eight months of her life. The nurse smiled proudly.

The shutter clicked and I let her go down again. Then I took her over to the swings.

I fastened her into the tiny seat and pushed. She gurgled with glee. The bright sun brought out all the roses in her cheeks and she looked like a little doll in her warm blue snowsuit. We were in the play area I had set up back of the model house to show how much space there was for outdoor living.

I looked down the street with satisfaction. There were cars parked all along the new street and salesmen were busy showing the various houses.

It wasn't that each house was so different. The important thing was that they appeared to be. Each was basically the same, the conventional T shape with an expansion attic for later conversion to split level if the purchaser so desired. But by limiting construction to four to the acre, eight to the block, we were able to position each house differently. This created what the building trade called a custom look.

The price was right too—$13,990. Don't ask me why it wasn't fourteen even; that was another practice of the trade. I guess the ten dollars off made it seem more like a bargain. And it was too.

The purchase price included forced air heat and a carport. It compared favorably with houses closer to town costing three to five thousand more. And even though we lost twenty-five acres for roads and access because of city zoning demands, we would still come out with a clear profit of fifteen hundred on each house.

Dani laughed loudly as I pushed the swing still higher. I knew just how she felt. It was her world.

I looked beyond the swing. The bulldozers were already working on the next block, leveling and clearing the land. Tomorrow the shovels would come in and dig foundations, then the cement mixers. After that the frames would begin to grow where nothing but empty land had been before. It was my world too.

I felt a hand on my arm. Nora's voice came from behind me. "Having too much fun to say hello to your wife?"

I turned in surprise. Though I had left a message with Charles, I hadn't really expected her. She had shown no interest in the project up to now. "This is a pleasant surprise, Nora."

As if by magic, the reporters and photographers, who had begun drifting off toward the bar we had set up in the trailer that served as our office, suddenly reappeared. I didn't kid myself. Nora was the main attraction. Nora Hayden was news. Especially in her home town.

"What brings you out here?" I asked.

Her eyes met mine. "Sam was good enough to drive me out so I could bring Dani home."

"Home? For what? She's having the time of her life."

"You know she still has a cold." She stopped the swing and began to unfasten the safety belt.

Sam was coming toward us, watching with a curious look on his face. "What cold?" I turned to Mrs. Holman. "You didn't tell me Dani had a cold."

The nurse looked at me, then Nora, then down at the ground. She mumbled something indistinctly. I couldn't hear what she said. Dani didn't want to leave. She twisted and squirmed in Nora's arms.

One of the photographers smiled at Nora. "Children are all right," he said in a friendly voice, "until you try to keep them from doing what they want to do."

Nora's face flushed, then turned white. She didn't like the idea of herself with a screaming child in her arms. It wasn't at all the way she pictured the scene. Mothers held sweet charming children posing prettily in their arms. She gripped Dani more tightly and began to walk away from the swing. Dani screamed even louder.

Nora turned and thrust her into the nurse's arms. "Take her back to Mr. Corwin's car."

She turned to me. "Now see what you've done," she said angrily. "You're never happy unless you've succeeded in embarrassing me!"

From the corner of my eye, I caught a glimpse of the reporters edging in. I didn't know whether they'd heard or not but I wasn't giving them any more. "I'm sorry," I said in a low voice. "I didn't know Dani had a cold."

"Letting her play on the cold ground and in all this muck and dirt. I'm taking her right to the doctor."

I could feel my temper going, but I kept control of my voice. "Don't overact, Nora. Nobody will believe you."

I was completely unprepared for the look of sheer hatred that flashed from her eyes. She didn't answer but that one glance told me that the things that were wrong between us had gone too far ever to be repaired.

Still, we were out there where everybody could see and I had to make it look good—for her sake as well as mine. I forced a smile. "Well, now that you're out here, you might as well have a look around. What do you think of the houses?"

"I haven't the time," she said contemptuously. "I've got to get Dani home, then make arrangements to leave for New York."

This time she had caught me flatfooted. "New York?"

"Yes. My United Nations sketch has been approved. They want me to come east and discuss it with them."

That was news. Even these building trade reporters knew that. They pressed forward with questions. A moment later Nora was in the midst of a full-scale press conference. When I left to check on a grading problem the bulldozers had run into, she was relaxed and smiling, happy at being in the center of the stage once more.

I felt easier too. At least we were saved some unpleasantness. But that was only until I read the papers the next morning. I was out in the field when the telephone call came and one of the workmen came to get me.

It was Stan Barrows, the real estate agent who was handling sales for the project. He whispered into the telephone as if he didn't want to be overheard. "Get down to the Valley National Bank right away, Luke. There's trouble."

"What trouble?" I asked. Valley National held the construction mortgages. "They have nothing to complain about. We're coming in under the budget."

"I can't talk. Get down here right away!"

The telephone went dead in my hands. I started to call him back but I put the phone down. If he'd wanted to tell me more he would have. I went out to my car.

They were all there when I walked into the bank president's office. They didn't know it but I was more surprised to see them than they were to see me. I looked around the room. My mother-in-law, George Hayden, Stan, the bank's president, the vice-president in charge of the mortgage division.

"I didn't know there was going to be a meeting," I said. "Somebody forgot to let me know."

They looked uncomfortable but no one wanted to be the first to speak. After a moment the vice-president took the plunge. "Have you seen the morning papers, Luke?"

"No," I said. "I leave for work while it's still dark. They don't come up the hill that early."

"You'd better read this, then." He held out a folded copy of the *Chronicle*.

I glanced down at a story outlined in red pencil. Next to it was a picture of Nora.

NORA HAYDEN TO DO
STATUE FOR U.N.

I looked up. "This is very nice," I said. "But I don't see what it has to do with us."

"Read on."

I continued. The first two paragraphs were nothing. They told about the award. It was the next three paragraphs that were the killers.

Interviewed at the grand opening of Carey Estates, a widely heralded building development sponsored by her husband, Colonel Luke Carey, former war hero, Nora Hayden, with her customary forthrightness, delivered her opinion of modern American homes, their owners and those who build them.

"The American builder is completely contemptuous of the American home owner and housewife. Being completely unimaginative and inartistic, he is turning the American home into a conformity-ridden and tasteless cube for purely selfish economic reasons which enable him to secure greater profits. Each house looks exactly like the next, devoid of individual character, and any woman who allows herself to be railroaded into living in one of these crackerboxes has only herself to blame."

When asked if her opinion applied to Carey Estates as well as others, she had this reply. "You may infer what you wish. Speaking only for myself, I would not even be found dead in so tasteless and styleless a structure, much less live in one."

Miss Hayden plans to leave for New York later today to discuss with the U.N. Art Committee plans for her proposed work.

I felt my stomach contract as I finished the article. I threw the paper back on the desk. "There must be some mistake. I'll get Nora to make a retraction."

"It won't do any good," George Hayden said. "The damage has already been done."

"What damage?" I asked angrily. "The average home owner doesn't even read this kind of bilge."

"You're wrong, Luke," Stan Barrows said quietly. "Our sales book last night indicated forty-seven commitments and nineteen possibles. By ten o'clock this morning there were only eleven commitments and three possibles left on the books. I called most of the cancellations personally, and while they wouldn't admit the reason, they all said they'd read the article."

"I'll sue the damn paper for this!"

"On what grounds?" George Hayden asked, contemptuously. "They're only quoting your wife."

I didn't answer. He was right. I sank into a chair and reached for a cigarette. "Maybe if we changed the name of the project, if we took my name off it, it would help."

"I doubt it, Luke. The whole thing's already been given the kiss of death."

I lit the cigarette without answering. My dream was going up in the air with the smoke.

"You've got to understand our position, Luke," the bank president said. "We've got almost a million dollars out on this project and we've got to protect it. We'll have to call the loan."

"You'll give me a chance to place it somewhere else?"

"Of course, but I doubt you'll find any takers. We checked at least a dozen other banks, trying to syndicate the loan, but they all turned us down. We were the only bank willing to stay in for even a hundred thousand."

I turned to my mother-in-law, who had remained quiet throughout all this. "What do you think? You know what this means. We bust and your three hundred thousand goes down the drain."

She looked at me steadily. "Sometimes it's better to take your losses and get out early. We could lose ten times that much trying to save a hopeless situation."

I looked around at them. "I can't believe this whole thing is going to blow up because of a few chance remarks."

My mother-in-law spoke again. "Perhaps it wouldn't have been so important if your wife hadn't made them."

Her inference was plain enough. "I can't recall that you were ever able to keep her from doing what she wanted," I said.

"Be that as it may, Luke. It was as your wife she spoke, not as my daughter. It was your responsibility."

"She's not a child!" I said angrily. "She knew what she was saying!"

"It was still your responsibility," the old lady insisted stubbornly.

"How could I stop her?" I asked. "By locking her in her room without her supper?"

"It's too late to be arguing over what's already been done." Cousin George turned toward me. "I was afraid of something like this. That's why I wanted you to wait until you were better prepared."

"Why wait?" I asked. "The idea was a good one. It still is. But that doesn't seem to make any difference now. You've all made up your minds."

I got up and started for the door.

"Luke!" My mother-in-law's voice stopped me.

"Yes?"

"Don't feel too badly about this. I'll see to it that you get your money out."

I stared at her. "I refused to accept any equity in the house you gave us. I refused the stock offered me in Hayden and Carruthers. What makes you think I'll accept this kind of a handout?"

Her eyes grew cold and hard, but I'll say this much for the old girl—her voice didn't change an iota. "Don't be foolish. There's always another time."

I smiled bitterly. "What you mean is that I can always go back to Hayden and Carruthers if I want to be a good boy and do as I'm told?"

She didn't answer, but her lips tightened into a thin, hard line.

"Thanks, but no, thanks," I said bitterly. "This won't be the first time I ever went down in flames, just the first time I was ever shot down by my own side."

I looked around the room. They were all silent, staring at me. "I'll survive. I walked away from the others and I'll walk away from this one."

"Luke!" My mother-in-law's voice was harsh and angry now. "If you walk out that door, you'll never have another chance! I can promise you that!"

Suddenly I was tired. "It's time we stopped kidding each other, Mother Hayden," I said wearily. "We both know that the only chance I ever had was to do exactly what you and Nora wanted. I know that I was a fool ever to think I could learn to live like that!"

I closed the door behind me and went to a bar and had a few drinks. Then I went home to tell Nora exactly how I felt. But I never got the chance. She'd already left for New York by the time I got there.

I went upstairs to Dani's room. She sat up in her crib and looked at me. I walked over and picked her up and held her close. Suddenly I felt the tears running down my cheeks. I pressed my lips gently against her soft little neck.

"Well, Dani girl," I whispered, "it looks like your old man turned out a real bomb!"

I was discharged in bankruptcy on the day that she was one year old.

15

Life came to a screeching halt. You move through the days but you might as well be a ghost. People don't see you. You don't touch them; they don't touch you. It's almost like you never were and maybe that would be fine except for one thing. You see too damn much.

Like the wide yellow streak threading its way through your gut like a snake you never knew was there. Fear isn't always a physical thing. It has many faces. One of them begins when you buy someone else's lies. Then you find yourself tied by the yellow thread of your own acceptance.

Nora's mother had kept her promise well. My name was mud and all the doors were closed and after a while I just stopped trying. There was always Dani during the day.

I watched her learn to walk in the park. I listened to her laugh in the zoo and out at the Cliff House, looking for the sea lions that were never there. But she liked best of all putting coins in the mechanicals at Sutro's old Crystal Palace.

There was one she especially loved. It was a farm and a farmer milked the cow while his wife fed the chickens and the windmill turned. We played that one six times on her second birthday alone.

At night there was always bourbon to take the sour taste of disappointment away. On the weekends, when Nora was generally home, I would go down to La Jolla and fool around on the boat. That was the only thing I hadn't lost in the bankruptcy, and the weekends there were the only time I felt halfway useful. There was always something to do—painting, calking, fixing. Sometimes the whole two days would go by and I wouldn't even have a drink. But Monday night, at home, I'd be back on the bottle again.

They ought to give a medal to the man who invented bourbon whiskey. Scotch tastes like medicine, gin smells like perfume, and rye sours your stomach. But bourbon is the sweet cream of them all. It's mild and smooth and soothes you all over. You never get drunk drinking bourbon whiskey. It just fills up all the holes and makes you feel big and strong again. And sleep always comes easier.

But even the bourbon couldn't close my eyes. I still saw too damn much. Like the night I couldn't sleep and I went downstairs at three o'clock in the morning looking for another bottle.

Nora came in the door just as I reached the foot of the stairs. She closed the door behind her and we just stood there, looking at each other, measuring each other, almost like two strangers trying to recall some vaguely remembered impression.

I knew what I looked like with my hair unkempt and my rumpled pajamas and carelessly tied bathrobe. Not very pretty. Especially with my bare feet sticking out.

As for Nora, it was almost like seeing her for the first time. There was the musky odor of sex about her. Her face was pale, and there were the faint blue translucent circles under her violet eyes that were always there afterwards until sleep had washed them away. She didn't have to be told that I knew.

I couldn't stand looking at that knowledge in her eyes and I turned away. I didn't speak.

There was a faint smile in her voice. "If you're looking for whiskey, I told Charles to put a case of bourbon in the den."

I didn't answer.

"It is bourbon that you drink, isn't it?"

I looked up. "Yes."

"That's what I thought." She walked by me to the staircase. When she was about halfway up she turned and looked down at me. "Don't forget to turn out the lights before you come upstairs."

I went into the den and got the bottle of bourbon and thought of a thousand things I should have told her but hadn't. I could feel the yellow creeping around in my belly and I threw some bourbon on it. My daughter needed me, I told myself. She needed someone to love her and to take her out to Sutro's to play the mechanicals, to share the sunshine and the water and all the other things her mother never thought about. I took the bottle upstairs with me and stretched out on the bed.

I'd just swallowed my third drink when I heard the lock turn in the door. I looked toward the bathroom. The door was open. I almost got to my feet, then stopped. Instead I reached for the whiskey again.

I swallowed the shot quickly and killed the light. I stretched out on the bed but I didn't sleep. I found myself listening in the dark for a sound from her room. I didn't have long to wait.

The light in the bathroom clicked on and poured into my room as she came through. She stood in the doorway knowing that I could see she had nothing on under the sheer negligee. She spoke softly. "Are you awake, Luke?"

I sat up in bed without answering.

"I unlocked the door," she said.

I still didn't speak.

She walked to the foot of my bed and stood there looking at me. Abruptly she shrugged her shoulders and the negligee fell to the floor. "I remember once you didn't want seconds." There was a faint echo of contempt in her voice. "Still feel the same way?"

I reached for a cigarette and lit it. My hands were trembling.

The contempt grew thicker in her voice. "I thought you were a man once. But I can see now that I was wrong. I'm more of a man now than you are. You lost your balls when you took off your uniform."

I dragged on the cigarette, letting the smoke burn its way into my lungs. I could feel the sweat running into my clenched fists. "Better go back to your room, Nora," I said thickly.

She sat down on the side of the bed and picked the cigarette out of my hand. She put it to her lips and took a quick puff, then gave it back to me. I could taste the faint scent of her lipstick.

"Maybe it would help if I told you what I did tonight."

"Don't push it, Nora!" I said huskily.

She paid no attention to what I said. Instead she leaned across me, her face very close to mine. I could feel her small warm breasts press against me through my pajamas. "It was only once," she whispered teasingly. "It was tremendous. But you know me. Only once is like Chinese food. An hour later I'm hungry again!"

The anger flooded up into me. I couldn't take it any more. I grabbed her by the shoulders and shook her violently. A strangely excited look came into her eyes and I felt her hand, warm and urgent against me. "Make love to me!"

"Nora!" I cried and rolled over on top of her.

It was over almost before it began. I lay there feeling sick and futile and inadequate, staring as she picked up her negligee from the floor. She looked down at me, a cold triumph in her eyes.

"Sometimes I wonder whatever made me think you were man enough for me," she said contemptuously. "Even a boy could make a better job of it than you do."

The door slammed shut behind her and I reached for the bottle again. But this time even the bourbon couldn't take away the sick feeling in my stomach.

I was on the boat in La Jolla when the news came over the radio that the Reds had crossed the line in Korea. I beat it down the dock to the pay telephone and called Jimmy Petersen in Washington. We. had flown together in the Pacific. He had stayed in after the war and was a brigadier in the Air Force now.

"I just heard the news," I said when he came on the wire. "Can you use a good man on the line?"

"Sure, but we're using jets now. You'll have to go through retraining and I'm not sure that I can get your rating back."

"To hell with the rating, Pete. When do I go?"

He laughed. "Check in with Bill Killian at the Presidio tomorrow morning. I'll have something worked out for you by then."

"I'll be there with bells on, Pete. Thanks."

"You may not thank me when you find yourself a captain again."

"General," I said sincerely, "I'd thank you if you took me back as a private!"

I went back to the boat where Dani was sleeping in her. portable travel bed. She was almost three. years old then and she opened her eyes when I picked her up, bed and all. "Where we goin', Daddy?" she asked sleepily.

"We have to go home, sweetie. Daddy has something to do."

"Alri'," she whispered and closed her eyes again.

I strapped the bed onto the seat of the car beside me and threw our bags in the back. I looked at my watch. It was almost eight o'clock. If the traffic was light I could be in San Francisco by four o'clock in the morning.

Dani made the whole trip without opening her eyes. There was no traffic. The lights were still on in Nora's studio when I carried Dani upstairs at three-thirty and put her in her crib.

I went through into my room and then remembered the lights. I would only have to tell her in the morning, I thought. I might as well do it now, since she was still awake. I went down the stairs and into her studio.

The lights were on but the studio was empty. "Nora," I called.

I heard a noise from the small room next to the studio. I walked over and opened the door. I started to say her name again and then my voice went.

They were still on the bed, frozen grotesquely in their embrace. Nora was the first to recover. "Get out!" she screamed.

My head felt as if it were nine miles above the clouds. This was the classic denouement and I was torn between anger at having to face the truth so unexpectedly and a wild desire to laugh at the ridiculousness of the whole thing. Anger won out.

I crossed to the bed and pulled the man from her by the scruff of his neck. I spun him around and caught him on the side of the jaw. He fell backward through the open door, crashing into a statue. Both went to the floor with a clatter that would wake the dead.

I started after him again but something held my arm.

I looked at him. Fear and guilt had combined to render him helpless. He was nothing but a boy. I let my arm drop to my side.

Charles came into the studio, still tying his robe around him. I could see the cook and the downstairs maid staring into the doorway behind him.

I went back into the small room and picked up the boy's things and threw them out into the studio. "Charles," I said, "get that cruddy little bastard out of here!"

I closed the door behind me and turned to Nora. Her face was pale with anger and hatred. "You better get something on too. You look like a two-bit whore dressed in nothing but that sheet."

"Why did you have to wake the servants? How will I ever face them?"

I stared at her. She wasn't worried about the fact that I had caught her in bed with someone else. The only thing that bothered her was how it might affect the servants. I shook my head. I guessed I would never stop learning. Suddenly I seemed to know all the answers.

"I don't think you have to worry, Nora," I said, almost gently. "You weren't really fooling anybody. Except me."

"You never believed me! You heard the stories about me and I know you believed them!"

"That's where you're wrong, Nora," I said. "I never heard any of the stories, I still haven't. Don't you know that the husband is generally the last one to find out?"

"What did you expect me to do? You never even came near me after Dani was born!"

I shook my head. "It won't work, Nora. Not any more."

She began to cry.

"I'm beyond that, Nora. Tears won't work either."

They stopped as quickly as they had begun. "Please, Luke," she said, getting off the bed and coming toward me. "It won't happen again."

I laughed. "You're right about that. Not to me it won't. I'm leaving!"

"No, Luke, no!" She flung her arms about me, clinging to me. "I'll make it all up to you. I promise!"

"You couldn't live long enough!"

I pushed her away from me. Her eyes were wide and frightened. "What are you going to do?"

Suddenly all the hurt and the pain came up inside me at one time. "Something I should have done a long time ago."

The back of my hand flashed across the side of her face and she spun halfway across the room, falling over the bed to the floor. I was out of there before she could pick herself up.

I went through the studio and down the corridor. I could see the servants' faces staring at me. Charles was just coming back from the front door as I reached the staircase. The poor old man couldn't look me in the face.

The studio door opened and Nora came into the hallway, completely naked. "You son of a bitch!" she screamed. "I'll tell the whole world what you are. You're not even a man. You're a homosexual, a pervert, a queer!"

I looked at Charles. "You'd better take care of her. Call a doctor if you think you need one."

He nodded silently. She was still screaming when I reached the top of the stairs.

Mrs. Holman was at her door, her eyes wide.

"Is Dani all right?" I asked.

She nodded, her face still pale.

I walked into the child's room. She was still sleeping

like the baby she was. I bent down and kissed her cheek. Thank God for the sleep of the innocent.

My luck was about the same in Korea as it had been during the war. I checked out fine in the jets and flew about nine missions, getting two MIGs before they got me. It wasn't a big enough war for me to make general staff after I got out of the hospital, so they gave me a medical discharge and shipped me home.

I arrived in San Francisco to a tumultuous welcome. The only one waiting at the airport for me was a process server.

"Colonel Carey?"

"Yes."

"Sorry," he said, thrusting a piece of paper into my hand, then scurrying off like a rat with a terrier after him.

I opened the paper and read it. It was dated that day—July 20, 1951. Nora Hayden Carey *vs.* Luke Carey. An action for divorce brought by the plaintiff, Mrs. Carey. The grounds were mental cruelty, desertion and nonsupport.

"Welcome home," I said to myself, shoving the paper into my pocket. There's nothing like a good old-fashioned homecoming.

PART THREE

LUKE'S STORY
The Weekend

1

I looked at my watch as I came up in the elevator from the garage. It was almost noon by the time I'd got back to the motel from Juvenile Hall. That made it two o'clock in Chicago. Elizabeth would be waiting to hear from me.

Suddenly my hands were trembling. I needed a drink. I got off the elevator in the main lobby and walked into the bar. I ordered one Jack Daniels. Just one. I drank it quickly and went up to my room.

I threw my jacket across the chair and sat down on the edge of the bed and put in my call. I pulled off my tie and stretched out on the bed while I waited for my connection.

Her voice sounded warm over the wire. "Hello."

"Elizabeth," I said.

"Luke?" There was quick concern in her voice. "Are you all right?"

The words could scarcely make it out of my throat. "I'm all right."

"Is it that bad?" she asked quietly.

"Bad enough," I said. "Nothing's changed." I pulled the package of cigarettes from my shirt pocket. "Nora still hates me."

"You didn't think that would have changed, did you?"

I lit a cigarette. "I guess not. Only—"

"Only what?"

"I wish there was something more I could do. To let Dani know how much I want to help her."

"You're there, aren't you?" she asked.

"Yes, but—"

"Then stop worrying about it," she said quietly. "Dani knows. The most important thing is that she doesn't feel she's alone."

That kind of brought me back a little. "How about you? Don't you feel alone?"

She laughed. "I'm not alone. Our little friend has been keeping me company."

"I wish you were here."

"Maybe the next time," she said. "You'll do all right without me."

"I love you," I said.

"And I love you, Luke. Next time call collect. We won't get the bill until the first of the month."

"Okay, darling."

" 'Bye, Luke."

I put down the phone. Somehow I felt better. Some of the tension was gone. Elizabeth had that effect on me. She made everything seem better. I closed my eyes and remembered how it had been on the boat a long time ago. That first time. When I took her and her boss out on a charter.

We'd tied up off Santa Monica and the old man had taken a cab into Los Angeles. Elizabeth had stayed on the boat. The old man had told her that she could have the weekend off.

We were all on a first-name basis by then and after the old man had gone off in the taxi, I turned to Elizabeth. "I have a friend here who'd put me up for the night if you'd feel better about it."

"Would you be more comfortable that way, Luke?" There was no artificial coquetry in her voice.

"I was just doing the gentleman bit."

"I'm sure." She looked at me out of her clear blue eyes. "If I'd had any doubts, Luke, I wouldn't have agreed to stay aboard."

"A kind remark like that gets you taken out to dinner," I said.

"It's a date if you'll let me pay."

"Uh-uh. I insist. You're my guest for the weekend."

"But that's not fair. I cut your charter fee a hundred bucks."

"That's my headache," I said stubbornly.

She saw the look on my face and put a hand on my arm. "If it means that much to you. Why?"

"I had a wife who fixed it so she paid all the bills. No more."

She took her hand away quickly. "I see," she said. "Well, I hope you're loaded. We Swedes have big appetites."

We went to the fish place on the Coast Highway between Malibu and Santa Monica and she was every bit as good as her word. Even I had to back off from the size of the portions but she cleaned her plate. Afterward we sat over our coffee, looking out through the plate glass at the surf breaking against the beach under the windows, and we talked. It was real easy and the evening went by and it was after eleven when we got back to the boat.

"I'm beat," she sighed as we walked down the dock. "I guess I'm not used to all that sea air."

"It has a way of knocking you out." I looked at her in the uneven yellow light of the single overhead bulb on the edge of the dock. "You turn in. If it's okay with you I'll go down the beach a while. I have a friend I ought to see."

She looked at me peculiarly for a moment, then nodded. "Go ahead. And thanks for dinner."

I grinned at her. "That was just an exhibition game. Tomorrow night we'll do the real thing. Soft lights, white tablecloths, music."

"Thanks for the warning. I'll starve myself all day." She climbed down into the boat and disappeared into the cabin.

I waited a moment, then turned and walked down the dock. I went through the doors of the first bar I came to and asked for my friend by name. Jack Daniels.

I got stewed and it must have been after three when I stumbled off the dock onto the boat. I tried so hard to be quiet that I tripped over a mooring rope coiled on the deck and sprawled out with a crash. By then I was too tired to make it to the cabin, so I just went to sleep where I'd fallen.

I woke in the morning to the aroma of coffee and the fragrance of frying bacon. I sat up before I realized I was in my bunk with nothing on but my shorts. I rubbed my hand over my head. I didn't remember getting there.

Elizabeth must have heard me move for she left the small stove in the galley and brought me a glass filled with tomato juice. "Here, drink this."

I stared at her doubtfully.

"Drink it. It will burn away the fog."

Automatically I swallowed it. She was right. It burned away the fog, all right and the teeth, the throat, the stomach lining, everything. "Wow!" I gasped. "What was in that? Dynamite?"

She laughed. "It's an old Swedish hangover cure. Tomato juice, pepper, Worcestershire, Tabasco and aquavit. It either kills you or cures you, my father used to say."

"Your father was right. It's sudden death. Where did you get the aquavit?"

"The same place you met your friend last night. I guess it's the nearest one, isn't it?"

I nodded.

"Your friend packs a pretty good wallop."

"I'm out of training," I said defensively. "I've had practically nothing to drink for four days. How did you get me to bed?"

"You were nothing. My father was six-four and weighed two hundred and thirty and I used to put him to bed. It was just like the good old days." She took the empty glass from my hand. "Hungry?"

A moment ago I would have thrown up at the mere mention of food, now I was suddenly ravenous. I nodded.

"Sit down at the table then," she said, walking back to the galley. "The service doesn't include breakfast in bed. How do you like your eggs?"

"Sunny side." I climbed out of the bunk and into my pants. "Wait a minute," I protested. "You don't have to do the cooking."

But the eggs were already in the pan. There were hot rolls and butter, jam and marmalade, four eggs and a half pound of bacon, a pot of steaming coffee. I was eating like a madman when she brought her cup to the table, filled it and sat down. She lit a cigarette.

I wiped up the last of the egg with the last of the roll and leaned back with a sigh. "That was good."

"I like to see a man eat."

"You've just watched a professional." I filled my cup again. "That's real coffee."

"Thank you."

I lit a cigarette and sipped at the coffee. I felt better than I had for a long time.

"You have a daughter?"

I nodded.

"How old is she?"

"Eight."

"Is her name Nora?"

I shook my head. "No. Dani. Short for Danielle. Nora was my wife."

"Oh."

I looked at her. "What makes you ask?"

"You kept talking about them when I was putting you to bed. You miss them both very much, don't you?"

"I miss my daughter," I said gruffly. I got to my feet. "Why don't you go out and get some fresh air? I'll do the dishes."

"You take your cup of coffee out on deck. The dishes are my job for the weekend."

I went outside and sat down in one of the fishing chairs. The morning smog was rolling out to sea. It was going to be a hot one. I'd just finished my cup when she came up behind me.

I turned to look at her. "Want to hit the beach today?"

"Why go to a crowded beach when you can take your own boat out and have a private ocean?"

"You're the skipper," I said, getting to my feet. "I'll go ashore and lay in a few things for lunch."

She smiled. "I already took care of that. Including a dozen cans of beer if the sun gets too hot."

I went forward to cast off.

The morning kept its promise. The sun was slow and reached down deep into your bones so that even the relief you found in the cool green water was only temporary. It didn't seem to bother her though.

She lay stretched out flat on the deck soaking up the sun. It had been almost an hour since she'd moved. I lay on the bench behind the wheel under the canopy. I was in no mood to be cooked alive.

I pushed my cap back from over my face so that I

could see. "There's some suntan lotion in the cabin if you want it."

"No, thanks. I don't burn. I just turn black. I could use another beer though. I'm all dried out."

I reached down into the cooler and came up with two cans. I opened them and walked out into the sun. It was like stepping into a furnace. She rolled over and sat up, reaching for the frosted can. She held it to her mouth and drank thirstily. Some of the beer escaped the corner of her mouth and ran down to her tawny shoulders. I couldn't help staring. Bikinis and beer cans.

She was a big girl, at least five-eight with everything scaled to size. You knew automatically that if you had a woman like that you had it all, that there was not another woman on this earth who could make it plus or minus.

She wiped her face on the back of her arm. Then she caught me staring. She grinned. "My mother always said I was a sloppy drinker. Like my father."

I grinned back. "You said you were thirsty."

She put her hands flat on the deck behind her and leaned back on her arms, turning her face up to the sun. "God, this feels good. The sun and the ocean. I never thought I'd miss the water so much."

I had to force myself to look away. For the first time in my life I dug the big blonde bit. Until now they had always been something up on the screen or in the chorus at Las Vegas. But seeing a real live one up close, now I knew all the reasons.

"If you miss the water that much," I asked, "how come you wound up in a place like Sandsville?"

She had her eyes closed to the sun. "I came out to Phoenix with my husband. He was a pilot in the Air Force. He flew his jet into the side of a mountain at six hundred miles an hour. When it was all over, I took this job. I've been there ever since."

"I'm sorry," I said. I looked out over the water. Some guys aren't ever lucky. Not even once. "How long ago was that?"

"Four years. You were a flyer, weren't you, Luke?"

"I was—once. But that was when I was very young."

"You're not that old."

"I'm thirty-six going on seventy."

"It's the booze that makes you feel that way. My father used to feel the same—" She stopped when she saw me staring at her. Her eyes fell. "I'm sorry, that popped out."

"How old are you?"

"Twenty-four."

"Everything's easy at twenty-four."

"Is it?" she asked, her eyes meeting mine once more. "As easy as being a widow at twenty?"

"Now it's my turn to be sorry."

"Forget it."

I reached down and took a sip of my beer. "Where did you get that bit about me being a flyer?"

"I've known about you for a long time. That's why I came out here looking for you."

"For me?"

"You were Johnny's hero. A hot fighter pilot. A chicken colonel at twenty-five. Johnny wanted to be just like you. I had to come out and see what he would have been like—if he'd lived."

"And now?"

"I don't have to wonder any more. I guess I'll never know. Johnny wasn't anything like you."

"What makes you say that?"

"Last night when I put you to bed you were crying. I can't imagine Johnny crying over anything once he got past the age of six. He was quick and aggressive and sometimes harsh and impatient. You're exactly the opposite. Soft and gentle inside."

"I was never really a hero," I said. "War forces you into being something you aren't if you want to survive. I was a survival expert." I grinned wryly. "Though what the hell I was trying to survive for I can't imagine."

Her eyes looked into mine. "I guess surviving can come to mean very little if you spend your life hiding in a whiskey barrel."

I looked deep into her eyes for a moment. They were clear and proud and met mine evenly. I sighed. "I guess I asked for that." I looked at my watch. "There's just about time for you to get in one more dip before we have to haul anchor."

I picked up my can of beer and went down into the cabin. It was a little cooler there. I took a sip from the can and put it on the table in front of me. Through the open hatch I heard the splash of the water as she dived.

The telephone beside my bed bounced me back into the present. I struggled up through the warmth of memory.

"Yes," I mumbled.

"Colonel Carey?"

"Yes."

"Harris Gordon here."

Now I was awake. "Yes, Mr. Gordon."

"I'm sorry to be so late in calling. But I was all tied up."

I looked at my watch. It was after seven. I'd slept the whole afternoon. "That's all right."

"Would it be all right if we put off our meeting until

tomorrow morning? It's Saturday night and I find my wife has asked some people in."

"I understand perfectly."

"Tomorrow morning at nine?"

"Fine," I said. "I'll meet you in the lobby."

I put down the telephone and turned to look out the window. Dusk was falling and the neon was coming on. San Francisco on a Saturday night and nothing for me to do in my old home town. So I lit a cigarette and leaned back against the pillow and went back to thinking about Elizabeth and me.

2

Elizabeth wore a simple white dress that night. Her hair fell down to her shoulders like spun gold against the creamy chocolate of her sun-darkened skin. It gave all the weekend cheaters in the place cricks in their necks. They're used to beautiful women in Southern California, especially up around Malibu where the film colony comes to play, but there was something about her that drew every eye.

The maitre d' was no fool. He knew an attraction when he saw one. He gave us a corner window looking out over the ocean, where everyone could see us. Then he sent over a bottle of champagne and the violins.

Elizabeth smiled at me. "You must be a very big man around here."

"It's not me." I lifted my glass. "It's you. As a matter of fact it's a lucky thing he doesn't remember me. The only other time I was ever in here I was thrown out for being drunk."

She laughed. "He'll change his mind once he sees me eat." After a while the violins went away and the dance band came on. I looked at her, and when she nodded we moved out onto the floor. I put my arm around her and where my hand touched the flesh of her bare back I could sense the strength that lay hidden there under her skin.

I stumbled, trying to find the beat of the music. "It's been a long time."

"For me too." Then she put her face against my cheek and after that it was easy.

I was surprised when the orchestra wrapped it up and I looked at my watch and saw that it was three o'clock. It had been a long time since an evening had gone by so quickly for me. I paid the check and laid a big tip on the maitre d' for being so nice to us. The scent of flowers came down from the hills as we walked out into the star-filled California night. Mingled with the salt air it was real heady.

"Want to walk down near the water?"

She nodded and slipped her arm through mine. We went down the path that wound its way around behind the restaurant past the small motel fronting on the beach.

The night was very still. No sounds came from the road high behind us. "I could ask you to watch the grunion running," I said.

"I'm a sucker for fish stories."

I laughed as we walked along the beach for a while until we came to a rock. We sat down and looked out at the ocean. We didn't talk. We didn't have to. The night was filled with a rare kind of peace.

I flipped my butt and watched it leave a trail of sparks on its way to the water. We sat there real close, watching the surf break on the sand, not touching each other, but close just the same.

She turned her face to me. "Luke."

I kissed her. No hands, no frantic clinch, just our lips touching and tasting and telling each other of the way it had been with us before. How lonely we were, how we would like it to be.

After a while she took her mouth away and put her head on my shoulder and we sat that way for a long while. Then she sighed a little and raised her head. "It's getting late, Luke. I'm tired. Let's go back to the boat."

We were silent in the taxi that took us back to Santa

Monica. Just our fingers spoke as they rested quietly intertwined.

We climbed down off the dock onto the boat and came to a stop outside the cabin. Her voice was quiet and calm.

"I'm not the type for weekend romances, Luke. When I go it's for the long time, the whole distance. I'm not a lonely widow trying to fill an empty gap in her life. I don't want to be used like a fire extinguisher, to put out a torch."

I looked into her eyes. "I understand."

She was silent for a moment while she sought the truth in me. "I hope you do," she whispered softly. "I want you to." She reached up and pressed her lips to mine. "Give me a few minutes before you come in."

She disappeared into the cabin and I lit a cigarette. Suddenly my hands were trembling and I was afraid. I didn't know what I was afraid of but I was. I looked around for a drink, but all there was was a few cans of beer. I opened one and drank it quickly. It wasn't cold any more but I felt better after I drank it. I threw my cigarette into the water and went into the cabin.

She was lying in my bunk, the sheet pulled up to her throat, her spun-gold hair spread over my pillow. "Turn out the light, Luke. I'm a little shy."

I reached over and switched it off. The light from the dock poured in through the porthole, framing her face. I fumbled my way quickly out of my clothes and knelt beside the bunk and kissed her.

Her arms came up around my neck. "Luke, Luke."

I raised my head and slowly drew the sheet back. Her eyes were open now, she was watching me. After a moment's silence, she spoke. "Am I beautiful enough for you, Luke?"

Her breasts were full and proud. Her waist was tiny

as it fell away from the bones of her high rib cage, her stomach flat with just a hint of roundness as it reached down into the swelling curve of her hips. Her thighs were strong and her legs long and straight.

Her voice filled the silence again. "I want to be beautiful for you."

"My golden goddess," I whispered, kissing her throat.

Her arms tightened around me. "Hold me, Luke. Love me."

I felt the passion flooding into me. I kissed her breasts. She moaned softly and I felt her warmth spread open beneath me. Then there was nothing but the pounding of my heart and the roaring of my brain. Suddenly all the whiskey and all the whoring I had engaged in for escape turned back on me and broke the dam.

"Oh, no!" I cried, feeling her arms freeze around me in surprise and shock. "Please, no!"

But it was over.

I lay very still for a moment, then I sat up slowly and reached for a cigarette. "I'm sorry, Elizabeth, I'm sorry. I should have known better. I guess I'm no good for anything any more. I'm not even a decent lover."

I sat on the edge of the bunk staring down at the floor, not daring to look at her. She was silent for a moment, then reached up and took the cigarette from my mouth. She put it down and with the other hand turned my face to her.

Her voice was soft and kind. "Is that what she did to you, Luke? Did she take you apart like that?"

"I took myself apart," I said bitterly. "Like I said, I guess I'm nothing but a lousy lover."

She drew my head down to the warmth of her breasts and stroked it slowly. "You're not, Luke," she whispered. "The trouble with you is you love too much."

When I woke in the morning she was gone. In her place was a note and four one-hundred-dollar bills. I opened the envelope with trembling fingers.

Dear Luke,
Please forgive my leaving like this. I know it may not seem fair but there is nothing else I can think of to do at this moment. Everyone carries his or her own cross and has to fight his or her own peculiar kind of war. I fought mine when Johnny died. You're still fighting yours.

If the time should come when you win enough of your war to come out of hiding and be the kind of man you really are, maybe we can take that long trip together. Because that's what I really want, that is, if you want it too. I know I'm not making much sense, but then I never make too much sense when I'm crying.

Love,
Elizabeth

For three months I tried to forget what she had written, then one morning I woke up in the drunk tank and everything was gone. The boat, my credit, whatever self-respect was left—all gone. They gave me thirty days on the work farm when I couldn't get up my fine.

At the end of the thirty days, when they gave me back my clothes, I found her note still in a pocket. I took it out and read it again, then looked at myself in the mirror. My eyes were clear for the first time in a long time. Really clear. I could see myself.

I thought of Elizabeth and how good it would be to see her. But not like this. I didn't want to show up looking like a bum. So I got a job as a laborer on a housing project and seven months later when the job was completed, I had worked my way up to assistant foreman. I had six hundred bucks in my jeans and an old jalopy that I could call my own.

I got into my car and drove non-stop to Phoenix. There I learned that she'd gone to Tucson, where her boss was just beginning a new development. I was in Tucson late that same afternoon. The office was way out on the speedway, and the first thing I noticed when I pulled into the parking lot was the sign:

CONSTRUCTION HELP WANTED

I opened the door and went in. A dark-haired girl was sitting in the outer office. She looked up at me. "Yes?"

"The sign outside says you're looking for help."

She nodded. "We are. Had any experience?"

"Yes."

"Sit down, please. Miss Andersen will be with you in a moment."

She picked up the telephone and whispered something into it. Then she gave me a form. "Fill this out while you're waiting."

I'd just finished when the phone buzzed and the girl pointed me toward an inner office.

Elizabeth didn't look up as I came in. She was staring down at a sheet of figures. "You've had experience?" she asked, still not looking up.

"Yes, ma'am."

Her eyes were still on the desk. "What kind of experience?"

"All kinds, ma'am."

"All kinds?" she asked impatiently. "That's not a very definite—" She looked up and the words disappeared in her throat.

She seemed thinner somehow, her cheekbones stood

out more. "But that's not the reason I came out here, ma'am," I said, watching her eyes. "The real reason is —I came out here looking for someone who said she might be willing to take a long trip with me."

For the longest kind of a moment she looked up at me, and then she was out of the chair and around the desk and into my arms. I was kissing her and she was crying and saying my name over and over again. "Luke . . . Luke . . . Luke."

The door on the other side of her office opened and the old man, her boss, came in. He noticed us and turned to go back out, then took a second look. He cleared his throat.

He reached into his jacket and came out with a pair of glasses. He peered at me again and again cleared his throat.

"So it's you," he said. "It's about time you got here. Now maybe she'll stop moping so we can get some work done."

He stomped out of the office, closing the door behind him, and we turned to each other and began to laugh. Somehow, listening to the sound of her laughter, I knew I would always feel better just knowing that she was around. Always, even like now, when I was in San Francisco and she was in Chicago, waiting for me on a lonely Saturday night.

3

Harris Gordon was in the lobby the next morning when I came down at nine o'clock. We went into the coffee shop, where there were nothing but empty tables. It was Sunday morning.

The waitress put down the coffee and I ordered a stack of dollar-sized pancakes and sausages. Gordon shook his head. "I've already had breakfast."

When the waitress went away I asked, "Where do we go from here?"

He reached for a cigarette. "We're fortunate in one respect. We're not facing a murder trial."

"We're not?"

"No," he answered. "Under California law, a minor who has committed a felony is not treated in the same way as a criminal adult. This is particularly true in cases involving minors under the age of sixteen."

"Then how do they determine guilt and punishment for a child?"

"Again, that is where the law operates to our advantage. There is no such thing as punishing a child. California maintains that a child cannot be held responsible for his or her actions, even if guilt is determined. Instead, the minor is subjected to a custodial hearing in Juvenile Court to determine the best possible solutions regarding rehabilitation and an eventual return to society." He smiled. "Do I sound too much like a lawyer?"

I shook my head. "I'm still with you. Go on."

The waitress returned with my breakfast. Gordon

waited until she had gone again before he continued.

"The court must determine in whose custody the best interests and welfare of the child will be served. One or both parents, as the case may be, a foster home, a remedial school like Los Guilicos, even a hospital or mental institution if necessary. But only after a complete investigation is made. In the event the court decided to retain her in custody, Dani might be sent to the California Youth Authority Reception Center, at Perkins, to undergo a psychological and psychiatric study in depth."

"What does that mean?"

"One thing it's sure to mean," he answered quickly, "is that if you have any idea of gaining custody, you might as well forget it. The court would never permit the child to be taken out of the state."

We stared at each other. At least I knew where I stood. I wasn't to be allowed custody of Dani no matter what. I kept my voice impassive. "So I don't get her," I said. "Who does?"

"Frankly I doubt that the court would ever return her to Nora. That leaves three possibilities—her grandmother, a court-selected foster home, or Los Guilicos. I think we can eliminate the foster home. Dani's grandmother can offer more advantages."

"Then it's between the old lady and an institution?"
He nodded.

I finished the last of my pancakes and signaled for more coffee. "Which do you think it will be?"

"Do you want my frank opinion?"
I nodded.

"The odds are perhaps ten to one on Los Guilicos."

I sat there silently for a moment. The thought of Dani spending months, maybe years, behind fences was more than I could take. "How do we get them to give us that one chance?"

Gordon looked at me closely. "We'd have to prove that we could give Dani everything—that an institution could. That means close supervision, schooling, religious education, psychotherapy, analysis if necessary. And constant contact with the probation officer assigned to her."

"Why is that necessary if Dani is with her grandmother?"

"Because only her custody will be entrusted. She will still remain a ward of the court until the court is completely satisfied that she can cause no more social problems."

"How long will that take?"

"Based on my experience, I would think she'd remain a ward of the court until she is at least eighteen."

"That's a long time for anyone to live under a microscope. Even a kid."

He looked at me strangely. "She killed a man," he said. "That's forever."

That was blunt enough. Even for me. "What can I do to help?"

"I feel it's important that you remain in San Francisco until Dani's court hearings are concluded."

"That's impossible," I said. "Trials go on forever."

"This is not a trial in the ordinary sense, Colonel. There is no jury to assess or determine guilt. This is just a custodial hearing before a judge, involving only the persons concerned. Even the police and the district attorney aren't involved, unless they are asked to appear to answer specific questions concerning the welfare and behavior of the child. The entire matter must be disposed of quickly. The law acts to protect the child from needless detention. If the child is held in custody more than fifteen days without a hearing, she must be released."

"In plain English," I asked, "how long?"

"The detention hearing will take place Tuesday. The court hearing will be a week from that day. A week from next Tuesday—roughly ten days."

"Ten days!" I exploded. "My wife is due to have a baby any day now! Why do we have to wait until Tuesday to get a hearing?"

"That's the way it works, Colonel," Gordon explained patiently. "The detention hearing is set for Tuesday because that's the day the judge sits on cases involving minor girls. The final hearing is scheduled for a week later because, as I said before, the probation officer must have time to investigate thoroughly every aspect of this case. And that investigation is as important to us as it is to the court. It is from the probation officer's report that the judge usually makes up his mind unless it is inconclusive in which case he orders further study of the child at Perkins. Our job is to convince the probation officer and the court that the best interests of both Dani and the state will be served if she is given into the custody of her grandmother."

"What do you need me around for? There's nothing I can do to convince anyone that the old lady should get Dani."

"I disagree, Colonel. There's a great deal you can do, merely by indicating that you feel this would be best for your child."

"Yeah," I said sarcastically. "My word counts for a lot. It couldn't buy you a beer if you didn't have a quarter."

He looked at me. "You underestimate yourself, Colonel. Your word means a great deal. It isn't easy for people to forget your service to your country."

"You're going to pull the war hero bit?"

"For everything it's worth. It's working for us already."

"What do you mean?"

Gordon signaled to a waitress and asked her to bring him the morning papers. When they were spread out on the table, he pointed to a front-page picture and its headline.

The picture was of me with my arm around Dani going into the detention hall. The headline was simple:

WAR HERO COMES
TO DEFENSE OF DAUGHTER

"Respectful, don't you think? The papers are on your side already. There's no mention of your losing your temper with the reporters. Ordinarily anybody would be crucified for acting as you did. But not you."

I looked at him questioningly.

"The people involved in the fate of your daughter are human. Even the judge reads the daily papers and whether he admits it or not he's influenced." Gordon leaned back in his chair. "If your remaining here is a question of finances, Mrs. Hayden has assured me that she's willing to help."

"My finances have nothing to do with it. I tell you my wife is about to have a baby."

"Public opinion has a way of changing overnight," Gordon added. "At the moment, there is a great deal of sympathy for you and your daughter. If you should leave before custody is settled, people might draw the conclusion that your daughter is an incorrigible, in your own eyes not worth saving."

I glared at him. He was clever all right. He had me neatly boxed in. I was damned if I did and damned if I didn't.

"Remember this, Colonel. Whether Dani spends the next four years of her life in a state correctional institution or at home with her grandmother may very well rest on your decision."

"Suddenly it's all my responsibility," I said angrily. "Why didn't the court consider that when it awarded Nora custody of Dani? The court had enough evidence to show what Nora was like. Where was the justice in that?

"And where was the old lady when this guy was living in Nora's house? She must have known what was going on. She didn't go suddenly blind. Why didn't she take steps to get Dani out of there before all this happened?

"I wasn't even here. I wasn't allowed to be. Oh, no, I wasn't good enough to come within ten feet of my daughter. I wasn't even supposed to be her father.

"And now you say it's my responsibility?"

Gordon looked at me silently for a moment. I guess there was a kind of understanding in his eyes. He spoke softly. "Granting the truth in everything you say, Colonel, it still doesn't alter the present circumstances. What we face now is bitter fact, not bitter past." He called for the check. "Don't make a hasty decision. At least wait until Tuesday, after the detention hearing, before you make up your mind."

He got to his feet. "Perhaps if you attended the coroner's inquest tomorrow it would help you reach a decision."

"The coroner's inquest? Will Dani be there?"

Gordon shook his head. "No. But her statement will be read in court. And Nora will be there to tell her story."

"What will that prove?"

He shrugged his shoulders. "Nothing, perhaps, that

we don't already know. But it might help convince you that it's important for you to stay."

I ordered another cup of coffee as he walked out of the restaurant. There was no point in going out to the old lady's house now. There wasn't time before I'd be going out to see Dani.

4

Nora's Jaguar was in the parking lot behind Juvenile Hall when I got there. I had got out of the car and started for the entrance when Charles's voice stopped me. "Colonel!"

I turned back. "Hello, Charles."

"Would you do me a favor, sir? I have some packages here that Miss Hayden asked me to deliver to Miss Dani."

"Where's Miss Hayden?"

Charles didn't quite meet my eyes. "She's not—she's not feeling too well today. Dr. Bonner advised her to stay in bed and rest. She's been very upset."

"I can imagine," I said dryly. "All right, I'll take them in."

"Thank you, Colonel." He turned and opened the car door. He removed a small suitcase and two packages, one of which looked like a box of candy.

"Wouldn't they accept them inside?" I asked.

"Oh, yes, sir. But they told me that you were coming out and I thought it would be nicer if you gave them to Miss Dani."

As I started to walk toward the building, Charles fell into step beside me. "May I have your permission to wait until you come out, sir? I'd very much like to hear how Miss Dani is getting on."

"Of course, Charles. I'll look for you when I come out."

"Thank you, sir. I'll be waiting in the car, sir."

He turned and went back toward the parking lot as I went into the building. The same gray-haired woman was at the desk. She smiled when she saw me. "I have your visitor's pass all ready, Colonel."

"Thank you," I said.

She noticed the suitcase and the packages. "May I, Colonel? It's a rule here."

At first I didn't know what she meant. Then I understood. Maybe this wasn't called a prison but some of the same rules applied.

She opened the suitcase first. There were several blouses and skirts on top. She lifted them out onto the desk. Underneath were two sweaters, some stockings, underwear, two pairs of shoes and a neat pile of handkerchiefs. She ran her hands down under and then carefully around the sides. She smiled at me as she put everything into the suitcase and closed it. The two packages came next. I had guessed right. One was a box of candy. The other contained several books, the kind that young girls were supposed to read.

The clerk looked at me apologetically. "Everything seems to be in order. You have no idea what some people will try to smuggle in."

"I understand," I said.

She handed me a slip of paper and pointed to a door. "Through there to the end of the corridor. Then up one flight and follow the signs on the wall. You'll come to a locked gate. Show your pass to the matron on duty. She'll take you to your daughter."

"Thank you."

The corridors were clinically clean, the walls painted a pale hospital green. I went up the flight of steps and came out in a corridor exactly like the one I had just left. A sign on the wall opposite pointed—TO THE GIRLS' COTTAGES.

I followed this until I came to a wire wall. It was heavy gauge wire and ran from floor to ceiling. In the center was a steel-framed door, also of the same heavy wire grill.

I tried it but it was locked. I shook it and the reverberations echoed down the empty corridor.

A door opened and a large Negro woman came hurrying out, her fingers buttoning the front of her white uniform. "I just came on," she apologized.

I held up my pass.

She read it quickly and nodded. Taking a key from the pocket of her white uniform, she turned the lock. I stepped in and she closed the door after me.

We walked down the corridor until it opened into a large reception room. There were chairs scattered around and on one side, against the windows where it was completely screened from the corridor, a table and several more chairs.

Several girls were gathered around the table, listening to a small radio. Two other girls were dancing, one white and the other a Negro. The music was rock and roll.

The girls looked up as we came in. There was a strangely disinterested curiosity in their expression that faded quickly when they saw I hadn't come to visit them.

"What room is Dani Carey in?" the matron asked.

They looked at her blankly.

"The new girl."

"Oh, the new girl." It was the colored girl who answered. "She in twelve."

"Why isn't she out here with you girls? Didn't you invite her?"

"Sho, we axed her. But she didn' want to, Miss Matson. She wanted to stay in her room. She still shy, I reckon."

The matron nodded as we left the room and started down another corridor. There was a door every few feet. The matron stopped in front of one and knocked. "You have a visitor, Dani."

"Okay," Dani called from inside.

"I'll let you know when your visiting time is up," the matron said.

"Thank you," I said as she went back down the corridor.

"Daddy!" Dani exclaimed and flung herself into my arms.

"Hello, baby." I juggled the packages and kissed her.

The door was all the way open now and I could see into Dani's room. It was small and narrow, with two cots along the opposite walls. High up on the wall between them was a small window. A young woman was sitting on one of the cots. She got to her feet when I entered.

"This is Miss Spicer, Daddy," Dani said. "Miss Spicer, this is my father."

The young woman held out her hand. "I'm pleased to meet you, Colonel Carey." Her grip was firm and friendly. "I'm Marian Spicer, the probation officer assigned to Dani."

I stared at her. Somehow the term "probation officer" conjured up a vision of a harsh-faced man. This one was young, not more than twenty-eight, of medium height, with brown hair, cut in ringlets framing her face, and alert brown eyes. I guess some of my surprise showed for her smile grew broader.

"How do you do, Miss Spicer?"

I guess she was accustomed to this reaction because she ignored it. Instead she looked down at the packages. "I see your father brought some things for you, Dani. Isn't that nice?"

Dani looked at me questioningly. I knew she recognized the suitcase. "Your mother sent them," I said.

A kind of veil came down over Dani's eyes. "Isn't Mother coming?"

"No. She isn't feeling well—"

The shadow was deeper over her eyes now. I couldn't see into them at all. "I didn't really expect her, Daddy."

"Dr. Bonner told her to say in bed. I know she wanted to—"

Dani interrupted me. "How do you know, Daddy? Did you see her?"

I didn't answer.

"She probably sent Charles and he gave the packages to you. Isn't that the way it was, Daddy?" Her eyes dared me to contradict.

I nodded.

She turned away with an almost angry gesture.

"I'll leave you to visit with your father, Dani," Miss Spicer said quietly. "I'll be back later this afternoon."

Dani walked over to the far side of the bed and sat down, her face averted. I glanced around the room again. It was at most eight by ten; the only other furniture besides the two beds was one chair and a small chest of drawers at the foot of each bed. The walls had once been green but had later been painted cream without too much success. They were heavily marked up. I looked more closely and saw that the scrawls were actually mostly boys' names or dates. Here and there were what appeared to be telephone numbers. Occasionally there was a lewd invitation, usually the kind found scratched into the walls of public restrooms. I looked at Dani.

The grown-up young lady who had come down the staircase yesterday morning had completely disappeared. Instead a little girl sat there on the cot. Her only makeup was a pale lipstick, and in place of the bouffant hair-do was a pony tail secured with a rubber band. In the blouse and skirt she looked even younger than her fourteen years.

I reached for a cigarette.

"Give me one, Daddy."

I stared at her. "I didn't know you smoked."

"There's lots of things you don't know, Daddy," she said impatiently.

I handed her a cigarette and held the match for her. She smoked all right. I could see that from the way she inhaled, dragging the smoke up into her nostrils as she blew it out.

"Does your mother know you smoke?" I asked.

She nodded, giving me that challenging look again.

"I don't think it's such a hot idea. You're still young—"

She cut me off quickly. "Don't start being that kind of a father now. It's a little too late for that."

In a way she was right. There were too many years that I hadn't been around. I tried to change the subject. "Aren't you going to look at what your mother sent you?"

"I know what Mother's sent me," she retorted. "Candy, books, clothing. The same stuff she always sends whenever I go away. Ever since the first summer she sent me to camp."

Suddenly her eyes filled with tears. "I guess she thinks this is just another camp. She always sent me something, sure. But she never came to visit, not even on Parents' Day."

I wanted to reach out for her, to hold her and soothe her, but something about the way she sat there so stiffly made me keep hands off. After a few minutes she stopped crying.

"Why didn't you ever come to see me, Daddy?" she asked in a small voice. "Didn't you care about me any more?"

5

The coroner's jury was already seated when I entered the small crowded courtroom the next morning. The only vacant seats were down in front and reserved for the witnesses. Harris Gordon noticed me standing in the rear of the room and stood up and waved. I walked down and he motioned to a seat beside Nora. There were others I would have preferred but I could feel the watching eyes of the reporters. I sat down.

"Charles told me he saw you yesterday," Nora whispered. "How is Dani?"

Her face was pale. She was wearing very little make-up and was dressed very simply. "She was very disappointed that you couldn't come," I said.

"So was I. I wanted to but the doctor wouldn't allow me out of the house."

"That's what I heard. Feeling better now?"

She nodded. "A little."

I looked away, a faintly reminiscent bitter taste in my mouth. Nothing really changed Nora, nothing really reached her, even now. No matter what happened, there would always be the polite small talk, the little lies, the careful skirting of the truth. She had no more been sick yesterday than I'd been.

There was the rap of a gavel from the small raised bench behind which the coroner sat. A hush fell over the room as the first witness was called—the medical examiner. An experienced witness, he reported rapidly and efficiently. He had performed an autopsy on the body of

Anthony Riccio, deceased, and found that death had been caused by a violent rupture of the large aorta, inflicted by a sharp instrument. He further estimated that the time of death could not have been more than fifteen minutes after the inflicting of such a wound and in all probability even less.

The next witness was another doctor, the police surgeon. Also an expert witness, he testified that he had arrived at the scene in response to a call from Police Headquarters and had found the deceased already dead. Beyond making the superficial examination necessary to completing the death certificate, he had done nothing but direct that the body be taken to the morgue.

He stepped down and the court clerk called the next witness: "Dr. Alois Bonner."

I looked up as Dr. Bonner rose from the far side of the witness bench. It had been a long time since I'd seen him. He hadn't changed very much over the years. He was still handsomely gray, with an important and distinguished manner that had earned him the richest practice in San Francisco.

He took the oath and sat down in the witness chair.

"In your own words, Dr. Bonner," the coroner said, "tell the jury exactly what happened on Friday evening last."

Dr. Bonner turned to the jury and his mellifluent bedside tones rolled beautifully through the dingy courtroom. "I was just leaving my office a little after eight when the phone rang. It was Miss Hayden's butler, Charles, who informed me that there had been an accident there and would I please hurry over.

"Since my office is only one block from Miss Hayden's house, I arrived not more than five minutes after his call. I was taken immediately to Miss Hayden's studio, where I saw Mr. Riccio lying on the floor, his head in Miss Hayden's lap. She was holding a blood-soaked towel to his side.

"When I asked her what had happened she told me that Mr. Riccio had been stabbed. I knelt on the floor beside him and lifted the towel. There was a large, ugly wound, bleeding profusely. I put the towel back and felt for Mr. Riccio's pulse. It was very faint and irregular. I could see that he was in great pain and sinking fast. I opened my case to give him an injection of morphine to ease his pain, but before I could administer it he was gone."

He turned and looked up at the coroner.

The coroner stared at him thoughtfully for a moment, then turned towards a man sitting next to the court stenographer. "Do you have any questions, Mr. Carter?"

"Carter's from the district attorney's office," Gordon whispered as the man nodded and got to his feet.

"Dr. Bonner, at any time during your examination before actual death, did the deceased say anything, make any remarks?"

"Yes, he did."

"What did he say?"

"He repeated the same phrase twice. 'She stabbed me.' "

"When Mr. Riccio made that remark, Dr. Bonner, did you have any idea to whom he referred?"

"At the time I did not," the doctor replied firmly.

Out of the corner of my eye I could see the glint of satisfaction in Gordon's eyes and I knew that he had already spoken to the good doctor.

"Was there any other person in the room besides Miss Hayden and the deceased when you entered?"

"Miss Hayden's daughter was also there," the doctor answered.

"Did she remain all during the time you ministered to the deceased?"

"She did."

"Thank you, Dr. Bonner." The assistant district attorney went back to his chair and sat down.

"You may step down, Dr. Bonner," the coroner said. "Thank you."

"Inspector Gerald Myrer," the court clerk called.

A well-built, quietly dressed, crew-cut young man rose from the end of our row of seats. He stepped forward, took the oath and sat down.

"Please state your name and occupation for the information of the jury."

"Inspector Gerald Myrer, San Francisco Police, Homicide Squad."

"Now, please tell us of your activities in regard to the matter before the court on the evening of Mr. Riccio's decease."

The inspector took a small notebook from his pocket and opened it. "We received the call at Homicide about 8:25 P.M., from the radio car which first answered the summons. We arrived at Miss Hayden's home at 8:37. Two radio cars were already there and the policeman at the door told me that a man had been murdered in the studio. I went directly there.

"The deceased was lying on the floor. Also in the room were Miss Hayden, her daughter, Dani Carey, Dr. Bonner, and the butler, Charles Fletcher. Mr. Harris Gordon, the attorney, who had arrived a few moments before me, according to the patrolmen, was also there. I immediately began my investigation."

He cleared his throat and looked around the courtroom. "My investigation revealed that Miss Hayden and her daughter were the only two people in the room at the time the blow was struck which resulted in the death of the deceased. Questioning of Miss Hayden and her daughter led me to understand that the daughter had struck the deceased with a sculptor's chisel, during an argument between Miss Hayden and the deceased. The sculptor's chisel was found on the floor near the deceased's body. I had it sent to the police laboratory for examination."

"Pardon the interruption, Inspector Myrer," the coroner said. "But can you please inform us at this time of the results of that examination?"

The policeman nodded. "Yes, I can. The police laboratory informed me that the blood on the chisel was type *O*, which corresponded to the blood type of the deceased. They also informed me that there were three different sets of fingerprints found on the handle of the chisel—those of Miss Hayden, her daughter and the deceased. Some of the fingerprints were smudged or overlaid, but enough separate prints were found to establish clearly that each of these three persons had handled the chisel."

"Thank you, Inspector. Please proceed."

"After completing my investigation, I then took the daughter, Danielle Carey, to headquarters. We were accompanied by the attorney, Mr. Gordon, whom I previously mentioned as being on the scene. At headquarters Miss Carey dictated a statement to the police stenographer which was read back to her in Mr. Gordon's presence and signed by her. Then, pursuant to law, I took her to Juvenile Hall on Woodside Avenue, where I placed her in the custody of the probation officer on duty. Mr. Gordon accompanied us there also."

"Do you have a copy of that statement with you?"

"Yes, sir."

The coroner turned to the jury. "Under the law of the State of California, a minor may not appear in any court where he or she may be in jeopardy as a result of a felony. The only court in which a minor may appear is in Juvenile Court. We are permitted, however, since our only concern is to establish the physical cause of the death of the deceased, to read to the jury the statement given by the minor concerned."

He turned back to the policeman. "Would you please ready the statement, Inspector Myrer?"

Inspector Myrer took a folded sheet of paper from his inner pocket. He opened it and began to read aloud in a flat, expressionless voice.

The Statement of Miss Danielle Nora Carey, a Minor:
My name is Danielle Nora Carey and I live with my mother, Nora Hayden, in San Francisco. I was upstairs in my room studying for midterm examinations when I heard voices coming from my mother's studio downstairs. I knew that my mother and Rick had been quarreling all day over something. Usually when they had a quarrel I stayed in my room because it was always very upsetting. But this quarrel had been getting worse all day and I began to be frightened for my mother. Once before when they had a quarrel Rick had hit her and she couldn't go out for three days because she had a black eye and my mother would not appear in public with a black eye.

Their voices kept getting louder and louder. Then I thought I heard my mother scream and Rick yell, "I'll kill you." I ran out of my room and downstairs to the studio. I was very frightened for my mother and when I opened the door of the studio I saw Rick had her arm and was twisting it back and forcing her backwards over a table. I grabbed the chisel from the table near the door and ran toward them. I yelled at him to leave my mother alone. He let go of her arm and turned around. He took one step toward me and told me to get the hell out of there. I forgot I had the chisel in my hand and I punched him in the stomach with my fist.

He stood there for a second, then put his hands to his stomach and said, "Jesus Christ, Dani, what did you have to go and do a stupid thing like that for?" Then I saw the chisel sticking out between his hands and the blood coming out from around it. I ran past him to my mother screaming, "I didn't mean to do it." My mother pushed me out of the way and went to Rick. He turned toward her and pulled the chisel out and dropped it in her hand. The blood seemed to come bursting out of him and my mother dropped the chisel on the floor. Rick took one step toward her and then fell down too. I couldn't watch it any more so I covered my face with my hands and began to scream.

Then Charles and Violet came in and Violet slapped my face and I stopped screaming. Then Dr. Bonner came and told me Rick was dead. I guess that is all except that I didn't mean to do it.

I have read the foregoing statement which I have given of my own free will and volition and I submit that it is a true and accurate account of the incidents described herein.

The policeman looked at the jury. He still spoke in the same flat emotionless voice. "It is, of course, signed Danielle Nora Carey."

The coroner turned to the assistant district attorney. "Do you have any questions, Mr. Carter?"

Carter shook his head.

"Thank you, Inspector. You may step down."

The court clerk stood up as the policeman walked by him. "Nora Hayden."

I stood up as Nora got to her feet and slipped past me into the aisle. Her face was pale and set, her lips pressed firmly together. For the first time I could see a little of her mother in her. She held herself erect, her chin high. She had all flags flying.

She took the oath and went to the witness chair. Harris Gordon took a seat next to the assistant district attorney.

The coroner's voice was sympathetic and gentle. The Hayden name still went a long way in this town. "Please tell the jury, Miss Hayden, what you know of the events already described."

Her voice was low but it carried. At least to the jury and the first few rows in the court. But I could sense the straining of the spectators behind me to hear what she was saying.

"Mr. Riccio and I had been quarreling. He had been my business manager for several years but I had become dissatisfied with his services and had discharged him. He was not satisfied with the severance that I was willing to offer and he persisted in carrying on the argument all day. Finally he came into the studio that night while I was working, and became very abusive. I told him to leave me alone, that I could not work, that I could not concentrate, that he was ruining the sculpture upon which I was working.

"At this point he seized me by the shoulders and began to shake me violently, saying that he would not be put off by excuses like that. I tried to push him away but he grabbed my arm and was bending it back, causing me to fall against the table in severe pain. Then the door opened and Dani came running in and shouted at him. He turned to Dani and told her to get out.

"I saw her hit him. I remember how surprised I was. I had never seen Dani strike anyone before. She had always been a very calm and good girl, quiet and self-controlled. You would never know she was around the house if you didn't see her.

"Then Mr. Riccio turned around and I noticed the blood. Dani ran past him to me, screaming that she hadn't meant to do it. I told her to step aside while I tried to help Mr. Riccio. I didn't realize what had happened until I saw the chisel in his hand. He—he gave it to me and—and it was wet with blood. I dropped it. He began to fall. I tried to catch him but he was already on the floor."

The tears came into her eyes. She choked up, tried to speak again but couldn't find her voice, than began to cry. But like a lady. Her handkerchief raised delicately to her eyes. There wasn't another sound in the court as the coroner spoke in his gentle sympathetic voice. "Please bring Miss Hayden a glass of water."

The clerk filled a glass from the vacuum pitcher on his table and brought it to her. She sipped it delicately.

"Would you like a short recess, Miss Hayden?" the coroner asked.

Nora gave him her grateful look. "I—I don't think so. I'll be all right now. Thank you."

"Take your time, Miss Hayden."

Nora took another sip of water and began to speak again. Her voice was strained and weak but could still be heard. "Dani was screaming and the butler came into the studio. I told him to call the doctor while I notified the police. Then I went to Mr. Riccio and tried to make him comfortable." The tears came to her eyes again. "But there was nothing I could do. There was nothing anyone could do. I know that Dani didn't mean to hurt him. It was an accident. Dani wouldn't harm a fly."

She was silent for a moment and you could see her fighting for self-control; then she raised her head and looked directly at the jury. "I suppose it was all my fault," she said bravely. "I should have been a better mother. But then, I suppose, every mother says that to herself."

That really put the icing on the cake. There were five women on the jury and they were all crying along with her.

Nora turned and looked at the coroner. "I—I'm afraid that's all I have to say."

He cleared his throat. "Have you any questions, Mr. Carter?"

Mr. Carter got to his feet. "Miss Hayden, you told us that you had the butler call the doctor while you notified the police, then you went to the aid of Mr. Riccio, is that right?"

Nora nodded. "Yes."

"Yet when Inspector Myrer arrived, Mr. Gordon, your attorney, was already there. When did you call him?"

"After I called the police, I believe. I really can't say. I was so upset that I don't remember exactly."

I wondered if Carter realized that Nora was lying. If I knew Nora I was sure that she wasn't aware of it. Apparently Carter decided to let it go.

"What was your relationship with Mr. Riccio?"

"He was my business manager," Nora answered.

"But he lived in your house, didn't he?"

"Yes."

"Is that customary in your profession?"

"I don't know," Nora answered. "But in my case it was a necessity. It was more than a full-time job."

"By that do you mean that you and Mr. Riccio had a much more personal relationship than merely business, Miss Hayden?"

Gordon was on his feet. "Objection! The question is irrelevant and immaterial to the purpose of this inquest."

"Sustained."

"Were you and Mr. Riccio planning marriage at any time?" the assistant district attorney asked.

"Objection! I respectfully ask the court to direct the assistant district attorney to confine himself to questions relevant to the purposes of this investigation."

"Sustained," the coroner said. His voice was annoyed as he spoke to Carter. "You will so confine your questions."

Carter looked at Nora. "Did you see your daughter pick up the chisel with which she allegedly struck Mr. Riccio?"

"I did not."

"Did you see it in her hand when she struck him?"

"I did not."

"Did you know that such a chisel was lying on the table near the door?"

"I suppose so."

"Did you ordinarily leave that chisel there? Surely you must have realized that so sharp an instrument could be potentially dangerous?"

"I left the chisel wherever I happened to be working with it. In this case it was on that table because I had been working on a rosewood figurine there." She spoke in a firm voice now. "It was my studio. In addition to that chisel there are many other tools of my trade, including an acetylene blowtorch. I am a sculptress and I am interested only in what I create, not in keeping track of my tools. I have never considered any of my tools to be a potential danger. They are the foundation of my art."

"No further questions," Carter said and sat down.

Nora came down from the stand with her head still high. Her art was her shield and she had raised it in front of her so that nothing in the world could touch her. She was safe and secure behind it.

There was only one more witness—Charles. His testimony merely confirmed everything that had been said before, which I surmised was why Violet was not called. The coroner then turned the case over to the jury.

They were out for less than five minutes. The foreman delivered the verdict. "It is the finding of this jury that the deceased, Anthony Riccio, met his death as the result of a blow delivered by a sharp instrument in the hands of one Danielle Nora Carey, a minor, in justifiable defense of her mother."

There was a buzz in the courtroom and I turned to see the reporters scampering out as the coroner rapped his gavel. I stepped aside and let Nora and Gordon precede me up the aisle. They went out the door and I saw the flashes of the cameras. I decided to wait until the photographers had gone and sat down again.

The courtroom was almost empty now. I looked across the aisle. A young woman was sitting there, making notes in a small book. She closed it and looked up at me and nodded. I nodded back automatically before I recognized her. The probation officer.

I got up. "How do you do, Miss Spicer?"

"Colonel Carey," she answered quietly.

"Did you see Dani this morning?"

She nodded.

"How is she?"

"She still feels a little lost. But she'll be all right when she gets used to it." She got to her feet. "I must be going now."

"Of course," I said.

I stepped aside and watched her hurry up the aisle. Dani will get used to it, she said. As if that were a good thing. To get used to being in prison.

The corridors were empty as I walked toward the exit. The bright sunlight was in my eyes and I didn't see Harris Gordon until he was directly in front of me. "Well, Colonel Carey. What do you think?"

I squinted at him. "Whether it was a trial or not, they managed to do a pretty good job of hanging Dani."

"Justifiable homicide is a long way from murder one," he said, falling into step beside me.

"Yeah," I answered dryly. "We can be thankful for small favors."

"There's one thing that wasn't said in there that I think you ought to know."

I looked at him. "What's that?"

"What Dani said after she signed that statement at police headquarters."

"Why did you let her make a statement?"

"I had no choice, she insisted on it. Then when I didn't want her to sign it, she insisted on that too."

I was silent for a moment. "What did she say?"

He looked at me. " 'Do they take me to the gas chamber now?' Then she began to cry. I told her that they wouldn't but she didn't believe me. The more I assured her, the more hysterical she became. I called Dr. Bonner from there and he came down and gave her a shot. He went out to Juvenile Hall with us, but even that didn't work. Dani was more hysterical than ever. That was the main reason they gave me custody of her for the night. She was still hysterical until her grandmother thought of telling her the one thing that finally quieted her down."

"What was that?"

"That you were coming," he said. "That you wouldn't let anything happen to her."

PART FOUR

The Part of the Book
About DANI

1

When Dani had been very young and did not want to stay in the dark, she would look up at me from her bed and say in her tiny little voice, "Daddy, turn the night out." And I would snap on a small light in her room and she would close her eyes and go to sleep, safe and secure in a familiar world.

I wished it were as easy as that now. But there was no turning on a light to turn out the night any more. The coroner's jury had made sure of that.

I watched Gordon get into his car and drive away. I turned and stared up at the courthouse for a moment, then walked over toward the parking lot on Golden Gate Avenue where I had left my car.

The old nursery rhyme kept running through my head: *Humpty Dumpty sat on a wall, Humpty Dumpty had a great fall.*

For the first time I knew how the king's men must have felt when they couldn't put Humpty Dumpty together again. Like fools. They shouldn't have let him fall off in the first place. I shouldn't have let Dani fall either.

Maybe it was my fault. I remembered sitting in her little room out at Juvenile Hall yesterday afternoon and trying to explain to her why I could not come to see her. I remembered too how it sounded. Even if it were the truth, and I knew it was, I found it hard to believe.

And Dani was still a child despite the cigarette she smoked so expertly. What did she believe? I couldn't

211

tell. But I could tell that she wanted to believe me, that she wanted to trust me. Still she wasn't quite sure that she should. I had gone away before and I could go away again.

It wasn't said like that. Not in so many words. But it was there just the same—lying under the surface of her thoughts, her actions. She was too old to say it aloud and too young to hide it from me. There were so many things we had to tell each other, so many things to re-learn about each other, and there just wasn't enough time.

The unspoken words clung to us like an invisible cloud when it came time to say goodbye. "I'll come to see you tomorrow."

"No," she said. "They don't allow visitors during the week. But I'll see you Tuesday. Miss Spicer told me that there would be a hearing."

"I know."

"Mother will be there?"

I nodded. "So will your grandmother." I bent down and kissed her. "You be a good girl and don't worry about anything, kitten."

Her arms went up around my neck suddenly. She pressed her face to my cheek tightly. "I'm not afraid of anything now, Daddy," she whispered fiercely. "Now that you're home again."

It wasn't until I was outside in the daylight that I realized what she had meant. But I hadn't come home to stay. It was only for a visit.

It was four o'clock when I got back to my motel. The red message light was blinking on and off. I picked up the telephone. The red light would have gone right on blinking until I called the operator. I gave her my name and room number.

"Mrs. Hayden called. It is very important that you call her back the minute you get in."

"Thank you." I pressed down the receiver for a moment, then dialed the number the operator had given me. A maid answered and the old lady came right to the phone.

"Are you alone?" she asked in a guarded voice.

"Yes."

"It's very important that I see you."

"What about?"

"I don't want to talk on the telephone," she said. "But believe me, Luke, it is very important or I wouldn't call you." A strained kind of note came into her voice. "Can you come for dinner? I'll make certain that we're alone."

"What time?"

"Seven o'clock?"

"Fine. I'll be there."

"Thank you, Luke."

I put down the telephone and began to undress. A hot shower would take some of the tightness out of my muscles. I wondered idly what the old lady wanted. If she was worried about my backing her up in court tomorrow, she needn't be. At this point I had no other choice.

Despite the fact that the evening was only mildly cool, there was a fire roaring in the fireplace when the maid showed me into the library of the big house. The old lady sat in one of the armchairs facing the fire.

"Help yourself to a drink, Luke."

"Thank you." I went to the sideboard and poured a small shot of bourbon over some ice cubes and added water. I turned to my former mother-in-law. "Your health."

"Thank you."

The whiskey was rich and smooth going down. It had been a long time since I could afford bourbon like this. I sipped it slowly. There was no sense in gulping it. "Well?" I asked.

The old lady looked up at me. "Has the maid gone?"

I nodded.

"Make sure the door is closed."

I crossed the room and checked the door. There was no one in the room beyond. I came back to her. "Why the mystery?"

Silently she picked up her purse and opened it. She took out an envelope and handed it to me. It was addressed to her. I looked at her questioningly.

"Read it."

I put down my drink and opened the letter. It was on plain white paper and typewritten.

DEAR MRS. HAYDEN,

You don't know me but I have been a friend of Tony's for a long time. Several weeks ago he gave me a package of letters which he told me were very important and to keep them for him. He also told me that he was having a lot of trouble with your daughter and when the time came for her to settle up, these letters would make sure that he got everything that was coming to him. I opened the package and looked through the letters. They are from both your daughter and your granddaughter, the last being as recent as two months ago. They should be very interesting to the police, even more interesting to the newspapers, since both of them were in love with Tony. But Tony is dead now and I am the last one interested in making more trouble for anybody than they already got. So if you are interested in these letters, place this ad in the personals in the Examiner *not later than Thursday*—COME HOME, ALL

IS FORGIVEN. AUNT CECELIA. *I will then get in touch with you before I go somewhere else with them. But remember, no lawyers and no cops or no deal.*

The letter was unsigned. I looked up at her.

"Well, what do you think?" she asked.

"It could be some crank. I've heard of nuts who write letters to people in the news."

"I don't think so, Luke. I called Nora and asked her if she had written any letters to Riccio and she told me she had. I asked her what was in them and she said it was none of my business. Then I asked her if she knew that Dani had written him letters too and she got very angry and hung up on me."

"That's typical of Nora. Whenever something comes up that she doesn't want to face. she avoids it. Do you think there is anything to this letter?"

"Maybe there isn't," she said. "But I certainly wouldn't want to take that chance."

"This is nothing but cheap blackmail. Even if you pay off you don't know whether they'll hold out some letters for another shakedown. I'd turn this over to the police."

"Hasn't there been enough in the papers already? Do you want more?"

I stared at her. "Haven't you done more than enough to protect the good Hayden name?" I shot back sarcastically. "Do you think anything can make Nora smell less like a rose than she already does? Do you think people are so stupid they don't know what's been going on in her house?"

"No. People aren't stupid. But you are!" She shoved the envelope angrily back into her purse. "I'm no longer concerned with what they say or print about Nora. There's nothing I can do to change that and, frankly, I don't even intend to try. But perhaps you didn't read the letter."

"I read the letter."

"Did you read where it said there were also letters from Dani, and that she was in love with Riccio too?" the old lady asked irascibly.

"I read it. But I didn't pay any attention to it. After all, Dani is just a kid."

"Then you're even more stupid than I thought. Dani may be a child in years, but have you taken a good look at her? She's mature physically and she's been mature since she was a little over eleven years old. She's her mother all over again. Nora had her first sexual experience when she was scarcely thirteen, her first abortion when she was a little over fifteen. There were at least two more that I know of before she married you!"

I stared at her. "You knew all that?"

Her eyes fell. "I knew it," she admitted in a low voice. "But I hoped it would remain a thing of the past if she married you. That she would grow up and see what a fool she'd been."

"But you still stood up for her. You still protected her."

"I am her mother," the old lady said simply. There was a proud kind of dignity about her. "It was never the Hayden name I really cared about. It was my daughter. Just as it's not the name I care about now. It's Dani. I don't want her damned before she has a chance. I don't want her to be like her mother. I want to help her."

"Nora said that I wasn't even Dani's father," I said.

"I know what Nora said. I think I'm old enough to accept the truth now. I wonder if you are?"

I put down my drink. "Try me and see."

Her eyes held mine steadily. "I don't think even Nora knows whether you're Dani's father or not."

I didn't speak.

"So you see," she continued gently, "it all comes back to you. To how you feel about Dani."

I picked up my drink and took another sip. The ice cubes had melted and the fine taste of the whiskey had been lost in the water. It always seemed to come back to me. Harris Gordon had said the same thing on Saturday, maybe a little differently, but in essence the same thing. Either I was her father or I was not.

I turned to the sideboard and added some whiskey to my glass. I thought about the baby that I'd loved before I ever knew what Nora would some day say. Then I thought about the child I'd played with on the boat down in La Jolla, after Nora had said that I wasn't her father. I knew that I loved that child just as much as I'd loved the baby. And as much now as I did then.

I turned back to my former mother-in-law. "I guess it takes more than an act of nature to make a father," I said. "It also takes an act of love."

Her bright old eyes glittered. "All it takes, Luke, is the act of love. The other thing doesn't really matter at all."

I took a small pull at my drink and sat down. "Now, what are we going to do about the letter?"

"I've already inserted the ad. It will run on Thursday. Today is Monday. That gives us three days to find out where the letters are and who has them."

"Two days. Tomorrow and Wednesday. Today is shot already and a good part of tomorrow we'll be in court. I don't even know where to start. I don't know anything at all about Riccio. Not even who his friends were."

"Sam Corwin would know."

"Sam?" I asked, wondering. I hadn't thought about Sam at all. It was strange that I'd forgotten about him. He and Nora had been married about a year after our divorce. I'd seen him at the house several times when I'd brought Dani back from her visits with me. He'd always been polite and friendly.

"Yes, Sam. Poor Sam. He knew what Nora was like when he married her, but he thought he could change her. But after she met Riccio, I guess even Sam gave up. It was because of Riccio that Sam divorced her and was able to enforce a strict community property split."

"Then Sam must have had something on her?" I asked.

"He had something on both of them."

The door behind her opened and the maid came into the room. "Dinner is served, ma'am."

We got to our feet and the old lady smiled at me. "Will you give me your arm, Luke?"

I smiled back at her. "I'd be proud to."

2

For the first time I approached the front entrance of the building. The parking lot was filled up and I'd had to leave my car several blocks away. I walked up the curved path leading to the entrance from the street. A gardener in work clothes was busy clipping the neat hedges that lined the walk. He looked up at me as I walked by. I could see the heavy beads of sweat on his forehead from the morning sun.

I looked at the glass doors. There was lettering in gold leaf.

> STATE OF CALIFORNIA
> SAN FRANCISCO COUNTY
> *Juvenile Court*
> *Probation Dept.*
> *California Youth*
> *Authority*

I went in and found myself in a large lobby filled with reporters and cameramen. A few flashbulbs went off and several reporters pressed around me. They were much less pushy than they'd been the other day.

"Is there anything you can tell us about plans for your daughter's defense, Colonel Carey?"

I shook my head. "No, I can't. It's my understanding that under the laws of this state there is no such thing as a trial for a minor. This is merely the first of a series of custodial hearings."

"Will you attempt to get custody of your daughter?"

"That's up to the court to decide. I feel sure the best interests of my daughter will be the primary consideration."

"Have you seen your daughter?"

"I visited her on Sunday afternoon."

"Was her mother with you?"

"No, her mother was ill."

"Has her mother visited her at all?"

"I don't know. But I do know that there were packages from her mother."

"Do you know what was in them?"

"Clothing, books, candy."

"What did you and your daughter talk about?"

"Nothing much. Father-and-daughter talk, I guess."

"Did she tell you anything more about what happened Friday night?"

I looked at the man who asked that question. "We didn't talk about that at all."

"Did you learn anything that might throw more light on what happened?"

"No," I said. "I know nothing beyond what I heard at the coroner's inquest yesterday. I believe most of you were there. Now, if you'll be good enough to let me through—"

They opened a path for me.

Juvenile Court was off to the left of the entrance hall. I followed the arrow down a long corridor and around the corner. Another pointed down a flight of stairs. I went down and came out opposite a glass-enclosed waiting room. I passed through the waiting room and opened the door to the Juvenile Court.

It was a small courtroom with a raised platform at the far end of the room. In front of the judge's desk was a long table with several chairs around it. Slightly to the side of the table, between it and the bench was a small desk and chair. The walls were painted an official-looking tan and brown, and there were four large windows in the long wall. The rest of the space was taken up by extra chairs and benches.

As I stood there a man entered from one of the doors behind the judge's desk. He stopped when he saw me.

"Is this where they're holding the Dani Carey hearing?" I asked.

"Yes, but you're early. Court doesn't convene until nine o'clock. You can wait outside in the reception room. You'll be called."

"Thank you."

There were several benches in the waiting room. I looked at my watch. It was eight-thirty-five. I lit a cigarette.

A few minutes later another man came in. He looked at me, lit a cigarette and sat down. "Judge not in yet?"

I shook my head.

"Damn," he said. "I'll bet I lose another half-day's pay. Every time I come down here it costs me. They never get to my case until late."

"Do you have a child here?"

"Yeah," he said, jerking his head. The ashes from his cigarette fell on his dirty work shirt. He paid no attention to them. "They got my kid down here. She's nothing but a whore, that's what she is. I told them the next time they picked her up they could keep her. But no, they get me down here anyway."

He peered at me. "Say, you look familiar," he said. "I seen you down here before?"

"No. This is the first time."

"Brother, you're in for it. They'll keep you coming back and coming back until you agree to take your kid home again. That's what they done to me. She's oney

a fifteen-an'-a-half-year-old girl, they say. You got to
give her a chance, they say. So I do, and what happens?
Two days later she's shacked up in a hotel taking on
all comers for five bucks apiece. The cops get her and
here I am again."

He squinted up through his cigarette smoke. "You
sure I didn't see you here before?"

I shook my head.

He stared at me for another moment, then snapped
his fingers. "I know you! I seen your pitcher in the
papers. You're the guy whose kid knocked off her
mother's boy friend!"

I didn't say anything.

He leaned toward me, his voice a confidential whisper. "Ain't it a bitch? What kids get into nowadays!
Tell me, the guy banging her too? It wouldn't surprise
me at all if he was. The papers don't give you half the
story."

I felt my fists clench. I forced my fingers to loosen.
There was no sense in getting angry. This was just something I had to get used to. I felt a twinge in my heart.
Dani would have to get used to it, too. That was even
worse.

Two women came in. They looked like Mexicans and
were jabbering excitedly in Spanish. They fell suddenly
silent as they saw us, then went over to a bench and sat
down. The younger one looked pregnant.

A moment later a colored woman came in, then a
man and a woman. The woman's face was puffed and
bruised and she had a black eye. The man tried to take
her arm to lead her to a seat, but she shook his arm
off angrily and sat down along the other wall. She didn't
look at him.

The colored woman spoke to one of the Mexicans.
"Think they goin' to give you yo' girl back, honey?"

The pregnant woman made the classic gesture of ignorance. "I don' know," she said, her accent faintly Spanish.

"It's the relief what wants them kep' here, honey. I'm sho' of it. If she stays here it costs only forty a month for her keep. They let you take her home they got to give you seventy. It's the money, honey."

The pregnant girl shrugged her shoulders. She said something in Spanish to the other woman and she nodded her head in violent agreement. On the bench along the wall the woman with a black eye began to cry silently.

More people came down the stairs and soon all the benches were occupied. The overflow began to gather in the corridor outside the waiting room. At five minutes to nine Harris Gordon appeared, followed by Nora and her mother. I got up and went out to meet them.

Harris Gordon looked through the glass. "Looks pretty crowded."

"S.R.O.," I said. "It looks like we're not the only people with troubles."

He gave me a peculiar look. "People in trouble seldom are alone. Wait here. I'll go check the clerk and find out when the judge expects to get to us."

He disappeared down the corridor. I turned to Nora. "How are you?" I asked politely.

She nodded, her eyes searching my face for any signs of sarcasm. "I'm all right. I went home and stayed in bed after I got through in court yesterday. I was completely exhausted."

"I can understand that. What you did wasn't easy."

"Did I do all right? I didn't want to say any more than I had to. I could hardly bring myself to testify but I had no choice, did I?"

"That's right. You had no choice."

Gordon came back. "We won't have long to wait," he said. "We're the third case on the docket. The first two shouldn't take more than fifteen minutes, the clerk told me."

I lit a cigarette and leaned back against the wall. The door to the courtroom opened and I heard a name called. I turned and saw the two Mexican women get up. The door closed behind them. It was exactly nine o'clock.

They couldn't have been inside for more than ten minutes. The pregnant woman was crying as they walked past. The clerk called another name. It was the man who had come in just after me.

He came out in less than ten minutes, a look of smug satisfaction on his face. He stopped in front of me on his way to the stairs. "They're going to keep her for good this time. I told 'em they can throw away the key for all I care!"

I didn't say anything. He turned and stamped up the stairs. I heard the clerk's voice behind us. "Carey."

We went through the waiting room into the court. The clerk motioned us to seats at the table in front of the judge's desk and surveyed us with a bored expression. "Is this the first time you've been here?"

We nodded.

"The judge stepped out for a moment. He'll be right back."

The words were no sooner out of his mouth than the door behind him opened. "All rise and face the court," the clerk called. "Be it known that the Juvenile Court, State of California, County of San Francisco, the honorable Justice Samuel A. Murphy presiding, is now in session."

The judge was a tall man in his early sixties. His hair was white and thin, and through his horn-rimmed glasses his eyes were blue and piercing. He wore a rumpled brown suit, white shirt and dark maroon tie. He sat down and picked up a paper from the desk in front of him. He nodded to the clerk.

The clerk got up and walked over to a door on the right side. He opened it. "Danielle Carey."

Dani came through and looked around hesitantly. Then she saw us and ran toward us. Nora half rose in her seat and they were in each other's arms.

Dani was crying. "Mother. Mother, are you all right?

I couldn't understand what Nora was mumbling. I looked away for a moment. Even I felt it and I didn't believe half the act Nora always put on. Another figure appeared in the doorway. It was Miss Spicer, the probation officer. She stood there watching Dani and Nora.

I looked up at the judge. He, too, was watching. I had the feeling that this was somehow important, that the judge had staged this very carefully.

Another door opened on the same side of the room, and a uniformed officer came in. He was brown-haired and of medium height. The blue-and-gold patch on his shoulder bore the insignia of the San Francisco County Sheriff's office. He closed the door and leaned back against it.

Dani had left Nora and gone on to kiss her grandmother, then came over to me. Her eyes were shining. She kissed my cheek. "Mother did come, Daddy. Mother did come!"

I smiled at her. "I told you she would."

Miss Spicer came into the courtroom and walked over to the edge of the table. "Sit down here near me, Dani."

Dani left me and sat down. She looked at Harris Gordon. "Hello, Mr. Gordon."

"Hello, Dani."

The judge cleared his throat. "This is a very informal sort of hearing. Just so I will know who you are will you please introduce yourselves?"

"May I, Your Honor?"

The judge nodded. "Please do, Mr. Gordon."

"On my left is Nora Hayden, the child's mother. On my right, Mrs. Cecelia Hayden, the child's maternal grandmother. Next to her, Colonel Luke Carey, the child's father."

"And you are acting as attorney for the child?"

"Yes, Your Honor," Gordon said. "And also as legal adviser to the family."

"I see. I assume you are all acquainted with Miss Marian Spicer, who is the probation officer assigned to this case?"

"We are, Your Honor."

"Then I think we may begin." He picked up the sheet of paper on his desk. "On Friday night last, the police department, operating under Section 602 of the California Juvenile Court Law, turned over custody of one Danielle Nora Carey, a minor, to the probation officer for detention. The grounds were that said minor had committed an act of homicide, a felony in the State of California. Since that time, with the exception of the first night when the minor was released in custody of Mr. Harris Gordon, an attorney, on the advice of a physician and to protect the health and well-being of said minor, the minor has been held in custody in the juvenile detention home in accordance with the law.

"We are here this morning to hear a petition submitted by the probation department to further detain this minor in custody until such time as the probation department can properly investigate all the factors pertaining to the minor's being brought before this court."

The judge put down the paper and looked at Dani.

His voice was kind and gentle. "Despite the legal sound of all that, Danielle, this is not a trial, nor are you facing any criminal proceedings. You are here because you have committed a wrong act, a very wrong act, but we are not here to punish you. We want to help you, if we can, so that you will never again do any evil deeds. Do you understand that, Danielle?"

Dani's eyes were large and apprehensive in her white face. "I think so," she said hesitantly.

"I'm glad that you do, Danielle. It's important for you to understand that although you will not be criminally punished for what you have done, you cannot escape certain consequences which result from your wrongdoing. I am bound by the law to inform you of these possible consequences and of your rights before this court. Are you following me?"

"Yes, sir."

"This court has the power to take you from your home and place you in a state youth home or reformatory until you are of age. Or it can place you in a state hospital for observation. It can even place you in a foster home, if it feels it is not to your advantage to be returned to your immediate family or any other of your relatives. It can, at any time while you are under the jurisdiction of this court, keep you on probation, so that no matter whom you live with, you will remain in contact with the probation officer assigned to you until you are released from so doing by the court or come of age. But I want you to bear this in mind. Whatever the court decides will not be punitive in nature but only what it thinks is in your best interest. Do you understand that, Danielle?"

Dani nodded. She looked down at the table in front of her. I could see her hands twisting nervously.

"During any of the proceedings before this court,"

the judge continued, "you have, of course, the right to counsel. You have the right to summon witnesses on your own behalf, and the right to question any witness whom you may consider prejudicial to your best interest. Do you understand that, Danielle?"

"Yes, sir."

"I'm bound further to inform your parents that they are entitled to the same rights to counsel, witness and cross-examination.

"We will now open the hearing on the petition. Miss Spicer, will you please state your reasons for requesting the court to detain this minor?"

The probation officer got to her feet. She spoke in a soft, clear voice. "There are two reasons for this request, Your Honor. One, the nature of the act committed by the child indicates an emotional disturbance far deeper than a preliminary psychological and psychiatric examination could reveal. For the welfare and well-being of the child, we request additional time to complete such examinations in depth. Secondly, we also need additional time to invesigate further the child's environment and family life in order to help us make a proper recommendation for the child's future care and treatment."

She sat down.

The judge turned to us. "Do you have any objection to the petition?"

Harris Gordon got to his feet. "No, Your Honor. We have the utmost faith in the experience and judgment of the probation department and in its ability to make a proper evaluation and determination of all the factors in this case."

The judge's voice was mildly amused. He knew that Gordon couldn't say anything else, that he had no choice. Petitions for detention were always granted.

"Thank you for your display of faith, Mr. Gordon. We trust that we may be truly worthy of it."

He looked down for a moment, then went on. "It is the decision of this court that the petition by the probation department *in re* Danielle Nora Carey, a minor, be granted, and further that she be declared a temporary ward of this court until such time as a final determination shall be made. I will set the date for a complete court hearing on this matter for a week from today. At that time I shall expect all parties present to return, and all evidences and examinations pertinent to this matter to be placed before me. I shall also expect all plans for the future custody and welfare of this child to be presented to me, in writing, not less than twenty-four hours before the hearing." He rapped his gavel smartly on the desk.

He looked down at Dani, his voice kind and gentle again, completely unlike its official tone. "This means that you will go back to the cottages again, Danielle, while your case is being investigated. Be a good girl and cooperate with Miss Spicer and the others and everything will be that much easier and better for all of us. Do you understand?"

Dani nodded.

He looked at the probation officer. "You may take Danielle and her parents into my chambers before you return her to the cottages, Miss Spicer."

The probation officer nodded and got to her feet. We rose also. "Thank you, Your Honor," Gordon said.

The judge nodded and we followed Miss Spicer through the door behind the dais.

3

The judge's chambers consisted of two small rooms, the smaller his clerk's, the larger belonging to the judge himself. Miss Spicer led us into the larger office. One wall was covered with law books, on the others were photographs and framed diplomas. A neat desk and several chairs completed the furnishings.

"Make yourselves comfortable," Miss Spicer said tactfully. "I have to go to my office for a few minutes. I'll be right back."

When the door closed behind her, Nora turned to Dani. "You look thin. And why didn't you wear that pretty dress I sent you? What kind of an impression do you think that made on the judge? He'll think we don't even care enough about you to dress you properly. Where did you get those terrible things? I never saw them before."

I watched Dani. A curiously tolerant patience came over her face. She waited until Nora had finished her outburst, then a faint note of sarcasm came into her voice. "This isn't Miss Randolph's School, Mother. I have to wear what all the girls wear. They give you the clothes."

Nora stared at her. "I'm sure if you'd asked them, they would have allowed you to wear your own things. Probably they do that because most of the other children haven't anything of their own."

Dani didn't answer. I took out a cigarette. She looked at me. I threw her the package and she caught it deftly.

"Dani!" Nora's voice was shocked.

"Oh, be quiet, Nora!" Old Mrs. Hayden's voice was annoyed. "You can stop acting now, there's no audience. You know she smokes. I asked you to stop her enough times. But you said you didn't see any harm in it."

She looked at Dani. "Come here, child."

Dani walked over to her. "Yes, Grandmother."

"Are they treating you all right?"

"Yes, Grandmother."

"Getting enough to eat?"

Dani smiled. "More than enough. I'm not very hungry though."

"You have to eat to keep up your strength. We can't have you getting sick on top of everything else."

"I won't get sick, Grandmother."

"Is there anything I can send you?"

Dani shook her head. "No, thank you, Grandmother."

The old lady kissed her forehead. "You do as the judge says, Dani. Be a good girl and cooperate and we'll have you out of there in short order."

Dani looked up at her and nodded. There was a strange wisdom in her eyes. As if she knew better than the old lady what was going to happen to her. But she didn't say anything.

Instead, she turned to me. "Do you still own that boat down at La Jolla?"

I shook my head. "No, Dani."

"Too bad," she said. "I'd have liked to go out with you again."

"Maybe we will some day, Dani. When you get out of here."

She nodded and I could see that she didn't believe that either. "One of the matrons told me that she saw a picture of your wife in the paper. She said she was very pretty." She looked into my eyes. "The paper said that the reason she didn't come out with you was because she's going to have a baby."

"That's right, Dani."

"When?"

"Very soon now," I said. "The doctor thought it would be better if she didn't travel."

A sudden smile crossed her face. "Then it's true what the papers said? I'm glad."

"It's true." I smiled back at her. "Did you think she'd have any other reason for not coming?"

Dani glanced at Nora out of the corner of her eye. Nora was applying her lipstick in apparent boredom over our conversation. "I don't know," Dani said in a low voice. "At first I thought she wasn't coming because she hated me."

I laughed. "Where'd you get that idea?"

Again the side glance toward Nora. "I don't know. It was just an idea."

The door opened and Miss Spicer came back into the room. Through the open door I could see the figure of a matron waiting. "You'll have to leave now, Dani."

"Okay," Dani answered. She tamped the cigarette out in an ashtray and kissed me. " 'Bye, Daddy."

She kissed her grandmother and then walked over to Nora. Nora put her arms around her. She looked into Dani's eyes. "You know I love you, don't you, Dani?"

Dani nodded.

"Better than anyone else?"

Again Dani nodded.

"How much, dear?"

I could see that they were playing a game they had played many times before. Whether it really meant anything to Nora or not I couldn't tell.

"The most, Mother."

Nora glanced at me to see if I had heard the answer. I laughed. Dani turned and looked at me, her eyes startled. There must be something to this thing called telepathy because I was sure she knew what I was laughing at. She turned and kissed her mother. " 'Bye, Mother."

Nora looked at me. Her face was flushed and angry. She started to say something but bit her lip and remained silent.

"While you're all here," Miss Spicer said smoothly after she closed the door behind Dani, "I was wondering if we might arrange our appointments. It would expedite matters." She went behind the desk and sat down. "Could I come out and see you tomorrow afternoon, Miss Hayden?"

"Thursday would be better," Nora said. "The servants would be off and we'd be alone. We would have time to talk."

"It would be more helpful if the servants were available," Miss Spicer said. "I'd like to talk with them about Dani, too."

Nora looked at Gordon. "I don't know." She hesitated. "I don't particularly relish the idea of discussing my affairs with the servants. It seems to me that they have nothing better to do than gossip as it is. You wouldn't learn anything from them."

"It's my job to find out as much as I can about your daughter, Miss Hayden. You may be sure that I'll be most discreet."

Nora looked at Gordon again. He nodded. She turned to the probation officer. "Could you come tomorrow morning?"

"The afternoon would be better. I have an appointment at Miss Randolph's School in the morning."

"Wednesday afternoon then," Nora agreed petulantly. "Two o'clock."

"Two o'clock will be fine." Miss Spicer looked at Nora's mother. "Is Thursday good for you?"

The old woman nodded.

"Nine o'clock in the morning too early?"

"I'm up early," the old woman replied.

Miss Spicer turned to me. "When would be a good time for you, Colonel?"

"Any time. You name it."

"I don't know your plans, Colonel Carey," she said. "I know your wife is pregnant. I wasn't sure whether you'd want to return to Chicago and come back again for the hearing. I can make it at your convenience."

I had purposely waited until the hearing was over, hoping that my staying might prove unnecessary. But there was no purpose in waiting any longer. I knew I was going to stay. I'd have to call Elizabeth that afternoon and tell her I wasn't returning as planned.

"I'll be here, Miss Spicer," I said. "You pick the time."

"Thank you, Colonel Carey. Four o'clock Friday afternoon at your motel?"

"Good."

"Then we can leave now?" Nora asked.

"Just one thing more, Miss Hayden."

"Yes?"

"The judge asked me to get your permission to obtain a transcript of the divorce proceedings between you and Colonel Carey."

Nora exploded. "This is utterly ridiculous! I can't see any reason for prying into my past. Why, Dani was just a baby when the divorce was granted."

"The court is entitled to any information that is relevant to the welfare of your daughter. I think you should make it available. They have the right to subpoena such court records, you know. Wouldn't it be easier to cooperate?"

"Are you threatening that you'll keep my daughter until you obtain those records?" Nora asked in a freezing tone.

Miss Spicer wasn't in the least intimidated. She looked at Nora calmly. "I'm not making any threats at all, Miss Hayden," she said quietly. "I'm just informing you of the powers of this court. If you have any concern for the welfare of your daughter you'll do everything you can to cooperate. Am I stating it correctly, Mr. Gordon?"

"You are, Miss Spicer." Harris Gordon turned to Nora. "Dani has been made a temporary ward of the court. That means their power over her is absolute. I suggest that you grant your permission."

"I thought you were supposed to be *my* attorney!" Nora said angrily. "But all you did in court was agree with the judge. Now you're agreeing with this—this woman! Must I stand here and be humiliated like this? Do we have to remain in this idiotic court? What do they know about dealing with our kind of people, after dealing with the sort they normally have here? Can't we appeal to a higher court or something?"

"Dani is a minor. This is the only court in which she can legally appear."

Nora glared at him, her eyes flashing anger. "In that case, what the hell do I need you for?"

"I didn't call you, Miss Hayden," Gordon said in a quietly dignified manner. "You called me. I'll withdraw any time you want me to."

Nora looked at him for a moment more, then turned away. "Oh, the hell with it! Do whatever you like. I don't give a damn!"

She stormed out of the office, slamming the door behind her.

Gordon turned to the probation officer. "I apologize for my client. This whole wretched business has made her overwrought."

"I understand, Mr. Gordon."

"I have a transcript of the divorce proceedings in my office. If you'd care to stop by at any time I'll have it ready for you."

"Thank you, Mr. Gordon." Marian Spicer got to her feet. "I guess that will be all for now."

We turned and started out the door. The old lady went first, Gordon followed, then I. The probation officer's voice called me back. "Colonel Carey, may I trouble you for just a moment?"

I turned and walked back to her. "Yes, Miss Spicer?"

She gave me a slight smile. "I'm glad you're staying, Colonel. And I'm sure that Dani will be very happy, too. She was very concerned that you might not be able to."

"It's the least I could do. Even a complete stranger would find it hard to walk out on a child at a time like this."

She looked at me peculiarly for a moment, then her eyes fell. "I guess so, Colonel."

My former mother-in-law was waiting in the back seat of the Rolls when I came out. She beckoned to me and I walked over. "Where's Nora?" I asked.

"Gone," the old lady said. "She'd left even before I came out." She glanced down the road. "Where are you parked?"

"A few blocks down."

"Get in. We'll drop you there."

I got in and the big car rolled majestically out into the traffic. "Did you call Sam Corwin?"

"No. I thought I'd call him this afternoon." I looked glumly out of the window.

"You seem depressed," she observed shrewdly. "Is there anything Miss Spicer told you that she didn't tell us?"

I glanced at her. "No. What reason would she have for doing that? She merely said that Dani would be pleased to learn that I'm staying on."

"So that's it. You haven't told your wife yet?"

"No."

"You think she might be upset?" the old lady asked. She didn't wait for my reply. "I'm an old fool. Of course she'd be upset. I would. Expecting a baby any day and being home alone."

The big Rolls pulled over to the curb. It was a lot more than that, I thought. Like whether we had enough money for me to stay on.

"Is there anything I can do to help? Perhaps I could talk to her and tell her how important it is that you do stay."

I shook my head. "No, thanks. I'm sure Elizabeth will understand."

I opened the door and got out. The old lady leaned toward the door. "Call me this evening. Let me know if you've learned anything."

"I will." I watched her car move on and then I got into mine and drove back to the motel.

It was just about noon when I put the call through. "Hi," I said. "Had your lunch yet?"

"Of course," Elizabeth replied. "How did it go?"

I started to tell her about the coroner's inquest but she stopped me. "I just finished reading about that in the papers. What did they decide about Dani?"

I kept it as brief as I could. Then I told her about

the letter. When I finished there was a silence. "Elizabeth," I said, "did you hear me?"

"I heard you," she said. Her voice was very low.

"Are you all right?" I asked.

"I'm all right," she said. "I never felt better in my life. I enjoy being by myself. I suppose you want to stay out there until next week?"

I took a deep breath. "I would like to if it's all right with you."

"What more could you expect to accomplish?" she asked.

"If I leave now, Dani will think I'm running out on her again."

"But you didn't run out on her before!" Elizabeth said. "Didn't you explain that to her?"

"I did," I said. "But she's still a child. I don't think she half understood." I reached for a cigarette. "She's depending on me."

"So am I," Elizabeth said. "How do you think I feel? With all the neighbors looking at me and asking how you are? They read the papers the same as I do. They know that you're seeing her every day!"

I knew who she meant. "That's stupid."

"Is it?" she asked. "Are you sure that Dani is the only reason you're staying?"

"Of course, I'm sure," I shouted. "What the hell other reason would I have?"

"You wouldn't be worried about those letters just on account of Dani," she retorted. "You've already told me there was nothing more they could do to her. The law protects her. It's Nora you're trying to protect. You'd see that if you only took the time to be honest with yourself!"

I heard the connection break at the other end of the

line. I flashed the operator and told her that I'd been cut off, then I heard the telephone ringing.

"Hello." She sounded as if she'd been crying.

"Elizabeth," I said. "I'm sorry. I'll make arrangements to come home."

"No, you won't," she sniffed. "You're going to stay there until this whole damn business is settled."

"But—" I protested.

She interrupted. "No. No, you're going to stay there and get it out of your system. When you come home I don't want anything haunting you. I want a whole husband back, not the guilt-ridden ghost of the man you were in La Jolla."

"But what about the money?" I asked.

"Don't worry," she said. "Your V.A. check just came in. That's a hundred and forty bucks, enough to keep us a week. And I can always get a couple of hundred for my ring if I have to."

"Elizabeth," I said in a wondering voice.

I heard her sniff. "What?"

"Elizabeth," I said. "I love you."

4

The Scaasi-Corwin Galleries had their own building on Post Street, not far from Gump's. It was a narrow old-fashioned building sandwiched in between two larger ones, with a brand-new front of Mediterranean brick. The entrance was through a heavy glass-paneled door, just to the side of a small showcase set in the brick like a picture frame. In it, like a jewel on blue velvet, was a small abstract sculpture in welded bronze, glowing red and gold in an amber spotlight. The artist's name was in small black letters on a white card, the lettering on the door was respectable gold leaf.

SCAASI-CORWIN
TOKYO, SAN FRANCISCO, NEW YORK, LONDON, PARIS.

I opened the door and went in. A young man with a neatly trimmed Vandyke stepped forward and in an accent matching his English-cut clothes, inquired, "May I be of service, sir?"

"I have an appointment with Mr. Corwin."

"That's the lift on your left, sir. The offices are on the fourth floor."

"Thank you," I said and walked over to the elevator. The door opened as if by magic as I approached. "Fourth floor, please."

"Fourth floor," the operator repeated, closing the door. "Thank you, sir."

I glanced at the operator and almost immediately

began to feel ashamed of my sixty-dollar, three-button threads. Even the elevator boy wore an English-cut suit.

I stepped out into a lushly appointed reception room. Behind the desk was another Vandyke.

"I have an appointment with Mr. Corwin."

"Your name, please?"

"Luke Carey."

He nodded. "Thank you. If you'll take a seat I'll see if Mr. Corwin is free."

I sat down and picked up a copy of a magazine from the free-form table in front of the couch. It was *Réalités*. That figured. But in French. So I could look at the pictures.

I turned the pages. There was a picture of Brigitte on a boat in St. Tropez. I studied it. Any magazine that had a picture of Brigitte in a bikini couldn't be all bad. A shadow fell across the page. I looked up.

"Colonel Carey?" the attractive young blonde asked. I nodded.

"Mr. Corwin will see you now. Please follow me."

I got to my feet. This girl knew what she looked like going away and she made the most of it. It was the first pleasant thing that had happened to me all day. It was even better than the magazine.

"Thank you," I said as I went through the door she held open for me.

Sam's office was like outside, only more so. Fruitwood paneling. Two Matisses with lots of color; one sloe-eyed Modigliani with a wonderful almondy tone; a Picasso that I thought had been hung upside down. And Nora's bronze casting—*Woman in the Net*—that had won her the Eliofheim Award, standing on a small pedestal in the corner with a single bright spot shining down on it.

Sam entered from another door on the far wall. He came toward me, his hand outstretched. "Luke."

I took his hand. I liked the way he shook hands. Firm, but not effusive or overfriendly. I appreciated it. "How are you, Sam?"

"Fair enough. Losing a little hair but that's about all." He looked at me. "You look well."

"The good life," I said. "That and the right woman."

"I'm glad." He walked around behind his desk. "Sit down, Luke."

I slipped into the chair opposite him.

"I was shocked to hear about Dani."

I didn't say anything but I thought he meant it.

"I liked the kid," he said. "She was a sweet child. I'm sorry this had to happen to her. It was almost as if it were bound to happen though."

"What makes you say that?"

He shrugged his shoulders. "Nora."

"Did you know Riccio?" I asked.

"Yes." He smiled but it was a twisted sort of smile. "I was the one who introduced them."

"How did that happen?"

He laughed. "You saw my boys?"

"The Vandykes and the coats?"

He nodded.

"I sure did. I can't tell you how relieved I was to see your secretary."

He laughed again. "It's Scaasi's idea. Out here it's mostly women who buy art. It works pretty good."

"How does that lead to Riccio?"

"When I opened this place five years ago, he was number-one boy. He was very good too. Women adored him."

"Vandyke and all?"

"It goes with the all-arty look," he said. "Sort of well-groomed beatnik."

"I see."

"So did Nora," Sam said wryly. "He wore Italian style trousers—tight around the crotch, like a ballet dancer's. Nora couldn't keep her eyes off him." He opened a cigarette box on his desk and pushed it toward me. "And you know how that is. It's like the song. What Nora wants, Nora gets." His eyes met mine candidly. "Only this time I think Nora got more than she bargained for."

"Brighten my day," I said, taking a cigarette. "What do you mean?"

"He was as bad as she was. He'd bang anything that walked. A couple of times he almost got into trouble with customers but he always managed to weasel his way out."

"Why did you keep him?"

"He was good. The best salesman we ever had. And he knew his stuff."

"How did you meet him?"

Sam peered at me. "Why all the questions about Riccio?"

"I want to know something about him," I said. "Nobody else seems to. I thought if I did, maybe I could convince the court it wasn't such a bad thing after all."

"I see," he nodded slowly. "It's reaching. But it might help."

"That's what I think. What do you know about him? Did he have any special friends you might remember?"

He thought for a moment, then picked up the telephone on his desk. "Bring in the personnel file on Tony Riccio."

A moment later the door opened and Sam's secretary came in. She placed the file in front of him, looked at me and then walked out. I noticed Sam's eyes following her.

"Healthy," I said. "Very healthy. I don't think I could have taken the shock if you'd turned fruit."

He laughed and opened the file. "Tony worked for Arlene Gately before he worked for me. He came over here when she did."

"Does she still work for you?"

"She died two years ago. In a plane crash."

"Oh," I said. "What about his friends?"

"I can't remember any. He concentrated on dames. I never heard of his being real buddy with any man."

"How about his family then?"

"They're here in San Francisco. His father has a fish stand on the Wharf. I think his brothers own a boat."

"Do you have their address?"

He pulled a buck slip toward him and wrote an address on it. I took the slip of paper.

"I wish I could think of something more."

"There is something," I said. "But you don't have to tell me if you don't want to."

"What is it?"

"Nora and Riccio. Mrs. Hayden told me you clubbed her into a settlement. How did you manage it?"

He hesitated a moment. "I knew what was going on. It was just a question of time before I got photographs. She squawked but she settled."

"Do you still have them?"

He shook his head. "I gave them to her when the decree became final. I didn't want any part of them. I had enough to remember."

I didn't speak.

He looked at me. "It was a fair settlement. I didn't touch anything that was really hers. We only split what we made together."

"I'm not criticizing."

"I hope you can do something. I keep remembering

Dani when she was a little girl. She was kind of lost there for a while after you stopped seeing her."

"I didn't want to," I said. "Nora fixed that."

"I didn't know that," he said in a surprised voice. "Nora told me that one day you just decided you weren't going to come around any more."

I stared at him. "That sounds like Nora."

"You know, I thought I knew everything, but—" He ground his cigarette out and lit another. "There was one thing I'll never forget."

"What's that?"

"It happened about five years ago. Dani was almost ten and said something about wanting a birthday party. Nora went through the roof. She told the kid to stop emphasizing her age, that she was old enough to realize that if she went around talking about her age it would be very embarrassing to her mother. Dani didn't understand, so she looked up at Nora and asked, 'Don't you want me to grow up, Mommy?' Nora started to answer, then she saw me watching her and she walked away, leaving the kid standing there with a hurt expression on her face."

He dragged on the cigarette. "I honestly believe Nora was jealous of Dani. Of her youth, of her growing up. Of everything about her. But there was nothing I could do about it. Nora always made it very clear to me that I wasn't her father and had no right to interfere."

He looked down at his desk for a moment, then up at me. "I suppose you're wondering why, with everything I knew about her, I married her?"

"I thought about it a couple of times."

"Maybe you won't understand it," he said quietly. "I was art critic on a small-town paper. No matter what they say, in the art world San Francisco is small town. I discovered something great. That happens maybe once in a lifetime, if you're lucky. But only if you're lucky. I discovered Nora Hayden, and whatever else she is, in her own field she's one of the greats. What she does with sculpture is the truth. So much truth that you don't stop to think that she uses it all up in her work and has nothing left for herself or anyone else as a human being.

"I knew what she was like. But I thought I could change her. I thought I could make some of that truth that I saw in her work apply to her own life. But I was wrong. I was completely wrong.

"What I didn't see was that the only truth she's capable of is in her work. Nothing else, no one else, matters. And there was one other thing."

"What was that, Sam?"

He looked at me. "I loved her," he said simply. Then he smiled grimly. "But look where love has gone. I've got nothing to show for it but some pictures on the wall and a couple of statues. But you've got something. No matter how bad it looks right now, you'll always have something to show you where love has gone."

I knew what he meant. I got to my feet. "You've been more than kind, Sam."

He rose also. "I'd like to send Dani a little something. Do you think it would be all right?"

"I'm sure she'd like that, Sam."

He held out his hand. "Give her my love."

"I will, Sam," I said. "Thank you."

Post Street was bustling with afternoon shoppers and the sunlight beat at my eyes after the sheltered cool dimness inside the gallery. I felt the sweat come out on my skin inside my clothing and I headed for the coolness of a bar. I ordered a bottle of beer. A couple of tourists came in and stood beside me. They ordered beer too.

"Jesus, it's hot," one of them said.

"It sure is, man," said the other as he lifted the foaming glass to his lips. "But think how much hotter it is for them poor guys out there on that rock in the middle of the bay. I bet they'd give anything for a cool beer on a day like this."

I glanced at them and thought of the rock they were talking about. Alcatraz. There were other rocks too. My daughter was on one of her own. And she was just a kid.

I wondered what she was doing to keep cool in this bright mid-afternoon heat. I wondered what Miss Spicer was finding out about her. Things, probably, I'd never know. Never could know.

5

Marian Spicer recognized the shoes even before she heard the voice. They were so highly polished that she could almost see her face in them, though she knew that if the foot were raised, the upper would come slightly away so the white yarn of the socks would show. She raised her head from the notes spread out on the table.

"Ah! Would it be the good maid Marian come to play with Robin Hood and whilst away the time in some shaded dell of Sherwood Forest the hotted afternoon?"

She coughed. "Sit down, Red, before you spill your coffee all over my work papers. It's a good thing I know you. Even the Sheriff of Nottingham wouldn't understand English the way you speak it."

He stood there grinning, his blue eyes crinkled and his red hair tousled as usual. He had two cups of coffee, one in either hand. "You looked about ready for a refill," he said, putting one down in front of her.

"Thanks."

He looked around the cafeteria. It was almost empty. "Something drastic will have to be done. The employees aren't taking proper advantage of their coffee break."

At one of the other tables a probation officer sat with a girl and her mother. The girl was about fifteen, pregnant and sullen. The girl's mother was talking a blue streak to the probation officer, who was nodding her head patiently.

Marian could guess what the woman was saying. She'd heard the same thing so many times before. "I didn't know—I never suspected . . . My own daughter . . . It was those kids she—"

It was always the same thing. Children got into trouble and parents were always surprised. Of course they never saw it coming. They were always too busy with other things. Some of them were valid, others were not, but it all added up to the same thing—Juvenile Court.

"Where've you been all day?" she asked, gathering her papers into a neat stack.

Red sipped noisily at his coffee. "Where do you think? Out looking for that lousy little fag."

Marian knew whom he meant—a sixteen-year-old boy whose parents had shipped him off to military school to make a man of him after he had turned up in a police dragnet about six months ago. Four days later they'd called to report he was missing from school. "Did you find him?"

"I found him. Right where we thought he'd be. In the men's room of a swish bar on North Beach."

"I don't see why that should have taken you four days."

"Do you know how many of those joints there are?" he asked indignantly. Then he saw her smile and eased back in his chair. "You should have seen the kid when I found him. He was still wearing his school uniform. It looked like he'd slept in it the whole four days. When he saw me he went hysterical. Kicking and screaming and scratching. I had to get a radio car to help me bring him in." He looked at her and grinned mischievously. "Even at that, I didn't do so bad today. I managed to get propositioned five times and one of them was a woman. Out there that's an achievement. She must have thought I was real queer."

"Did you notify his parents?"

Red nodded. "They'll be in tomorrow." He shrugged his shoulders. "That's life. Boys will be girls."

"Poor kid." That was the one kind of case none of them liked. They felt so completely useless. There was nothing they could really do that was constructive. The only thing they could do was to turn it over to the psychiatrists. And there were times, she felt, when even they were helpless.

"You're a busy little bee. What are you working on? The Hayden case?"

"The girl's name is Carey."

"I know that. But all the papers call it the Hayden case. After the mother, who is pumpkins in this town." He took another noisy sip of his coffee. "What's with the kid?"

Marian looked at him speculatively. "I don't really know. I haven't been able to figure her out yet. She doesn't fit in like most of the other children I've come across."

He raised an inquisitive eyebrow. "She's even got you going has she? Those the preliminary reports?"

She nodded.

"Let me take a look."

She watched him read the top page. It was the report of the examining physician. Every girl who was brought in was given a thorough physical before being sent to the cottages. Dani had had hers last Saturday, but the psychometric evaluations hadn't been processed until Monday, because that office was closed on the weekend.

Marian had the feeling that somewhere along the line they were missing something very important about the child, but she couldn't put her finger on it. But Red was really very good. He'd been a probation officer for many years. Maybe he could come up with the something that would help.

He finished reading the medical report and glanced at her cynically. "I'm glad to see that at least this kid is normal."

She knew what he was talking about. *The hymeneal rupture is complete and the scar well healed and of indeterminate age. However, there are signs of irritation in the vaginal walls and a slight swelling of the clitoris, which indicates the probability of a high level of sexual activity during the period shortly preceding this examination.*

"I'm beginning to believe there are no fourteen-year-old virgins in San Francisco." He looked at her and grinned. "Historically speaking, Marian, were you still a virgin at fourteen?"

"Cut the jokes, Red. Don't let this job distort your outlook. Nice kids seldom wind up here."

"Who was it? The guy she killed?"

She stared at him. "She wouldn't say. Whenever anyone asks about it, she clams up. Doesn't talk, doesn't say anything. Read the psychometric and see for yourself."

She saw his eyebrows shoot up as he reached the middle of the page. She knew about that too.

"The kid has an I.Q. of 152."

"That's right. We're dealing with an extraordinary level of intelligence and perception. That's what makes it so hard to understand what follows. Read it."

He continued on silently. He went through the next few pages rapidly and then put the report down. "She's playing with us. I don't get it. Why?"

"That's exactly what I feel. Did you read what she told the psychiatrist at the end of their session? That she freely admitted doing wrong, that she realizes she shouldn't have done it, that she is perfectly willing to discuss anything that pertains to her wrongdoing, but is not interested in discussing anything more than that. The rest of her life is both personal and private and she does not feel impelled to reveal anything about it because it is not pertinent to what she did."

"That's quite a mouthful."

Marian nodded. "Somewhere over this weekend she regained control of herself. Too bad we couldn't have got to her when she came in Saturday. She was upset and nervous then."

"Do you think anyone fed her that line?"

"The only one she saw was her father. He'd never think of it. To him she's still a little girl. The last time he saw her she was about eight years old, and while he realizes that she's bigger, I don't think he's got it clear yet that she's any older."

"What's he like?"

"He seems like a nice gentle man."

"With that war record?" Red's voice was incredulous.

"That's the paradox. But I feel sorry for the poor guy. It's obvious from his clothes that he's not too well off, yet he came all the way out from Chicago to see if he could help. His wife is back there expecting a baby any day and he's being pulled in both directions. He wants to do right but he's not that sure that he knows what right is."

"What's Miss Hayden like?"

"Nora Hayden knows what she wants. All the time. She may be an important artist but she's also a real bitch. I feel sorry for the kid, having to live with her all these years. It couldn't have been easy."

"I guess you don't like her."

"I guess I don't. But that doesn't alter the basic problem. How do we reach this kid and get her to open up?"

"Sometimes the best thing to do is to leave them alone. Maybe when she gets to trust us a little more she'll see we want to help, and she'll come around."

"That might work if we had the time. But Murphy only gave us until next week. I've got the feeling there's a lot of pressure on him to clean this up quickly and he's not going to let it go over the legal limit of fifteen days."

She reached for her coffee cup. The coffee was cold now but she drank it anyway. "I have the strangest feeling that we're nowhere near the truth in this case yet. From the kind of control the kid is showing I can't believe that she'd commit murder."

"Who do you think did it then? The mother?"

"Much more likely, it seems to me."

"But all the evidence is against you. You've read all the statements. You were in coroner's court and heard them again. They all point to the child."

"That's just it. It's like when I come into my house and find everything in place. Then I know that something is wrong. It's just too perfect. And besides, there was only one witness."

"The mother?"

She nodded.

Red stared at her thoughtfully for a moment. "Don't let the fact that you don't like the mother push you off the deep end. I feel that way most of the time when I see how stupid most parents are. I'd much prefer blaming them than the kids. But it doesn't work like that."

He got up and went over to the kitchen door and came back with two more cups of coffee. "Where's the kid now?"

"In psych. Maybe Jennings can get to her today."

"Sally Jennings is good. If she can't get her to open up, nobody can."

"I hope so. Meanwhile I've got to get started on my leg work. Judge Murphy wants me to look at the transcript of the parents' divorce action. I'm going down to their lawyer's office to pick it up."

Marian pushed her chair back. "How's Anita, and the boys?"

"The same as usual. Anita wants to get a part-time job to help out with the money, but I told her over my dead body. I see too much of what happens to kids whose parents have part-time jobs."

She nodded sympathetically. There were times she wondered how some of the men who were married managed on their salaries. She could understand why Red's shoes were always at least two months in need of repair.

He sighed. "Stevie, that's the oldest, is bugging us for a scooter. He says all the kids in school have them."

"Are you going to get him one?"

"If I can find a good used one for fifty bucks." He looked down at the table. "I guess I'm just kiddin' myself. There aren't any around for that kind of money."

"Maybe you'll be lucky, Red."

"I'll keep my fingers crossed. But sometimes it frightens me."

"What do you mean?"

"Stevie's a good kid and all that, but I keep thinking about all the things he has to make do without. You know what I mean. Maybe it's no good to know so much."

She nodded.

"I wake up sometimes in the middle of the night," he said, "dreaming that I'm on desk duty and they bring in a kid and it's Stevie. Then when I ask him why, he says to me: What did you expect, Pop? For me to go on forever believing that the moon is made of green cheese?"

She stared at him for a moment. That was the trouble with all of them. They saw too much and they felt too much. She put a friendly hand on his shoulder. "It's been a long hot day. Why don't you take off for the rest of the afternoon and go home?"

He reached up and patted her hand gratefully.

"What for?" he asked with a grin. "And worry Anita half to death that I'm sick or something?"

6

The framed diploma on the wall behind the tiny cluttered desk in the equally tiny glass cubicle was an M.A. in psychology from the University of Wisconsin. The name on the diploma in flowing gothic script was Sally Jennings. The date was June 1954.

Sally Jennings was thirty-eight when she received that diploma. Behind it lay fifteen years as a probation officer, while she studied and saved toward her goal. When all the money had been carefully accumulated she took a leave of absence for two years and came back with the diploma. It had been another two years before there was a vacancy in her present department.

She had a youthful face, graying hair, a quiet, pleasant manner and a real feeling for the children that came to her. Most of the times they felt this and responded to her. Once in a while, there was one who escaped her intangible pull. This was one of those times.

She looked across the desk at Dani. The child sat silently, her face composed, her hands folded neatly on her lap. Sally had noted the other day that the child had neatly manicured fingernails. The control was there all right. She reached for a cigarette and noticed the child's eyes following her hand.

"Would you care for a cigarette, Dani?" she asked politely, extending the pack.

Dani hesitated.

"It's all right, Dani. You can smoke in here."

Dani took the cigarette and a light. "Thank you, Miss Jennings."

The psychologist lit her own cigarette and leaned back in her chair. She let the smoke out slowly and watched it drift idly toward the ceiling. "I like to watch the smoke drift up," she said casually. "It's like tiny clouds in the sky taking on all kinds of forms and shapes."

"We had a game like that the girls played at Miss Randolph's School. We called it Instant Rorschach." Sally Jennings glanced at Dani. There was a faint trace of amusement in the child's eyes. "You'd be surprised at what some of the girls saw. Some of it was pretty far out."

"You know a great deal about psychology for one so young."

"I read a lot about it. One time I thought I'd like to be one but I changed my mind."

"Why was that, Dani? I imagine you might be very good at it."

"I don't know. Maybe it was that I didn't like the idea of prying into people's minds. Or maybe it's just that I don't like prying. period."

"Do you think I'm prying, Dani?"

Dani looked at her. "That's your job, isn't it?" she asked bluntly. "To see what makes me tick?"

"That's only a part of it, Dani. The smallest part. The main thing is to see if we can find a way to help you."

"What if I don't want help?"

"I think we all do in one way or another, whether we admit it to ourselves or not."

"Do you need help?" Dani asked.

"I think I do. There are times when I feel very helpless."

"Do you go to a psychologist then?"

Sally Jennings nodded. "I've been in analysis for the

past few years. Ever since I realized I had to know more about myself before I could do my job properly."

"How often do you go?"

"At least once a week. Sometimes more, when I have the time."

"Mother says that the only people who go to analysts are sick. She says it's a substitute for the Roman Catholic confessional."

Sally Jennings glanced at Dani. "Is your mother right about everything?"

Dani looked at her without answering.

The psychologist could see the wall rising in the child's eyes. She changed the subject quickly. "The doctor who examined you told me you complained that your breasts hurt. Have they been hurting for a long time?"

Dani nodded silently.

"For how long?"

Dani hesitated.

"That certainly isn't prying into your mind. That's a medical question."

"Is there anything wrong?" Dani asked, quick concern in her voice.

Sally watched the child's hands go involuntarily to her bosom and felt a twinge of conscience at having reawakened the child's fear. "No, there's nothing wrong. It's just that doctors like to know the reasons for everything."

"When I first began to develop, I used to bind my breasts. Then they began to hurt me so I stopped doing it. They've hurt on and off ever since."

Sally laughed. "Why did you ever do a thing like that? It's kind of old-fashioned. Girls haven't done that for years."

"I heard my mother telling a friend of hers about it.

She said the geishas in Japan do it to look young and keep from growing up."

"Didn't you want to grow up, Dani?"

"Of course I did," Dani said quickly.

"Then why did you do it?" Sally repeated. The child didn't answer. "Was it because you thought it would please your mother?"

She saw the truth of her guess reflected in the child's suddenly wide eyes. She hardened her heart and kept on talking. "That's the reason, isn't it, Dani? You bound your breasts until they hurt because you thought it would please your mother if you could keep from growing up? Why did you think that, Dani? Did your mother ever tell you that you made her feel old because you were growing up?"

Suddenly the child was crying, her face hidden in her hands.

Gently the psychologist took the cigarette from Dani's fingers and ground it out in the ashtray. "Most mothers don't really want their children to grow up, Dani. They like to keep them young because it makes them feel more important, more useful, younger themselves."

"My mother loves me," Dani sobbed between her fingers. "My mother loves me."

"Of course she does, Dani. But love alone doesn't keep a mother from making mistakes sometimes."

The child looked up, the tears shining bright in her eyes. "I—I don't want to talk any more, Miss Jennings. May I go back to my room?"

Sally studied her for a moment, then nodded. "Of course, Dani," she said, pressing a button on her desk for a matron. "We'll talk again tomorrow."

Through the glass-paneled walls of her office, she watched Dani go down the corridor. She sighed wearily. It had been a long day. A little progress had been made.

Maybe tomorrow she would make more.

The sound of the music from the television set came to her small room through the closed door. Unconsciously Dani's feet began to pick up the beat. After a few minutes she surrendered to its pull and opened the door and went out into the corridor. The music was louder there and she followed it into the large recreation room where the girls were gathered in front of the television set.

The music stopped and the smooth, unlined face of Dick Clark filled the screen. His voice flowed effortlessly from the speaker. "Welcome to the American Bandstand. And to get today's session off to a flying start, our first record will be the one and only Chubby Checkers singing his immortal 'Let's Twist Again!' "

Dani stood watching, enraptured, as the camera pulled back to reveal the crowded dance floor. Most of the boys wore sports jackets and the girls were equally casual. There was a moment's silence as they stood there expectantly, then the sound of the record blared from the speaker. The hoarse rhythmic chant of the singer filled the room.

> Let's twist again—
> Lak' we did last sum-muh—
> Let's twist a-gain—
> Lak' we did last ye-uh.

Several of the girls paired off and began to dance in front of the TV set. From the far side of the room, a matron watched, her feet also keeping the beat.

"Do you twist, Dani?"

Dani turned. It was the girl who sat next to her at mealtime. She nodded. "Yes, Sylvia."

The girl smiled. "Then how about showin' them?"

Dani smiled back. "I'm with you."

The two girls assumed round-shouldered postures and stolid faces as they picked up the rhythm. As they gyrated back and forth, seemingly glued to one spot on the floor, they never once looked into each other's faces. Each focused her eyes at about the level of her partner's knees.

After a few moments' silence, during which each probed the other's proficiency in the dance, they began to talk. "You're good," Sylvia said.

"Not as good as you are, though."

"I love to dance," Sylvia said. "That's what I'm goin' to be. A pro."

"You could be a pro right now."

Sylvia smiled proudly. She was slightly taller than Dani, about a year older, with almost blond brown hair and blue eyes. "Let's try a few variations."

"Okay."

"Hully-Gully."

Dani grinned and followed her into the steps.

"Now the Madison." Sylvia spun out and Dani circled around her, then Dani spun out while Sylvia circled around her.

Sylvia laughed aloud. "Now we'll kill 'em with the Watusi!"

The almost primitive steps of a jungle dance came to life as she postured in time to the music. Dani followed as the music crescendoed and crashed, the last wail of the singer fading with the sound.

The two girls stood there breathing heavily, looking at each other. "Like it's too much," Sylvia said.

"All go." Dani answered.

The music came on again. Sylvia looked at Dani. "Try another?"

Dani shook her head. "Cigarettes got my wind. I'll stay on the launch pad for this one."

Sylvia smiled. "I've got an extra dime for a Coke. I'll split."

"Thanks." Dani could have bought one of her own but that wouldn't be polite. She'd buy the next one.

Sylvia walked over to the machine and picked up a Coke. There were some straws on a nearby table. She stuck two in the bottle and came back. "Let's sit over here."

They sat down where they could watch the television screen and sipped at their Cokes. A commercial came on and their eyes followed it with even greater attention than they'd paid to the program itself.

"That chewing gum commercial is the end."

Dick Clark came back on and then the music. Sylvia turned to Dani. "You go to the head-shrinker's again today?"

Dani nodded.

"Who'd you draw? Jennings?"

"Yes."

"She's not so bad, you can go with her. But that old man who's the boss. He's like 'Thriller' when he looks at you with those fish eyes."

"I don't know him," Dani said.

They watched the dancers on the screen for a few moments. The camera moved in close on a dancing couple. The boy was tall and handsome, his hair peaked and dipped in the latest style. The girl wore a loose sweater and skirt. They became aware that the camera was on them and put on a little show.

"That boy looks real smooth. He reminds me of my boy friend."

"He looks a little like Fabian," Dani said.

"My boy friend is a dead ringer for Fabian," Sylvia

said proudly. "That's what got me in the first place. I think Fabian's the greatest."

"I like Rickie and Frankie Avalon better. They can sing rings around him."

"So can Elvis. But I'm not talking about their voices. Fabian's got it. All he has to do is look at me and I'm all cream." She looked at Dani. "You got a boy friend?"

"No."

"You had one?"

Dani shook her head. "Not really. Not a steady."

"Wasn't that guy your boy friend? The one—"

Dani shook her head.

"I thought he was," Sylvia said. "Because they put you over here with us. They keep the cherries in another cottage. You mean it was someone else?"

"I don't want to talk about it."

Sylvia leaned back against her chair. "I miss my boy friend."

"Where is he?"

Sylvia jerked her thumb toward the windows. "Over in the boys' cottage."

"What's he doing over there?"

"They brought us in together," Sylvia said. "Richie borrowed a car for us to take a ride in. Then we went up to Golden Gate Park. The cops picked us up there."

"I don't get it. Why should they bother you?"

Sylvia laughed. "Don't be real cute. I told you Richie borrowed the car. Besides it was two in the morning and we were in the back seat doing you know what." She finished the last of the Coke. "Man, it was real dreamy, you know what I mean?" She sighed. "The top down on the convertible, the moon, music from the car radio. We were just making it into orbit when the Untouchables came on. Then it was a real mess."

"I'll get another Coke," Dani said. When she came

back Sylvia was watching a younger singer who was making a guest appearance.

"He's not really singing," Sylvia said. "He's just moving his lips to a playback."

"How do you know?"

"You don't see the orchestra, do you? Besides, they got a big echo in his voice. They can't do that except in a recording studio." She studied the close-up of the singer for a moment. "But he's real cute, only not as cute as Fabian. Did you get any mail today?"

Dani shook her head. "No, but I didn't expect any."

"The others got mail. I expected a letter from Richie but I didn't get one. He said he'd write every day." Concern came into her voice. "You don't think the finks are holding it out on me, do you?"

"I don't think so."

"If I don't hear from him by tomorrow, I'll die!"

"Don't worry, you'll hear from him," Dani said consolingly.

Silently the two girls sat sharing the Coke.

7

I got over to the Wharf just a little ahead of the dinner rush. The vendors were busy stocking their stands, laying the cracked crabs artistically on the shaved ice, trimming the borders of their carts with the gay glass cups of fresh-cooked pink shrimp. There were stacks of fresh-baked sourdough bread and rolls, and over the whole area hung the heady aroma of the fish market.

I walked past Tarantino's toward the Maritime Museum. The fishing boats were tied up for the night, bobbing slightly with the swell of the water, and along the Wharf were more stands. One, almost in the middle of the block, was covered with a faded tarpaulin. Across it was printed RICCIO.

I stopped. A man working at the next stand, his hands deftly setting out crabs, said out of the side of his mouth, "They're closed today."

"Do you know where I can find them?"

He put down the crabs and walked toward me. "You a reporter?"

I nodded.

"They're at the funeral parlor. The funeral's tomorrow morning. You come to interview the family?"

"In a way."

"The boy was no good," he said. "When he was a kid he'd never come to help out on the stand. He wouldn't dirty his hands with the fish, like his brothers. He was too good for them. I told his father he'd come to a bad end."

"Which funeral parlor?" I asked.

"Mascogani's."

"Where is it?"

"You know Bimbo's?" he asked.

I nodded.

"Across the street from Bimbo's, about a block down."

"Thanks." I started back up the block toward my car. I found a place to park on Jackson near the funeral parlor. It was a white stone and marble-front building. I opened the doors and went inside.

I stood in the dim, softly lighted foyer until my eyes adjusted, then walked over to the glass-covered directory on the wall. In a moment a dark-suited man came up behind me.

"Can I help you, sir?" he said in a hushed voice.

"Riccio?"

"Right this way."

I followed him to the elevator. He pressed a button and the door opened. "I don't know if the family is still up there. They may have gone to supper, but you can sign your name in the book just inside the door. Room A."

"Thanks."

The door closed. When it opened again I stepped out. Room A was just across the corridor.

I looked in the open door. Through an archway at the far end of the room I could see the coffin resting under a blanket of flowers. My footsteps made no sound on the heavy carpeting as I walked toward it. I stopped alongside and looked down.

So this was the man my daughter had killed. At first glance, he seemed to be merely sleeping. The morticians had done their job well.

He had been handsome, with thick black hair coming

to a slight widow's peak on his high forehead, His nose was straight and strong, his mouth firm though even now slightly sensual. His lashes were almost as long as a girl's. I felt a sense of pity well up inside me. He couldn't have been much past thirty.

I heard a sigh behind me, almost a groan. I turned, startled.

A little old man was sitting in a corner of the alcove, to the side of the archway, on a small straight-backed chair. I hadn't noticed him when I came in, though I must have walked right past him. He looked up at me, his dark eyes glittering in the candlelight.

"I'ma th' fath'," he said. "You knew my son?"

I shook my head. I walked toward him. "My sympathy, Mr. Riccio."

"Grazie," he said heavily, his tired eyes searching my face. "My Tony, he not sucha bad boy like they say," he said. "He justa want too much."

"I can believe that, Mr. Riccio. No one is ever as bad as people say they are."

Voices came from just beyond the archway. "Papa! Who are you talking to in there?"

I turned to see a young man and woman in the archway. The young man looked very much like the man in the coffin, though his features were slightly heavier and coarser. The young woman was dressed in black, the kind of black that only Italian women seem able to achieve in times of mourning. Her hair was covered by a lace shawl, her face patient with a sad, tired kind of beauty.

"This another my sons. Steve," the old man said. "And my Tony's *fidanzata,* Anna Stradella."

The young man stared into my face with a shocked expression. "Papa!" he said harshly. "You know who this man is?"

The old man shook his head.

"He's the girl's father! You can't talk to him. You know what the lawyer said."

The old man looked up into my face. He turned back to his son. "What I care whata the lawy' say? I look into this man's face when he is stan' by the coff'. An' I see in it the same kin' sorrow that I gota in my heart."

"But, Papa," the young man protested, "the lawyer said not to talk to him if we're going to sue. It might prejudice our case!"

Mr. Riccio raised a hand. "Stop!" he said firmly with a curious kind of dignity. "Later the lawyers can fight. Now, we are joosta th' same. Two fathers, whos'a childr' bring them sorrow and shame."

He turned back to me. "Sit down, Mist' Carey. Forgive my boy. He'sa still young."

"Thank you, Mr. Riccio."

The young man turned angrily and walked from the room. The girl stood there watching us. I pulled two chairs from the wall and held one out for her. She hesitated a moment, then sat down. I sat in the other.

"My condolences, Miss Stradella."

She nodded without answering, her eyes dark in her white face.

"Your little girl?" Mr. Riccio asked. "How is she?"

I didn't know what to say. How harsh would it sound for me to say all right, while his son lay there in the coffin a few feet from us?

He sensed my feelings. "Poor kid," he said softly. "She'sa nothing but a baby." He looked into my face. "Why did you come, Mist' Carey?"

"To find out about your son." I saw his eyes widen. "Not to bring him shame," I added quickly. "But to learn something about my daughter."

"Do not be embarrass, Mist' Carey. It'sa only right to want to help you' daughter."

"Thank you for understanding, Mr. Riccio."

"Now, what you want to know?"

"Did your son have any close friends?"

He shrugged his shoulders. "Friends?" he asked. "No. No friends. Anna who he was going marry would be his friend. His brothers, Steve and John, they woulda be his friends. But he no want any of them. He want to be a big society man."

The old man smiled bitterly, his eyes clouding with a memory. "When Tony wasa littla boy, he say to me, 'Pop, Pop, look up from the dock. Up there on the top of Nob Hill. I'm going to live there some day. Way up there where you no can smella the fish!'

"I laugh. 'Tony,' I say. 'Go study your lesson. Play baseball like a good boy. Maybe some day you be lika the Di Mag brothers an get your Pop a big restaurant ona the Wharf. Stop dreaming.'

"But Tony, he always dream. When he finish school he don' want to be a baseball play' lika the Di Mag brothers. He wanta be an artist. He grow a beard and hang out in the coffeehouse. He come home late every night and sleep late every morning. He no go out on the boat with his brothers. Hisa hands are too delicate. When he'sa twenty year old he get job with an art dealer. A fat lady. Then a year later he get another job. Big place this time. Near Gump's.

"One day he come down to my stand with a pretty lady. 'Thisa my boss' wife,' he say. They eat the shrimp and the crack crab and they laugh like two kids. Then they go away. A little later I read in the pap' where the boss and his wife, they geta divorce. I worry about my Tony's job, then one day he comes down to the stand in a brand-new car. Expensive. Not American car. Foreign.

" 'Pop!' he say. 'I got it made. I worka for the boss' wife now. She'sa big time. Big money. An' you know where I live?'

" 'No,' I say. 'Where you live, Tony?'

"He point up to the hill. 'Right up there, Pop,' he say. 'Right up there on Nob Hill like I always say I will. And you know, Pop, it'sa true. You never smell the fish from up there!' "

He glanced over at the coffin, then back at me. "Tony, he can't smell the fish from there either. From there, he can't smell nothing at all."

I sat there silent for a moment, then got to my feet. "You've been very kind to talk to me, Mr. Riccio. I apologize for disturbing you at a time like this."

The old man looked up at me and nodded. but already his eyes were far away. He looked back at the coffin, his lips moving silently. "I will pray for your daughter," he said, "as well as for my son."

I looked down at the girl. "Miss Stradella."

She glanced at the old man but he was still staring into the coffin. Her eyes came brightly alive in her face. "Wait outside for me!" she whispered.

I stared at her for a second, then nodded and started across the room. I passed the younger son in the outer room. He glowered as I passed and then started toward the alcove. I didn't wait for the elevator. I went down the stairs to the street.

I leaned up against the car, waiting. She came out into the street and I saw her looking for me. "Miss Stradella," I called.

She hurried toward the car. When she reached me, she looked back over her shoulder at the funeral parlor. "Better get into the car. Steve and his father will be coming out any minute now. I don't want them to see me talking to you!"

I opened the door and she got in. I shut the door and went around to the other side. I got in and started the motor. "Where to?"

"Anywhere," she said nervously. "Anywhere away from here."

I cut out into traffic and turned back away from the Embarcadero. We went a good half-mile before she spoke again. Her voice was harsh and tense. "You're looking for the letters?"

I shot a surprised look at her. I hadn't thought it would be this easy. "Do you have them?"

She didn't answer.

"Blackmail's a pretty dirty business," I said. "You can spend more years in jail for it than you've got left."

"I haven't got them, Mr. Carey. But I know who has." Then the tears welled up into her eyes. "Damn Tony and his soul to hell!" she swore angrily. "I never should have listened to him. I should have burned those damned letters as soon as he gave them to me!"

I pulled the car over to the curb and cut the motor. "Who has them?"

She dabbed at her eyes with a handkerchief. She didn't look at me. "My brother."

"Where is he? I want to talk to him."

She still didn't look at me. "I don't know. I gave them to him Friday night. I haven't seen him since."

"You gave them to him?"

"Yes. He tricked me out of them. He came by my apartment at ten-thirty and said Tony had asked him to get the letters. Of course I gave them to him. I was glad to get rid of them. Then at eleven o'clock I heard the news on TV and I knew what he was going to try to do."

"How did you know?"

She looked at me. "Lorenzo was just like Tony. Always with an eye for the big buck. He was in my apartment when Tony gave the letters to me. He heard what Tony said about them. I wanted to burn them then but Tony wouldn't let me. 'Those letters are our insurance policy,' he said. He said that when the time came for him to be free of the old-lady, they'd be his guarantee that we'd have enough money to live on for the rest of our lives.

"Tony could always talk me into anything. He was real good at that. It was always the big deal. Tomorrow. When he went to work for your wife he said it was just a question of time. He couldn't stand her, he said. Just to touch her made him sick but she was crazy about him and when the time was right there would be the money. Always the money. He used to come down to my place to get away from her."

"Did you read the letters?"

She shook her head. "No. He gave them to me in a big brown envelope. It was sealed."

"Did he ever say anything to you about my daughter?"

"No. Wait a minute. Yes, he did. Once, about a year ago. He said the kid was growing up fast and if the mother didn't watch out there'd be a real beauty in the family. And the old lady wouldn't like that."

"He never said anything else?"

"No, nothing else."

"Does anyone besides you and your brother know about the letters? Tony's brothers?"

"Tony and his brothers fought like cats and dogs. They thought he was no good and he thought they were jerks. He never told them anything."

I took out a cigarette and lit it.

"Did Renzo call you?" she asked.

"No. He sent a letter to my former mother-in-law. He said that he'd read the letters and if she wanted them she'd have to pay plenty for them." I looked at her. "Where does your brother live? Maybe we can find him there."

She laughed. "Don't you think I tried that? I went there looking for him. His landlady said he moved out late Friday night. She doesn't know where he went."

"Has he got a girl friend?"

She shook her head. "He runs around a lot but I don't know any of his girls. When Mama died two years ago, Renzo moved out. I only see him when he needs money."

"You live alone?" I asked.

She nodded. She began to cry. "I always thought Tony would come home some day."

He came home all right, I thought, but not the way she'd thought. "I'm sorry, Miss Stradella."

"Don't be. I'm not crying because of Tony. That was over a long time ago. I knew that even if his father didn't. Now, maybe Steve will feel free to speak up. He'd never have dared while Tony was alive."

I thought of the glowering young man I had seen in the funeral parlor. I'd thought there might have been something between them because of the protective way he held her arm. "I'm sure he will."

She dried her eyes again. "What are you going to do about Renzo?"

"Nothing," I said, "if I can locate him and get the letters before Thursday."

"And if you can't?"

I made my voice harsh. "On Thursday, Mrs. Hayden will make her deal with him. When they meet to exchange the letters for the money, I'll be there with the police."

She sat silent for a moment, thinking. "Where can I reach you tomorrow afternoon?"

"I'll be moving around. Better let me call you."

"Okay." She took a small notebook out of her handbag and scribbled a telephone number. She tore the page out and gave it to me. "That's my home number. Call me there at four o'clock. I'll see if I can find Renzo for you."

8

"What do you think, Sally?" Marian Spicer asked, putting the two containers of coffee on the desk between them. "Is the child really disturbed?"

The psychologist opened her container and took a sip of the black coffee. "Of course she's disturbed. If she weren't, she wouldn't be here. Exactly how much, however, is difficult to tell. If you're asking if she's violently disturbed, if she has tendencies toward paranoia, say, I don't think so. At least none that I've been able to discover up to now. Of course there's always the chance that they'll reveal themselves later."

"She's still not talking?"

"Not very much. I did learn one thing, though."

Marian looked at her questioningly.

"It's not much. But at least it's a place to start. Dani seems to have a strong need of reassurance about her mother's love for her."

"That seems to indicate a sense of guilt toward her mother."

The psychologist smiled. "Come now, Marian. You know better than to jump to conclusions like that. A certain amount of guilt toward your parents is inevitable."

"I mean guilt over a specific act."

"What you really mean is that Dani feels guilty about taking away her mother's lover?"

"Yes. First sexually, then physically, by death."

Sally Jennings lit a cigarette and took another sip of

coffee. "Part of what you say is right, of course. But it's recent and not necessarily conclusive. What we are looking for is something basic, something buried inside Dani that she's reluctant having us know about. If we could pry that out of her, we'd have an idea which way to go."

"Judge Murphy had me get a transcript of the parents' divorce proceedings."

"Oh?" Sally's eyebrows went up. "What did you find out?"

"Nothing much. You know how those things are. Everything is arranged before they get into court. But there was one thing. At the very end of the hearing, Dani's mother tried to cut Colonel Carey out of any visiting privileges."

"That's normal in a way. Every parent is jealous of the other parent."

"But she gave a beaut of a reason. She said that Colonel Carey was not really Dani's father."

Sally sat thoughtfully for a moment.

"What are you thinking, Sally?"

"Not about that. That doesn't surprise me. Nothing surprises me any more when two parents meet in a divorce court. What I'm wondering is whether Dani knows it."

"Do you think she might?"

"Children have a way of learning the best-kept secrets. If she does know we could be on the completely wrong track." Sally looked at the probation officer. "If she'd only loosen up. Then, at least, I'd know what to recommend."

"And if she doesn't?"

"You know the answer to that one as well as I do, Marian. I'd have to send her up to Perkins for ninety days' observation."

Marian didn't answer.

"There's nothing else I could do. We can't afford to take any chances. We must be certain that the child isn't really disturbed, perhaps even paranoid, before we dare let her resume anything remotely resembling a normal life."

Marian heard the frustration in the psychologist's voice. "Maybe you won't have to. Maybe she'll start talking this afternoon."

"I hope so," Sally said fervently. "When do you see Dani's mother?"

"This afternoon. I'd better get moving."

Later that afternoon Marian followed the butler through the large foyer, past a beautiful circular marble staircase, down a hallway that led to another wing of the house. It was a beautiful home, she thought, not like the usual places she came to during her investigations. Everything about it reflected the artistic sense of values of its owner.

At the end of the hallway, the butler opened a door. "Go right in, madam. Miss Hayden's expecting you."

The studio was large and sunny, the north wall a solid sheet of glass. Through it Marian could see the harbor, the Bay Bridge and beyond that Oakland.

Nora was working in front of the window, an arc welder, spitting a flame, in her hand. Her face was covered with a heavy protective mask and glasses. She wore a faded and stained pair of coveralls and thick gloves. She glanced toward Marian. "I'll be just a moment," she said, her voice muffled by the mask.

Marian nodded and stood watching her. She was working with thin strips of metal, quickly welding them across the basic framework of an armature. The outline was still too indefinite for Marian to be able to determine what it was intended to be. She turned and glanced around the studio.

Scattered on tables were various sculptures and statues, all in different stages of work. Wood, stone, metal, wire. Anything and everything that lent itself to shaping by the human hand. On one large wall was a series of framed photographs and drawings. Marian walked over to look at them.

There was one large charcoal sketch, the original drawing of the statue of *The Dying Man,* which was now in the Guggenheim Museum in New York. Next to it was a photograph of *Woman in the Net,* which had won Nora the Eliofheim Award. Higher on the wall was a giant mural photograph of the stone bas-relief *Peaceful Is a Woman's World,* commissioned by the United Nations. There were also sketches and photographs of other works, but those were the three Marian recognized.

She heard a metallic sound and turned. Nora was cutting off the flame of the welding arc. It went out in a burst of blue and she put down the torch. She pushed the mask up on her head and pulled off her gloves. "I'm sorry about holding you up, Miss Spicer. But some things just won't wait."

Marian didn't answer. She waited for the next question. The inevitable one. How is Dani? It didn't come.

Instead, Nora took off the mask, her hand leaving a black smudge on her cheek. "I'm way behind in my work. This whole affair has raised hell with my production schedule."

"I'll try not to hold you up too long," Marian said.

Nora looked at her and Marian wondered if she had sensed the sarcasm underlying the words. "We'll have tea while we talk." She pressed a button on the wall near her workbench.

Almost immediately the butler opened the door. "Yes, mum?"

"We'll have tea, Charles."

He nodded and closed the door. Nora crossed to a small couch arranged in a conversation grouping with a few chairs and a coffee table. "Please sit down."

Marian sat down opposite her.

"I suppose you want me to tell you about Dani."

Marian nodded.

"I don't really know what to say." Nora took a cigarette from a box on the coffee table. "Dani is really a very ordinary child."

Marian couldn't be sure whether Nora said this with approval or disapproval. It almost sounded as if she considered it some sort of failing. " 'Ordinary' varies from child to child," she said. "We've already learned from our examinations that Dani is a highly intelligent and perceptive child."

Nora looked at her. "Is she? I'm glad to hear that."

"You seem surprised."

"I am, in a way," Nora admitted. "But then I suppose no parent is truly aware of the capability of her own children."

Marian didn't answer. Parents who were interested were aware. "Tell me about Dani's behavior at home generally. I already have a pretty good idea of how she behaved at school."

Nora looked at Marian with curiosity. "You went to Miss Randolph's this morning?"

Marian nodded. "They seem to like her very much there. Both the teachers and Dani's fellow pupils seemed to think she was a very nice girl."

She didn't add that they thought it strange that Dani never expressed much interest in the usual activities of the girls there. As a matter of fact she was known as a loner. She seemed to prefer the company of adults to that of her own age group, though at parties or dances she mingled very well.

"I'm glad to hear that," Nora said.

The butler came in and they were silent while the tea was served. When Charles bowed and left, Nora looked across at Marian. "Where shall I begin?"

"Anywhere you like. The more we know about Dani, the better equipped we'll be to help her."

Nora nodded. "Dani led an ordinary life here at home. Until a few years ago she had a nurse—a governess who had been with her since she was a baby. Then Dani decided she was getting too old for that, so I let her go."

"She decided?" Marian asked. "You mean Dani?"

"Yes. She felt she wasn't a child any longer."

"Who looked after her then?"

"Dani was always quite self-sufficient. Violet, that's my maid, looked after her clothes just as she did mine. Outside of that, Dani didn't seem to need any special attention."

"Did she go out much?" Marian asked, "I mean with girls and boys her own age?"

Nora thought for a moment. "Not that I can recall. But then I've been very busy, you know. I didn't keep track of Dani's social life. I remembered how much I used to resent my mother's always asking me where I'd been. I didn't want Dani to go through that. Once, a few months ago, she came in from a party and I asked her how it had been. She said all right, but when I asked her what they'd done, she said the usual things. Danced and played games. Then she looked at me in an odd way and said in a peeved voice, 'You know the things, Mother. Kid games. They're so dull and childish, I'm bored with them.' I knew just what she meant. I felt the same way when I was her age."

"How did she get along with Mr. Riccio?" Marian asked.

Nora gave her a curious glance. "Fine," she said quickly. Much too quickly, Marian thought. Something evasive seemed to come into her voice. "She liked Rick very much. But then she always seemed to like my friends much better than her own."

"You mean male friends?"

Nora hesitated, then nodded. "I suppose so. I don't have many women friends, because of my work."

"Do you think Dani might have formed some kind of attachment for Mr. Riccio?"

Again the slight hesitation. "It's possible. Dani always seemed to favor men. I remembered how much she liked my second husband. When Rick came into the house she may have transferred that feeling to him. I suppose it was some kind of a father thing."

Marian nodded.

"Her father stopped coming to see her when Dani was about eight, you know. She was very upset about it. No matter how many times I tried to explain why he didn't come."

"I've been curious about that," Marian said. "Exactly what was the reason he gave for stopping the visits?"

"I can't really say. He was drinking a great deal at the time. We'd been divorced because of his excessive drinking. And in the years immediately afterward he seemed to get worse. Drinking more heavily than ever and living in La Jolla, on a boat he rented out for charter. I guess after a while it just got to be too much trouble to come to San Francisco to see Dani."

"I see," Marian said. "And what did you tell Dani?"

"That her father was busy and couldn't get time off

from his work to come and see her. What else could I
say?"

"Did Dani ever mention any boy or boys that she was
particularly interested in?"

Nora shook her head. "I don't think so."

"Any man perhaps?"

It seemed to Marian that Nora's face paled slightly.
"Exactly what are you getting at, Miss Spicer?"

Marian watched her steadily. "I'm trying to find out
whom Dani may have had sexual relations with."

Nora's face was now definitely pale. "You mean?"

Marian nodded.

"My God!" Nora was silent for a moment. "She's
not—"

"No, she's not pregnant."

Nora let out a sigh of relief. She forced a smile. "At
least we can be thankful for that."

Marian noticed the hint of tears in the corners of her
eyes. For the first time she began to feel sorry for the
woman opposite her. "Do you think it might have been
Mr. Riccio?" she asked.

"No!" Nora said sharply. Then she hesitated. "I mean
—I don't know what to think. The fact that she has at
all is quite a shock."

"It always is."

Nora's voice was almost normal again. "I suppose so.
It's always a surprise to find that your child is so much
more grown-up than you realized."

That was a good way to put it, Marian thought. No
hysterics, no condemnation, no blame. Just much more
grown-up. "Was she alone with Mr. Riccio very often?"

"I suppose so. After all, he lived here."

"But you had no idea that anything was going on
between them?"

"No," Nora said definitely. "None at all." She looked

at Marian, quick concern in her eyes. "Did—did Dani say anything?"

Marian shook her head. "Dani won't talk. That's one of the things that makes it so difficult. Dani won't talk about anything at all."

She thought she saw some of the color come back into Nora's face. "More tea, Miss Spicer?" Nora asked, the politeness coming back into her voice.

"No, thank you."

Nora refilled her own cup. "What do you think they will do with Dani?"

"That's hard to say," Marian answered. "It's completely up to the court. Right now there's a good chance she may be sent to the Northern California Reception Center at Perkins for observation. The psychiatrists here can't get enough out of her to make a recommendation."

"But Dani's not insane!"

"Of course not," Marian Spicer said quickly. "But she did kill a man. That may indicate paranoia." She watched Nora closely.

"That's ridiculous! Dani's no more insane than I am!"

That might be the truth, Marian thought to herself. Almost immediately she felt a sense of self-reproach. She had no right to pass that kind of judgment.

"I'll send in some doctors of my own selection," Nora said suddenly.

"That's your right, Miss Hayden. And it might be helpful. Perhaps a doctor of your own selection might more easily gain Dani's confidence."

Nora put down her teacup. Marian knew the interview was over. "Is there any other information I can give you, Miss Spicer?"

Marian shook her head. "I don't think so, Miss Hayden." She started to rise. "There is one more thing."

"Yes."

"Could I see Dani's room?"

Nora nodded. "I'll have Charles show it to you."

Marian followed the butler up the circular marble stairway. "How is Miss Dani, ma'am?" Charles asked over his shoulder.

"She's all right."

They reached the top of the stairs and started down the hall. Charles stopped in front of a door. "This is Miss Dani's room."

He opened the door and Marian went in. As Charles followed her into the room, Nora's voice came from the house interphone on the wall. "Charles."

"Yes, mum."

"Would you ask Violet to show Dani's room to Miss Spicer? I have an errand for you."

"At once, mum." The butler turned toward the doorway just as the colored maid appeared. "You heard the madam?"

Violet nodded. "Yes, suh."

Charles bowed and left the room. The maid came in and closed the door behind her. Marian stood in the center of the room and looked around.

It was a beautiful room. There was a canopied four-poster on a small platform against the far wall. Television and radio and record player were all in one unit against the opposite wall. Marian didn't have to look to know that they could be operated by remote control from the headboard of the bed.

The curtains were a bright yellow chintz, the bed-spread the same matching material. Near the window was a desk, on top of which were a portable typewriter and some books. There were also a dresser, a chest of drawers and several chairs.

Marian turned to the maid. "Didn't Dani have any pictures or pinups on the wall?"

The maid shook her head. "No'm. Miss Dani didn' go for things like that."

"What's in there?" Marian asked, pointing to a double door in the opposite wall.

"That's the closet. Her own bathroom is through that other door."

Marian opened the closet and looked in. A light went on as soon as the door opened. There were rows of dresses hanging neatly, and shoes on a circular revolving rack. She closed the doors and heard the click as the interior light went out.

"Where does Miss Dani keep her personal things?"

"Over there in the dressuh."

Marian opened the top drawer and looked in. It too was neatly arranged—handkerchiefs and stockings in separate compartments. The same held true for the other drawers. Brassieres, panties, slips. All were neatly folded.

Marian went over to the desk and opened a drawer. Pencils, pens, paper, everything neat and orderly. She wondered about the usual teen-age mess. This didn't seem much like a child's room. She looked at the maid. "Does she keep her room like this all the time?"

The maid nodded. "Yes'm. She's very neat. She don' like havin' her things messed up."

"What does she keep in there?" Marian asked, indicating the chest of drawers.

"She call that her treasure chest. She keep it locked all the time."

"Do you have a key?"

The girl shook her head.

"Would her mother?"

"No'm. Miss Dani always kep' the key herself."

"Would you know where it is?"

The maid looked at Marian for a moment, then nodded.

"Could I have it, please?"

The maid hesitated. "Miss Dani won' like it."

Marian smiled. "It's all right. You can ask her mother."

The maid looked doubtful for a moment, then walked over to the headboard of the bed and stuck her hand behind it. She came up with a key which she handed to Marian.

Marian unlocked the chest of drawers. All the pictures and photographs were in here. Maybe they weren't on the walls but Dani had kept them. Quickly she leafed through them. There were pictures of her father taken years ago, when he was still in uniform. And of her mother, one of them the cover picture from *Life* magazine, dated 1944. There were several of herself alone and with her parents, pictures of a boat. Marian could just read the name on the white bow. *The Dani Girl*.

The second drawer was filled with newspaper clippings about her mother. Dani had arranged them neatly so that they formed a chronological history of her mother's career.

The third drawer contained exactly the same thing as the second. Only here her father was the subject. Marian glanced through the items briefly, thinking that the child must have spent a great deal of time gathering all this material. Much of it dated back to even before she was born.

The bottom drawer at first seemed to be filled with junk. There were several broken toys. Child's toys. A worn and faded wool Teddy bear with one glass eye missing. And a green leather box. Marian took it out and opened it.

It contained a single eight-by-fourteen glossy photograph of a smiling, very handsome young man. The writing across the corner was in black India ink.

To My Baby With Love. It was signed *Rick*.

When Marian picked up the photograph to study it, she noticed a small metal container underneath. The bold dark lettering jumped up at her: AMERICA'S FINEST.

She didn't have to open it to know what was inside. She had seen enough of them. It seemed to be the teen-ager's favorite brand. They could buy them in almost any public restroom in the country by inserting a fifty-cent coin in a vending machine.

9

Sally Jennings looked up from her desk as Dani came into the small office. "Sit down, Dani." She pushed a package of cigarettes toward her. "I'll only be a few minutes. I have to finish this report."

Dani took a cigarette and lit it. She sat watching the psychologist's pen flying over the lined yellow notepaper. After a few moments she tired of that and looked out the window. It was late in the afternoon and the bright yellow sun had begun to pick up faint tinges of orange. Suddenly she wished she were outside.

Idly she wondered what day it was. She seemed to have lost all track of time. She glanced at the calendar on the wall. Wednesday. She had come in Saturday, so today was her fifth day. She stirred restlessly in her seat. It seemed like a very long time.

She looked up at the sky. It would be nice to be outside. She wondered what it was like on the street. Whether there were many people out walking; whether the traffic was heavy; even how the sidewalks would feel against the soles of her shoes. She wished that she could see the street. But she couldn't. Not from any of these rooms. The windows were too small and high up.

She glanced at Miss Jennings again but she was still writing, a furrow of concentration knotting her brow. Dani wondered how long she would have to sit before the psychologist was through. She looked up at the sky again. There were small orange-tinted clouds scudding by, high up. She remembered clouds like that once in

Acapulco. High in the sky over the cliffs, where the boys leaped with flaming torches at night into the sea.

There had been a boy there. He had smiled at her, his white teeth flashing in his dark face. And she had smiled back at him. Rick had been angry.

"Don't give any of those greasers the come-on like that," he'd said.

She'd looked at him with the look of wide-eyed innocence that always made him even more angry. She knew that he thought it made her look more like her mother than ever. "Why not?" she'd asked. "He seems like a nice boy."

"You don't know these boys. They're not like other boys. They'll bother you. They don't know you're still a kid."

She smiled sweetly. "Why not, Rick?"

She'd seen his eyes dart over her white bathing suit. He flushed. She knew why he flushed. She'd caught him looking at her like that many times. "Why not, Rick?"

"Because you don't look like a kid, that's why," he'd said angrily. "You don't look like thirteen."

"How old do I look, Rick?"

She saw him look again. It was almost involuntary on his part. "You're a big girl. Seventeen, maybe eighteen."

She'd smiled at him, then turned to look at the boy because she knew that would make Rick even angrier.

Just then her mother had come up. "Damn it, Rick. Scaasi wants me to fly up to San Francisco tonight to sign those contracts."

"Do you have to?"

"I have to."

"I'll go pack our bags," Rick said, scrambling to his feet.

"No, there's no need for all of us to go. You and Dani stay here. I'll be back by lunchtime tomorrow."

"I'll go to the airport with you."

Dani got to her feet. "I'll go too, Mother."

When they came out of the airport, after the plane had taken off, they passed a souvenir shop, one of those tourist traps that sold everything from cheap jewelry to peasant skirts and blouses. Dani had looked in the window at the skirts.

"Would you like one?" Rick asked.

They'd gone inside and he'd bought her a blouse and skirt. She wore them that evening for dinner, her hair hanging to her shoulders in a sort of Mexican page-boy style.

She saw his eyes widen. "How do you like it?" she asked.

"I like it real fine. But—"

"But what?"

"Your mother. I wonder what she'll think."

Dani had laughed. "Mother won't like it at all. Mother would like to keep me a baby forever but she can't."

They went out for dinner and the waiter asked if she'd like a cocktail, just as if she were grown-up. And later, when the orchestra began to play, she asked Rick to dance with her.

It had been real dreamy. Not like dancing with the boys from school. She liked the smell of him, the faint cologne, the light aroma of whiskey on his breath. She pressed very close to him. She liked the feeling of strength in his arms as he held her. She sighed and moved her hips sensuously with the beat of the Latin music.

Suddenly he missed a step and cursed, then abruptly drew away from her. "I think we'd better sit down."

Obediently she let him lead her back to the table. He

ordered another drink and sipped it quickly. He didn't speak.

After a moment, she said, "Don't be embarrassed. I've seen it happen to you when you danced with Mother."

He gave her a peculiar look. "Sometimes I think you see too damn much."

"I'm glad it happened. Now I'm sure I'm grown-up."

He flushed and looked at his watch. "It's after eleven o'clock. Time you were in bed."

She lay stretched out on the bed, listening to the night sounds coming in from the open windows. The lush tropical sounds of birds and crickets and creaking trees and rustling palms. Then she heard the telephone ring in his room. In a little while there was silence again.

Abruptly she got out of bed and walked across the living room of the suite to his door. She stood listening for a moment. There was no sound from the other side. She turned the knob gently and went in. In the dark she could see that the door to her mother's room, just beyond, was open. She turned and looked at his bed. "Was that Mother?"

He'd turned on his side, the sheet pulled halfway up. "Yes."

"What did she want?"

"Nothing. She said she'd be back tomorrow."

She moved closer to the side of his bed and looked down at him. "She was checking up on you. Mother doesn't like to take any chances. It's a good thing you were in."

"I do what I please," he said angrily.

"Yeah," she said. "Sure."

"Don't you think you'd better go back to bed now?"

"I'm not sleepy."

"You can't stay in here. I haven't anything on under this sheet."

"I know," she said. "Even in the dark I can see that."

He sat up in the bed. She could see the muscles in his arms and chest ripple as he moved. His voice was hoarse. "Don't be a fool. You're still a kid."

She moved closer and sat down on the edge of the bed. "You didn't think so this afternoon when that boy smiled at me. You were jealous."

"I was not."

"And you didn't think I was a kid when we were dancing." She opened her pajama top. She saw his eyes turn toward her breasts as if drawn by a magnet. She smiled. "Do I look like a kid?"

He stared into her face without speaking.

She put her hand on the sheet. He caught it in a tight grip. "What are you doing?" he asked in an almost shocked voice.

"What are you afraid of?" A challenging look came into her eyes. "Mother will never know."

He stared into her eyes as she raised his hand to her breasts. "I'll hurt you," he whispered.

"I know about that. But it's only the first time."

He seemed incapable of movement. "You're worse than your mother!"

She laughed and suddenly slipped her hand under the sheet. "Don't be a fool, Rick. I'm not a kid any more, I know that you love me. I've seen the way you've been looking at me."

"I look at lots of girls," he said.

She let her fingers caress him gently.

"Dani." Miss Jennings' voice reached into her reverie. "Dani."

She turned toward the psychologist. "Yes, Miss Jennings?"

The gray-haired woman smiled. "You were far away. What were you thinking about?"

Dani could feel the flush creep up into her face. "I—I was thinking how nice it was outside."

The psychologist looked at her. Dani had the feeling that somehow Miss Jennings knew what she had been thinking about and the flush grew hotter in her cheeks. "You'd think about it too if you had to stay in this place all the time!"

Sally Jennings nodded. "I suppose so," she said thoughtfully. "But I don't have to. And you do."

"I won't have to for long! Only until next week. Then I'll be home again!"

"Do you really believe that, Dani?"

Dani stared at her. For the first time she began to feel doubts rise in her. "That's what everybody told me."

"Who?" Miss Jennings' voice was calm. "Your parents?"

Dani didn't answer.

"Apparently you didn't pay much attention to what Judge Murphy said to you in court. It isn't up to your parents. It's the judge who decides what you'll do. And he can just as easily keep you here or even send you to Perkins for observation as send you home. It's up to him to decide what's best for you."

"He can't keep me here," Dani retorted.

"What makes you say that, Dani?" Miss Jennings asked. "Isn't the reason you were brought here sufficient in itself to keep you here?"

Dani looked down at the floor. "But I didn't mean to do it," she said sullenly.

"Merely saying you didn't mean to isn't enough to convince Judge Murphy that he should send you home. Every child brought in here says the same thing." Miss Jennings reached for a cigarette. "You have to show him by your actions that you won't get into any more trouble if he lets you go home."

She shuffled the papers on her desk. "I'm just closing the file on a girl who's been here several times before. This time the judge is sending her away. She hasn't proven herself trustworthy." She looked at Dani. "I think you know her. She's in the room next to yours."

"You mean Sylvia?"

Miss Jennings nodded her head.

"Why?" Dani asked. "She's a nice girl."

"Maybe she is to you. But she's always getting into trouble."

"Her only trouble is that she's boy crazy."

Miss Jennings smiled. "That's one of her troubles," she said. "She's promiscuous. This is the third time she's been here. Each time she's been found with another boy and each time she talked that boy into stealing a car so they could go for a ride. She's not only careless about her own morals but she's a bad influence on anyone she comes into contact with."

"What are they going to do with her?"

"She'll probably be sent to a correctional home until she's eighteen."

Dani was silent.

"I tried to help her. But she wouldn't let me. She thought she knew everything. But she didn't, did she?"

"I guess not," Dani admitted.

Miss Jennings pushed the stack of papers to one side and picked up another sheet of paper, which she held so that Dani could read it. "I've a report from Miss Spicer," she said, pressing with her knee the button of the tape recorder built into the desk. "She went out to Miss Randolph's today and after that she talked with your mother."

"Yes?" Dani said politely.

"The teachers and your fellow pupils at school seem to think a great deal of you. They say you got along very well with everyone."

"That's nice."

"Your mother was very surprised to learn that you were having sexual relations with Mr. Riccio."

Dani's voice went tight with anger. "Who said that?"

"It's true, isn't it?"

"It's not true!" Dani retorted. "Whoever said so is a liar!"

"Then what were you doing with these?" Miss Jennings took a small metal container from her desk. "They were found in a box under his picture."

Dani glared at her. "It's Violet!" she said angrily. "She knew where I kept the key."

"Who's Violet?"

"My mother's maid. She's always sneaking around spying on me!"

"You're not answering my question, Dani," Miss Jennings' said sharply. "If it wasn't Mr. Riccio, then who was it?"

"Why does it have to be anybody?" Dani retorted. "Just because I happened to have some of those in a drawer?"

"You forget, Dani. You were examined by a doctor when you came in." She picked up another sheet of paper. "Do you want me to read what she said?"

"You don't have to," Dani said sullenly. "That could have happened from horseback riding."

"You know better than that. That's the oldest one in the book." She leaned forward. "I'm only trying to help you, Dani. I don't want the judge to send you away, like Sylvia."

Dani stared at her silently.

"Tell me what happened? Did he rape you?" She

looked at Dani earnestly. "If he did, tell me. It might help the judge understand why you did what you did. He'd take that into consideration in making his decision."

Dani was silent for a moment, staring into the woman's eyes. "Yes," she finally admitted in a low voice, "he raped me."

Sally Jennings stared back at her. She didn't speak.

"Well?" Dani asked. "Isn't that what you wanted me to say?"

The psychologist leaned back with a sigh of frustration. "No, Dani. I wanted you to tell me the truth. But you're not. You're lying." She pressed the button again, this time turning the recorder off. "I can't help you when you lie to me."

Dani's eyes fell. "I don't want to talk about it, Miss Jennings. I don't even want to think about anything that happened before. I just want to forget about the whole thing."

"It won't happen that easily, Dani. The only way you'll ever be free of what's troubling you is to bring it out in the open and face it squarely. Then you'll understand why you did what you did and you'll know how to keep it from happening again."

Dani didn't answer.

The psychologist pressed the buzzer to summon a matron. "All right, Dani," she said in a weary voice. "You may go."

Dani got to her feet. "The same time tomorrow, Miss Jennings?"

"I don't think so, Dani. I think we've about accomplished all that we can. There wouldn't be any point in further discussions, would there?"

Dani looked at her. "I guess not, Miss Jennings."

"Of course, I'll be here if you should want to talk to me."

"Yes, Miss Jennings."

There was a knock at the glass door. The psychologist got to her feet. "Good luck, Dani."

"Thank you, Miss Jennings." Dani started for the door, then turned back. "Miss Jennings?"

"Yes, Dani?"

"About Sylvia," Dani said. "Don't you think she'd never have gotten into trouble if all the boys she knew had their own cars?"

Miss Jennings suppressed an involuntary smile. That was as good a cure for certain kinds of juvenile delinquency as any. Give them all their own cars. "I don't think so," she said, keeping as straight a face as she could. "You see, what Sylvia did was wrong. If it wasn't cars she wanted the boys to steal, it would have been something else. What Sylvia was really doing was making them prove that they were worthy of her favors. She felt that if they'd do something really wrong, then she wouldn't feel that what she was doing was so bad. That's the way she justified her own behavior."

"I see," Dani said thoughtfully. She looked at the psychologist. "Maybe I'll see you again before I go?"

"Any time, Dani," Miss Jennings answered. "I'll be here."

10

The Barbary Coast is nothing but a series of dirty gray buildings that are used mostly as warehouses and small factories now. Scattered among them is an occasional night club, struggling for existence, trading on the sin and glamor of the long-gone past. The best of these are in street-level stores and go in for jazz. Far-out combos or Chicago and New Orleans style.

They attract the *aficionados* and the college kids, who sit around in a kind of reverie listening to the outlandish sounds produced in the name of a new art form. The worst of them are imitations of the plusher traps out at North Beach. Second-rate Hungry I's or overripe Purple Onions.

The Money Tree fitted into the latter category. I looked at my watch as I stopped in front of the place. It was almost midnight. There was a long narrow photograph on either side of the door. Both pictures were exactly the same. A heavy-set, leering old woman, dressed in a tight-fitting sequined evening gown four sizes too small for her tightly corseted figure, and with a mouthful of the latest thing in dentures. The lettering over the pictures was large: MAUDE MACKENZIE INSIDE!

If I'd been in the market for entertainment that picture would have been the last thing in the world to entice me. But I wasn't. This was where Anna Stradella worked and I'd agreed to meet her after the last show. She was the club photographer.

"Go on in, buddy," the doorman said. "The show's just about to start."

I looked at him. "I think I will."

He leered at me and winked. "If you get nervous sitting by yourself in the dark," he said, "just tell your waiter that Max said for him to take care of you."

"Thanks," I said and went inside.

Like the street outside was dark, inside was really dark. Your own hands looked like they belonged to somebody else. The white shirt front of the headwaiter gleamed from the gloom. "Do you have a reservation, sir?"

I grinned to myself. I could see enough white tablecloths to do a good-sized TV commercial. "No. That's all right. I'll sit at the bar."

"I'm sorry, sir," he said smoothly, "we don't serve at the bar except on weekends."

They really hustled you in this joint. Business had to be way off if the three extra bucks they got for the linen was that important.

"I have a nice table right up in front."

He had nothing but nice tables right up front.

Maybe about ten tables out of the sixty were occupied. He held the chair while I sat down, then hung around waiting for bread. I gave him a single and he blew. Maybe he wasn't very happy with it, but it was better than getting stiffed.

The waiter climbed on my back and I ordered a bourbon. I didn't have to add water. Apparently they put it right in the bottle. I sipped at the drink and looked around. I didn't see Anna Stradella anywhere.

I'd called her that afternoon like she'd told me to.

"Did you locate your brother?" I'd asked.

"Not yet. I expect to hear something tonight though."

"I can call you later."

"I don't get home until late. Maybe you'd better pick me up where I work. Then if I have any information maybe we can act on it right away."

"Okay, where is it?"

"The Money Tree. It's a night club on—"

"I know where it is," I'd said. The surprise must have shown in my voice.

"I'm the club photographer. I work for the concessionaire. From five to eight I work the dinner hour at one of the restaurants on the Wharf. From nine o'clock on I'm at the club."

"What time is the last show?"

"There are only two shows tonight. Ten and midnight. The last show should be over a few minutes after one."

"I'll pick you up there then."

"Good. You'd better come inside. Then if I don't know anything, I can let you know and I won't hold you up."

"Okay."

"And don't give your car to the doorman. They stick you for a two-buck service charge. It's a real trap. There's plenty of room to park in the next block."

"Thanks."

Then I'd put down the telephone and dialed my former mother-in-law.

"She doesn't know where he is yet. I'm supposed to meet her later, and if she knows, she'll take me to him."

"The morning papers will be out by then. The ad will be in already. He'll know we're willing to buy."

"What do you want to do?" I'd asked.

"I want those letters. Make a deal with him if you have to. We can't take any chances on their getting into the wrong hands."

"They're in the wrong hands already."

"Don't do anything to make it worse."

"I won't."

"What are you doing tomorrow afternoon?"

"Nothing that I know of," I said.

"Nora and Gordon are coming over here. We have to present a plan for Dani to the court. Dr. Bonner and the headmaster of Dani's school will be here too. I thought you might want to come over."

"What time?"

"Three-thirty."

"I'll be there."

"You'll let me know what happens tonight? Call me no matter how late it is."

"Will do."

It was another half-hour before Maude Mackenzie came on. By that time a few more suckers had drifted in and now the room was about a third full.

Maude Mackenzie looked exactly like the pictures outside. She came on in the white glare of the spot, looked around the room, counting the house, then sat down at the piano and declared that this was what she liked—working small intimate parties. At her age she couldn't take the big things like circuses.

The audience laughed, but I could see she was disgruntled. She must have been working on percentage and this show was practically for free.

She immediately launched into a song about the good old days and how she'd worked her way to the Barbary Coast in a covered wagon. I looked at the old bag sweating in the spotlight and thought to myself how much better it would have been if the Indians had got her.

"Would you like a nice picture of yourself, sir?"

I turned and in the spill-over from the spot Anna Stradella looked like she'd come out of an Italian movie. The brief costume and the long opera-length black net hose did it. Broad shoulders, deep bosom, narrow waist and wide comfortable hips. *La Dolce Vita*. Sophia Loren making it the hard way.

I started to shake my head.

She smiled. "Let me take your picture." Then under her breath she whispered quickly, "My boss is watching. I got to have a reason to keep on talking."

"Okay," I said. "But make it a good one."

She smiled and did something with the camera. Held it up to her face, fiddled with the view finder. She leaned over me. Now I knew what those Italian girls did with all that pasta. "Turn your chair like this," she said aloud, pushing me to the left. She checked the view finder again. "That's better."

She backed away and held the camera up to her face. The flashbulb went off and I blinked the red and green spots out of my eyes. She came back to the table.

"I'll write on the back of the picture where you should pick me up," she whispered.

"You find him?"

She nodded and straightened up. I saw her eyes flicker and sensed rather than saw the man walking by. "That's fine, sir. It'll be ready in about fifteen minutes."

She turned and walked away. I watched her for a moment. This would have been the last job I'd have figured her for when I met her in the funeral parlor. But then you never can tell, can you?

"Another drink, sir?" the waiter asked.

I looked up and nodded. What the hell, they were half water anyway. The rest of the show was as bad as the opening song. Maude Mackenzie was no Pearl Williams or Belle Barth but she was just as rough. And the customers who were there didn't seem to mind. They ate it up. At that I guess it was better than TV on an off Wednesday night.

It was one-forty-five when I pulled the car into the

800 block on Jackson and parked under a street lamp. I cut the engine and looked down at the picture again. It wasn't a bad picture considering where it had been taken. I turned it over. The writing had been made with a soft pencil, the kind photographers use for retouching. The words scribbled hastily—*800 block on Jackson St.*

I put the picture down on the seat beside me and lit a cigarette. She came along about ten minutes later, getting out of a taxi on the corner behind me. I looked in the rear-view mirror when I heard the door slam.

She spotted my car right away and came toward it. She had a camera case slung over her shoulder on a long leather strap and it flopped against her side as she walked. I leaned over and pushed the door open.

"What did you find out?" I asked when she was inside.

Her eyes were troubled. "I don't like it, Mr. Carey. Renzo isn't in this alone. Maybe it would be better if we didn't interfere."

"Did you find out where he's staying?" I asked impatiently.

She nodded.

I turned on the motor. "Let's go, then. Which way?"

"Renzo has an apartment over a saloon out near the Cliff House."

I put the car into gear and we moved out. I glanced at her. Her face still wore the troubled expression. "Why all the mystery?"

"I told you, my brother isn't in this alone. There are some very important people involved."

"You mean he thought the job was too big for him?" I asked sarcastically.

"Yes. He went to a friend of his who was also a very good friend of Tony's."

"Who's the guy?"

"Charley Coriano."

I glanced at her. Her face was impassive. If she was right, the kid had gone into the big time. Charley Coriano had the reputation of being in on every crooked racket in San Francisco. Of course nobody had ever proved it, any more than they'd ever pinned anything bigger than a tax rap on Mickey Cohen. But the reputation was still there.

"Where did you hear that?"

"At work. One of the girls told me."

"How would she know?"

"She's the girl friend of one of Coriano's boys."

"So why would she tell you?"

She looked at me. "She thought I was in on it. Coriano owns the concession company I work for."

"Then who has the letters? Coriano or your brother?"

"I don't know."

"Well, there's only one way to find out."

"I don't want my brother to get hurt."

"That's up to him," I said. "I didn't choose his friends, he did."

It had been a long time since I had been out this way. Not since I'd taken Dani out to Sutro's to see the mechanicals when she was still a baby. I remembered how crazy she used to be about them. I slid into an open parking space and looked around.

Nothing had changed. The same hot-dog stands and pizza parlors and cheap bars. Only the beer and the hot dogs were a quarter now, instead of a dime.

She gestured toward a saloon. "We'll look in there first. He hangs around there a lot."

I followed her into the saloon. It was late and the bar wasn't very busy. A couple of diehards nursing their goodnight shot and some kids drinking beer.

The bartender came over, swishing the bar with his towel. "Hello, Anna."

"Hello, Johnny. Was Renzo in here tonight?"

His eyes flicked over me briefly and then went back to her. "He was in earlier. But he went out."

"Thanks, Johnny." She turned to leave but he called her back.

"I'm sorry about Tony. He was a nice guy. I always liked him."

"Thanks, Johnny," she said again.

I followed her outside. "Where now?"

"Down this alley and up the stairs at the back of the building."

I started for the alley, but her hand on my arm stopped me. "Let's not go," she said, looking into my eyes. "That bartender was warning us."

"What makes you say that?"

"He tipped me off when he talked about Tony like that. I know he hated his guts. They had a fight once and he almost killed Tony."

I stared at her. "Coriano own that place too?"

She nodded. "Maybe we better just let them settle this their own way." She kept her hand on my arm. "You're a nice man. I wouldn't like to see you get hurt."

"It's my daughter's future they're playing around with. You don't have to come up with me, if you don't want to. You can wait in the car."

"No," she said nervously, her hand tugging at the strap of the camera case. "I'll go with you."

I looked at her. "Why didn't you leave that in the car? There's no sense lugging a heavy camera around."

"They steal anything around here," she said. "This camera cost me two hundred bucks."

11

It was a wooden stairway and it went up the outside of the building. Our footsteps echoed hollowly as we climbed to the top. A strip of light seeped through the bottom of a wood door. I knocked on it.

There was a scuffle of footsteps behind the door. "Who is it?"

I looked at Anna.

"It's me, Anna," she said. "Let me in, Renzo."

I heard a muffled curse and the door started to open. "How the hell did you find out where I was?" he asked harshly. Then he saw me and started to close it.

I put my foot in the crack and pushed. He reeled back into the room. He stared at me, his dark eyes blinking. He had the same kind of good looks that his sister had, only on him it didn't fit. It looked too soft. He was wearing dark, tightly fitted continental slacks and a T shirt.

"Who's this guy?"

"This is Mr. Carey, Renzo," Anna said. "He came about the letters."

A girl's voice came from a back room. "Who is it, sweetie?"

"My sister and a friend."

"A friend? I'll be right out."

"Don't rush yourself," he said sullenly. He looked at me. "What letters is she talking about?"

I pushed the door shut behind me with my foot. "The letters in the manila envelope she gave you the night Tony Riccio was killed."

"She's full of crap. I don't know nothin' about no letters."

I looked over at a table behind him. A copy of the next morning's *Examiner* lay open on it. "You know the letters I'm talking about. The same ones you wrote Mrs. Hayden about." I saw a typewriter in a corner of the room. "You wrote her on that typewriter."

A girl came out of the back room. She had orange-red hair and a blue Grant Street kimono tied around her middle with a bright red sash. "Interduce me to your friends, sweetie."

He looked at her, then back at me. "I never wrote no letters on that typewriter."

I crossed the room and picked up the typewriter. I stuck it under my arm and started for the door.

"Hey!" the girl squealed. "Where you going with my typewriter?"

I looked at Lorenzo. "The police can match up type," I said. "If I'm right, the penalty for blackmail and extortion is ten to twenty."

"I told yuh not to use my typewriter!" the girl yelled at him.

"Shut up!" He turned back to me. "Wait a minute," he said. "You buyin'?"

I put the typewriter down and looked at him. "Maybe," I said.

A shrewd look came into his eyes. "The old lady send you?"

"How would I know about them if she hadn't?"

"What's she willing to pay?"

"Depends on what you got," I said. "We're not buying anything blind."

"They're the McCoy all right."

I had a sudden idea. "You're not the only guy trying for a shakedown."

He looked flustered. "You mean there are others?"

"Your letter was the fourth we've received."

He began to look worried.

"How do we know you're legit?" I asked. "I got to see something first."

"You don't think I'm goofy enough to keep the letters around here? I got partners in this action. We got 'em in a safe place."

I picked the typewriter up again. "In that case I'll talk to your partners when they come up with the goods."

"Hold it! I figured something like this might come up. I took a couple of the letters from the envelope just in case."

I put the typewriter down. "Now you're making sense. Let's see them."

Renzo looked at the girl. "Get some clothes on and go downstairs and ask Johnny to give you the envelope I gave him."

"You don't have to bother." I looked at Anna, who had been standing there silently, watching us. "Would you mind?"

She shook her head.

Her brother sneered. "What's he pay you for running errands, Anna? It better be good money because you ain't going to be working long."

"I'm not paying her anything, you slob. All she wants to do is keep you out of jail."

Anna went out the door. Renzo turned to me. "Might as well take a load off your feet. Sit down and have yourself a snort."

"No, thanks."

He went over to a closet and took out a bottle. "Get some ice, baby," he called to the girl.

"Get it yourself," she said sullenly.

Renzo shrugged his shoulders. "Dames," he said disgustedly. He crossed over to the alcove that served as the kitchenette and opened the refrigerator. He tipped some cubes from a tray and put them into a glass. Then he came back and sloshed in some whiskey. He sat down at the table across from me. "That Tony was a real smooth operator."

I didn't answer.

He drank from his glass. "He had everything going for him. My sister. Your ex-wife. Your daughter. He didn't have to miss a night if he didn't want to."

I held onto my temper. I was getting used to this kind of talk.

"Your kid was nuts about him. Wait'll you glim those letters. They're so hot the paper sizzles. He must have trained her right, she had a real yen for him. And she wasn't the least bit bashful about putting it down on paper—what she'd like to do to him when they got together."

I gritted my teeth. I hadn't come here expecting to find the Sonnets from the Portuguese.

"Your wife wasn't bad either," he continued. "Though she didn't come right out and say it like the kid did. But she was sure jealous. In one of the letters she said she wouldn't stop at killing him if she caught him cheating on her. But the kid beat her to it, didn't she?"

I still didn't answer.

"And my stupid sister. Waiting around like a jerk for Tony to come back." He laughed. "He only came around when he wanted a little spaghetti and some plain old-fashioned Italian humping. Like he got tired of all that fancy stuff he was getting up there on the hill. You gotta have meat and potatoes once in a while, kid, he used to tell me. You can get awful tired of caviar and *pâté de foie gras*. Man, that Tony was the bending end."

I heard footsteps on the outside wooden staircase.

Renzo heard them too. He raised his drink to me in a kind of salute. "Here's luck."

I heard the door behind me open, but I didn't turn around. Then a sharp pain exploded in the back of my head and I pitched head over heels into the blackness coming up at me from the floor.

Lights kept flashing in my eyes. One after the other and in between I could feel myself being pushed first one way and then the other. I groaned and tried to get up, but the fog was all around me and I couldn't quite make it. Then some more lights went off and then there weren't any at all. Just the pain in my head.

The ice-cold water brought me up sputtering. I shook my head and opened my eyes. Johnny and Lorenzo were standing over me. I looked down at myself. I was sitting on a bed stark naked.

I heard a rustle of clothing and turned my head, the pain ricocheting around in my skull. The girl with the orange-red hair was just slipping back into her Grant Street kimono.

I tried to stop the pain from tearing the top of my head off. I squeezed my eyes shut tight and opened them quickly. That seemed to help. It wasn't until then that I began to realize what had happened. I'd been a setup from the word go.

"You're clothes are over on the chair," Renzo said. "We'll leave while you get dressed."

They went out, closing the door behind them. I sat on the bed, hearing the dull sound of their voices through the closed door. I stretched my neck and moved my head around. It hurt like hell. It didn't feel at all like in the Mickey Spillanes. No Cloud Nine, no wild erotic dreams. Just plain hurt like hell.

I staggered off the bed and into the bathroom. I turned on the cold water in the shower and stuck my head under it. The spray was like needles but it did the trick. Slowly the pain began to go away. I put my hand to the back of my head and found a small egg there. It was a good thing I had such a thick skull.

I turned the water to hot, then back to cold again until the ache in my neck and shoulders went away. I pulled down a dirty towel, which was the only one I could find, and dried myself. Then I got dressed.

They were sitting around the table having a drink when I came out of the bedroom.

"You look like you could use a drink," Renzo said. He poured some whiskey into a glass and pushed it toward me.

I took it and swallowed it down. The warmth hit my gut and I began to feel better. "Where's Anna?"

"I sent her home," Renzo answered. "She did her bit." He pushed a photograph toward me. "Nice piece of work, ain't it?"

I picked it up and looked at it. It was a Polaroid ten-second print. I remembered now that the camera case Anna had been carrying wasn't big enough for the Speed Graphic she'd used in the club. The picture was about what you'd expect. I was naked and so was the girl with the orange-red hair. The pose was Oriental classic. I gave the picture back to him. "She's a little too skinny for my taste."

"Keep it," Renzo said genially. "We shot a whole roll."

"Now what?"

"Sit down and wait. We got some company coming."

I stuck the picture in my pocket. "I don't think so. I've had about all the fun and games I can take."

I started for the door and Johnny, the bartender, got up quickly. I stepped toward him. "I wouldn't if I were you," Renzo said casually. "He used to be light-heavy champ of the Pacific Coast."

I moved forward and Johnny let go with a round-house right that he'd telegraphed all the way from Los Angeles. I went in under it easily. You don't spend a lot of time out in the field with a construction gang without getting some sort of exercise.

I let his fist go over my shoulder and cut up in a judo jab at his sternum. He doubled forward and I chopped him on the side of the neck with the best karate cut I ever took. He went down like he was poleaxed. My old Air Force instructor would have been proud of me.

I turned just in time to catch Lorenzo coming at me. I caught him and pushed him back against the wall. I held him there, squirming. The girl began to scream as I held my hand, palm flat down, in front of his neck. "Now, where are the rest of those letters?"

Terror began to flood into Renzo's eyes. He shook his head.

I rapped him lightly on the Adam's apple. Just enough to make him choke a little. "I do that hard enough and you're in the same daisy field with your hero Riccio."

"I haven't got them," he gasped hoarsely. "I gave them to Coriano."

I made a threatening gesture.

"Honest!"

"The pictures," I said.

"Johnny's got them." Renzo was shaking with terror. I slapped him on the side of the face and let him slump to the floor. He sat there, moaning. The girl ran over to him. "Renzo, baby! Did he hurt you?"

I went over to Johnny. He was beginning to move a little. I rolled him over on his back, glad that I hadn't killed him. I knelt down on the floor and began to go through his pockets. I'd just found the pictures when the door behind me opened.

The first thing that I saw when I turned around was the muzzle of a .38. It was pointed right at my belly and from where I stood it looked like a fifty-millimeter cannon. The next thing I noticed was the chubby little man behind it, his beady eyes almost lost in the rolls of fat around them.

"I'll take those pictures if you don't mind," he said.

I held them out without speaking.

"Just put them on the table and back up against the wall."

You don't argue with a cannon. I did what I was told.

"Now turn around and put your hands high on the wall and lean against it. You know what I mean. Like they do on TV."

I knew what he meant.

I heard him move to the table. There was a rustle of paper. "You can turn around now, Colonel."

I turned around. "You're Coriano?"

He nodded. He looked at Johnny, then over at Lorenzo. He smiled amiably. "Been having a little fun with my boys?"

"They were very cooperative," I said.

"All ass and no forehead, both of them. But it doesn't matter. I already made a deal on the letters with your ex."

He pulled out a chair and sat down. "Nothing personal in this, you understand, Colonel," he said. "Merely a matter of business."

I looked at the pudgy little man. He seemed so content sitting there that the least I could do was shaft him a little. "How much did she give you?"

He waved the revolver negligently. "Twenty-five thou."

"You've been had. The old lady would have gone to a hundred grand."

He stared at me steadily for a moment, then shrugged. "That's life," he said philosophically. "I have the same kind of luck when I get into the market. The stock always goes up after I sell."

"What about the pictures?" I asked.

"Insurance, Colonel. For me and for the lady who bought the letters." He glanced at them. "A good likeness, aren't they?"

I walked past him to the door. Coriano was still watching me; so were Renzo and his girl friend. The only one that wasn't was Johnny. He was lying on his back on the floor. I shook my head sadly, as if to commiserate with all of them, and went out.

My car was still where I'd left it. I started to open the door when I heard Anna's voice. "Mr. Carey?"

I climbed into the car beside her.

"Are you all right?"

"I guess so," I said.

"I couldn't help it, Mr. Carey." She began to cry. "They made me do it. Coriano was in the bar when I came downstairs."

"Sure, Anna, sure." I tapped the leather camera case on the seat between us. "You just happened to have your Polaroid along?"

"That's right. Coriano saw the camera and that gave him the idea. He said it would keep you from squawking to the cops. I made sure I got each shot when your eyes were closed, so at least you can prove you were unconscious."

I turned to look at her. Prove I was unconscious? Hell. I looked positively ecstatic.

"I had to do it, Mr. Carey," she said earnestly. "If I hadn't, Coriano would never have let me work again."

"All right, Anna," I said. "Now tell me where you live and I'll drive you home."

I dropped her off, and when I got to my room almost an hour later the red message indicator on the telephone was blinking. I picked it up. The old lady had just called and wanted me to call her back. I dialed the number.

Her voice was wide-awake and sharp. "Well, Luke," she demanded. "Did you get them?"

"No."

"What do you mean?" she asked angrily.

"There was nothing to buy. Nora got to them before we did."

"Nora?" Her voice was surprised.

"Who else?"

She chuckled. "I should have thought of that. Nora wouldn't want us to have those letters. Well, at least we don't have to worry any more."

"Sure," I said and put down the telephone. Nobody but me. I barely had the energy left to get out of my clothes and into bed. It had been a long night.

12

The matron opened the door to Dani's room. "Your mother's here to see you."

Dani got off the bed. "Where is she?"

"She's waiting in the cafeteria."

Dani followed the matron down the corridor and through the steel gate. They took the elevator down to the cafeteria level. It was just about three o'clock and the cafeteria was almost empty. A strange man and Miss Jennings were sitting with her mother.

Nora raised her cheek for Dani's kiss. "Hello, dear."

Dani looked at Miss Jennings, then at the man. "Hello, Mother. Hello, Miss Jennings."

Sally Jennings got to her feet. "Hello, Dani." She turned to the others. "Well, I've got to get back to my office."

They nodded and she went out.

"Don't stand there, Dani," Nora said, with some asperity. "Sit down."

Dani sat down obediently. "What did she want?"

"She didn't want anything. We wanted to talk to her."

"What about?" Dani's voice was suspicious.

"You. You seem to be making a great deal of trouble."

Dani looked at her mother steadily for a moment, then at the man. "Who's he?" she asked bluntly.

"Dani!" Nora's voice was shocked. "You have better manners than that."

Dani's voice was impatient. "Not here, Mother. There isn't enough time for manners here. Who is he?"

Nora looked at the man eloquently. "This is Dr. Weidman, Dani. I've asked him to examine you."

"What for?"

"For your own good! They can't seem to find out what's the matter with you."

"Is he another head-shrinker?"

Nora's voice was angry. "He's a psychiatrist, Dani."

"I don't want to talk to him."

"You must!" Nora insisted.

"Why, Mother? Do you think there's something the matter with me?"

"What I think doesn't matter, Dani. It's what they think that does. They could send you away for a long time."

Dani was still watching her mother's face. "What you think matters to me, Mother. Do you think there's something the matter with me?"

Nora stared back at her, then drew a deep breath. "Of course not, dear," she said. "But—"

"Then I don't want to talk to him."

The doctor got to his feet. He was smiling. "I don't think you have any need for concern, Miss Hayden. Miss Jennings has an excellent reputation and I think you can rely on her appraisal." He turned to Dani. "It wouldn't hurt, young lady, if you were to have a little more trust in Miss Jennings. The worst she could do is help you."

He made a sort of bow and left them.

They sat there silently, staring at each other. "Do you have a dime, Mother? I want to get a Coke."

Nora looked at her absently. Dani knew that her mother was thinking of something else. She always was when she looked like that.

"A dime, Mother?" she repeated gently.

Nora opened her purse. "Do you think you could get me a cup of coffee?"

"Sure, Mother."

Dani got up and went back to the kitchen door. "Hey, Charley! Can I get a cup of coffee for my mother?"

A shining dark face appeared in the doorway. "Sure thing, Dani."

Dani brought the coffee back to the table, then went for her Coke. When she came back and sat down, Nora lit a cigarette. Dani looked at her and Nora pushed the package toward her with a reluctant sigh. She took one and lit it.

"I thought you didn't believe in head-shrinkers, Mother."

"I don't know what to believe in any more."

Dani looked at her mother curiously. This wasn't like her. Nora usually had very definite ideas about everything.

Nora sipped at the coffee and made a face.

Dani grinned. "It isn't much like the coffee at home, Mother."

"I guess not," Nora said. She looked at her daughter. "Is the food as bad?"

"The food's all right."

"I saw the letters you wrote to Rick," Nora said in a low voice. "Why didn't you tell me about them?"

Dani felt the flush burn its way into her face. "I didn't think about it. I forgot."

"If someone else had gotten them it would have been much worse. I—I didn't know it had been going on for such a long time," Nora said awkwardly.

Dani felt her throat constrict. She stared back at her mother silently.

Nora's eyes fell again. "When did it start?"

"That time in Acapulco. Remember, you had to fly to San Francisco? That was when it happened."

"You should have told me, Dani. What did he do to you?"

"He didn't do it to me, Mother," Dani said steadily. "I did it to him."

The tears came to the edge of Nora's eyes. "Why, Dani, why?"

"I wanted to, Mother. I got so very tired of pretending to be a little girl."

She fell silent, staring at her mother and dragging on her cigarette. "I guess there's not very much else to talk about, is there, Mother?"

Nora shook her head. "I guess not."

There was so much for them to talk about, but Dani couldn't talk to her and she couldn't talk to Dani, any more than she'd been able to talk to her own mother. Each generation was an island to itself.

She made one more attempt. "Dani," she said earnestly, "please talk to Miss Jennings. She may be able to help you—help us."

"I don't dare, Mother. With her you can't always stop where you want to. One thing will lead to another and the next thing you know she'll know the truth about what happened that night. And I don't want anyone to know, any more than you do."

Nora looked at her daughter. This was what it all came to, she thought. The only thing they had to share was a common guilt.

Dani looked up at the wall-clock. It was almost three-thirty. "I have to go back," she lied hesitantly. "I have a class."

Nora nodded. Dani got out of her chair and walked around the table and kissed her mother's cheek. Impulsively Nora put her arms around her.

"Don't worry, Mother. Everything will work out all right."

Nora managed a smile. "Of course it will, dear. I'll see you Sunday."

She watched the matron get up and follow Dani out into the corridor, then the swinging doors closed and cut off her view. She looked down at the ashtray. Her cigarette was still smoldering. Slowly she ground it out and then picked up her handbag. She took out her mirror and made a minor repair to her makeup, then left.

"Your mother's very beautiful, Dani," the matron said as they walked back to her room.

Dani glanced at the matron. Everyone always said that the first time they saw her mother, then when they saw *her* she could almost sense their disappointment. "What a pretty child," they'd say. But she knew how they really felt.

Dani went into her room and closed the door. She looked at the scratched and pencil-marked walls for a while, then stretched out on the bed.

Beautiful and talented. That was her mother. Everything that she was not. She remembered how she used to sneak down to the studio when her mother was away and try to copy some of the wonderful things her mother sculpted. But everything she did turned out a mess and she'd throw it away so nobody would see it.

Suddenly she found herself crying silently. After a while the tears stopped and she got out of bed and looked at herself in the small mirror. Even after crying, her mother still looked beautiful! Her eyes clear, her skin pale and luminescent. Not like this—eyes puffed and red, face swollen.

She took a Wash 'N Dri from the package her mother had sent her and tore the foil wrapper. She pressed it to her face, feeling the cool, slightly mentholated wetness soothing her skin.

She remembered how Rick used to tease her because she liked them so much. She always carried some in her handbag. Once after they had been together and he had been lying next to her with his eyes closed, she had taken one out with the idea of refreshing him.

But he had almost jumped out of his skin when she'd touched him with it. "For Christ's sake, kid, what are you doing?"

"I was only trying to make you feel better," she'd said.

He'd laughed and pulled her over against him. She felt the slight scratch of his beard as he nuzzled her throat. "You know, you're a crazy kid!" Then he held her and his hands did all those wonderful things that made her feel so necessary to him.

She felt the tears come to her eyes again and she blinked them back. There was no use crying now. There was no one to turn to. When she'd been blue like this before she could always go to him. He'd smile and touch her and her blues would go away. But not any more.

Carefully she ticked off the days. Sylvia had been shipped off yesterday. That made today Friday. Rick's funeral must have taken place already. Idly she wondered if her mother had sent flowers.

She probably hadn't. Probably not, if she knew her. Mother had forgotten all about him already. Besides she would still be too jealous deep down inside.

She remembered how angry her mother had been when she'd found her in Rick's room. She'd screamed at him, and her fingers had left angry red marks on his bare shoulders. She'd thought her mother would kill him.

"No! Mother, no!" she'd screamed.

Then her mother had pulled her, naked, down the

hall and had flung her into her room. She remembered huddling there, alternately shivering and crying as their fight raged all through the house.

No, she was sure now that Mother hadn't sent any flowers. But she was also sure that her mother hadn't forgotten about Rick either. Her eyes felt dry and burning. She took out another Wash 'N Dri and patted her face with it. She crumpled the tissues and threw them into the wastebasket.

Suddenly she felt very much alone. As if the discarded tissues had been a link with the past and now that link had been broken. Only Rick had tried to understand, but now there was nobody. Nobody. She began to cry again.

Sally Jennings looked up at the clock. It was a quarter to six. She looked down at her desk impatiently. There were so many reports to get out. She began to put them neatly into her briefcase. Maybe she'd be able to get at some of them after she got home from the theater.

She had waited a long time to get tickets for this play and this was one time nothing was going to interfere with seeing it. By the time she got home and changed, then downtown again, she'd just have time for a quick bite before curtain time.

There was a hesitant knock at the door. "Yes," she called impatiently.

At first all she could see was the white uniform of the matron behind the glass door, then the door opened and Dani came in.

Dani stood there in the doorway. "Miss Jennings," she asked in a thin, small voice, "can I talk to you?"

The psychologist looked at her for a moment. The child had been crying, she could see that, but there was also a forlorn look about her that hadn't been there before. "Of course, Dani."

Dani looked down at the open briefcase. "If you're leaving, Miss Jennings, I can come back in the morning."

Sally Jennings closed the briefcase and put it on the floor behind the desk. "No. As a matter of fact I'd been planning to stay and work tonight."

Dani came further into the office. "I didn't want to bother you."

Miss Jennings smiled at her, and when she smiled she suddenly seemed very young. "Tell you what. Suppose we have supper in the cafeteria together? It will be so nice to have someone to talk to for a change."

Dani glanced over her shoulder at the matron, still waiting outside the office. "Do you—do you think they'd let me?"

Sally Jennings reached for the telephone and dialed the chief probation officer. She put her hand over the mouthpiece. "I think it could be arranged."

Maybe it wasn't relief or gratitude that the psychologist saw in Dani's eyes, but suddenly it seemed that the forlornness had disappeared from her face. Suddenly the play she'd been waiting so long to see just wasn't important any more.

13

"The first time I found out that people weren't forever was when my father stopped coming to see me." Dani looked across the desk at Miss Jennings. They had just come back from dinner. "You know what I mean? When you're little it's like you're the center of the whole world, but when you get older you find out you're not. I cried every day for a month. Then I got used to the idea.

"Uncle Sam, that's Mr. Corwin, was very nice. Mother married him after she divorced my father. I think he felt kind of sorry for me. He used to take me out like my father used to. To the parks and the zoo. Once he even took me sailing. But he wasn't like Daddy. When I was with Daddy it was like he never thought about anything else but me. With Uncle Sam, it was different. He tried very hard, but I was only one of the many things he thought about. But I liked him just the same. And then one day, he was gone. I remember that day."

Dani fell silent, looking down at the smoldering cigarette between her fingers.

"Go on, Dani," the psychologist urged. "You remember that day. What happened to make you remember it?"

The blue-and-white station wagon with the words *Miss Randolph's School* lettered delicately on the door pulled into the driveway and stopped. The driver, in a smart gray uniform, got out and opened the door. Dani came flying out of the car, her long black hair streaming behind her, her white blouse and navy-blue pleated skirt bright in the sunlight. She ran up the steps to the front door.

"Have a nice weekend, Miss Dani," the driver called after her.

She flashed a bright smile back at him from the door. "You too, Axel."

She dropped her books on the table in the foyer and, holding her report card in her hand, dashed around the circular staircase and down the corridor to the studio.

She flung the door open and ran inside calling, "Mother! Mother! I got an A in Art!"

She'd run all the way into the studio, the card still held high in her hand, before she realized that no one was there. She went over to the small room that was just off the studio.

The door was closed. She knocked at it lightly. "Mother. Mother, are you in there?"

There was no answer.

Carefully she opened the door and peeked inside. The room was empty. Slowly she closed the door. She was puzzled. Usually her mother was working at that time of day.

She went back to the foyer. She picked up her books from the table and started up the stairs. Charles was just coming out of Uncle Sam's room. "Good afternoon, Miss Dani."

She looked up at him. "Where's Mother?"

The butler looked uncomfortable. "She went out, Miss Dani."

"Did she say when she'd be back?" Dani held up the report card. "I got an A in Art. I want her to see it."

"Isn't that wonderful, Miss Dani." Then the butler's tone changed. "Madam didn't say when she'd return."

"Oh," Dani said in a disappointed voice. She started

toward her room, then stopped and looked back. "Let me know when she comes in, Charles. I want her to see it."

"Of course, Miss Dani."

Mrs. Holman was hanging some dresses in the closet when Dani came into her room. A big smile came over her face as she saw the child. "So there you are. I was wondering when you'd come home. Did you get it?"

Dani grinned. "What do you think?"

"Let me see," the old governess said. "I can't wait!"

Mischievously Dani held the report card behind her. "I won't let you see it, Nanny, until you keep your promise!"

"I have the cake already baked."

"All right, then!" Dani held the card out to her.

"I've got to get my glasses," Mrs. Holman said. "I'm so excited I can't read!"

She found them in a pocket of her uniform and put them on. Quickly she looked down at the card. "Oh, Dani," she exclaimed, "an A in Art!"

The governess pulled Dani to her. "I'm so proud of you," she said warmly. She kissed Dani on the cheek. "Your mother will be proud too when she sees it."

"Where is Mother? She wasn't in the studio."

The same look she had seen in Charles's eyes came over the governess' face. "Your mother had to go away suddenly on a business trip. She'll be back Monday."

"Oh." Her mother had taken quite a few of these unexpected weekend business trips lately. She took the report card back from the governess. "I hope she's back in time to sign my report card. I have to return it on Monday."

"I'm sure she'll be back in time. Now, why don't we go down to the kitchen and ask Cookie to put out the milk and the cake? We'll have a little party, just the three of us."

Dani looked at the old woman. She was tired of having parties with her. It would be nice if Mother came to one of her parties for a change. "I don't feel like a party."

"You do what Nanny tells you," the governess said with halfhearted sternness. She knew what Dani was thinking.

"Okay." Dani turned and went out the door. She met Uncle Sam and Charles in the hallway. Each was carrying several suitcases.

"Uncle Sam!" Dani shouted, running to him.

He turned to wait for her. Charles went on down the stairs with the luggage. "Yes, Dani?"

"I got an A in Art!"

"That's great, Dani."

There was something in Uncle Sam's voice that made her look up into his face. He looked tired and she felt in him a kind of sadness. She glanced at the bags. "Are you going away for the weekend too? Are you going to meet Mother?"

"I'm going away, Dani. But I won't be meeting your mother."

"Oh! I thought if you saw her you could tell her."

He seemed to be thinking of something else. "Tell her what?"

"That I got an A in Art."

"I won't be seeing her, Dani."

"Will you be back on Monday?"

He looked down at her silently for a moment, then put the luggage down. "No, Dani, I won't be back on Monday. I won't be back at all."

"Not ever?" she asked in a puzzled voice.

"No. I'm moving out."

The tears rushed to her eyes suddenly. It was just like Daddy. One day he moved out and after a while he stopped coming to see her. "Why? Don't you like us any more?"

He saw the tears in her eyes and heard the concern in her voice. He took her hand. "That's not it, Dani. It isn't you. But sometimes things don't work out the way they should. Your mother and I are getting a divorce."

"Like Mother and Daddy?"

He nodded.

"That means you won't come to see me any more?" She began to cry. "Now nobody will come to see me."

He put his arm around her awkwardly. "I'd like to come to see you, Dani. But I can't."

"Why not?" she asked. "Susie Colter's mother was divorced five times and all *her* fathers come to see her. I know because she sits next to me in class and she always shows me the presents they bring her."

"Your mother wouldn't like it."

"Why can't she move out when she gets a divorce?" Dani demanded, beginning to get angry. "Why does the daddy always have to move out?"

"I don't know."

Impulsively she threw her arms around him. "Don't go, Uncle Sam! I'll miss you something awful!"

He smiled and put his cheek alongside hers. "I'll miss you too, Dani. You be a big girl and let me go and I'll send you a present every now and then. You can show it to your friend so she'll know she's not the only one whose Daddy gives her presents."

"All right," Dani said hesitantly. She kissed his cheek. "But I'll miss you anyway."

Sam kissed her again and straightened up. He picked up his bags. "I'll have to hurry."

She followed him down the stairs. "Are you going to La Jolla and live on a boat like my daddy?"

He laughed. "No, Dani. I'm going to live in New York for a while."

Her voice was disappointed. "If you lived on a boat we could go sailing."

He laughed again. "I'm not as good a sailor as your daddy."

Dani followed him to the door and watched Charles put the bags into the taxi. Uncle Sam bent down and kissed her again. "Goodbye, Dani."

She waved to him as the cab began to move. "Goodbye, Uncle Sam!" she called, and then because she didn't know what else to say, "Have a good time!"

She walked thoughtfully through the house to the kitchen. Charles, Cookie and Nanny were waiting for her. All of them except Violet, who was her mother's maid. Violet was never around when her mother went away.

"Mother and Uncle Sam are getting a divorce," she announced. "Uncle Sam's going to live in New York."

Mrs. Holman brought out the chocolate layer cake and put it on the table. "How do you like that for a cake?"

Dani looked at it. "It's wonderful." But there was no enthusiasm in her voice.

"You sit down at the table and I'll cut you a piece," Cookie said.

Obediently, Dani sat down. Cookie cut a big wedge and put it on her plate, next to a glass of milk. Then she cut pieces for the others and they all sat down. Dani knew they were waiting for her to taste it so they could start. She cut a piece with her fork and put it in her mouth. "This cake is delicious," she mumbled.

"Not with your mouth full, Dani."

They all began to eat. "The cake is very good, Mrs. Holman," Charles said.

"Take it easy, now," Cookie warned him, laughing.

"Of course your cakes are very good too, Cookie," Charles said, aware that good cooks weren't that easy to come by these days.

"Why are they getting divorced?" Dani asked suddenly.

The servants exchanged awkward glances. It was the governess who answered. "We don't know, child. It's not our place to know."

"Is it because Mother is so pretty and has so many friends?"

They didn't answer.

"I heard Uncle Sam and Mother quarreling a few days ago. Uncle Sam said he was sick and tired of her sleeping partners. I know that Uncle Sam and Mr. Scaasi were partners but I didn't know that Mother had partners too. Why didn't I know that?"

"That's none of our business, child," Mrs. Holman said sternly. "And none of yours either. You just eat your cake and worry about the things that concern you."

Dani ate silently for a few minutes more, then looked up. "Uncle Sam said he would send me presents so I could show Susie Colter she isn't the only one who gets presents from her daddies."

Two weeks later she was ten years old and a big crate came for her from New York. It was filled with presents. Uncle Sam had kept his word. She felt a little better then. But in her own way she missed him.

When school closed her mother took her to a dude ranch near Lake Tahoe for the summer. Mother said she had to do it to get her divorce, but Dani didn't mind. It was a lot of fun. She went horseback riding every morning and she was on the lake every afternoon. Rick was there too. He was her mother's new manager. He must have been one of the partners she'd heard Uncle Sam and Mother quarreling about, because once in a while she'd see him coming from her mother's room in the morning.

But she liked Rick. He enjoyed doing the same things she did. He'd go horseback riding with her and he taught her to water ski. And he used to laugh a lot. Not like Uncle Sam, who never laughed very much at all. Mother used to say that Rick seemed as much of a kid as she was.

Mother didn't like to ride horseback or spend a lot of time on the water. She said it was bad for her skin, she got sunburnt too easily. Instead, she spent most of her time in the room she had fixed up as a studio. At night she'd get up and she and Rick would go in to Reno. Then Mother would sleep late. But Rick was up early every morning for their ride together. He used to call her Little Swinger.

He had a mustache at the time. A trim line, a little wider than a pencil stroke, that reached to the corners of his wide mouth. She thought it made him look cute. Something like Clark Gable. One day she told her mother that and for some reason her mother got angry. She told Rick to shave the silly thing off.

Dani began to cry. She didn't know why she was crying. "Don't shave it off!" she begged. "Please don't!"

"Stop acting like a silly little fool!" her mother shouted.

Dani turned on her mother angrily. "You only want him to shave it off because I said I liked it! You don't want anybody to like me or me to like anybody!" She turned to Rick. "Tell her you won't shave it off!"

Rick looked at her, then at her mother. He hesitated.

Her mother smiled then. It was a funny sort of smile,

the kind that came over her face when she made you do something you didn't really want to do. "You're free, white and over twenty-one, Rick. Make up your own mind what you want to do."

Rick stood there for a moment, then turned and went to his room. When he came out a few minutes later the mustache was gone.

Dani stared at him. He looked different somehow. There was a funny white line where the mustache had been. He didn't look like Clark Gable any more. She burst into tears and ran to her room.

After that Rick didn't go riding with her any more. Neither did he take her out in the speedboat to water ski. But it really didn't matter very much because their vacation was almost over. Her mother sent her off to a camp for the rest of the summer.

14

Nora looked up from her work in answer to the soft knock at the studio door. "Come in."

The door opened slightly and Mrs. Holman stood hesitantly in the doorway. "May I have a word with madam?" she asked formally.

Nora nodded. "Of course." She put down the lump of clay and rubbed her hands clean.

The governess came in awkwardly. It was one of the few times she had ever entered the studio. "I'd like to talk to you about Danielle."

She glanced at Rick who was standing nearby.

"What about her?" Nora said.

Mrs. Holman looked at Rick again. She hesitated. Rick took the hint. "I'll leave you two alone." He went into the other room leaving the door open.

"Well?" Nora asked.

The old woman was still awkward. "Danielle is growing up."

"Of course," Nora said. "We all know that."

"She's not so much a baby any more. She's quickly becoming a young lady."

Nora looked at her silently.

"What I mean," the governess continued, embarrassment in her voice, "it's not easy to explain things."

"What things?" Nora asked in an annoyed voice. "I'm sure she doesn't have to have the facts of life explained to her. They do that very efficiently at Miss Randolph's School."

"That's it!" Mrs. Holman said excitedly. "She knows."

Nora shook her head. "Of course she does. She should know."

"She knows," the old lady said. "And she sees."

Nora was silent for a moment. "Exactly what are you getting at, Mrs. Holman?"

The governess didn't look at her. "Danielle sees what is happening in this house. And she knows what she knows. Together it is not good for a girl to see such things in her own home."

"Are you telling me what to do in my own house?"

The governess shook her head quickly. "No, Miss Hayden. I'm just telling you about your daughter. These things she sees and these things she knows, they are too much for a child like her to understand. She thinks all the wrong things about them." Her eyes met Nora's candidly. "It is no longer possible for me to explain to her that she does not really see what she does see."

"I don't think that's any of your concern, Mrs. Holman," Nora said coldly.

The old woman's face grew stubborn. "In a way it's not, Miss Hayden. But I have been Dani's nanny since she was born. I would not feel right if I did not tell you how this is affecting Dani."

"Thank you, Mrs. Holman," Nora said, still in that cold voice. "But please remember that I have been Danielle's mother since she was born. She is my responsibility, not yours."

The governess looked at her. "Yes, Miss Hayden." She turned and left the studio. The door closed behind her and Rick came out of the other room.

"Did you hear what she said?" Nora said.

Rick looked at her. "That old lady's got to go."

"She's right, in a way. Dani is growing up." Nora

picked up a piece of clay. "We'll have to be more careful."

"Careful?" Rick exploded. "How careful can we be? You just try sneaking out of this house in the small hours of the morning and back to that apartment over the garage. I bet half the neighborhood knows what I'm doing!"

Nora laughed. "You could try making a little less noise when you close the doors."

"You try it! Especially when it's raining and everything sticks. I get half drowned."

Nora put down the clay. "Yes, we'll have to do something about that."

"We could get married," Rick said. "That would put an end to all this jazz."

"No." Nora looked at him frankly. "We're not meant for marriage. I've tried it twice and I know. And at heart you're no more for it than I am."

He walked over and put his arms around her. "But we haven't tried it with each other, baby. It would be different then."

She pushed him away. "Stop kidding yourself. Neither of us is the type to be tied down. We're alike. We both like something new once in a while."

"Not me, baby. I could be very happy with just you."

She avoided his grasp. "And how would you explain to your friends when you couldn't get out Tuesday and Thursday nights? Especially to your little Italian girl, the night-club photographer, who makes spaghetti for you on her night off? What would you tell her after she's been waiting all this time for you to marry her?"

He stared at her, his face flushed. "You know about her?"

Nora smiled. "I know everything about you. I'm not that much a fool." She shrugged her shoulders and picked up a cigarette. She waited for him to light it before she continued. "But I don't mind, really. You can do what you want so long as I get what I want."

He started to smile slowly. "And I got what you want. Is that right, baby?"

He reached for her. This time she didn't avoid his embrace. He took the cigarette from her lips and put it in an ashtray. He kissed her, his mouth hard and brutal against hers.

She kept her eyes open, looking into his face.

He pressed her back against the table, his hand reaching up under her skirt.

"The window," she said, gesturing toward the expanse of glass before which they were standing.

"To hell with that, I can't wait. Let the neighbors eat their hearts out."

Charles met Dani at the station when she came home from camp. She looked around. Mrs. Holman usually came with him. "Where's Nanny?"

Charles didn't meet her eyes as he picked up her assorted gear. "Didn't you know, Miss Dani? Mrs. Holman's left."

Dani stopped suddenly. "Nanny left me?"

Charles was embarrassed. "I thought you knew, Miss Dani. She's taken another job."

Dani's face was angry. "Did Mother send her away?"

"I don't know, Miss Dani. It happened right after you left for camp." He opened the car door for her.

"Do you know where Nanny is working?" she asked.

Charles nodded.

"I want you to drive me there."

Charles hesitated. "I don't know. Your mother—"

"I want you to drive me there!" Dani said angrily. "Now!"

"Miss Dani. Your mother will be very angry with me."

"I won't tell her. Drive me there!"

Dani got into the back seat and Charles closed the door. He made one more attempt to dissuade her when he got in the front seat. "Miss Dani—"

Suddenly the child's voice became as icy as her mother's. "If you don't take me there, I'll tell Mother that you did."

It was one of a group of new houses in St. Francis Wood. Nanny was just coming down the walk, pushing a small gray baby carriage. Dani was out of the car almost before it stopped. "Nanny!" she cried running toward her. "Nanny!"

The old woman stopped and squinted into the afternoon sun. She shielded her eyes with one hand. "Dani?"

Then her vision cleared and she flung her arms open to embrace the onrushing child. "Dani!" she cried, her eyes beginning to fill with tears. "Dani, *mein kleines Kind.*"

Dani was crying too. "Why did you leave me, Nanny? Why did you leave me?"

The nurse kissed her cheeks, her face. "My baby," she crooned. "My little girl. Let me look at you. How big you've grown, how brown."

Dani buried her head in the ample bosom. "You should have told me," she sobbed. "You shouldn't have left me like that!"

Suddenly the old lady realized what Dani meant. She raised her head and looked over at Charles. The butler shook his head slowly.

Intuitively she knew what he meant. She turned back to the child. "You're a big girl now, Dani. Too big a girl to need a nanny."

"You should have told me," Dani said, the tears still in her eyes. "It wasn't right."

"My job is really with little babies, Dani child. Babies need me."

"I need you," Dani said. "You've got to come home with me."

Slowly the governess shook her head. "I can't, Dani."

"Why not?"

Mrs. Holman put her hand on the carriage. "This baby needs me too," she said simply.

"I need you more than she does. You've always been with me."

"And now it's time you learned to do without me," the old woman said. "You're a big girl now. What is there for me to do except sit around and watch you come and go? You can take care of yourself. Didn't you do it all summer without me? Why should it be so different just because you're home?"

"But I love you, Nanny."

The governess hugged her again. "And I love you, my little Dani."

"Then you have to come home with me."

"No, Dani," the old woman said. "I can't go home with you. Your mother was right. She said it would have to happen sometime."

"My mother? Then I was right! She *did* send you away!"

"Sooner or later, Dani," the governess said sadly, "it would have happened. You're twelve years old already. Almost a young lady. Soon boys will be coming to see you. You will be going out on dates and to parties. What would you want an old nanny hanging around for? You'll have a life of your own."

"Did Mother send you away?" Dani asked stubbornly.

"We agreed it would be best. Your mother was very kind about it. She gave me a whole year's severance pay."

"You still should have talked to me about it," Dani said. "You weren't her nanny, you were mine."

The old lady was silent. The child's logic was too much for her. "I think you had better go now. Your mother will be worried what's happened to you. Besides, she has a very nice surprise for you."

"I don't care about her surprise," Dani said. "Can I come to see you? Once in a while, I mean. That is, if you can't come to see me?"

Mrs. Holman hugged her closely. "Of course, Dani. I have every other Thursday off. Maybe I can meet you after school."

Dani kissed the governess on the cheek. "I'll miss you something terrible."

"I'll miss you too," Mrs. Holman said. She seemed on the verge of tears again. "Now go, or Charles will get in trouble."

They kissed again and Dani walked slowly back to the car. She was silent almost all the way home. When they were nearly there she leaned forward to the front seat. "What kind of a surprise has Mother got for me?"

"I can't tell you. Your mother made me promise to keep it a secret."

But in the end it came from Charles anyway. Her mother was having a meeting in the studio and had left word that she was not to be disturbed. Dani went up the stairs, Charles following with her things, and turned toward her room.

"Not that way, Miss Dani. This way." Charles turned and started down towards the other end of the hallway, away from her old room and her mother's.

She followed him. "Is this the surprise?"

He nodded as they stopped at the door of what had formerly been the largest guest room. He opened the door with a flourish. "After you, Miss Dani."

The room was more than twice the size of her old one. Everything in it was new, from the sparkling canopied bed to the built-in hi-fi and television set along the wall. There was a large walk-in closet, just like her mother's, and a new bathroom with a sunken tub and a dressing alcove.

"You can adjust the TV and hi-fi from the headboard," Charles said proudly.

"It's very nice," Dani answered unenthusiastically. She looked around the room. "Where's my treasure chest?"

"It didn't match the new things, so your mother had it put in the attic."

"Bring it down."

"Yes, Miss Dani."

"What happened to my old room?"

"Your mother had it made into an office for Mr. Riccio. And Mrs. Holman's old room is now his bedroom."

"Oh," Dani said. She was old enough to know what that meant. The girls at camp all whispered about what was going on between the men and women counselors who had rooms close to each other.

Charles brought her gear into the room. Her camp trunk was already there. "I'll send Violet in to help you unpack. We were waiting for you to bring the trunk key."

"I don't need any help."

"Of course you do." Her mother's voice came from the open doorway. "You can't possibly unpack all that yourself."

Dani turned to face her mother. "I packed it all myself," she said. "I don't need Violet's help."

Nora looked at her. She knew that there was something wrong. She glanced at Charles. He nodded. "Is that any kind of greeting to give your mother after being away all summer? Come over here and let me look at you."

Nora leaned forward slightly to allow Dani to kiss her cheek. Obediently Dani followed the custom. Charles left the room and closed the door behind him.

"Why did you send Nanny away?" she asked, the moment the door clicked shut.

"Is that the first thing you can think of saying after I've gone to all the trouble of fixing up this room for you? The least you could do is let me know you like it."

"It's very nice." Dani's tone of voice indicated she couldn't care less.

"The television and record player have remote controls in the headboard."

"I know. Charles already told me."

Dani seemed to be waiting for an answer to her question and Nora was just as determined not to give her one. "You've grown. You're almost as tall as I am. How tall are you now?"

"Five, one-and-a-half."

"Turn around," her mother said. "Let me look at you."

Obediently Dani turned around slowly.

"You've grown in other ways too. You're quite a young lady."

"I wear a thirty-two bra," Dani said, a note of pride coming into her voice. "But I have a very broad back. The way I'm growing my counselor thinks I'll need at least a thirty-four by next summer."

Nora's voice showed annoyance. "Young ladies don't talk about such things. I'll send Violet in to help you unpack."

"I don't want Violet," Dani said, her voice growing sullen. "I want Nanny."

Nora turned in exasperation. "Well, Nanny isn't here any more. If you don't want Violet to help you, you'll have to do without."

"I don't need anyone then!" Dani retorted. Her eyes began to moisten. "Why didn't you tell me you were going to send Nanny away? Why did you keep it a secret?"

"I didn't keep it a secret!" Nora's voice was angry. "You're a big girl now. You don't need a wet nurse."

Dani began to cry. "You could have told me."

"Stop acting like a child! I don't have to tell you anything. I'll do what I think is right!"

"That's what you always say! That's what you said when you sent Daddy away. That's what you said when you sent Uncle Sam away. Every time you see that somebody loves me more than they love you, you send them away! That's why you did it!"

"Shut up!"

And for the first time in her life, her mother slapped Dani across the face. The child's hand flew to her cheek and she looked up at her mother with horror-filled eyes. "I hate you! I hate you! Some day you'll love somebody as much as I do and I'll send him away from you! You'll see how much you like it then!"

Nora dropped to her knees in front of her daughter. "I'm sorry, Dani," she whispered. "I'm sorry, I didn't mean to do it!"

Dani stared into her eyes for a moment, then turned and ran into the bathroom. "Go away! Leave me alone!" she shouted through the closed door. "I hate you. I—"

"—hate you!" she finished saying.

Sally Jennings looked across the desk at her. The child's eyes were red with weeping. The tears had left smudgy tracks down her cheeks. Sally pushed the package of Kleenex toward her.

Dani took one and dried her face. She looked at the psychologist gratefully. "I didn't mean it. I didn't really mean it. But there was no other way I could talk to my mother. If I didn't scream or holler or have a fit of hysterics she'd never pay any attention to me."

Sally nodded. She looked up at the clock. "I guess that's all for right now, Dani," she said gently. "Go back and try to get some sleep."

Dani got to her feet. "Yes, Miss Jennings. Will I see you on Monday?"

The psychologist shook her head. "I'm afraid not, Dani. I have some work to do at the hospital. I won't be in all day."

"And Tuesday I have the hearing. I won't be able to talk to you then either."

Sally nodded. "That's right. But don't worry about it, Dani. We'll find a way to work something out."

She watched the matron lead the child down the corridor. She sank back into her chair and reached for a cigarette. She lit it and switched on the recorder. She didn't have it all but she had enough to start with. That was the tough thing about this job. There never was enough time to see any one thing really through.

15

I walked over to the window and looked out. The morning fog was still heavy on the street. I lit a cigarette restlessly. I turned and looked at the telephone. Maybe I should try to reach Elizabeth again. Then I thought better of it. There would be no answer. She just wasn't picking up the phone. I'd been a fool. I never should have sent her that picture.

Elizabeth had been quiet enough on the phone when I'd told her about it. "It's crazy," she'd said. "What could Nora expect to get from something like that?"

"I don't know. Maybe like the man said, insurance, or maybe just to hold over me like a club. That's why I'm sending you the picture."

"Don't send it to me, Luke. I don't want to see it. Get rid of it."

"I can't," I said. "The only chance I have is if I send it to you. If it weren't a phony I wouldn't. You know that. I'll send it airmail, registered special. You don't have to open it. Just put it in a safe place."

"You're asking a lot. You know I won't be able to resist looking at it."

"Look at it then," I said, "and see what a jerk you married."

She was silent for a moment. "I wish I'd never let you go out there."

"It's too late to think about that now."

She was silent again.

"Are you all right?"

"Yes."

"Sure?"

"Sure. We're both waiting for you to come home."

That had been Thursday morning. I mailed the letter and called her the next day, after I figured she'd received it. The moment I heard her voice I knew I was in trouble. She sounded as if she'd been crying.

"You come home right now!"

"But Elizabeth," I protested. "It's only a few more days now 'til the custody hearing."

"I don't care!" she said. "You come home!"

"You saw the picture?"

"The picture has nothing to do with it!"

"I told you it was a frame."

"Even if it was," she sobbed, "you didn't have to look so damn happy about it!"

"Elizabeth, be reasonable."

"I've been reasonable long enough. Now I'm just being a woman. I don't want to talk to you any more. Send me a wire when you're ready to leave!"

Then she hung up. I called right back. But for the next hour all I got was a busy signal. She must have left the telephone off the hook. Then I got a call from the lobby that Miss Spicer was waiting for me and I went downstairs.

We had our interview in the coffee shop. "How is Dani?" I asked after the waitress had brought us our coffee.

"Much better," she said. "She's been much more cooperative these last few days."

"I'm glad to hear that."

She looked at me. "She's still a very sick girl."

"What makes you say that?"

"Whatever is troubling her is buried deep. We haven't yet come up with the reason for her exploding the way she did. There are some things about her we just don't understand."

"Like what?" I asked. "Maybe I can help."

"As a child was she given to tantrums, outbursts of temper, violent rages when she was frustrated?"

I shook my head. "Not that I remember. Usually she was just the opposite. She used to go away by herself when she was upset. Generally up to her room or to her governess. Otherwise she'd try to pretend there was nothing the matter. She'd be extra nice, try harder to please."

"Did she act like that to you?"

I laughed. "I'm afraid she never had to. Dani could always twist me around her finger."

"Toward her mother then?"

I hesitated.

"Please tell me," she said. "I don't want you to feel I'm prying, or that I'm urging you to be uncharitable. But at this point every bit of information is important."

"Nora never really abused her," I said. "The things that Dani felt bad about were generally acts of omission, rather than commission."

"Did you and Miss Hayden often quarrel in front of the child?"

I looked at her and laughed. "Our relationship was a very civilized one, at least according to Nora. We existed in a constant state of cold war. It never burst into open conflict."

"What made you stop visiting your daughter when you did?"

"I was told to."

"By Miss Hayden?"

I nodded.

"There's no record of the court terminating your

visiting rights. You didn't raise the issue when Miss Hayden forbade the visits?"

"I was in no position to do anything. I was broke."

"What did you do then?"

I looked into her eyes. "I got drunk," I said simply.

"You didn't try to tell your daughter why you couldn't visit her?"

I shook my head. "What good would that have done? It wouldn't have changed anything."

Miss Spicer didn't answer. After a few moments she said, "I saw your former mother-in-law yesterday. I presume you're aware of her plans for Dani?"

"I am."

I'd been at the meeting when it was discussed. The old lady had worked wonders in the short time she'd had. It must have cost her plenty, but Dani had already been accepted by a new school with a great reputation for dealing with problem children. Dr. Weidman, a prominent child psychiatrist, who was also connected with the school, was at the meeting and was prepared to take on the responsibility for her rehabilitation.

"Do you approve?" Miss Spicer asked.

"I think it's an extremely good plan. It seems to me that Dani would have far better care than the state could provide."

"You don't object to Dani's becoming a ward of her grandmother's?"

"No. It seems the only practical solution to me. Mrs. Hayden is an extremely responsible person. She'll make certain that Dani has everything she needs."

"I'm sure she will," Miss Spicer said dryly. "But, then, if what you tell me is true, so did her mother."

I knew what she meant. Nora had given Dani everything she seemed to need and still it hadn't prevented anything. "Mrs. Hayden will be able to devote much

more time to Dani. She doesn't have the outside interests that Nora has."

"You know, of course, Colonel, that your daughter
is not a virgin. In all probability she was having an affair
with the man she killed."

"I've guessed as much," I said frankly.

"Miss Hayden said she hadn't been aware of it."

I had nothing to say to that.

"It seems to us that Dani has little conception of
sexual morality. And from what we've been able to find
out, her mother hasn't set a particularly good example."

"I think we all realize that," I said. "That's one of
the reasons why I feel Dani would be better off living
with her grandmother."

She looked at me. "That might be true. But we're a
little concerned about it. If the grandmother wasn't
successful in curbing the impulses of her own daughter,
how successful could she be with her grandchild?" She
finished her cup of coffee. "Perhaps the best thing for
the child would be to remove her from that environment
completely."

She got to her feet. "Thank you very much for talking
with me, Colonel."

In the lobby she stopped for a moment. "There are
two things that still puzzle me."

"What are they?"

"Why did Dani kill him if she loved him?"

"And the other?"

"If she did kill him, why is it that no matter where we
turn we can find no evidence that Dani possessed a
violent enough temper to explode into murder?" She
hesitated a moment. "If we only had more time."

"How would that help?"

"We have to find the cause before we can recommend
the cure," she said. "We're working against time. We

recommend a course of action and hope that we're right. But if we can't turn up the reason, we have to recommend that the child be sent to Perkins for a study in depth. We have to be sure."

"What's your batting average?" I asked.

She looked up at me and smiled suddenly. "Surprisingly good. It's always a source of wonder to me."

"Maybe you people are better than you think."

"I hope so," she said seriously. "More for the children's sake than our own."

I watched her walk out of the lobby, then went back to my room. I called Elizabeth again, but again the telephone just rang and rang. Finally I gave up and went across the street to *Tommy's Joynt* and had some big German knockwurst and beans and a stein of beer for dinner.

On Sunday I drove out to Juvenile Hall. Dani seemed to be in a good mood.

"Mother came out to see me twice this week. You just missed her. She said they were fixing it so I can live at Grandmother's when I get out. Both times she came with Dr. Weidman. You know him, Daddy?"

"I met him."

"He's a head-shrinker. I think Mother likes him."

"What makes you say that?"

She gave me a sly grin. "He's Mother's type. You know, talks a lot and says nothing. Art and all that jazz."

I laughed. "How about a Coke?"

"It's a deal."

I gave her two dimes and watched her walk over to the vending machine. Quite a few of the tables were occupied. It looked more like Parents' Day at a school than a detention home. Only the matrons at the doors and the bars on the high windows told me it wasn't. Dani came back and put the Cokes down on the table.

"Do you want a straw, Daddy?"

"No, thanks. I'll take mine straight." I raised the bottle to my lips and took a swallow.

She looked at me over her straw. "When I do that, Mother says it's vulgar."

"Your mother's an expert on vulgarity," I said quickly, then regretted it. We were silent for a minute.

"Do you still drink the way you used to, Daddy?" Dani asked suddenly.

I stared at her in surprise. "What made you ask that all of a sudden?"

"I just remembered something," she said. "How you used to smell when you'd come to pick me up. It's nothing. I just thought of it, that's all."

"No, I don't drink like that any more."

"Was it because of Mother?"

I thought for a moment. It would be easy enough to say it was. But it wouldn't be altogether true. "No," I said. "That wasn't the reason."

"Then why did you, Daddy?"

"For a lot of reasons. But mostly because I was trying to hide from myself. I didn't want to face the fact that I was a failure."

Dani was silent while she thought about that. Then she had her answer. "But you weren't a failure, Daddy," she said. "You had your boat."

I smiled, thinking how simple her logic made it. But in a way she was right. She probably didn't know that I'd ever tried anything else. "I was an architect. I wanted to be a builder but it didn't work out."

"But you're a builder now. One of the papers said so."

"I'm not really. I just work for a builder. I'm really a construction foreman."

"I'd like to be a builder," she said suddenly. "I'd build happy houses."

"How would you go about doing that?"

"I wouldn't build a house for any family unless they were happy together and wanted to stay together."

I smiled at her. Right was right. She had the only foundation you could build on. But who gave the guarantees? God?

"Since we're playing truth or consequences," I said as lightly as I could, "would you mind telling me a few things?"

A look of caution came into her eyes. "Like what, Daddy?"

"Exactly whose boy friend was Riccio? Yours or your mother's?"

She hesitated. "Mother's."

"But you—" It was my turn to hesitate.

She met my gaze candidly. "Did they tell you we were making out?"

I nodded.

She looked down at her Coke. "That's right, Daddy. We were."

"Why, Dani?" I asked. "Why him in particular? Why not anyone else?"

"You know Mother. She likes to be the wheel in everything. Just this once I wanted to show her she wasn't."

"Did you?" I asked. "Is that why you killed him?"

Her eyes fell away from mine. "I didn't mean to," she said in a low voice. "It was an accident."

"Were you jealous of your mother, Dani? Is that why?"

She shook her head. "I don't want to talk about it," she said stubbornly. "I told them everything at the police station before they brought me here."

"Unless you tell them the truth, Dani," I said, "they may not let you live at Grandmother's."

She still didn't look at me. "They can't keep me forever. When I'm eighteen they'll have to let me out. I know that much."

"Three-and-a-half years is a long time out of any-one's life to stay locked up."

"What do you care?" She looked at me defiantly. "Next Tuesday when this is over, you'll go home and you'll probably never come to see me again. Just like before."

"But I do care, Dani. That's why I'm here now. I told you why I couldn't come before."

Her voice was sullen. "That's a lot of crap! You'd have come if you had cared enough!" She looked down at the Coke bottle again. I wondered what she saw in the brown liquid through the green glass that was so absorbing.

"It's easy for you to come back and say things like that," she said in a low voice. "It's always easy to say the right things. But it's not so easy to do them."

"I know that, Dani. I'm the first one to admit that I've made mistakes."

"All right, Daddy." She looked up and suddenly she wasn't a little girl any longer. She was a young woman. "So we've all made mistakes. Let's drop it. I said I didn't want to talk about it any more. It's my life and there's nothing you can say that will change anything for me. It's too late now. You've been away too long."

She was wrong and she was right. Like there's nothing ever completely black or white.

"Was there ever anyone else? Other boys, I mean?"

She shook her head. "No."

"You're not lying to me, are you, Dani?"

Her eyes looked right into mine. No, Daddy. I'm not lying. I couldn't do it with anyone else. I might have started because I wanted to show Mother, but it wound up something else."

"How did it wind up?"

Her eyes were clear and soft and there was a sadness in them. "I loved him, Daddy," she said quietly. "And he loved me. We were going to run away and get married, just as soon as I was old enough."

The sun was finally beginning to break up the fog. I walked away from the window restlessly. I picked up the paper and turned to the amusement page. I thought of going to a movie but I'd seen almost every picture in town. I turned on the television. Ten minutes later I switched it off. I was the in-between generation for the daytime offerings. One generation too old, one generation too young.

Then the telephone rang and I jumped to answer it. Maybe Elizabeth had got over her mad.

"Colonel Carey?"

"Yes."

"This is Lorenzo Stradella. Remember those two letters we sent Anna to get?"

"What about them?"

"Well. I still have them," he said.

"What are you calling me for? You know who bought them."

"That's right. But she's already paid. I figure you ought to be good for these two."

"Not interested," I said. "Take them to Miss Hayden."

"Wait a minute! Don't hang up."

"I'm waiting."

"I can't take them to her. I'll give you a good deal."

Suddenly I understood. Of course he couldn't take them to Nora. Nora would tell Coriano. And Coriano didn't like his boys holding out on him. I tried it out.

"Okay, but I'm not dealing with any small fry. Tell Coriano to get in touch with me. That way maybe I'll be sure no more of them turn up later."

I had guessed right.

"No Coriano. This deal is between you and me."

"Coriano won't like that."

"I'll make it so cheap he won't have to know."

"How cheap is that?" I asked.

"Five Cs."

"Goodbye, Charley," I said and hung up. I had just time to light a cigarette before he called back.

This time his voice was a little softer. "What do *you* call cheap?"

"Fifty bucks."

"That *is* cheap."

"You're talking to a real cheap guy. I'm from the poor side of the family."

"I'll make it easy on you. Two-fifty."

"One hundred is as high as I'll go."

He didn't say anything for a moment and I figured he was thinking.

"It's found money," I said.

"You're on."

"Bring them on over."

"Not so fast. You're the square type. You might have the cops there."

"Don't be a jerk."

"You be in your room eleven o'clock tonight. I'll send someone over with them."

"Okay," I said.

"Remember. No tricks. Hand over the dough, you'll get the letters."

The telephone went dead and I put it down. I went over to the table and wrote a check for a hundred dollars. Then I went downstairs and cashed it. I kept my fingers crossed all during the time the cashier was counting out the money. I only hoped there was enough dough in the bank to cover it.

16

When I got back to my room the message light was blinking on and off. Nora had phoned and wanted me to call her back. I dialed the number.

"This is Mr. Carey, Charles," I said. "Is Miss Hayden there?"

"Just a moment, sir. I'll put her on."

I heard a click and then her voice. "Luke?"

"Yes," I said. "What did you want?"

"I want to talk to you. Can you come for dinner?"

"I don't think so. It wouldn't feel right."

"Don't be old-fashioned. I won't eat you. I want to talk to you about Dani."

"What about her?"

"We'll talk at dinner."

I hesitated a moment. A good meal wouldn't do me any harm. I'd about had it with the knockwurst and beans. "What time?"

"Come early enough for a drink. About seven o'clock?"

"See you then," I said and put down the telephone wondering what in hell brought that on all of a sudden.

When I rang the bell at seven Charles opened the door almost immediately. "Good evening, Colonel."

"Good evening, Charles."

It was almost as if I'd never been away. "Madam is in the library. You know the way," he said with a faint smile.

"I know the way," I answered wryly.

355

I knocked at the library door and went in. Nora rose from the big couch facing the desk. Dr. Weidman was a fraction of a second behind her. She came toward me, her hand outstretched. "Luke. I'm so glad you could come."

I knew that tone of voice. It was warm and friendly as if there'd never been any real differences between us. The *company* voice she had always used whenever she had an audience.

Still holding my hand she turned toward the doctor. "You remember Dr. Weidman? He was at Mother's."

How could I forget? Especially after what Dani had said. What was I supposed to do, give the bride away?

"How are you, Doctor?" I would have held out my hand only for some reason or other Nora still held on to it.

He bowed slightly. "Good to see you again, Colonel."

Then Nora let go of my hand. "There's a fresh bottle of bourbon on the bar. Bourbon is still your drink, isn't it?"

I nodded. She'd made her point. I walked over to the bar. "Can I fix something for you?" I asked automatically. It was as if I still lived there. I used to ask that whenever we had drinks in the library.

"No, thanks. The doctor and I are having martinis."

I turned to look at them. That was one of the tipoffs that Nora was interested in the doctor. She was a Scotch drinker basically, but there were two things she picked up the moment she found a new man—his brand of cigarettes and his drink.

We all sipped. It wasn't until I sat down that I realized I'd gone behind the desk to my old chair. I took another sip of my drink and put it down on the desk. "Nothing's been changed," I said, looking around the room.

"There was no reason to change it, Luke," Nora said quickly. "This was always your room."

I wondered why she'd said that. Nora had no sentimentality about things like that. "It seems to me I'd have changed it around," I said. "If only to avoid annoying memories."

She smiled. "I had nothing to avoid."

Dr. Weidman finished his drink and got to his feet. "Well, I really must be going, Nora."

"Are you sure you can't stay for dinner, Doctor?"

He shook his head regretfully. "I'm due back in my office," he said. "I have an eight-o'clock appointment."

Nora put down her drink and got up. "I'll see you to the door."

Weidman turned to me. This time we shook hands. "Nice seeing you again, Colonel."

"Goodbye, Doctor."

I watched them walk out of the room and then I sat down behind the desk again. Idly I opened one of the drawers. There was an old blueprint there. I took it out and looked at it. It was for the pilot house of my first project.

So many years ago and yet like yesterday. I studied the plans. It was still a good house. There were only a few things I'd change if I were building it today.

Nora stood in the doorway watching me. "You see, nothing has been changed, Luke. I didn't even empty the desk."

"So I see." I put the plans back and closed the drawer. "Exactly why did you ask me to dinner?"

She smiled and closed the door behind her. "That can wait until after dinner. You're always much more reasonable on a full stomach."

She came over and stood in front of the desk, looking down at me. "I always said that rooms are for people.

Somehow this one always seemed empty to me without you in it."

"Come off it, Nora." I smiled to take the sting out of my words. "The audience is gone. You're not sentimental about silly things like that."

She laughed suddenly. "We have no illusions left, have we, Luke?"

I shook my head. "I guess not."

She walked over to her drink and picked it up. She looked at it for a few moments, then suddenly set it down with a thud. "Be a good sport, Luke. Fix me a Scotch and soda. I don't see how anyone can drink these damn martinis. They smell like cheap perfume."

I got up and fixed her a drink, then walked it to the couch. She took a sip from it and nodded. "That's much better."

I walked back and picked up my drink. I leaned back against the desk and raised my glass to her. She raised hers. We both drank.

"Dr. Weidman has such an interesting face. Don't you think so, Luke?"

I gestured with my hands.

"Do you know what his first name is?"

"No."

"Isidore. Can you imagine that? Isidore. In this day and age. You'd think he'd change a name like that."

"Maybe he likes it."

"I don't think so," she said thoughtfully. "But he's too proud to admit it. That's one thing I've noticed about these Jewish doctors. They're very proud."

"They've got every reason to be."

"They wear their religion like a cloak. And you know another thing I've noticed about them?"

"What?"

"They've all got such sad eyes," she said. "Like the paintings of Christ."

The door opened and Charles came into the library. "Dinner is served, madam."

The dinner was too much. It began with cracked crab, served on lettuce leaves spread over shaved ice, and with it that wonderful tangy mustard sauce that only Charles seemed able to conjure up. After that, cioppino, a kind of San Francisco bouillabaisse which is more a fish stew than a soup, with everything in it that the Pacific has to offer. Then roast beef, a great thick slab with the rib still attached, medium rare with the blood running out on the plate. And finally, great halves of yellow cling peaches, over rich chocolate ice cream, just the way I'd always liked them. I looked up at Charles as he filled my coffee cup.

He smiled. He remembered how much I liked canned peaches. At first he'd been horrified by my taste and had ordered giant fresh peaches especially for me. But after a while he gave in and bought the cans. He had also remembered that I liked a large coffee cup after dinner, not a demitasse.

"That was a great dinner, Nora," I said.

She smiled. "I'm glad you liked it, Luke."

I liked it all right. I'd eaten like a horse but she'd merely picked at her food in her usual manner.

"I think I know you well enough that you won't mind if I go into the kitchen and tell Cookie how great it was."

Nora rose from the table. "You go right ahead. We'll have more coffee and brandy in the studio when you come out."

I went into the kitchen. Cookie was there, her face red and steaming from the stove, as I always remembered it. Only her hair was gray now, to remind me of the passing of time.

"Colonel Carey!" she exclaimed in a pleased voice.

"Cookie! I couldn't leave without telling you what a wonderful meal that was."

"I loved preparing it for you, Colonel. You was always a good eater." Then her face clouded over. "There was only one thing missing. I wish Miss Dani had been here too."

"Maybe she'll be home soon," I said gently.

"Do you really think so, Colonel?"

"I hope so, Cookie."

"I hope so too. If only we'd been home that day maybe it would never have happened."

I'd started to turn away but I turned back to her. "Weren't you home that day?"

"No, sir. Thursday is our day off. But since Miss Hayden was in Los Angeles and would not be home until late Friday evening, Mr. Riccio had also given us Friday."

"I didn't know that."

"I went to Oakland to visit my sister and didn't get back until late. Until it was all over."

I looked at Charles. "And you?"

"I was back at six o'clock," he said. "Miss Hayden was already home."

"What about Violet?"

"Violet came in a few minutes after I did."

"Then you must have heard something of the quarrel," I said.

Charles shook his head. "No, sir. No one wanted the cold supper I'd prepared, so Violet and I stayed in the kitchen. You can't hear anything in the house from here."

He was right about that. I remembered laying out the house so that the kitchen and servants' quarters would be away from the rest of it. Nora had always said there was nothing quite so annoying as trying to talk over the sound of dishes being washed in the kitchen.

I turned back to the cook and smiled. "It was still a wonderful dinner, Cookie," I said. "Thank you very much."

She smiled at me. "Thank you, Colonel."

The brandy and coffee were on the cocktail table in the center of the small conversational grouping in the corner of the studio. Nora looked up from her chair and smiled as I came into the room. I knew from that that she was ready to get down to business.

"How was it?" she asked. "Was Cookie glad to see you?"

"It was like Old Home Week." I closed the door and sat down opposite her.

She poured some brandy into the glasses, then handed one to me. I closed my hands about the bottom of it and sloshed the brandy around to warm it. I sniffed the bouquet as it came up from the glass. It was rich and warm and exploded like tiny firecrackers in my nose.

Nora was watching me. "Well?" I asked.

She picked up her brandy glass and took a small sip from it. When she spoke her voice was husky. "I want you to help bring Dani back here, where she belongs."

It was as if the mountain finally came to Mohammed.

"Why me?" I asked finally.

Her voice was still husky. "Because together we could do it. You and I. We could bring Dani home."

I took a swallow of the brandy. "You're forgetting one thing. I don't live here any more."

"That could be arranged," she said softly.

I sat there watching her and suddenly I realized she hadn't changed at all. The laws she lived by were the same as they had always been. The only thing important to her was what she wanted to do. What damage she'd do, whom she would hurt, didn't matter at all.

"Uh-uh," I said.

"Think about it. Dani would be better off with us than with Mother, certainly better off than in one of those youth homes. Gordon thinks we might carry it off if we got together. Dr. Weidman feels the psychology is sound, that the court would have to agree."

"It might be a good idea if I were still single," I said. "But I'm not."

"You said your wife was an understanding woman. She must know how you feel about Dani, or she wouldn't have let you come out here. We can make it very attractive for her. She need never have to worry about money for the rest of her life!"

"Don't waste your breath, Nora," I said. "It's impossible."

I put down the brandy snifter and started to get up. She leaned forward in her chair and put her hand on mine. She looked up into my face. "Luke."

I stared down at her. I could feel the electricity reaching through the pressure of her fingers. I remained very still, not speaking.

"Remember how it used to be, Luke?" she said softly.

"I remember."

The pressure of her fingers grew stronger. "It can be like that again, Luke. It never was with anyone else the way it was with you and me, was it?"

It was almost as if I were hypnotized. "No," I answered.

"It could be like that again."

I tore my hand away angrily, more angry with myself than with her. I knew that the way I felt was the wrong that Nora always tried to make right. The spell was broken. "No," I said harshly. "Nothing could ever be like that again. Whatever it was, it was never the truth. It was never real. I can't go back to living with lies again."

"That's just it, Luke! We don't have to. Now there are no illusions left, remember? It can be a very sensible arrangement."

"Don't be a damn fool, Nora!"

"I have my work," she said, still looking at me. "You'd have yours. I spoke to Cousin George. He said they'd be delighted to have you back. And most important, we'd have a home for Dani to come back to."

Suddenly I was weary. There wasn't anything that Nora had missed, but she couldn't see that none of it was real. I began to feel sorry for her. "No, Nora," I said gently.

She leaned back in her chair, a hint of anger coming into her voice. "You cried so much over your daughter," she said harshly. "About how much you loved her, about how much you wanted to do for her. And now that you have the chance to really do something for her, you won't lift a finger!"

There were so many things that I'd just begun to understand. Like what Elizabeth had meant when she said she wanted me to come home without the ghosts that had plagued me for so long. Somehow she must have known it would come to this. That I would have to choose between her and Dani.

I felt my heart begin to swell. She'd known, and still she had let me come. There wasn't much more a man could ask of his wife.

I looked down at Nora and in a way it was as if I were seeing her for the first time. Sam Corwin had been right when he'd said the only thing she had was her art.

Outside of that there was nothing else that she could share with anyone.

"I came here to help Dani," I said quietly. "But not by building a life for her on pretense and destruction."

"How very noble. The next thing, I suppose, you'll be telling me that you love your wife!"

I looked at her thoughtfully. Then suddenly I smiled. She had put everything into words for me. "That's right, Nora," I said. "I do."

"How much do you think she'll love you after I send those pictures?"

I'd been waiting for that. I didn't answer.

"What reason will you have then for refusing me?"

"The best reason in the world, Nora. I just don't like you."

Love dies with words like those. It burns up and destroys itself with the language of hate and recrimination. It tears apart in anger and violence. But after the explosion, some vestige of it still remains, clinging to the mind and heart like an unfulfilled hope, the memory of a passion that never came to fruition. Then it dies finally, with a few simple, almost childlike, words.

And the ghosts are gone, the guilts vanish. This was the way it was, this is the way it would have been. No matter what you did.

I put down all the windows of the little car as I drove back to the motel. The cool clean night air washed even the hate I had felt out of my soul. Nora didn't matter that much to me. Not any more.

17

I got back to the motel at a quarter to eleven and went directly to my room. At exactly eleven o'clock there was a knock at my door. I opened it.

Anna Stradella stood there, an almost frightened expression on her face.

I stepped back. "Come in, Anna," I said. I closed the door behind her. "Why did he send you?"

"Because he didn't think you'd turn me over to the cops if they were here."

"You don't have to be frightened. They aren't here."

A hint of relief came into her eyes. "I didn't think they would be."

"You have the letters?"

Silently she opened her handbag. She took them out and gave them to me.

"What if I said I didn't have the money?"

She shrugged her shoulders. "It wouldn't matter."

"What would you tell your brother?"

She turned to me, her eyes filled with a secret hurt. "I don't have to tell him anything. I gave him the hundred dollars before he gave me the letters."

"Why did you do that?" I asked.

"Because I wanted you to have them. We did you enough harm."

She began to cry. I stood there looking at her. "Anna," I said, "please don't. I have the money."

"I'm not crying about that," she said. The tears were rolling down her cheeks now, leaving heavy mascara streaks. "Everything's so mixed up!"

"What is?" I asked. "What are you crying about?"

"Steve. He asked me to marry him today. And I didn't know what to tell him!"

I smiled. I still didn't understand women. "I thought that was what you wanted."

"I do." She sniffed into a Kleenex she had pulled from her bag.

"Then what's the problem? He knows about his brother?"

She looked at me. "He knows about Tony. But he doesn't know about anything else."

"What else does he have to know about?"

"The same things Tony knew about," she answered. "A girl works for Coriano, she does things."

I took a deep breath. "Do you want to marry him?"

She nodded.

I put a hand on her shoulder. "Then go ahead. Whatever else you did doesn't matter."

She looked up at me. "Do you really believe that?"

"He loves you or he wouldn't want to marry you. That's the only thing that counts."

She started to smile.

"Now go into the bathroom and wash your face. I'll call down and have them send up some coffee. We can both use some."

She went into the bathroom and closed the door. I called room service and then I sat down and looked at the letters.

I opened Dani's first. I felt sick inside when I read it. It was the kind of a letter only a child could write, yet the things that were written there no child should know. It was exactly the kind of a letter Lorenzo had said it was.

A knock came at the door. Room service in this place

was prompt, I thought, as I went to answer it. I opened the door.

It was Nora. I stood there gawking at her.

"May I come in?" she asked and walked past me into the room. "I came to apologize, Luke." She took an envelope from her handbag. "Here are the pictures. I wouldn't have used them."

Automatically I took the envelope. I still hadn't said a word when the bathroom door opened and Anna came out.

She still held a towel in her hands, her face was clean of makeup. "Is the coffee here yet, Mr. Carey?" she asked. Then she saw Nora and stopped.

They stared at each other for a moment, then Nora turned back to me. Whatever it was that I had seen in her face before was now gone. She looked hurt and angry and duped.

"I should have known better," she said coldly. "I was beginning to believe everything you said."

I put a hand on her arm to stop her. "Nora."

She shook my hand off roughly and looked up into my face. "*You* can stop acting now, Luke," she said. "You're not God. You just talk like you are!"

The door slammed behind her.

"I'm sorry, Mr. Carey. I'm always messing things up, aren't I?"

I stared at the closed door. I'd never heard Nora apologize for anything before. Never. I looked down at the envelope in my hand. The pictures were in there. I put them in my pocket.

There was another knock at the door. This time it was room service. I paid for the coffee and filled the cups. "Here," I said, holding one out to her. "Drink this. It will make you feel better."

Then I went back to the table. Anna sat down opposite me, her eyes large and sad. I picked up Nora's letter and began to read it.

Suddenly it was as if no one else was in the room. Everything was there in the letter. Everything. All the missing keys. All the answers I'd been searching for without knowing it. I reread the last paragraph again, just to make sure.

And now, my darling, that we've definitely set Thanksgiving as a wedding date, let me warn you about just one thing. I'm a jealous and possessive woman and if I ever catch you so much as looking at another woman, I'll cut your heart into tiny little pieces. So be careful.
All my love,
Nora

Anna's voice seemed to come from a long way off. "What's the matter?" she asked. "Your face is as white as a sheet!"

I looked up from the letter. There was pain binding my temples; it began to go away as I saw the look of concern on Anna's face.

"I'm all right," I said gruffly. "Nothing's the matter."

Everything fell into place now. All the bits and pieces. All the tortuous turns and twisted lies. I knew the truth now, though I was the only one besides Dani and Nora who did. Now there was just one problem remaining.

To prove to the court that my daughter had not committed murder. And that her mother had.

PART FIVE

LUKE'S STORY
The Trial

1

Dani seemed pale and tense as she came into the courtroom. She paused in the doorway behind Marian Spicer and looked around the room.

We were seated at the long table as we'd been seated for the last hearing, only this time Dr. Weidman sat next to Nora and Harris Gordon sat between Nora and her mother. That left me at the opposite end of the table from where Dani would sit with the probation officer.

The judge was already on the bench, the court clerk and the recorder with his stenotype machine were seated too. The court attendant, in his deputy sheriff's uniform, leaned in his usual negligent manner against a closed door.

I reached up and touched Dani's hand as she passed behind me on her way to her seat. Her hand was ice cold. I smiled encouragingly.

She forced a smile to her lips but it was only a travesty of one. I held my thumb up in a gesture of courage. Dani nodded and went on. She paused a moment to kiss the old lady and Nora, then went to her seat.

The judge didn't waste any time. His gavel rapped almost before Dani was settled in her chair. "It is the purpose of this hearing," he said, "to determine the future custody and care of Danielle Nora Carey, a minor, in accordance with her own best interests and the best interests of the state." He looked down at Dani. "Do you understand that, Danielle?"

Dani nodded. "Yes, sir."

"You may also remember," he continued, "that when you were in this court last week I informed you that you have certain rights: the right to call witnesses on your behalf; the right to counsel; the right to question any statement made about you which you regard as derogatory or harmful."

"Yes, sir."

"I understand also that you, together with your family, have agreed on Mr. Gordon to represent all of you mutually. Did you agree to that, Danielle?"

She didn't raise her eyes. "Yes, sir."

The judge looked at all of us. "We will proceed then," he said, picking up several sheets of paper from the desk in front of him. "We have before us two separate petitions for the custody of this child. One has been filed by the probation officer, Miss Marian Spicer, requesting that the state retain custody until such time as the child has undergone satisfactory rehabilitation and care and we can be reasonably sure that she will not again bring harm to herself or others by her actions. The other is a petition filed by Mr. Gordon, acting for the parents and relatives of the child, requesting that the child be made a ward of, and custody be entrusted to, Mrs. Hayden, the child's maternal grandmother. She would undertake the education, care and guidance of the child until she comes of age.

"Both plans are complete in their recommendations with specifics concerning the care and guidance of the child. If there are no objections we will begin our hearings with the consideration of the petition by the probation department."

"I have no objections, Your Honor," Gordon said.

"Good." The judge looked over at the probation officer. "Miss Spicer, would you please give the court your reasons for requesting that the state retain custody of the child?"

Marian Spicer cleared her throat nervously and got to her feet. "There are several reasons, Your Honor."

She began in a thin, tense voice. Then, as she spoke, her nervousness gradually disappeared and her voice become more normal. "We must recognize that this child was brought to the attention of the probation department and this court because of a serious criminal charge—homicide."

"Objection!" Harris Gordon was on his feet. "The verdict of the coroner's court was 'justifiable homicide.'"

I could see that Miss Spicer was flustered. She looked at the judge.

"The objection is sustained and noted," he said, looking down at Gordon. "But may I call to your attention that Juvenile Law automatically provides that all such objections be made and noted on behalf of the minor? However, since there is no jury impaneled in this court, which needs instruction in these matters, we do not find it necessary to give voice to these objections."

Gordon nodded. "Yes, Your Honor."

The judge looked at the probation officer. "You may continue, Miss Spicer."

Marian Spicer looked down at some papers on the table in front of her and began again. "The probation department, of course, is concerned not only with the charge itself but with the reasons why the minor has committed such a crime and what possibly can be done to prevent another such occurrence on the part of the minor in the future.

"As you will note in our report, Your Honor, we have made an intensive investigation of the background of the child and of the circumstances surrounding her action. We have also examined the child physically and

psychologically as best we could under the circumstances."

She glanced briefly at Nora. "From the physical and
medical examination of the child we have determined
that she is generally in good health but that she had in-
tensively engaged in sexual relations during the period
immediately before she was brought to us. It is the
opinion of the examining physician that she indulged in
sexual relations for a period of at least a year prior to
that. This would make her little more than thirteen when
she began this sort of activity."

I looked at Dani. Her face was pale and she stared
down at the table. The probation officer continued.

"When we questioned Dani about this she refused to
discuss it. She would not tell us with whom she had committed these acts, nor would she confirm or deny that
these acts of sexual contact were indulged in by her.
When we pointed out that her refusal to discuss these
matters might react unfavorably on her disposition, she
stubbornly maintained that this conduct had nothing to
do with the matter for which she was brought here."

The judge cleared his throat. "Dani," he said in a
stern voice, "do you understand what Miss Spicer is
saying?"

Dani didn't look up. "Yes, sir."

"You know, of course, that such actions are very
wrong?" he said in the same tone of voice. "That nice
girls don't do such things? That this sort of behavior is
contrary to all standards of morality and is considered
very sinful?"

Dani still didn't look up. "Yes, sir."

"Then there is nothing that you have to tell us about
it in justification of yourself?"

She looked up at him. "No, sir," she answered in a
firm voice.

The judge looked down at her for a moment, then turned back to Miss Spicer. "Please continue."

"The child had a number of meetings with Miss Sally Jennings, our staff psychologist, during which she also refused to discuss these matters, on the ground that they were too personal. However she freely discussed many other subjects with Miss Jennings, whose report is also included in the department's petition."

Miss Spicer picked up a sheet of paper. "Here is a summation of Miss Jennings' report. I quote:

" 'After various meetings with Danielle Nora Carey, I have come to the following opinions. Beneath the child's apparent surface adjustment, there is a deep-rooted and well-hidden feeling of resentment and jealousy toward her mother. This has shown itself many times, in the child's own words, by her explosions and arguments with her mother. She finds reassurance in the fact that her mother does care for her, because of the attention paid to her during such moments of rebellion. At other times, Dani feels very certain that her mother is not in the least interested in her. Dani expresses feelings that her mother has separated her from anyone who loved her more than her mother, that her mother is jealous of her, then contradicts herself by maintaining that her mother loves her. There are some indications that a mild paranoia may lie beneath these observations, but at this stage of our observation it is difficult to be sure. Whether this latent paranoia has the potential to erupt in violence again under certain given circumstances, I cannot definitely say. I recommend strongly that the child be detained in custody until all such areas are completely examined and evaluated.' "

Miss Spicer put down the paper and looked up at the judge again. "As is usual, we also made a thorough investigation of the child's school and home life. Her school record is an extremely favorable one scholastically. She stands high in her class. Socially she is acceptable to her classmates, though they feel she exhibits a superiority toward them in the area of sophistication and worldly knowledge. The few boys whom she went out with all felt that she acted slightly bored while she was in their company.

"We spoke also to Miss Hayden, the child's mother, who expressed surprise at our knowledge of Dani's sexual activity. She claims that she had never been aware of it. Our investigation of Miss Hayden revealed that although she took good physical care of the child, the standards of her own behavior, both in her home and out, were highly questionable and certainly did not provide her daughter with an acceptable moral climate. Without attempting to pass judgment on Miss Hayden, because we realize that as an artist she lives in a peculiar world of her own, certainly the sophistication and conduct of that world would not properly influence Dani in what is normally considered right or wrong. Without going into specific instances of Miss Hayden's actions, of which we have many, we feel that this in itself would make it extremely hazardous to entrust the child to her supervision."

I glanced at Nora. Her lips were pressed tightly together as she glared at the probation officer. If looks could kill, the probation officer would be dead.

Miss Spicer did not even look at her, directing her whole attention to the judge. "We spoke also to the child's maternal grandmother, Mrs. Hayden, who would like to undertake the responsibility for this child. Mrs. Hayden has an excellent reputation in the community and is highly regarded by everyone. There is, however, one handicap which we feel is extremely hazardous. Mrs. Hayden, at present, is seventy-four years old, and although she seems to be in excellent physical health we realize that she cannot personally look after the child herself. She must necessarily rely on others to perform the physical acts she cannot undertake, and while her intentions are admirable we have doubts as to whether she will be able to discharge all the duties she is willing to assume. So, although we have the greatest respect for Mrs. Hayden, we are reluctant to recommend that the child be given into her care at this time."

The old lady's eyes were impassive. She watched the probation officer calmly. Apparently she had expected this objection all along.

Miss Spicer got to me last. "We have also spoken to Colonel Carey, the child's father. He is automatically ineligible to care for the child by virtue of the fact that he resides out of the state. But in addition there are other factors that might preclude his undertaking the responsibility. For many years he has not seen or communicated with his daughter. They have grown apart and are separated by more than the ordinary circumstances of a child's growing up. We doubt if he has the experience or ability, both financial and personal, to undertake the responsibility for his daughter."

I could understand now why she had said they didn't goof up many cases. I looked up to see if the judge had been as impressed. His ruddy face shone from the heat in the humid courtroom. But his eyes were unreadable behind his glasses.

"In view of the foregoing information," Miss Spicer went on, "we request that the court turn the child over to the California Youth Authority at the Northern California Reception Center at Perkins. It is our hope that after their examination they will send her to Los Guilicos, the rehabilitation school at Santa Rosa, where she will be under competent supervision and will receive

proper psychiatric therapy until she is of legal age and
released on her own recognizance."

A silence came over the courtroom as the probation
officer sat down. None of us looked at each other. In a
way I imagine we were all filled with a kind of shame.

The judge's voice broke the silence. "Do you have any
questions regarding the recommendation contained in
the petition of the probation department?"

Harris Gordon got to his feet. "There are a number
of objections, as I'm sure the court realizes, that under
ordinary circumstances I should make to a report of this
kind. But I'm sure the court recognizes them as well as
I, and they will so be made."

The judge nodded. "They will so be made, Mr.
Gordon."

"Thank you, Your Honor," Gordon said smoothly.
"We believe that our petition clearly states our position
and any questions we might have in regard to the
petition of the probation department. We believe that
the investigation of the probation department has, in
many respects, been extremely superficial and prejudiced. Under many circumstances, I suspect this would
not make a great difference, but the department must
recognize that the ability of the family to provide proper
care for the child is well within its means, both physically and financially. Better care, perhaps, than the state
itself could afford to give."

"The court has read your petition, Mr. Gordon. We
are now ready to take it under consideration. Would you
please proceed?"

Gordon nodded. He still remained standing. "Your
Honor, for the purposes of this petition, let it be known
that the petitioner in this case is Mrs. Marguerite Cecelia
Hayden, the child's maternal grandmother."

"The court so acknowledges."

"Thank you, Your Honor. Without prejudice to the child, let me say that the petitioner recognizes many of the factors inherent in this case, also stated in the petition of the probation department. It is the contention of the petitioner, however, that the probation department, because of its physical limitations, and the state, because of the many burdens placed upon it, cannot give this child the care, so necessary for her complete rehabilitation, that is within the power of the petitioner.

"Rather than the vague generalities of confinement and treatment stated in the petition of the probation department, we have proposed and are ready to implement a specific method of care and treatment for this child.

"Already we have entered into an agreement with the Abingdon School for Girls for the child's immediate enrollment. I do not have to state the reputation of Abingdon School. I am sure it is well known to the court. It has perhaps the most successful record with so-called problem children of any school in the country. One of the reasons for that success, it has been said, is that the child is not removed from all contact with normal home life. The child is cared for in a completely normal environment and returns home each night, as from any other school.

"I have in this court Dr. Isidore Weidman, a prominent child psychiatrist. He is closely associated with Abingdon School and will undertake the psychological and psychiatric care and treatment of this child. He has made himself available should there be any questions concerning his specific plans for this child." Gordon looked questioningly at the bench.

"The court knows of Dr. Weidman," the judge said, "and has a great deal of respect for his abilities and opinions. However it has no reason at this time to question the doctor."

Gordon nodded. "Mrs. Hayden has also made arrangements for her granddaughter to attend St. Thomas Church, so that she may begin to enjoy the guidance of sound Christian precepts. The Reverend J. J. Williston of St. Thomas Church, who unfortunately could not attend the hearing this morning, is willing, however, to come down to this court at its convenience later today should he be needed for consultation."

"The court will bear that in mind, Counselor."

"Mrs. Hayden has also set aside a suite of rooms in her home to be redecorated and made available to the child. She is prepared to exercise every care, both physical and moral, that a parent should. As to the concern of the probation department over the physical condition of Mrs. Hayden—"

Gordon picked up a glass of water from the table and took a sip from it. He put the glass down and turned back to the judge.

"Mrs. Hayden is at present a member of the board of directors of eleven different corporations and is actively concerned in the affairs of four of them. She is also a trustee of the College of Arts and Sciences at the university and an officer of the Daughters of the Founders of San Francisco Society.

"Several days ago Mrs. Hayden went into General Hospital at my request and underwent a complete physical examination. I have the written reports of that physical here and I should like to read from it."

He picked up a sheet of paper. " 'It is the opinion of the examining physicians, whose signatures are appended to this report, that Mrs. Marguerite Cecelia Hayden, age 74, is in excellent health and vigor and shows no extraordinary defects commonly associated with people in her age bracket. We are of the further opinion that, barring accident or unforeseen circumstances, Mrs. Hayden should be able to enjoy the benefits of her present good health for many years to come.' "

Gordon paused and looked up at the judge. "This report is signed by Dr. Walter Llewellyn, Professor of Geriatrics, College of Medicine, University of Southern California, the head physician of the examining group. There are five other doctors who also affixed their signatures. I will read them if the court so desires."

"The court accepts the statement of counsel. There is no reason to name the other physicians."

Gordon took another sip of water. "There is very little more that I can add to the petition, except one thing." He looked across the table at Dani. "We ask the court to bear in mind that for a child there is no greater or more powerful cure than to be loved, to be secure in the knowledge that it is loved. Without that, all our knowledge of medicine and psychiatry is powerless. With it, no cure is impossible.

"It is our contention that Mrs. Hayden can do everything and more for her granddaughter than the state could. Plus this one important added factor—the love they bear for each other. Love that an institution, no matter how well intentioned, cannot provide."

The judge looked at Miss Spicer. "Do you have any questions regarding this petition?"

The probation officer got to her feet. "The probation department has considered the petition made by Mrs. Hayden most carefully and still feels that the best interests of the child and the state would be served by its own proposal. Had we felt otherwise, we would have joined our recommendation with theirs."

The judge looked down at Dani. "Danielle, do you

have any questions to ask about either of these petitions?"

"No, sir," she answered in a low voice.

"You understand what I have to decide now?" he asked. "Now I must decide what is to be done with you. Whether you are to remain in the custody of the state or go to your grandmother. The more I know about you, the better I will be able to decide. Is there anything more you wish to tell me now?"

Dani didn't look at him. "No, sir."

"Not only have you committed a terrible deed," he said in his most somber voice, "but you admit to highly immoral and improper behavior as well. The kind of behavior we both know is very wrong and which under no circumstances can be permitted to continue. Is there anything you can tell me that would persuade me to grant your grandmother's petition?"

She still didn't look up. "No, sir."

"If you won't tell me in court, would you talk to me in private? In my chambers, where no one else will be able to hear us?"

"No, sir."

He sighed. "You know, you're not leaving me with very much choice, are you?"

Her voice was very faint. "No, sir."

I thought there was a hint of sadness in the judge's eyes as he leaned back in his chair. He sat like that for a moment, then turned slightly and looked at all of us. His face was solemn. He cleared his throat as if to speak.

We were watching him as intently as if he were the last man in the world. He cleared his throat again, his hand reaching for his gavel.

"Your Honor!" I said, suddenly getting to my feet.

"Yes, Colonel Carey?"

I looked around the table. I was aware of the surprise

and shock on all the faces, but the only one that I really saw was Dani's.

She stared up at me, her eyes large and round in her pale face. I noticed the faintly blue circles under them and I knew that she must have been crying before she came into court. I turned and looked up at the judge.

This was the last chance I'd have to do anything for my daughter.

2

I cleared my throat. "Do I have the right to ask a few questions, Your Honor?"

"You have the same rights in this court as your daughter Colonel Carey," the judge answered. "You have the right to counsel, the right to summon and question witnesses on matters pertinent to this hearing."

"Thank you, Judge," I said. "I have a question to ask Miss Spicer."

"You may ask the question."

I turned to the probation office. "Miss Spicer, do you believe my daughter is capable of murder?"

Gordon was on his feet. "Objection, Your Honor!" he said angrily. "Colonel Carey is asking a question that could be prejudicial to my client."

The judge looked at him. "Mr. Gordon," he said in a faintly annoyed voice, "I thought we had already explained to you that all objections on behalf of the minor are automatically made." He turned to Miss Spicer. "You may answer the question."

The probation officer hesitated. "I don't know."

"You told me the other day that you found it hard to believe that a child like Dani could commit murder," I said. "That you'd feel better if you were able to establish a sound psychological reason for her actions. Why did you feel like that?"

She looked up at the judge. "Neither Miss Jennings nor myself has been able to establish close enough contact with Danielle to determine what she really is capable of. We feel that she exhibits an extraordinary amount of self-control in one so young."

"You were in court and heard the testimony presented to the coroner's jury. Did you agree with their verdict?" I asked.

She looked at me. "I accepted their verdict."

"That's not what I asked, Miss Spicer. From what you now know about my daughter, do you think she could have killed a man, as was stated in that court?"

She hesitated again. "I think it's possible."

"But you still have doubts?"

She nodded. "There are always doubts, Colonel. But we must deal with the facts we have, we can't let our own personal feelings overrule them. The facts we have bear out the conclusion of that court. We must therefore act upon it."

"Thank you, Miss Spicer."

I turned back to the judge. He was leaning across the desk watching me. He seemed curious about what I would do next.

Gordon got to his feet again. "I must protest, Your Honor," he said. "I can't see what Colonel Carey hopes to accomplish by asking these questions. This whole form of procedure seems highly irregular to me."

The judge turned to me. "I must admit to my own puzzlement, Colonel Carey. Exactly what do you hope to accomplish?"

"I don't know exactly, Your Honor, but several things disturb me."

"What are they, Colonel Carey?"

"If my daughter had not been a minor, but an adult, and the verdict had been 'justifiable homicide,' in all probability she'd now be free to resume her normal life. Isn't that true?"

The judge nodded.

"But since she is a minor, she is still subject to punishment, and that is why she is now in this court?"

"That is not true, Colonel," the judge said. "Your daughter is not on trial here for murder. This is a custodial hearing held primarily for her own welfare and benefit."

"Forgive me for being dense, Your Honor. I am not a lawyer. To me the mere fact that she is threatened with confinement is punishment. Whatever the reason—the crime with which she has been charged or some other reason given by the state—it still seems to me to amount to the same thing."

"You can be assured, Colonel, that punitive measures are the furthest thing from the mind of this court," the judge said formally.

"Thank you, Judge. But there is one other thing that troubles me."

"And what is that?"

"If I were charged with a crime by the coroner's jury, I would then be bound over to trial in court. There I would have the right to defend myself against such charges, to definitely, once and for all, establish my innocence or guilt."

Again the judge nodded.

"But in my daughter's case that wasn't considered necessary. From the very first moment of my arrival here, it was carefully explained to me that there was no need to concern ourselves about punishment, because Dani was a minor. Our only concern would be in regard to her custody. It wasn't until today that I realized one very important thing was missing."

I was very thirsty and poured myself a glass of water. The judge looked at me curiously as I began to speak again.

"Nowhere in this entire procedure have I seen anything resembling a defense being made for my daughter. Surely she is entitled to an opportunity to defend herself."

"She has not been denied any of her rights, Colonel," the judge said rather testily. "It seems to me that you and her mother have employed a most capable counsel to act in her behalf. Mr. Gordon here has been present at all hearings. If you have any complaints regarding the conduct of his defense, surely this is not the place to make them."

I was beginning to feel entangled in a maze of legalities. It was stupid of me to have thought I'd be able to pierce the web of obscurities that the law had woven around her. "Your Honor," I said desperately, "what I'm trying to ask in simple words is . . . What can I do to get the truth about my daughter into this court?"

The judge looked at me for a long moment. Then he leaned back in his chair. "If that is all you desire, Colonel," he said slowly, "go ahead in any manner you feel will be helpful. This court is as anxious for the truth as you are."

Gordon got to his feet again. "This is highly irregular, Your Honor," he protested. "All Colonel Carey can do is prolong this matter unnecessarily. The coroner's jury has already rendered its verdict. I can't see what purpose it will serve to rehash the matter. We all realize this is a custodial hearing, and I object to its being turned into anything else."

"In any other court my daughter would have the right to appeal, Judge," I said. "Couldn't this court in effect be the same thing for her?"

The judge looked down at us. "It is not within the province of this court to review the decisions of any other court. However, it is the intent of this court to listen to anything that might aid its judgment in regard to any matter before it. It is the duty of this court to make certain that a minor is protected, in any manner whatsoever, even from his or her own actions. Since these hearings are conducted more or less informally, I cannot see that it would do any harm to hear the Colonel out."

"Thank you, Your Honor."

Gordon shot a curious look at me as he sat down. I turned back to the judge. "May I call a witness?"

The judge nodded.

I walked to the back of the courtroom and opened the door to the waiting room. Anna was sitting in the far corner, near the glass windows. I beckoned to her and she came into the court.

"Your Honor," I said, "this is Anna Stradella."

Nora's face was white with anger. I saw her whisper something to Gordon. The old lady's face was calm, Dani's merely curious.

"Please sit down, Miss Stradella," the judge said. He indicated a chair near his bench. Anna sat down and the clerk stepped forward with a Bible in his hand. Quickly he administered the oath to her and then sat down again.

"You may proceed, Colonel," the judge said. His eyes were alive behind his glasses now. An interest had come into his face that had not been there before.

Anna was dressed in black, but the darkness of her clothing could not conceal the lushness of her body. She sat quietly, her hands folded across her purse.

"Would you tell the court how we met, Anna?" I asked.

"I met Colonel Carey when he came to the funeral parlor to talk to the family of Tony Riccio."

Out of the corner of my eye I saw Dani suddenly lean forward across the table and look at the girl. "Why were you there, Anna?"

"Tony had been my fiancé," she answered quietly. "We had been engaged to be married."

"For how long?"

"Nine years."

"That is a long engagement for these times, is it not?"

"I suppose so," she said. "But Tony wanted to wait until he struck it rich."

"I see. You knew of his employment by Miss Hayden, did you not?"

She nodded.

"Did you ever discuss that job with Tony?"

She shook her head. "No, I never did. But Tony often spoke about Miss Hayden."

"What did he have to say about her?"

Gordon erupted from his seat. "I must object to this line of questioning most strongly. Your Honor. This entire subject is completely irrelevant and immaterial to the matters before this court."

"Overruled," the judge said almost negligently. I could see he was curious about what I was doing. "Continue, Colonel Carey."

"He said she was a rich middle-aged lady and some day he would get a bundle from her."

I stole a glance at Nora. Her face was white and angry. I turned back to Anna. "Did he have anything to say about his relationships in his employer's household?"

"Yes," she almost whispered. "He said that between the kid and her mother, he didn't know which was going to break his back first."

"By that I assume he meant that he was having sexual relations with both?"

"Yes."

"During that time did he also have relations with you?"

Anna looked down at the floor. "Yes," she whispered.

"You didn't object to his behavior with Miss Hayden and her daughter?"

"What good would it have done if I had?" she asked in a dull voice. "He told me he had to do it. It was part of the job."

"That's a lie!" Dani shouted suddenly. "It's a dirty lie!"

The judge rapped his gavel sharply. "Be quiet, Danielle," he admonished her. "Or I'll have to send you out of the courtroom."

Dani's face froze and she glared at me. Now I knew how Judas felt when he looked into the face of Christ. I turned back to Anna.

"When was the last time you saw your fiancé alive?" I asked.

"About two weeks before he died."

"What did he say to you at that time?"

"He gave me a large manila envelope and asked me to keep it for him," she said. "He said it contained letters from Miss Hayden and her daughter and that before long the letters would be worth a lot of money to us. Enough for us to get married on."

"Did you read those letters?"

"No," she said. "The manila envelope was sealed."

"What did you do with them then?"

"I put them away," she said. "Then one night my brother told me that Tony wanted them back and I gave the manila envelope to him. It wasn't until my brother had left that I found out that Tony was already dead."

"What did your brother do with those letters?"

"He sold them."

"To whom?"

"To Miss Hayden."

"But Miss Hayden didn't get all the letters, did she?" I asked.

"No. My brother held out two of them."

"And what did he do with them?"

She looked into my face. "He sold them to you for one hundred dollars."

This time it was Nora who came out of her seat. "The dirty little thief!"

Gordon pulled her back down and I could see that he was as surprised as anyone else. He probably hadn't even known that the letters existed.

I took them from my pocket. "Are these the letters that your brother gave you to deliver to me?" I asked.

She looked at them. "They are."

"That's all, Anna. Thank you."

She got up from the chair and started out. She stopped in the open door and looked back for a moment, then the door closed behind her.

"I would like to read an excerpt from one of these letters," I said, then read the last paragraph from Nora's letter without waiting for permission from the judge.

"You didn't tell me you were going to marry him, Mother!" Dani said. She looked down the table accusingly. "You didn't tell me!"

"Be quiet, Dani!" The probation officer put her hand on Dani's arm.

Gordon was on his feet again. "I move that the entire testimony of that woman and the excerpt from the letter be stricken from the record as irrelevant and immaterial!"

"Sustained," the judge said casually. "It is so ordered." He looked at me. "Have you any further surprises, Colonel Carey?"

"I have, Your Honor. I'd like to question Miss Hayden."

Gordon was on his feet again. "I object, Your Honor."

"Overruled."

"I request a short recess to confer with my client," Gordon said.

The judge leaned forward on the bench and looked down. "You seem to have a plethora of clients in this court, Mr. Gordon. Which client are you referring to?"

Gordon's face flushed. "Miss Hayden, Your Honor."

The judge nodded. He rapped the desk with his gavel. "The court declares a fifteen-minute recess."

We all stood up as he left the courtroom. Miss Spicer took Dani out into the girls' waiting room. The moment the door closed behind her, Gordon turned to me.

His voice was gruff and angry. "What the hell are you trying to do, Luke?"

3

"Your job, Counselor," I retorted. "Defend my daughter!"

"You're being a fool, Luke. You'll only make it worse for her!"

"How much worse can it be? The judge is ready to send her away."

"You don't know that," he said. "He hasn't handed down his decision yet. And if he did go against us we'd petition to reopen tomorrow. We have that right."

"What good would it do?" I asked. "Dani would still be locked up. Why should you be so afraid that I might dig up the truth? Or are you in on it, too?"

"In on what?"

I could see that he was genuinely puzzled. "Nora was afraid I might stumble onto the truth of what really happened that night. That's why she had Coriano frame me when I went to pick up the letters."

"Frame you?"

I took the pictures from my pocket, showed them to him, and explained what had happened. His face paled as I put them back in my pocket. "She warned me to keep out of it or she'd send them to my wife."

"I should never have given them back to you!" Nora said angrily. "I must have been out of my mind!"

Gordon was angry too. He grabbed her arm, almost roughly, and pulled her away.

I watched them walk to the rear of the courtroom. The sibilants of their whispers reached back to me but

I couldn't get what they were saying. I sat down and reached for a glass of water. I wanted a cigarette but I didn't know if I was allowed to smoke in the courtroom.

"Your daughter is being very upset by this, Colonel," Dr. Weidman said.

I looked up. There seemed to be genuine sympathy in his eyes. I drank the water. "I'd rather upset her a little now, Doctor, than try to repair the damage done by three years in a reform school."

Weidman didn't speak. I reached for a cigarette and lit it. The hell with the regulations. I could feel my hand shaking.

The old lady reached out and put her hand over mine. Her voice was as soft and as kind as her touch. "I hope you know what you're doing, Luke."

I looked at her. She seemed the only one of us to have kept her sanity. I returned the pressure on my fingers. "I hope so," I said.

Suddenly I wished Elizabeth were here. She would know what I ought to do; she would be able to calm the sudden fears and doubts that began to well up inside me. Maybe Gordon was right. Maybe I would do more harm than good. I didn't know. I couldn't remember ever feeling so much alone.

The door to his chamber opened and the judge came back into court. We stood up until his gavel signaled for us to be seated. Gordon and Nora had come back to the table. I could see Gordon's face still flushed and angry.

"Let the bailiff summon the child," the judge said.

The deputy sheriff walked over to the girls' waiting room and knocked on the door. In a moment Dani and the probation officer came back into the room.

The blue circles seemed deeper under Dani's eyes. I

could see that she had been crying again. She didn't look at me as she slipped into her seat.

"You may resume, Colonel Carey," the judge said.

Gordon was on his feet before me. "I must again protest this procedure, Your Honor. It is highly irregular and, if permitted to continue, could lead to charges of bias and prejudice on the part of this court."

Judge Murphy's eyes were suddenly cold and frosty. "Are you threatening this court, Counselor?"

"No, Your Honor. I'm merely voicing a considered legal opinion."

"The court respects the opinion of the learned counselor," the judge said, his voice still cold. "It appreciates his concern. But the court wishes to point out that if it is accused of bias and prejudice in favor of the minor appearing before it, it is only fulfilling its function. This court's avowed purpose, according to law, is to protect fully the minors appearing before it."

Gordon sat down silently. The judge looked at me. His voice was mild. "You may resume, Colonel."

I rose from my chair. "I would like to question Miss Hayden, please."

"Miss Hayden, will you take this seat near the bench?" the judge asked, indicating the chair that Anna had occupied.

Nora looked at Gordon for a moment. He nodded and she got up and walked to the chair. The clerk came forward to administer the oath.

Nora sat down and looked at me. Her face was calm and impassive, almost as if it had been carved from one of the slabs in her studio.

I took a deep breath. "Nora," I began, "at the coroner's inquest last week you testified that you had been quarreling with Tony Riccio the day he was killed. Can you tell us what time those quarrels began?"

"I don't remember exactly."

"Approximately. Was it eight o'clock in the morning? Ten? Twelve? Two in the afternoon?"

I could see the light dawn in her eyes. She knew what I was getting at. "It's difficult for me to say exactly."

"Perhaps I could help you refresh your memory," I said. "You were in Los Angeles all day Thursday. Western Airlines tells me that you were listed on their passenger manifest on the flight from Los Angeles that arrived in San Francisco at ten minutes after four on Friday afternoon. Allowing for reasonable traffic delays, you would have been home at, say, five o'clock. Was that about the time the quarrel began?"

Her eyes began to turn cold and angry. "About that time."

"So the quarrel you referred to did not go on all day but began at approximately five o'clock in the afternoon? Is that right?"

"That's right."

Gordon was up again like a jack-in-the-box. "Your Honor," he said, "I fail to——"

"Mr. Gordon!" The judge's voice crackled angrily. "Please refrain from further interruptions in this court! As the attorney ostensibly representing the minor appearing before this court you should welcome any information that might shed light on her actions and aid in her defense. It is beginning to appear to this court that you are trying to serve too many masters and prejudging too many facts. Let me reiterate that I am the judge in this court and that you will have every opportunity to give voice to your opinions in due course. Now, please resume your seat."

Gordon sat down. His face was almost purple with rage. The judge turned back to me. "Please continue, Colonel Carey."

"Was anyone at home when you arrived there?" I asked.

For the first time Nora hesitated. "I don't know what you mean."

"Were any of the servants at home?"

"No, I don't think so."

"Was Dani or Tony Riccio there?"

"Yes."

"Both of them?"

"Both of them."

"Did you see them when you came in?"

"No." She shook her head. "I went directly to the studio. I wanted to sketch out some ideas I had before I lost them."

"What time did you finally see them?"

She looked at me. For the first time I saw a look of pleading come into her eyes. She seemed to be begging me to stop.

"What time?" I repeated coldly.

"About—about seven-thirty."

"Then the quarrel didn't begin until seven-thirty, not five o'clock?" I asked.

She looked down at her hands. "That's right."

"You also testified at the coroner's inquest that your quarrel with Tony Riccio was over business matters," I said. "That wasn't the real reason, was it?"

"No."

"And when you told Miss Spicer that you didn't know about Dani's affair with Riccio," I said, "that wasn't the truth either, was it?"

She began to cry silently, the tears gathering on the lower lids and rolling down her cheeks. Her hands began to twist nervously. "No."

"Where did you see them?"

"When I went upstairs to change for dinner," she half-whispered.

"Where, not when. In what room?"

She didn't look up. "In Rick's room."

"What were they doing?"

"They were—" Her voice was shorn of all feeling. Her eyes were dull and glazed. "They were in bed."

I looked at her. "Why didn't you say so at the inquest?"

"It was bad enough the way it was," she whispered. "I didn't think—"

"You didn't think!" I interrupted angrily. "That's just it. You *did* think. You knew if you told that much you would have to tell the whole truth. About everything that happened that night!"

"I—I don't understand," she said, a puzzled, frightened look in her eyes.

"You understand!" I said brutally. "I don't know how you got Dani to agree to it, but you knew if you told the truth, the rest of it could not be kept silent . . . that you were the one who stabbed Tony Riccio, not Dani!"

I could see her grow old before my eyes. Her face froze and lines came into it that I'd never seen before.

Then a scream came from behind me. "No, Mommy. No! He can't make you say that you did!"

I half turned toward Dani but she was already out of her chair and running to her mother. She hugged Nora to her and stood there with her arms around her protectively. The tears were still running down Nora's cheeks but Dani's eyes were flashing anger and hatred at me.

"You think you know a lot!" she shouted. "You come back after all these years and you think you know everything. You're a stranger. Nothing but a stranger.

You don't know me. I don't know you. All we know about each other is our names!"

I stared at her. "But, Dani—"

"I told you the truth!" she cried. "But you wouldn't believe me! I told you it was an accident, that I didn't mean it, but you didn't believe me. You hated my mother so much that you wouldn't listen!

"You want to hear the truth so much, Daddy, then listen to it! It wasn't Rick that I tried to kill that night in the studio. It was my mother!"

4

I looked around the court. The room was deathly still. Everyone was watching Dani. Even the court stenographer, whose face had been imperturbable all morning, his eyes gazing unseeingly into space as his fingers flew rapidly over the keys of the stenotype.

"We were in Rick's bed when Mother found us," she said in a quiet, matter-of-fact voice. "We knew that it was late but I wouldn't leave him. He wanted me to go but I wouldn't. We didn't hear anything so we thought we were still alone. We'd been in bed for almost two days, except for meals, ever since the servants left. And still I didn't want to go."

The defiant look came into her eyes that I'd learned to recognize. "Would you like to know what we were doing when Mother found us, Daddy?" she asked. "Would you?"

I didn't answer.

"We were both naked in bed. He was lying down and I was on my hands and knees. Do you know what I mean, Daddy? I was trying to make it so he'd want me again and I wouldn't have to go."

I began to feel sick inside. It must have shown on my face, because the defiance crept into her voice now.

"You know what I mean, Daddy, don't you?" she said softly. "But you don't like to think it. Not even to yourself. You still like to think that I'm the same little girl you left six years ago. Well, I'm not. You don't like to think that I know about such things—all the ways there are to do it. But I do. You don't like to think that your little girl would do all those things. But I did."

Her voice began to rise slightly and a faint hint of tears came into her eyes. "And I did them over and over and over. As many times as I could!"

She was staring into my eyes and the knots in my stomach were growing tighter and tighter. "You don't like to hear that, do you, Daddy?"

I didn't answer. I couldn't.

"Mother came in through your old room. Remember how you used to come from your room into mine? That was the way she came. Only that room is Rick's now—was Rick's. She pulled me off the bed and dragged me down the hall to my room and locked me in. I was crying. I told her Rick and I were going to get married, but she wouldn't listen to me. I'd never seen her so angry before.

"Then she went downstairs to the studio and I stayed on my bed until I heard Rick's door open. I heard his footsteps on the staircase and I knew that he was going down to talk to her. I got dressed as quickly as I could and I left my room through the bathroom, which Mother had forgotten to lock.

"I crept downstairs as silently as I could. I heard Charles and Violet in the kitchen, on the other side of the house. Then I stole down the hallway and stood outside the studio door, listening. I could hear almost every word they said.

"I heard Mother tell Rick he had just one hour to get out of the house. Then Rick said that he had enough on both of us to tell the whole world what whores we were. Mother told him that if he didn't leave he'd wind up in jail for—" she stumbled over the world—"statutory rape."

There was a rustle in the court.

"I heard Mother laugh then, and say that she'd expected something like that from him, how much did he want? And Tony laughed too. That was more like it, he said. Fifty thousand dollars. Mother told him he was crazy, that ten thousand dollars was all she'd give him. Twenty-five then, he said. 'All right,' I heard Mother say. And then I went crazy!"

The tears came into her eyes and began to spill down her cheeks. "I went real crazy! All I could think of was that she was doing it again. The same thing she did with everybody that I liked. The same thing she did with everyone who liked me. She was sending Tony away!

"I pushed open the door and screamed at her. 'You can't do it,' I screamed. 'You can't send him away!' Mother looked at me and told me to go back upstairs to my room. I looked at Rick and he told me to do what my mother said.

"Then I noticed the chisel on the table near the door. I picked it up and ran at Mother. 'You can't send him away,' I shouted. 'I'll kill you first!'

"I raised my arm and struck at Mother, but like from nowhere Rick was suddenly between us, the chisel sticking out of his stomach. He stood there, put his hands to his stomach. 'Jesus Christ, Dani, why did you have to go and do a stupid thing like that?' he said. Then I saw the blood coming out between his fingers and I ran past him to Mother screaming, 'I didn't mean to do it! I didn't mean to do it, Mommy!'

" 'I know you didn't, baby,' she said softly, over and over. 'I know you didn't mean it.'

"She said we'd tell everyone that he had been hurting her, and that I'd done it to protect her. Then nobody need ever know what went on between Tony and me. She told me over and over, to make sure that I'd say the same things. Then I covered my face with my hands and the door opened and Charles came in."

They were clinging together now, both crying. I stared at them. It was almost like looking at a stereopticon slide without the viewer. Like two separate pictures of the same person. They looked so much alike, the same tears rolling down their cheeks. Mother and daughter. One and the same.

It was almost as if I were mesmerized. Then, suddenly, it seemed as if the spell were broken. Dani's eyes were dry now, though Nora still wept.

"Now that you know the truth, Daddy," she asked quietly, "do you feel better?"

I looked deep into her eyes. I don't know what it was I saw there, but the knots in my stomach disappeared. I knew the truth. I don't know how I knew it, because she still hadn't told it, but it didn't really matter now. Because this was the way Dani wanted it. Because this was the way it would have to be. And because I still knew deep inside that she hadn't committed a murder.

The judge ordered a ten-minute recess. When he came back into the courtoom we all sat quietly while he gave his decision.

"It is the decision of this court that the State of California retain custody of the minor, Danielle Nora Carey, as recommended in the petition by the Probation Department. Therefore she is hereby remanded to the custody of the California Youth Authority and will be delivered by the probation officer to them at the Northern California Reception Center at Perkins, California, for the standard diagnostic period of six weeks. Then, at the end of that time, and with their agreement, she will be transferred to Los Guilicos School at Santa Rosa, California, where she will undergo rehabilitation as proscribed for a period of not less than six months. At that time the court will consider the petition to remand her into the custody of the maternal grandmother which it now must reluctantly deny.

"The minor, Danielle Nora Carey, is hereby declared a ward of the State of California until she reaches the legal age of eighteen or until she is so discharged by this court. The parents of this minor are hereby instructed to make arrangements with the Probation Department to pay to the State of California the sum of forty dollars per month for each month the minor remains in custody of the State."

The judge rapped the desk with the gavel, then turned to Dani. "Los Guilicos, Danielle, is a very fine school, and if you behave yourself and show that you are making every effort to redeem yourself, you will have nothing to fear. If you cooperate with them, they will cooperate with you and try to return you to your home as soon as possible."

We all rose and he passed majestically into his chambers.

"You will be able to visit Dani tomorrow," Miss Spicer said as she led Dani to the door and opened it. Dani looked back at us for a moment, then went through. The door closed.

Nora began to cry. Dr. Weidman put an arm about her and she leaned her head against his shoulder as they started out.

Gordon came over to me. He was smiling. "Well, it didn't turn out so badly after all."

I stared at him.

He looked at me sharply. "He could have put her in custody of the state the full time, until she was eighteen. This way there's a good chance she'll be out in six to eight months."

I didn't answer as he walked after Nora.

Then an old hand pressed against mine. The old lady

looked into my eyes. There was an understanding in her own. "Thank you for everything you tried to do, Luke," she said gently. "I'll try to take care of her when she comes home."

"I know you will, Mrs. Hayden. I'm sorry. About Nora, I mean."

"It's all over now, Luke. We all did everything we could. Goodbye. And good luck."

"Thank you."

She went on out into the corridor. I looked up the staircase. They had all disappeared. I hesitated just a moment, then went down the corridor and around the hallway to the girls' probation office.

Miss Spicer was at her desk when I got there.

"I have to go back to Chicago this afternoon," I said. "Could I see Dani now instead of tomorrow?"

"I'll see if Dani wants to see you," she said politely and left the office.

I just had enough time to light a cigarette before she was back with Dani. "You can talk in here," she said. "I'll wait outside."

The door closed behind her. I held out my arms and my daughter came into them. "I'm sorry, Daddy," she said.

"It's all right, Dani," I said softly. "It took me a long time to get it, but now I understand."

She looked up into my face. "You don't hate her so much that you'd want to see her in the gas chamber, do you?"

"No, Dani," I said. "I don't hate her at all now. Not any more. I used to be afraid of her but now I just feel sorry for her."

"She's always got to have somebody who loves her more than anyone else, Daddy. Everybody does. You have your wife. She loves you more than anyone else."

"And your mother has you, Dani."

Her eyes were suddenly shining. "Some day maybe you can come and visit me. Or I can come and visit you."

"Some day," I said.

The door opened. "I'm sorry, Dani, but the time is up."

Dani reached up and kissed me on the cheek. "You'll write to me, Daddy?"

I kissed her forehead. "I'll write to you, baby."

I watched her walk down the hall, her tiny heels with their metal taps clicking against the floor. Then they turned a corner and Dani was gone.

Goodbye, Dani. Goodbye, my little red-faced baby. I remember the day you were born. I remember how I looked inside the glass window and you wrinkled up your tiny face and cried and how I was all busted and fractured inside because I knew that you were mine and I was yours and you were the most wonderful baby in the world.

Wherever love has gone, it goes with you.

It was nine-thirty that night when the big jet touched down at O'Hare Airport in Chicago. The cool air came rushing into the cabin as the door sprang open. I was the first one off. I had no time to be polite. I wondered if Elizabeth had gotten my wire.

I almost ran across the field to the unfinished arrival building. I didn't see her at first, there were so many people around. Then I did, waving and smiling and crying all at once.

I ran to her and the world stopped shaking, the pains all vanished. I held her very close. "I love you and I missed you," I said. "And I missed you and I love you."

Then we went over and I picked up my bag and we

went out to the car. I opened the rear door to put in my luggage and saw another bag there. I turned to her.

She grinned at me. "Oh, didn't I tell you? We have to go to the hospital from here."

"You mean now?"

"Now!"

"Why didn't you say something?" I yelled. "Instead of wasting all that time. Hurry! Get into the car!"

"You don't have to rush. There's time yet. The pains are only coming about once every hour." She looked up at the big electric Benrus over the parking lot entrance. "As a matter of fact, there should be one right about now."

"Don't stand there then!" I shouted. "Get into the car."

She just sat down when it hit her. I saw her face go white and tense, then it passed and her color came flooding back. "See, it wasn't so bad."

We made it to St. Joseph's in nothing flat. The police must all have been out to dinner.

We went in and they took her right upstairs. Fifteen minutes later she was on the rolling table and they were shipping her up to the labor room.

I stood in front of the elevator and looked down at her. Her face was pale but she was smiling. "Don't look so worried," she said. "We Swedes don't make trouble. We just make babies."

I bent over and kissed her. "You just make sure you're all right."

The doors opened and the nurse began to push her into the elevator. "I'll be all right. Just look out for yourself. Don't go getting into any trouble now, hear?"

"I hear," I said as the doors closed.

I walked down the corridor to the room they called The Club. There were several other expectant fathers there. They looked up as I came into the doorway. I took one look around and went back outside. I didn't feel much like sitting with them. They looked too grim.

I went downstairs and bought another pack of cigarettes. I lit one and puffed a few times, then put it out. I walked down the corridor.

I walked back upstairs to The Club. Even those grim faces were better than nobody.

"Nine hours I been here already," one man said to me as I sat down.

"Yeah," I said, lighting a cigarette. I looked around the room. All the stock cartoons were on the wall— "We haven't lost a father yet." Very funny.

A nurse came into the doorway and all our faces turned toward her as if we were puppets. "Mr. Carey?" she asked.

"That's me," I said, getting to my feet.. I felt kind of lightheaded.

"Of all the damn luck," I heard the man mutter. "I been here nine hours an' he's only been here five minutes!"

The nurse heard him too for she smiled as she walked toward me. "That's right," she nodded. "You're a very lucky man. . . ."